TEMPEST

KAREN LYNCH

ALSO BY KAREN LYNCH

Relentless Series

Relentless

Refuge

Rogue

Warrior

Haven

Fated

Hellion

Fae Games Series

Pawn

Knight

Queen

For teachers everywhere

A special shout out to the teachers who fostered my
love of literature and writing, and to my other teachers
who had to chide me for reading and writing in class.

ACKNOWLEDGMENTS

Thank you to my family and friends for your support and encouragement. Thanks to my beta readers: Anne-Marie, Sarah, Amber, and Irina, and the many people who make this possible.

1

I crept along the upper level of the old factory, stepping over the bits of debris and broken glass littering the floor. The musty scent of mildew mingling with the smell of rust and small animal scat made my nose twitch, but I ignored it as I trained my ears to pick up sounds in the cavernous building.

Up ahead, the wall on my left ended and a railed catwalk looked out over the main floor. I stopped and went down on my hands and knees to peer around the wall into the darkness below. My eyes had already adjusted to the gloomy interior, and I did two slow scans of the space before I picked up movement at the other end. My eyes followed the dark figure until they moved out of sight, but they were too far away for me to make out whether they were friend or foe.

Pressing my comm button, I whispered, "Check in."

Silence greeted me, so I pressed the button again. "Dima? Kai?"

Thirty seconds passed, and then a voice whispered back, "Kai's down. I don't think they –" He grunted, and the line went quiet.

"Dima?" I didn't expect him to answer, and my heart began to race with the realization I was on my own. I took a slow deep breath. The odds of making it without my team were slim, but there was no going back.

I retreated a few feet and moved to the wall opposite the railing. Crouching low, I continued across the catwalk, holding my breath until I reached the other end. I swept my gaze across the main floor again. From this position, I had a wider view, which included an office with Plexiglass windows accessible only via a flight of metal stairs.

I studied the darkened office for a long moment. If I needed a defensible position where I could see adversaries coming from all sides, that was where I'd go. You could easily pick off your enemy before they got halfway up those stairs.

From inside the open doorway came a flicker of movement I would have missed if I hadn't been looking directly at it. I watched the doorway for another five minutes until I was rewarded with a second glimpse of a shape among the shadows.

Gotcha. The thrill of the hunt went through me, but it soon faded when I remembered I was alone, and the hostile in that room was faster and stronger than I was. Coming at them directly was a suicide mission, and there was no other way into the office.

Releasing a quiet sigh, I tilted my head back in thought and stared at the ceiling of the factory, which was supported by metal rafters. My eyes followed the rafters to a beam directly above the office, and I smiled.

I cast another look around and retreated to the other end of the catwalk to study the rafters six feet above my head. It was doable. I'd reached tree branches higher than this. Bending my knees, I leaped straight up into the air until my fingers grasped cold metal. I adjusted my grip and pulled myself onto the beam.

After a few deep breaths, I made my way through the rafters until I was above the office. I stood on the beam and listened until my ears picked up the faintest rustle of clothing below me. My body tingled with nervous excitement as I took a roll of paracord from my pocket, tied one end to the beam, and soundlessly lowered myself to the roof of the office.

Ducking low, I crept to the edge of the roof and listened for sounds within. Silence. I inched forward to peer over the edge and almost jumped when a figure appeared in the doorway. He was dressed completely in black with his face covered, and he outweighed me by at least fifty pounds. I had the element of surprise on my side, but I was going to have to move fast to take him down.

He stood there for a long moment before he turned to go back inside. It was now or never.

Gripping the edge of the roof, I swung out and down in an arc. He spun, but my legs wrapped tightly around his middle, and I used my momentum to knock him off balance. He recovered with superhuman speed, but I had anticipated it. With one deft motion, I drew my knife and pressed the silver blade against his throat.

"Yield," I uttered in a calm, steady voice.

He went still, and exhilaration pulsed through me.

It happened so fast my brain had no time to process it. One second, I had him at my mercy, and in the next, I was weaponless and pinned against the wall with a steely hand around my throat. Blood roared in my ears as I stared at the face hidden behind a black ski mask.

A light came on, nearly blinding me. He reached up with his other hand and yanked off the mask. Brown eyes bore into mine. "You're dead."

"How did you do that?" I asked when he released me.

Gavin smoothed down his mussed black hair. "I felt your body relax a fraction when you thought you had me. That was all I needed. You can't let your guard down for even a second."

I straightened my coat. "I did have you. That should count for something."

"Nothing counts if you die," said another voice from behind me.

I turned to see Erik's perpetually-scowling face. I didn't think I'd ever seen the Korean warrior smile in all the years I'd known him.

We were interrupted by a muffled shout. I looked past Gavin at the three bound and gagged people sitting on the floor against the far wall. My fellow trainees: Naomi, Sean, and Anna glowered indignantly at us until Gavin walked over to free them.

Feet pounded the stairs, and Dimitri entered the room. His eyes lit up when he saw me. "Not bad, Sis. You almost did it."

"Almost," I muttered. "What happened to you guys?"

My twin grimaced. "Erik set a trap, and Kai and I walked right into it."

"Where is Kai?" I looked around Dimitri to the empty doorway.

"He was right behind me. He's probably sulking," Dimitri joked under his breath.

"Dima," I scolded softly.

Kai appeared in the doorway, and I smiled at the dark-haired trainee as he entered the room. He walked over to stand on my other side, but he barely returned my smile. Across from us, Naomi, Sean, and Anna wore equally sour expressions. Weren't we a fun bunch?

"You call that a hunt?" Erik's hard stare moved over each of us. "First year trainees would have done better."

Kai shifted his weight, and Naomi opened her mouth as if to speak. The rest of us stayed still and waited for what we knew was coming.

Erik looked at Naomi, who had led her team. At six feet tall, the black girl had an inch on him, and she seemed to shrink so as not to remind him of the fact. Everyone at Westhorne knew his height was a sore spot for him, and he was already pissed off enough.

"Your team was disorganized the moment you entered the building. You did not work as a unit, and you were careless, which is why you were taken out immediately. If this had been a real job, I'd be looking at a pile of corpses now."

Ouch. I flinched with them. The trainer didn't pull any punches as he spent the next five minutes listing every one of their mistakes. I dreaded his critique of my team's performance, and I swallowed hard when he turned his attention to Dimitri, Kai, and me.

"Your team showed some promise until one of you missed the clear signs of an ambush and led another into it," Erik said to Dimitri.

I looked from Dimitri to Kai, who stared ahead stonily and refused to meet my eyes. Erik went on, doling out the same harsh criticism he'd given the other team.

Gavin spoke up when Erik finished lambasting us. "Dani, your stealth and speed are impressive. You managed to take me by surprise, but you got sloppy during the attack. You need to work on that because you'll find yourself in many situations where a second's hesitation can be a deadly mistake."

I nodded, replaying the scene in my head.

"That said, you were the only one to breach our lair, so I'm giving your team a narrow win for this exercise," Gavin said with a small smile.

Dimitri threw an arm around my shoulders. "Way to go."

Erik glowered at us. "It's nothing to celebrate. You will all have to perform a lot better than this if you expect to graduate next year." With that parting shot, he turned and strode from the office.

Gavin picked up the knife I'd lost in the fight and handed it to me as he followed the other warrior. The room was silent until we heard the distant sound of the outer door closing.

"Fecking hell," Sean burst out in his thick Irish accent. "When is the new trainer supposed to get here?"

I grinned at the normally cheerful redhead. "Next week, I think, but for all we know, he could be worse than Erik."

"I don't think that's possible," Dimitri said, earning nods all around.

Grandfather had asked Erik to step in as a temporary trainer while our usual trainer, Callum, was having an extended visit with his family in Scotland. I'd always thought Callum was a tough trainer until our first session with Erik. We had no idea who was coming to replace Erik, but the new trainer had to be better than the ill-tempered warrior.

"This wasn't a fair test," Anna griped, tightening her blonde ponytail, which had come loose. "How are we supposed to best two trainers who are faster and stronger, and who knew we were coming?"

"Most hostiles will be stronger than us until we're older, so we have to be smarter," Naomi told her. "Dani almost took out Gavin, and she's smaller than the rest of us."

"Hey," I protested.

Erik wasn't the only one who hated being shorter than his peers. Dimitri and I had inherited our father's black hair and our mother's green eyes, but he had Dad's height and build while mine was closer to Mom's. I was five eight, three inches taller than her, but still short by Mohiri standards.

Naomi raised her hands. "I meant that as a compliment. You use your smaller size to your advantage, and you play to your strengths, such as being able to move as quietly as a shadow."

"And you treat every training exercise like it's real," Sean added.

Dimitri grinned. "Dani's always been like that. Playtime was brutal when we were little."

The others chuckled, and I felt a prick of pain as an old memory tried to surface. I poked Dimitri's ribs playfully. "When your brother is an over-achiever, you have to compensate somehow."

"Erik and Gavin are waiting for us. We should go," said Kai, who wasn't laughing with the rest of us.

He walked out of the office, and we filed out after him. No one said much as we exited the dark building into the midafternoon sun. In the parking lot, two dark SUVs sat with their engines running. Dimitri, Kai, and I headed for one while the other trainees went to the second vehicle.

Dimitri climbed into the front with Erik, and Kai and I took the back. As soon as we pulled out of the lot, Dimitri began grilling the trainer about his mistakes in the exercise and what he should have done differently.

I settled back in my seat and watched the streets of Boise go by, occasion-ally flicking a glance at Kai, who stared silently out his window. After we passed the city limit sign, I reached over and touched his arm, and he swung his head in my direction.

"It was only a training exercise," I said in a low voice. "They expect us to make mistakes."

His lips parted as if he was going to speak, but he faced the window again. I frowned at the back of his head and turned to my own window. If he wanted to sulk, I wasn't going to waste my breath trying to talk to him.

The drive home took an hour, and my irritation was at a low simmer by the time we passed through the gates of Westhorne. Erik parked outside the garage, and we got out as the other SUV pulled in beside us.

Dimitri and I called our goodbyes to the others as they headed to the manor. We started toward the woods, and we'd walked about ten feet when Kai called my name. I stopped and looked back at him.

"Are we still going to a movie tomorrow night?" he asked as if he hadn't spent the past hour ignoring me.

I lifted my eyebrows. "Are you going to be in a better mood by then?"

He smiled contritely. "Yeah."

"Then I'll see you tomorrow." I turned back to Dimitri, and we resumed our walk.

He was quiet until we reached the gravel road to the lake. As soon as we entered the woods, he said, "I still can't believe you're dating Kai. What do you see in him?"

"He's fun to be with, and it's not serious."

Dimitri scoffed. He and I had few secrets between us, so I already knew he didn't care for Kai, though he'd never let anyone but me see it.

I hid my smile. "You don't like him because he's your closest competitor in class. He did try to be your friend."

"He probably hoped he could get to hang out with Dad."

"So what? Not everyone is lucky enough to grow up as Nikolas Danshov's kid." I slanted a look at my brother. From this angle, he was almost a mirror image of our father, whom he idolized. He had spent countless hours learning Dad's fighting techniques and sparring with him. He even rode a Ducati like Dad.

Dimitri's lip curled. "Kai's arrogant."

"So are you."

He glared at me. "And he's a sore loser."

I couldn't deny Kai's moodiness annoyed me. It wasn't as if he was the only one Erik had raked over the coals. But I saw a different Kai outside of training, so I was willing to give him a pass this time. I shrugged one shoulder. "No one's perfect, Dima, not even you."

He made a pained sound. "I thought you were going to stop calling me that."

"But I like it." Dima was the nickname our Russian grandmother had given him when we were babies, and I'd grown up calling him by that name. I gave him a sly grin. "I'll tell you what. If you can beat me to the house, I'll stop using it."

His face brightened. "You're on."

We raced side by side down the road. We'd gone a quarter of a mile when I caught a blur of movement on my left. I skidded to a stop as a huge black shape leaped from the woods and landed directly in my path. His big head swung toward me and fetid breath washed over me as his long tongue lashed at my face.

"Woolf!" I sputtered, wrapping an arm around his thick neck to restrain him.

The hellhound gave my chin another lick and pressed his body against my side. I scratched between his ears and looked behind me at Dimitri, who was rolling on the ground with Woolf's brother Hugo.

"Need some help?" I called to him.

Dimitri turned his head to the side and grimaced as Hugo slobbered over him. It took him almost a minute to push the hellhound off him and scramble to his feet. The hair on one side of his head was wet and stuck to his face, and he was covered in damp leaves and pine needles.

My lips twitched. "If Erik was here, he'd say you need to work on your reaction time."

He shot me a dark look as he stomped back to the road. I couldn't hold in a laugh when he ran his fingers through his hair, leaving behind a leaf stuck to his cheek. Hugo, trying to be helpful, began washing Dimitri's face like an overexuberant puppy.

"Okay, boy, that's enough," Dimitri said, but Hugo didn't let up.

"He misses you," I said, stroking Woolf's coarse fur. Ever since we could walk, Hugo and Woolf had been our constant companions and protectors. Over the last few years, as we became busier with training and friends, we spent less and less time at home and with each other.

Dimitri patted Hugo's head. "I know, but they need to get used to us not being here once we become warriors. Just think, this time next year, we'll be out there travelling and doing real jobs."

I was excited to experience life out in the world, but I had mixed feelings about leaving home. I loved our valley, and I was never happier than when I was here. Mom was the same way. She'd spent a lot of her childhood in the woods in Maine. She believed our Fae side gave us a deeper connection with nature.

Unlike me, Dimitri craved the fast pace of city life. Most of the action happened in big cities like New York, LA, Vegas, and Chicago, and that was where he wanted to be. I wanted to see all those places and get in on that action, too, but I couldn't see me living there.

"Alright, be off." Dimitri playfully pushed Hugo away from him. "Go make sure no vampires are trying to sneak into the valley."

At the word *vampires*, the hellhounds' heads shot up, and their bodies went rigid. They let out low growls and sped off into the woods, even though a vampire couldn't get within ten miles of here. The whole valley, including the small town of Butler Falls five miles away, was protected by powerful Fae wards.

"Now, where were we?" Dimitri smirked and took off toward home.

"Hey." I was on his heels in seconds, letting him have the lead until I spotted the sparkling lake through the trees. Pulling ahead, I reached the front steps to our log house a good five seconds ahead of him. He might be stronger and a better fighter, but he was no match for my speed. It didn't stop him from trying, though.

"You suck," he called when he caught up to me.

I snickered. "That's what you get for cheating, *Dima*."

He reached out to ruffle my hair, but I ducked and ran into the house. After kicking off my boots and hanging my coat in the mudroom, I entered the kitchen.

On the kitchen island, Eliot, Orwell, and Verne argued and brawled over a blueberry muffin. The muffin was in pieces, and Verne looked like he had been rolling around in blueberry jam. The imps were so caught up in their argument they didn't hear me come in until I cleared my throat loudly. Three guilty faces turned to look at me.

"Oooh, you're in trouble," Dimitri said in a singsong voice behind me.

I pointed at the mess on the counter. "You guys better get that cleaned up before Mom sees it."

Verne stabbed a finger toward the other two and chattered indignantly. I wasn't fluent in the imp language, but I'd learned enough words to understand the gist of what he was saying.

I looked at his shirt and pants. "Don't worry. I'll wash them for you." To Eliott and Orwell I said, "You two, stop picking on your brother."

Leaving them to clean up, I walked down the short hallway off the living room to my bedroom. It was my favorite room in the house and done in soft earth tones with a pale green bedspread and a faded floral rug. Natural light flooded the room from the two large windows, one of which overlooked the lake. From here, I saw the house where Uncle Chris and Aunt Beth lived with their fifteen-year-old daughter Grace. They were currently in Europe visiting Uncle Chris's parents, and the lake was too quiet without them.

Changing out of my training clothes, I flopped down on the bed with my phone. I was plumping up my pillow when my phone rang with an incoming video call. I grinned when I saw the caller's name.

I hit the answer button. "Hey, Bestie."

Summer Kelly's smiling freckled face filled my screen. Her fiery red hair was piled on top of her head in a messy bun, and her green eyes lit up when she saw me. "Guess what. I aced that big chem test."

"Didn't I say you had nothing to worry about?" I adjusted my pillow into a reclining position. "Doing anything to celebrate?"

"My roommate, Sydney, asked me to go to a party with her tonight. I haven't been to one since I got here."

I felt a pang of envy. "Ooh. Your first college party."

She sighed. "I wish you were here to go with me."

"Me, too."

Summer was in her first year at Northeastern University. When we were younger, we used to dream of going to college together and sharing a dorm room. We'd had it all planned out until Mom and Dad told me it was too dangerous for a young Mohiri to be on their own at college.

"What I'd really like to do now is shift and go for a long run." She propped her phone up on her desk and stretched her arms over her head with a groan. "I miss being able to do that whenever I want to."

I made a sad face. It had to be hard for a werewolf living in a city, especially when she had grown up in a place like the Knolls, which was almost completely surrounded by woods. The Knolls was an outlying part of New Hastings, Maine where Mom grew up, and it was home to mostly werewolves.

"When are you going home again?" I asked.

She sank onto her chair. "Next weekend. It's Mom's birthday, and Dad is planning a family barbecue, which means everyone in the Knolls will be there."

"No one throws a party like your family."

Dimitri let out a bellow. I rolled off the bed and ran through our connecting bathroom to his room. I found him standing in front of his dresser with a hand on his chest.

"Damn it, Brontë. How do you keep getting in there?" he asked in exasperation.

I pressed my lips together to keep from laughing and walked over to him, holding up the phone so Summer could see what I saw. His top drawer was open, and nestled among his socks and underwear was a small, sleek black feline with silver eyes and stunted ears. She stretched, giving us a peek of delicate black bat wings.

Laughter came from the phone, and Summer said. "Aw, she's so cute."

"You are welcome to her," he replied.

Summer snickered. "I don't think my dorm allows demon cats."

Dimitri gave me a pleading look, and I shrugged. "She's your cat."

"She's not mine," he said for the hundredth time.

I let out a soft snort. "I don't think she knows that."

Lifting her out of the drawer, he set her down on his navy-blue comforter. She growled softly in annoyance before she curled up and closed her eyes.

I kept my distance from her. Brontë was a Krazan, a demon cat, Aunt Beth had found and brought home to us two years ago when Brontë was only a kitten. Our old cat Oscar died when I was thirteen, and we missed having a cat in the house.

There was only one problem. Being half Fae, Mom and I weren't Brontë's favorite people. She didn't mind Dad, but it was Dimitri she took to the most. She had decided she belonged to him whether he wanted a pet or not.

"Never a dull moment with you guys," Summer said. "But I need to run...literally."

I held up the phone. "I want to hear all about the party."

"I'll call you tomorrow," she promised. "Later."

Dad's voice drifted down the hallway from the living room. Another voice replied. Grandfather Tristan. Technically, he was our great grandfather, but that had been too much for us when we were little, so we'd shortened it.

"That's four demons who have disappeared in the last week," Grandfather said with a note of concern in his voice. "I need you to go to California to look into this."

"How many does that make now?" Dad asked.

"Thirty-two that we know of."

I started toward the living room as Dad said, "Sara thinks they are related."

Grandfather started to answer and stopped to smile at me when I entered the room. "I heard you had your first field exercise today. How did it go?"

I made a face and sat beside him on the couch. "I guess you haven't talked to Erik or Gavin."

Dad sat in the chair across from us and gave me a sympathetic smile. "The first one is always the hardest. Want to talk about it?"

"I'd rather hear about the missing demons. We still have no idea what's happening to them?"

Dad shook his head. "All we know is it started about three months ago, and it's not limited to a certain area or a particular race of demon."

I tucked my legs beneath me. "Why does Mom think they're related?"

"Two reasons." He rested his elbows on his knees. "First, all the missing demons we've heard about have strong ties to their communities and are not the kind to up and take off. Second is the way they disappeared. They vanished without any physical evidence of what happened to them. Someone is doing a good job of hiding their tracks."

"Why would anyone abduct demons?" I asked, although I already had some ideas. "Could it be Gulaks running a slavery ring?"

"Gulaks are messy," Grandfather said. "This is too clean to be their work."

"Maybe it's a collector," Dimitri said as he entered the room on his way to the kitchen.

A shiver went through me. Two years ago, warriors had raided the home of a Houston collector. She had a demon menagerie in the lower level of her house containing six different types of demons in glass cages with room for more. The oldest of the captives had been only thirteen.

"That is a possibility, and we have people looking into it," Grandfather said grimly.

"What else can we do if there are no clues?" I didn't want to think about what could have been done to them. Mom had a lot of friends among the demon community, and I hoped they were okay."

"There is always a clue if you know where to look for it," Dad said. "David and Kelvan are retracing the steps of each one of the missing demons. There are security cameras, traffic cameras, cell phone tracing, and any number of other ways our movements are recorded. If there is a trail, we'll find it."

Mom's friends David and Kelvan were genius hackers who had been working with Westhorne since before I was born. If anyone could find something, it was them.

The door opened, and Mom came in carrying a large basket, which she set on the island. Dimitri immediately went to open it, and she playfully smacked his hand away. "That's dinner."

She shot him a warning look and joined us in the living room. Standing behind Dad's chair, she bent and wrapped her arms around his neck to kiss his cheek. He turned his head so their lips met, and although the kiss was chaste, I could feel their love from across the room. I hoped someday I'd be lucky enough to have a love like theirs.

Mom straightened and pushed back the hair that had fallen into her face. Her eyes were tired, and she stifled a yawn.

"Hard day?" Dad asked her.

"I've had worse." She found a hair tie in her pocket and secured her hair in a ponytail. "I'm working with three orphans, and one of them needs more of my time than the others. And I have a warrior coming tomorrow."

"Ariana?" Grandfather asked, referring to one of the orphans.

Mom nodded. "She's been through so much. I'm not surprised she doesn't trust anyone."

"Maybe you should lighten your workload," Dad suggested as he did every time she came home tired or stressed about her patients.

She smiled. "If I don't help them, who will?"

He didn't answer because no one else could do what she did. Mom was a healer with a unique gift. She could heal warriors suffering from Hale witch attacks, and she had helped many of them over the years. She had also learned to communicate with other Mori, an ability that allowed her to help Mohiri orphans with mental and emotional issues. Sometimes, she traveled to other strongholds to see them, but most of them were brought to Westhorne.

Mom turned her admonishing gaze on me. "You blew off your lesson with Aine today. You can't keep doing this, Dani."

I sank lower into the cushion. "The lessons are a waste of time. All we do is talk about my feelings."

"Because our Fae magic is deeply connected to our emotions," she said patiently, sounding like Aine. "This is an important part of learning to control your magic."

"But there is no magic." My throat tightened in frustration. "It's gone, and I'm better off focusing on my warrior training."

She came over to sit on my other side and put her arm around me. I wanted to lay my head on her shoulder like I used to, but I was angry at her for bringing this up again. We'd been over it so many times, and I wished she would drop it.

"Your magic is not gone," she said softly, her hand stroking my hair. "And when you go through liannan –"

I pulled away from her and jumped to my feet. "Just because you went through it doesn't mean I will. I don't want to talk about this anymore."

"Dani," Dad called as I ran from the living room. Reaching my room, I shut the door and leaned against it, fighting the tears burning my eyes. Why couldn't everyone let this go?

A soft knock came at my door a minute later, and Dimitri said, "You want to talk?"

"No," I answered thickly.

"I'm here if you change your mind."

"Thanks." I lay down on my bed, but after a few minutes, the walls started to close in on me. I needed to be outside.

I pulled on a pair of boots, strapped on one of my knives, and grabbed a light jacket. Stuffing my phone into my back pocket, I opened the window facing the woods and threw my legs over the sill. It was an easy ten-foot drop to the ground.

Dimitri stood at his window. Our eyes met, and he gave me a sad smile.

We never talked about it, but I knew him too well. After all these years he still blamed himself for what happened even though it had been my fault.

I set off in a brisk walk around the lake. The farther I got from the house, the more my guilt weighed on me. I hated arguing with my mother, and I always felt like crap afterward. She was the warmest, most loving person in the world, and she wanted only to help me. I wished I could make her understand I didn't need help. I needed everyone to let me be me.

The walk was not helping like it usually did, so I turned away from the lake and broke into a run, picking up speed with every step. I skirted trees and leaped over rocks and other obstacles with ease as I went deeper into the woods. The scents and sounds of the forest filled me, leaving no room for negative thoughts and emotions.

Five miles from home, my phone beeped to notify me I had passed the inner perimeter sensors. It automatically sent back a signal identifying me. The sensors alerted security when someone got within five miles of Westhorne. Once or twice a year, hikers wandered onto our land, despite the posted NO TRESPASSING signs, and someone was sent out to turn them away.

Dax, our head of security, took his job seriously. If a sensor was tripped by an unauthorized person, one of a hundred perimeter surveillance drones was automatically deployed to send back video of the trespasser. His state-of-the-art system had eliminated the need for regular patrols, for which I was grateful. I loved having the woods to myself.

I slowed to a walk when the terrain started to rise toward the mountain at the end of the valley. I thought about going as far as the mountain, but a glance at the sky told me I was already going to be late for dinner.

Half a mile into my return trip, the hair rose on the back of my neck. Slowing to a walk, I looked around but saw nothing out of place. That was when the silence registered. A hush had fallen over the woods as if a dangerous predator was nearby.

I went still and listened. Of all the creatures in the valley, only one could stalk its prey without being seen.

The only warning I got was the flap of leathery wings as he swooped down at me. I hit the ground and rolled to one side, coming back to my feet in time to see a scaly spiked tail disappear into the canopy of branches overhead.

I darted to a large cedar and pressed my back against the trunk as I surveyed my surroundings. A rustle came from high up in the tree, and several twigs fell beside me.

Pushing away from the tree, I crept through the woods, stopping every few yards to listen for sounds of pursuit. I'd gone about an eighth of a mile when I heard him coming, and I took off like a doe sprinting from a hunter.

I leaped across a brook and felt something brush the top of my head mid jump. It startled me so much I screamed and stumbled on the landing. I straightened and found myself staring into the green reptilian eyes of the wyvern standing ten feet away.

"Alex." I wagged a finger at him. "You tried to knock me into the water."

He cocked his head to one side. If I didn't know better, I'd think he was grinning at me. He settled his wings against his sides and watched me expectantly.

I held out my hands. "Sorry, buddy. I don't have any treats today."

He snorted, and smoke billowed from his snout. He was quite capable of feeding himself and finding his own snacks, but he loved the raw meaty bones I sometimes brought him. The cooks in the big kitchen gave me the bones for Hugo and Woolf, but I saved some for Alex.

The wyvern's head snapped up, and he let out a warning growl, which sent a chill down my spine. Nothing in this valley could hurt me unless something had managed to get past Eldeorin's wards. And that was impossible.

A twig cracked somewhere off to my left. I reached for my knife as I whirled to face the threat.

2

Something blurred in my vision, and the next thing I knew, a man stood between Alex and me. At least, he looked like a man from behind. He was tall with dark, shaggy hair tied back with a strip of leather, and he wore a long coat, which appeared to be made from sheepskin but was too dirty to say for sure.

My first thought was that he was a vagrant, although I'd never seen one in the area. But no human was that fast. He wasn't Mohiri, or I would have sensed him. I swallowed dryly and gripped my knife. Could he be a vampire? I'd never been near one, so I had no idea if I'd inherited Mom's ability to sense when one was near. But what else could move like that?

Alex growled menacingly, and sparks flew from his mouth. His flames only had a three-foot reach, but they could burn a person to a crisp. I glanced sideways at the brook, ready to dive into the shallow water if necessary.

The man shifted, and the sun glinted off metal. I stared at the sword in his hand. Vampires did not carry weapons.

A roar erupted from Alex, and he charged. The stranger waited until the last second and jumped to the side. He spun, and I watched in horror as the tip of his sword slashed at the wyvern. The blade glanced off Alex's hard scales, but the man was already positioning himself to strike again.

"No." I ran at the man, who was too focused on Alex to pay attention to me. I tackled him around the waist, my momentum knocking him off balance. I let go as he fell sideways and landed in the brook with a splash.

He sat in the brook, staring up at me with water dripping from his hair and his sword still clutched in his hand. His mouth and jaw were hidden behind an overgrown beard, and some of his hair had come loose to obscure most of his face. I imagined his expression, and a laugh threatened to burst from me.

In an instant, he was on his feet. I retreated, forgetting about the danger to me until I felt the wyvern's warm breath on my back. Alex had never hurt me, but I had no idea what he would do if he felt threatened.

The man stepped out of the brook, and I took in his appearance. His clothes were dirty and he looked like someone who had just spent a year alone in the wilderness. He shook the water from his hair and took a step toward us.

"Leave him alone" I spread my arms wide as if it would protect Alex from him.

I thought I saw him frown behind his curtain of scraggly hair. He lowered his sword arm, and my demon gave a gentle stir of recognition as it acknowledged the presence of another Mori.

"You're Mohiri," I said, unable to hide my surprise. He continued to stare at me until I felt a flicker of annoyance. "Do you speak English?"

He gave the barest of nods as his gaze shifted to Alex again. He must have believed the wyvern was attacking me, which was an honest mistake if you didn't know Alex.

Twenty years ago, Alex escaped from the Westhorne menagerie, and he'd decided to make a home in the mountains. Grandfather had originally planned to recapture him and ship him to Argentina where they trained wyverns to hunt vampires. But Alex only hunted game and never bothered humans, so he was allowed to stay. Most people here had forgotten about his existence by now.

My irritation at the warrior grew. "Do you talk?"

He nodded again and returned his sword to the scabbard under his long coat. I took the opportunity to study him. I'd met many other Mohiri at Westhorne and while traveling with my family, but I'd never encountered one like him. Even the ailing warriors who visited Westhorne for my mother's help were less unkempt.

A new realization struck me, and shame washed over me. He was the sick warrior coming to see Mom. Most Hale witch victims became hostile and reclusive and stopped taking care of themselves. Some even became hermits. I should have seen it right away. Anyone meeting this strange warrior would know immediately something was off with him.

"I'm so sorry," I blurted and softened my voice like I was speaking to a lost child. "Do you need help?"

This time there was no mistaking his frown, but I couldn't stop myself, and I babbled on as I pulled a small bag of trail mix from my pocket. "Are you hungry? It's not much, but it'll tide you over until you get there. You can get a hot meal and clean clothes, and they'll have a nice comfortable bed for you."

His eyebrows arched, and hazel eyes stared at me like I was the crazy one. I wanted to kick myself. I'd handled this all wrong, and I hoped I hadn't scared him off. He clearly needed Mom's help.

I tried to remember everything Mom had said about Hale witch victims. They didn't like it when you treated them like they were sick, and here I was doing just that.

"I..." I fumbled for the words to fix it, but he walked away. He stopped a dozen yards away and picked up a worn canvas duffle bag covered in patches. Throwing it over one shoulder, he left without looking back.

I blew out a gust of air. "I handled that well, didn't I?

Alex snorted, and I turned to him. "I better head back. I'll bring you some bones next time."

I started toward home again. It wasn't long before I noticed the wyvern's shadow as he followed me from the air. He did that sometimes, and I didn't know if he was lonely or if it was his way of protecting me.

The sick warrior occupied my thoughts all the way home. The more I thought about our encounter, the more heat crept into my face. Thankfully, no one but he and Alex had seen me act like an idiot, and Mom's patients never stayed around after they were healed. I could only hope he didn't mention my blunder to her before he left.

The roof of our house came into view, and I immediately forgot about the warrior as a fresh surge of regret filled me. Mom would be sweet and understanding when I apologized, and it always made me feel worse somehow.

Hugo and Woolf brayed and raced toward me, announcing my return. I drew in a deep breath and went to set things right with my mother.

I entered the main hall the following evening and checked my phone. I was half an hour early for my date with Kai. The common rooms were empty, so I ran up the stairs of the north wing, where the other trainees lived. I passed by the second floor where the boys' rooms were and climbed to the third floor.

Every time I came up here, I thought about Mom sleeping in one of these rooms when she was a trainee. I couldn't imagine what it had been like for her, a seventeen-year-old orphan who'd had no idea she was Mohiri until Dad found her in Maine. She'd left everyone she knew to come here and start a whole new life, all to keep Uncle Nate and her friends safe from a Master hunting her. If I could be half as brave as her, I could face anything.

A door halfway down the hallway was cracked open, and laughter spilled out. I went to it and leaned in to see Victoria and Elsie, two raven-haired cousins who couldn't look more like sisters if they tried. The girls were sitting on Victoria's bed, propped up with pillows and watching something on her laptop.

"Hey, girls," I called.

They looked up at the same time, and Victoria gave me a finger wave. "Come on in."

I joined them and sat on the foot of the bed. "What are you two up to tonight?"

"Same as you probably." Elsie fluffed the pillow behind her. "A bunch of us are going to a movie later."

"You'd think there would be at least one party in town on a Saturday night, but that place is practically a ghost town," Victoria said, pouting. "I wish they'd let us go to Boise."

I didn't respond. We all knew why we weren't allowed to go to the city on our own. The only reason we were free to go to Butler Falls was the Fae warding that kept vampires out. It hadn't always been like that. When Mom and Aunt Jordan were trainees, they had been attacked by vampires at a party in town. Life around here was a lot more exciting back then.

"Did Dimitri come with you?" Elsie asked hopefully.

"No. I'm not sure what he's doing tonight," I said. Dimitri hadn't been hanging out much with everyone since his best friend, Theo, left this summer. Theo was a year older than us, and he'd finished training in the spring. He was working at the Atlanta command center run by his aunt.

Victoria looked at her laptop and let out a tiny gasp. "Cassidy and Julian broke up."

"What?" Elsie leaned toward her to see the screen. "I thought they would last."

"Are you serious?" Victoria gave her cousin the side-eye. "They had no chemistry. She's better off without him."

"Friends of yours?" I asked, knowing full well who they were talking about.

Every few months, Victoria had a new celebrity crush. The last one was a rock drummer named Samson who was old enough to be her father. Her current one was Cassidy Downs, a twentysomething actress.

Victoria turned the laptop toward me. "Don't you think she would look better with me than him?"

I studied the couple on the screen. The beautiful red-haired actress was tall and leggy in a short red dress and matching heels. Beside her was a man in a dark Armani suit with artfully messed blond hair and high cheekbones that would fill a model with envy. They looked like a good match to me, but I wouldn't tell Victoria that.

"I think you and she would look great together," I said,

She spun the laptop toward herself again. "He's not even a real celebrity. He's some boring millionaire who's famous because he hangs out with the Hollywood A-list crowd."

"He has a big fan following online, and I think he's actually a billionaire," Elsie said unhelpfully, earning a scowl from her cousin.

"Is this a private party, or can anyone join?" Naomi asked from the doorway. I looked over my shoulder as she entered with another trainee named Luis, who had moved here from Chile last spring. He and Naomi had been dating for three months, and they seemed to be getting serious.

"The more the merrier." Victoria got off the bed and picked up some clothes she'd left on her couch.

Naomi and Luis sat and started a discussion about what movie they were going to. I checked my phone to see if I had a text from Kai and found one from Summer instead.

Just met the cutest guy at the library! I love college men.

Details?? I wrote back.

Her typing bubble appeared immediately. **His name is Damon. He's a senior and he's studying engineering. Brains and brawn. Swoon.**

I laughed to myself. **What does he look like?**

About six feet with dark wavy hair and dreamy eyes. He definitely works out. You know I'm a sucker for muscles. She followed her text with a string of emojis.

Any plans to see him again? I asked.

Not yet, but he seemed interested.

I want pics if you do, I replied. **I'm living vicariously through you.**

Her next text was a laughing emoji.

Luis's voice caught my attention, and I tuned in to the conversation in time to hear the last of his sentence.

"...missing demons. They'll be there at least a week."

"What's that about demons?" I asked.

"Mom and Dad are going to San Francisco tomorrow to help investigate some missing demons," Luis said of his parents who were stationed at Westhorne.

I stuck my phone in my pocket. "They must be going with my Dad. Grandfather asked him to look into the disappearances on the West Coast."

"Mom didn't tell me that." Luis's eyes took on the sheen of hero worship I was used to seeing whenever Dad's name came up around the other trainees.

"It must be serious if Tristan is sending your father to investigate," Elsie said.

I nodded. "I think it is."

"What do you think is happening to them?" Naomi asked the room.

"I don't know," I said. "But I hope we find them before it's too late."

"Hey, guys," Kai said from the doorway. He looked at me and smiled. "I thought I'd find you here."

"Come on in," Victoria called to him.

He entered the room and came to sit beside me on the bed. I still felt a lingering irritation about his behavior yesterday, so I didn't say anything at first.

His arm slipped around my waist, and he pressed a light kiss to my cheek. "I'm sorry I was such an ass yesterday," he whispered in my ear. "Will you forgive me?"

"Maybe." I didn't meet his eyes. I couldn't hold a grudge, and he knew it.

His nose nuzzled my ear, tickling me. "What if I promise to let you eat all the popcorn tonight?"

A smile tugged at my mouth. "It's a start."

Victoria's laugh interrupted us. "All right, you two. No making out on my bed."

Naomi stood. "We should leave if we're going to make the eight o'clock movie." She looked at Kai and me. "Are you two coming with us?"

"I'm up for whatever you want to do," Kai said to me.

I got up and took his hand. "Let's go."

"So, you don't have to do the lessons with Aine anymore?" Dimitri asked as we arrived at the main grounds for training two days later.

"Mom said I can take a break from them for a few weeks." I spotted Naomi, Anna, Victoria, and Elsie standing in the small courtyard outside the training wing entrance with a red-haired girl named Teresa. I started their way and looked back when I realized he wasn't following me. "You coming?"

He eyed the girls like an antelope watching a pride of hungry lions and shook his head. "I'll see you inside."

I laughed, and we parted ways. I drew close to the others, who were facing away from me and speaking in hushed voices. My curiosity was piqued when Anna said Grandfather's name.

"What's up?" I asked from behind them, and they all jumped.

Victoria put a hand to her chest. "Damn it, Dani. Why do you always do that?"

I shrugged. "I don't do it on purpose. I can't help if I'm a quiet walker."

"Wraiths make more noise than you," Elsie quipped with a little smile. "I wish I could move like that."

"So, what juicy gossip did I miss?" I asked, steering them back to whatever they had been discussing.

"That." Anna turned to look toward the four guest cabins at the far corner of the grounds. Grandfather added them years ago for when the werewolves visited because they liked to be close to the woods. More recently, they were also used by afflicted warriors who came to my mother for help.

I followed Anna's gaze to Grandfather, who stood near the cabins. A male warrior I didn't recognize left the first cabin and walked over to him. He was Grandfather's height with dark hair and broad shoulders, and he was dressed like every other warrior.

I turned back to the girls. "Who is he?"

"I have no idea." Elsie fanned herself. "He was leaving the dining hall with Tristan this morning when we went in for breakfast. When he looked our way, I swear my girl parts melted. Those eyes."

Anna nodded and let out a lusty sigh. "He walks like a wolf stalking its prey."

"He can stalk me any day," Victoria said.

I cast a look at Naomi and Teresa who were barely holding back grins. Our friends were like this every time a new male warrior visited Westhorne. It was no wonder Dimitri avoided them whenever he could.

"Do you think he could be the new trainer?" Teresa asked.

Elsie shook her head forlornly. "We are not that lucky."

Grandfather and his companion walked out of sight, and Victoria and Elsie deflated like kids who'd had their toys taken away.

Naomi slapped her hands together. "I guess that's our cue to get to class."

She opened the door, and we followed her inside. The first floor of the wing consisted of a hallway lined with training rooms, an equipment room, and the healing baths. The baths were particularly helpful after being pummeled or slammed into the floor a few times. Warrior training was not for the faint of heart.

The sounds of fighting and swords clashing already came from behind several closed doors. The warriors in residence used the wing for sparring when they weren't working, and they didn't hold back. They didn't mind trainees watching them, but only when we didn't have to be in class.

We entered the largest training room and found Dimitri there along with Kai, Sean, Luis, and another trainee named Jamar. I took my usual spot next to Dimitri as Grandfather's voice drifted down the hall.

An air of anticipation filled the room. Grandfather stopped by the training area occasionally, but for him to be here immediately after we'd seen him with the stranger could only mean one thing.

Grandfather appeared in the doorway and smiled at us. "Good morning."

"Good morning, Tristan," said everyone except Dimitri and me. After he and I had started training, Grandfather told us we could call him by his name, but it was too weird for us.

He stepped into the room, and Elsie made a happy sound under her breath when the newcomer entered behind him. This close, his hair was lighter than I'd thought, a warm brown streaked by the sun, and his clean-shaven face revealed a square jaw and full lips.

"Everyone, I'd like you to meet your new trainer, Ronan Hale," Grandfather said.

The trainer gave a slight head bow. His impassive expression made me suspect he did not smile often. I saw why the girls were gaga over him. He had a brooding presence, and there was something different about him I couldn't put my finger on.

Grandfather's eyes met each of ours as he spoke. "Ronan has agreed to take over for Erik until Callum returns from his leave. I think he'll bring a fresh approach to your training curriculum."

A fresh approach? Grandfather hadn't mentioned plans to change the training program. I slanted a questioning look at Dimitri, who gave a small shrug.

I shifted my gaze to the new trainer and found myself looking into his hazel eyes. For a heartbeat, the mix of browns and greens seemed to turn to gold, and I forgot to breathe as a jolt of recognition shot through me. *It can't be.*

He was the warrior from the woods.

The transformation was unbelievable. The only thing that *hadn't* changed about his appearance was his eyes. No one would ever mistake this male for a mentally ill warrior.

Ronan's eyes widened the slightest bit, and I broke our stare as my neck grew warm. He recognized me too, and I could only imagine what he was thinking. He was probably wondering how the hell the crazy girl with the wyvern had ended up in his class.

"Any questions?" Grandfather asked, drawing my attention back to him. No one spoke, and I wished I could think of something to keep him here.

"Then I will leave you to get to know each other." The amusement in his eyes as he left only ratcheted up my discomfort.

Ronan stood near the door watching us – or more likely sizing us up. Even my normally cool brother was shifting his weight restlessly by the time our new trainer walked over to stand in front of us.

"Choose a sword," he ordered in a brusque tone, which carried a trace of an East European accent. Everyone hurried to the racks holding an assortment of weapons used in hand-to-hand combat.

"You." Ronan pointed at Dimitri. "Attack me."

My brother pulled back slightly. "What?"

"Show me how you take down a hostile."

Dimitri exchanged a glance with me and looked back at the trainer. "You don't have a sword."

"Neither does a vampire," Ronan replied.

Dimitri's fingers flexed on his sword hilt. "Yes, but I don't care about hurting a vampire."

"You won't hurt me," Ronan said without a trace of arrogance. He raised his hand and beckoned him. "Let's go."

The rest of us moved back to give them space as Dimitri stepped forward. He and Ronan faced off against each other, and neither of them moved for a good thirty seconds.

Ronan attacked. Dimitri reacted by bringing his katana up to block the advance. I stopped breathing, and several of the others let out soft gasps as we waited for the blade to impale our trainer.

Lightning-fast, Ronan sidestepped out of the sword's path. Dimitri's arm was still moving when Ronan grasped his wrist and twisted it. Dimitri let out a grunt of pain as the sword slipped from his fingers. Ronan's boot connected with the sword and sent it flying away before it even hit the floor.

Ronan wasn't done. The next thing I knew, my brother was face-down on the floor with his arm twisted behind his back. The whole thing had taken only seconds. Dimitri was the best swordsman in our class, and he hadn't had a chance.

Ronan released Dimitri, who stood looking a little dazed, not that I could blame him. The trainer said something to him I couldn't hear, and Dimitri nodded. They spoke quietly for a minute before Dimitri came back to stand beside me.

"You and you." Ronan pointed at Naomi and Kai. "Leave your weapons."

After watching Dimitri's takedown, neither of my friends looked eager as they went to the front of the room. I was simultaneously glad they were the ones up there and dreading my turn.

"Attack me," Ronan said.

"Together?" Kai asked hesitantly.

The trainer didn't blink. "Yes."

Kai looked at Naomi. A second later, he aimed a straight punch at Ronan while Naomi went for his throat. Ronan slapped away Kai's fist as if it was nothing more than an annoying gnat. Muscles rippled under his shirt as he twisted his body to evade Naomi's attack and swept her legs out from under her.

Naomi went down as Kai came back with another strike, which Ronan easily blocked. Behind Ronan, Naomi shot to her feet and tried to attack him again. He spun and grabbed her wrist, pulling her off balance. At the same time, he delivered a kick to Kai's body, which would have broken his ribs had he put his full strength into it.

Kai and Naomi hit the floor at the same time, and their groans signaled the fight was over. Ronan offered Naomi a hand and pulled her to her feet, and then he spoke to the two trainees as he had done with Dimitri. They returned to their places, looking as dazed as he had been.

The class continued in the same manner. Ronan asked individual or pairs of trainees to attack him in different scenarios with or without weapons, and each time, he defeated them like they were first years. The knot in my gut grew as I watched it all and waited for him to call on me.

It wasn't that I was afraid of looking bad in front of the others. I didn't want to face him after our embarrassing first encounter, even if I was sure anyone in my shoes would have made the same mistake.

Five minutes remained in class when Ronan finally looked at me and said, "You."

"Good luck," Dimitri murmured.

My pulse sped up as I walked over to stand six feet away from Ronan. This close, the raw strength emanating from him sent a tiny thrill of danger through me.

Our eyes met, and my breath caught when his did that color change again, the gold bleeding into the rest of his irises. My heart thumped, and I knew what a rabbit felt like staring into the eyes of a hungry wolf.

I still held my sword, but it felt more like a hindrance than a weapon after I'd seen Ronan disarm my friends. I was almost relieved when he said, "No weapon."

I set the sword on the floor near the wall and faced him again. He was Grandfather's height, but he somehow made me feel less than five feet tall.

"Attack me," he said.

I had watched him closely when he'd sparred with the others, so I knew how he would block every strike. I looked for a weakness but saw none. I'd be better off if he made the first move so I could at least try to counter his strike.

The words were out before I realized what I was saying. "You first."

I expected a strike or kick like he'd done with the others, but he opted for a grapple. Used to fighting larger opponents, I dropped and rolled out of his reach, coming back to my feet behind him. What I lacked in strength, I made up for in speed.

Ronan spun, and I caught the flicker of surprise in his eyes. It was replaced by a predatory gleam that sent a little shiver down my spine.

He struck without warning. He slowed his speed, but I had little time to bring my hands up to block him. My first instinct was to deflect his punch, but at the last second, I grabbed his fist instead.

I gasped at the tingle of electricity that shot up my arm to my fingertips. My heart thudded as the air between us crackled with the strange energy. I stared at him, and the shock in his eyes told me he felt it, too.

I recovered first. I pushed him backward as one of my legs swept his legs. He went down, but he grabbed my wrist, taking me with him.

He landed on his back with me on top of him. A second later, he rolled and pinned me beneath him with his arm across my throat. Panting, I stared up into his eyes as my body thrummed with adrenaline and a strange heady sensation. I didn't know if it was from the thrill of the fight or his nearness. The idea it could be the latter unsettled me.

Ronan released me and stood, his expression unreadable as he extended his hand to me. I took it reluctantly, but there was no electricity this time. His hard gaze made me want to look away, but I refused to be intimated – at least not outwardly.

"You are fast, but your technique needs work," he said in a low, disapproving voice. "Never wait for your opponent to attack. It puts you on the defensive and gives them the upper hand. In our next class, we'll see if you can do better with a weapon."

I nodded stiffly. I hadn't expected him to heap praise on me, but his expression seemed harsher than it had been with the others. Was he upset about the shock I'd given him? I had no explanation for it other than some lingering trace of my Fae magic had reacted to his Mori. But that hadn't happened in many years, not since –

Ronan looked past me at the class and said, "I will see you again in two hours." With that, he strode from the room, leaving a flurry of chatter behind him.

Gavin appeared in the doorway and smiled at us. "Judging by your expressions, Ronan is going to be a tough act to follow, but I'll do my best."

Everyone but me laughed as I picked up my sword and returned to my spot beside Dimitri. He shot me a questioning look, which I ignored. My pride still stung from Ronan's sharp criticism, and I didn't want to talk about it. Not even Gavin's announcement that we were going to work on agility and climbing – two things I excelled at – could cheer me up.

Callum wasn't due back until March. If my first class with Ronan was an indication of how things were going to be with him, this would be the longest six months of my life.

3

———————

"I thought that only happened in cartoons," Dimitri called from behind me, his voice laced with amusement.

I stopped walking to glare at him. "What?"

"That little black thundercloud hovering over your head. I'm expecting lightning to shoot from it any second."

"Ha-ha." I spun and continued toward home.

Dimitri caught up to me as I reached the woods. "You've been in a bad mood all day – all week, actually. I know you don't like Ronan, but you have to admit he's really good."

I scowled at the admiration in his tone. Of course, he liked our new trainer. Dimitri was at the top of our class and not receiving the brunt of Ronan's criticism. Ronan was tough on all of us, but I could do nothing right in his eyes.

If someone had told me a week ago I'd miss Erik, I would have laughed in their face. After three days of training under Ronan, I was almost ready to call my old trainer and beg him to come back.

My brother sighed. "Okay, I have noticed he's been a little harder on you than on the rest of us."

A snort slipped from me.

"Did something happen?" Dimitri asked. "Did you have a run-in with him outside of class?"

"You could say that," I muttered.

Dimitri's eyes widened. "When? And where was I? We're together most of the day."

I let out a long breath. "It was last Friday."

"Friday?" Dimitri laughed. "And how did you manage to have a run-in with our new trainer three days before he arrived?"

"He started his new job on Monday, but he arrived on Friday." I told Dimitri about my encounter with the warrior in the woods, and how shocked I was when Grandfather introduced him to us. By the time I finished, Dimitri was doubled over holding his stomach.

"You tackled our new trainer and knocked him in the water...to protect Alex from him?" he wheezed between fits of laughter.

I crossed my arms. "It's not funny, Dima. How was I supposed to know who he was?"

"It's hilarious." He straightened and wiped his eyes. "I don't know what's better – you treating Ronan like one of Mom's patients or you thinking Alex needed your protection."

"You didn't see him," I argued. "He looked wild."

"Alex or Ronan?"

I threw up my arms and stalked away. "I never should have told you."

"I'm sorry. Don't be mad." He caught up to me. "You have to admit it's pretty funny."

"You wouldn't say that if it had been you," I retorted.

He nudged my arm with his. "*I* wouldn't have been playing cat and mouse with that crazy wyvern."

I kicked at a stone. "Alex is not crazy. I think he's lonely."

Dimitri grew serious. "If Mom and Dad find out you've been going to see him, they will ground you for life."

"If they think Alex is too dangerous, how do they expect me to fight vampires when I'm a warrior?"

"That is where I come in," said a voice from behind us.

Dimitri and I spun at the same time to face the tall blond faerie standing a few feet away.

"Hello, my favorite twins," Eldeorin smiled, and his eyes sparkled with mischief.

"Hey, Eldeorin," Dimitri said to my godfather. "It's been a while."

It had been over six months since we'd last seen the faerie. I usually enjoyed his visits, but something in his expression made me wary.

"What brings you here today?" I was striving for casual, but my voice came out a little higher than usual.

Eldeorin's smile widened into a Cheshire grin. "I'm so happy you asked. I'm here to start your new training."

"My...training?" A small pit opened in my stomach. "What are you talking about?"

"Aine says your training with her is not progressing, and we decided it would be best if I took over."

I took a step backward. "Mom won't allow you to train me."

When I was ten, Eldeorin had tried to convince my mother to let him oversee my training, and she had refused. She'd told me it wasn't that she didn't trust Eldeorin to keep me safe, but she thought his methods were too drastic for a young girl. Not to mention Dad didn't like Eldeorin, and he would have lost it if Mom had sent me off alone with the faerie at that age.

"Sara and I have discussed it, and she agreed with me," Eldeorin replied.

Mom appeared next to him as if saying her name had summoned her. No matter how many times she did it, it was still the coolest thing I had ever seen.

"I agreed to a trial." She fixed Eldeorin with a hard stare. "And I told you I'd hunt you to the ends of Faerie if anything happens to my daughter."

Eldeorin placed a hand over his chest. "After all we have been through, I cannot believe you have so little faith in me."

Mom scoffed but followed it with a smile. "You forget how well I know you."

Their light banter only increased my apprehension. "Mom, you said I could stop the sessions for now."

"Sara and Aine are too indulgent with you," Eldeorin said. "I reminded them how difficult liannan was for Sara, and she, at least, had some control of her magic before it began. You are the same age she was when she entered liannan. If you are not prepared for it, it could kill you."

"Eldeorin," Mom snapped. She came over and put her hands on my shoulders. "I would do anything to keep you from having to go through liannan, but it will happen whether we want it or not."

I opened my mouth to speak, but she shushed me. "Eldeorin is too blunt as always, but he's here because he cares about you. He helped me through liannan and taught me to control my new magic. I trust him to do the same for you."

"But my magic is gone," I protested, even as the memory of what had happened with Ronan played in my mind.

Eldeorin made a pfft sound. "Faeries do not lose their magic."

"I'm only half Fae," I reminded him.

He stalked over to me. I leaned away, but he would not be deterred. He laid a hand against my cheek and nodded in satisfaction. "You shielded your brother from detection when you were still in the womb, but you are not powerful enough to hide your magic from me. We will start your training today."

"Mom." I gave her a beseeching look, and my heart sank at the resolve in her eyes. "Does Dad know about this?"

"Not yet." Dad was still in California investigating the demon disappearances. Her tone said he wasn't going to be happy about this, but they had agreed long ago that she knew what was best when it came to Fae matters. He would go along with whatever she decided even if he hated it.

"It's settled then." Eldeorin looped his arm through mine. "Shall we?"

A sense of impending doom filled me. I met Dimitri's worried eyes for a second before he, Mom, and the woods disappeared. The next thing I knew, we were surrounded by haphazard piles of rusty vehicles, appliances, scrap metal, and other junk. The air was heavy with the smell of gasoline and dust, and a moving crane stood nearby. The fading light told me it was late evening, which meant we were somewhere on the East Coast.

"You brought me to a junkyard?" I turned in a circle, half afraid I'd see a vampire lurking behind every stack of tires.

Eldeorin walked away from me. "You'd prefer the penthouse at the Four Seasons? I can arrange that, but training can be messy."

"Funny guy." I trailed after him, trying not to think about why his training was messy. "Where are we going?"

"Not far," he said without looking back.

I followed him around a tower of old clothes dryers and came up short at the sight of a large circular cage in the middle of an open area. The cage had to be thirty feet in diameter and fifteen feet high, and it appeared to be made of silver. Inside the cage, two figures were huddled at the center, as far from the bars as they could get.

My first thought that they were vampires sent a rush of fear and excitement through me. It was immediately followed by a sharp pang of disappointment because I couldn't sense them like Mom did.

The closer I got to the cage, the more distinct their shapes became until I made out their scaly skin, bat-like wings and reptilian eyes. Gulaks. Not nearly as dangerous as vampires but still a threat. They were mean brutes and responsible for most of the crime in the demon community.

Eldeorin stopped a dozen feet from the cage and motioned for me to stand beside him. "These two were part of a gang that stole human children and planned to sell them into slavery. The Mohiri dealt with the gang and rescued the children. I absconded with two of their captives for educational purposes."

My mouth went dry. "What exactly are you going to do with them?"

"Not me, you." Eldeorin snapped his fingers, and I found myself looking at him from the other side of the bars.

"What the hell?" I spun to look for the door and discovered there wasn't one. "Let me out."

"You may leave when both demons are dead or unconscious," Eldeorin said.

The Gulaks shuffled nervously but stayed where they were.

"I can't fight two Gulaks on my own."

"Sara slayed a Gulak master when she was your age," he said with pride in his voice.

The Gulaks began talking in urgent guttural whispers, probably planning how they were going to kill me.

I patted my leg for the knife I usually wore, but it was gone. I swung my gaze back to Eldeorin. "You took my knife?"

He walked over to stand a few feet from the cage. "You don't need a knife. You have a weapon better than any blade. Use it."

"I can't." I banged my palms against the bars. "Don't you think I would if I could?"

"I think you fear your magic more than you fear those demons."

I glared at him. "You don't know what you're talking about."

"We both know that is not true." Eldeorin brushed an imaginary fleck off his sleeve. "You should get started unless you want to stay in there all night. I have nowhere else to be." To prove it, a red wingback chair appeared behind him. He sat and crossed his legs as if he was at a Broadway show, waiting for the curtain to rise.

I looked at the demons, who stared back at me. I'd watched videos of Gulaks fighting and heard many stories about them, but none of that compared to the real thing. They were stocky and fought with brute strength, and their hard scaly hide protected their torso from heavy blows. The shape of their mouths made it look like they were snarling even when they laughed, which helped them intimidate weaker opponents.

Some Gulaks wore a cutlass, but most of them preferred to fight with wooden clubs. A quick scan of their bodies found no weapons, and I had a moment of relief until I remembered it was still two against one, and they each had at least a hundred pounds on me.

The three of us stood staring at each other. The tip of one Gulak's horn was broken and jagged, giving him an even fiercer appearance.

Eldeorin's voice cut through the silence. "I've had more fun watching trees grow."

"Then you come in here and fight them," I called without turning to look at him.

He chuckled. "Excellent idea. Demons, you can fight her, or you can fight me."

"You –" It was the only word I got out before the Gulaks rushed me. Years of training and instinct took over, and I automatically fell into a fighting stance. The one with the broken horn reached me first and charged, his big clawed hands going straight for my throat. I sent a swift kick to his knee, one of his few vulnerable spots, and he howled as he stumbled back.

I straightened to face the second Gulak, but he moved faster than I expected. He'd gotten behind me, and his thick scaly arms wrapped around me in a bear hug. His deep guttural chuckle filled my ears as he tightened his hold. I struggled to break free, but his arms were like a vice slowly squeezing the breath from my lungs.

Through the black dots filling my vision, I watched the first Gulak regain his footing. He leered and started toward me again. I had seconds to get out of this, and I was no longer sure Eldeorin would step in to save me.

I let my body go limp. My captor's arms loosened a second later, and I leaped into action. I grabbed one of his arms and thrust my hip into him as I spun and bent my body. Grunting with the effort, I used my momentum to throw him over me and into his friend. They went down amid a chorus of growls.

Panting, I backed away, putting as much space between us as I could. It wouldn't take long for them to recover, and this time, they would be driven by rage. The one thing a Gulak hated more than losing a fight was losing it to a female.

I had reached the cage bars by the time the Gulaks charged, and there was only one place I could go. I wrapped my fingers around one of the bars and climbed. The bars were too close together to allow me to use my legs, so I had to rely on nothing but upper body strength. I'd done it plenty of times in training, but never when my life depended on it.

The bars in the ceiling of the cage were spaced wider, and I hooked my legs around them. I looked down at the Gulaks staring up at me. Even if they could touch silver, they'd never be able to climb up after me.

After an hour, Eldeorin spoke. "Do you intend to stay up there all night?"

"I have nowhere else to be," I called back.

His sigh was audible even at this distance. In the next instant, I was standing on the ground beside him.

Eldeorin took my arm again. "Never let it be said I am not up to a challenge."

The cage and the junkyard disappeared. I expected to arrive at home, but we materialized on the roof of a building. A quick glance around told me were in Washington, DC. Before I could ask why we were here, we transported to the back of an alley stinking of garbage and urine. The brick walls on either side of us were covered in graffiti, and a low, muffled thumping of bass came from the building on our left.

I was about to ask where we were when something moved on the other side of the overflowing dumpster. A figure stepped out, silhouetted by the light from the street, and I sharpened my eyesight until I saw it was a young woman in her early twenties. She had straight dark hair and wore black jeans and a red leather jacket. She stalked to the top of the alley, and the soft click of her heeled boots echoed through the narrow space.

I wondered why she was alone in an alley. I stepped forward to tell her it wasn't safe, but Eldeorin put a hand on my shoulder to stop me. He pointed at the woman, who turned to walk back to the dumpster, and my eyes widened at the flash of fangs.

"A vampire," I whispered hoarsely and clamped my mouth shut. *Idiot.*

Eldeorin gave my shoulder a reassuring squeeze. "She cannot see or hear us."

"Please don't tell me you expect me to fight a vampire after what happened with those Gulaks," I said, staring at her with a mix of fascination and fear. I couldn't wait to tell Dimitri I'd seen a real live vampire.

"The Gulaks did not present enough of a threat to you. I believe something more dangerous is needed to call your magic," he said. "She is a new vampire and not much stronger than you, and she does not have your warrior training."

I shot him a glare over my shoulder. "How do you know that? She could have been a ninja when she was human."

He smirked. "Then you'll have to use your magic, won't you?"

"I really don't like you anymore." I turned my back on him again.

"You will once you have mastered your magic," he said with a smugness that made me want to elbow him in the ribs.

The vampire leaned against the brick wall as if waiting for someone. *Waiting for dinner is more like it.* A chill went through me and settled in my chest. I'd heard so many stories about vampires over the years, and it finally hit me that soon my friends and I would be out in the world fighting them ourselves.

"So, what now?" I asked.

Two things happened at once. The vampire's head whipped in my direction, and I looked behind me to discover I was alone with her in the alley. Eldeorin had abandoned me.

For a moment, I couldn't breathe as panic paralyzed me. Then the part of my brain that could still reason assured me Eldeorin would not let me get hurt. In fact, he was most likely here and hidden behind a ward so he could observe me. That made me feel only slightly better.

"Hello there." The vampire walked around the dumpster, her fangs now hidden. "How did you get back there, little girl. Are you lost?"

"I'm waiting for someone," I said as my eyes darted around looking for something to use as a weapon.

She smiled. "What a coincidence. So am I. Maybe we can wait together."

"Okay." My body tensed, and I gave up searching for a weapon when she started toward me. Her stride was slow and casual, but I could feel her menacing presence as she drew near. It wasn't until she was only a few yards away that I realized what else I was feeling. Coldness pulsated at the center of my chest like a living block of ice.

Excitement momentarily overcame my fear, and adrenaline surged through me. *I can sense her!*

The vampire stopped and sniffed the air. "What is that smell? It's amazing."

I wrinkled my nose. "It's garbage."

"It's so much more than that." Her mouth widened in a slow smile, showing off her emerging fangs. "Don't worry. I'm hungry, so it'll be over fast."

It took her a few seconds to realize I wasn't screaming or cowering in terror. Her smile faltered, but I could still see her fangs. I'd be lying if I said the sight of them didn't scare me, but Mom always said a little fear is good. It keeps you from getting overconfident and complacent.

I didn't know if it was the vampire's hunger or her lack of experience that made her run at me. A more experienced vampire might have questioned why a human girl alone in a dark alley with them didn't show fear.

She closed the distance between us quickly. I had barely enough time to side-step the attack and land a hard kick to her ribs. She stumbled but recovered fast with a new gleam in her eyes. Vampires liked it when their prey put up a fight.

I was ready when she lunged at me the second time with her fangs bared. I brought up my forearm to block her and punched her so hard in the jaw my hand went numb. Her head snapped back, and I followed the strike with a powerful kick to her chest. She slammed into the wall, stunned.

I scanned the ground again for a weapon, and my eyes landed on a two-foot length of rusty pipe sticking out from beneath a bag of garbage. I grabbed it, happy to see the other end was broken and jagged. It wasn't an ideal weapon, but it would have to do.

The vampire snarled and pushed away from the building, and we circled each other. All at once, her nostrils widened and her expression became feverish. That was when my nose picked up a scent of copper in the air, and I saw blood seeping through a tear in my sleeve. One of her claws must have slashed me during her last attack.

I swallowed hard and tightened my grip on the pipe. A new vampire was one thing, but one crazed by bloodlust was a whole different story.

The growl she let out as she pounced at me made the hairs on the back of my neck stand on end. I swung the pipe as hard as I could, slamming it into the side of her head and sending her off balance. With a small battle cry, I ran at her and drove the sharp end of the pipe into her chest. It was more difficult to do than with a blade, but I pushed until it went straight through her heart.

I let go of the pipe, and she crumpled lifeless to the ground. Breathing harshly, I stood over her. I had just killed my first vampire, and the whole experience felt like a strange dream.

A slow clap brought me back to my senses, and I looked up at Eldeorin, who stood a few feet away.

"Not what I had hoped for but impressive nonetheless," he drawled.

I stepped back from the corpse, fuming. "Has anyone ever told you you're an asshole?"

He laughed softly. "I believe Sara called me that once or twice."

"Gee, I wonder why." I held up my arm to inspect the wound. It had already stopped bleeding, but my sleeve was soaked. There would be no hiding it when I got home.

I didn't know Eldeorin was beside me until he laid a hand on my arm. My cut disappeared, and the sleeve became like new again.

"Sara will want to hear about your training, but it's better if you return intact," he said.

"Better for who?" I pointed at the dead vampire. "What was the point of this other than learning I have Mom's vampire radar?"

I didn't realize what I'd said until Eldeorin's mouth curved in a satisfied smile.

"You sensed the vampire." It was a statement, not a question.

I tried to backtrack. "Maybe. I'm not sure."

"Yes, you are." His smile grew even wider. "Your magic is closer to the surface than you want to admit. Now we must figure out how to free it."

"If being near a vampire couldn't do that, what makes you think you can?"

"There is always a way." He took my arm, and the world blurred. When it came back into focus, we were where we'd left Mom and Dimitri hours ago. In the dark woods, crickets chirped, bats fluttered overhead, and an owl screeched. I was glad to be home.

Eldeorin let go of my arm, and we walked toward the lake. "Does it require conscious effort to suppress your magic?" he asked.

"I'm not suppressing it. It's gone."

"I am uncertain whether you truly believe that or you want others to believe it," he said without the mockery I expected. "Perhaps it will help if we talked about the incident."

"No." I walked faster. "You know everything."

He kept pace with me. "I am flattered by your high opinion of me, but no one knows everything."

"You were there, and you know what happened." I stared ahead as the lights from my house came into view. I didn't talk about that day to anyone, not even Dimitri. If I could, I'd wipe it from my memory entirely.

"I won't force you to talk about it," he replied, and I shivered because I knew he could if he wanted to. "But I want you to think about it before my next visit. The best way to free your magic is to go back to the exact moment it was bound. In the meantime, I will look at some other options."

"But I don't want –" I broke off because Eldeorin was gone.

I resumed walking and stopped at the edge of the lake. I wasn't ready to enter the house and answer their questions about my adventure with Eldeorin. Staring across the glassy, black water, my gaze fell on the weathered wooden platform in the middle of the lake. An image surfaced of the platform closer to the shore with sun reflecting off its fresh coat of white paint.

I tried to push the image away, but the conversation with Eldeorin had triggered something inside me. A floodgate opened, and I was lost in the memories of that day.

The lake sparkled under the bright sun, and a warm summer breeze sent gentle ripples across the surface. Along the shore, the birds sang in the trees, ignoring the two huge hellhounds snoring in the grass.

I stood up to my waist in the water, giggling at the speckled trout trying to nibble on my toes. Bending over, I stuck my face in the water and blew bubbles at him. Instead of darting away, he swam up until he was inches from my face, his large round eyes staring back at me. Mommy said fish didn't have thoughts like we did, which made me sad. I wished I could talk to them and learn what it was like to live their whole life in the lake.

The trout wriggled and sped away. I lifted my head from the water and saw Dimitri swimming toward me.

"Are you talking to the fishes again?" he teased. "Papa said you are going to grow a tail and fins."

I pushed my wet hair out of my eyes. "He did not."

Dimitri grinned. "Let's race."

"Not until you say you're sorry." I turned my back on him.

He sighed dramatically. "I'm sorry."

I spun and splashed him in the face. "Now we're even."

He sputtered and laughed, and we spent the next few minutes splashing and dunking each other. We could never be mad at each other for long.

"You want to race now?" he asked. He loved racing, and he usually won, but I was getting faster every day, especially in the water. Daddy said he couldn't swim as fast as me when he was five.

"Okay." I twisted to look at Nana Irina who sat on the deck overlooking the lake. "Watch us, Nana!"

"I'm watching," she called.

Dimitri and I dived into the water and swam for the wooden platform twenty feet from the shore. I could hold my breath a long time, so I stayed under and swam like Ariel. A school of fish darted along beside me as if they were cheering me on.

I reached the platform and took in a gulp of air as I turned to go back. Dimitri got there as I kicked off, and I grinned from ear to ear. I was winning.

Knowing he could still catch me, I swam harder than ever. As soon as I made it to the shallows, I popped out of the water, gasping, and looked for Dimitri. He was still ten feet away.

"I won," I shouted, waving my arms wildly. "Did you see, Nana?"

Clapping came from the deck. "Yes. You swim like a little minnow now."

I beamed at Dimitri when he finished. "I beat you by a mile."

"No, you didn't." He stood sullenly. "And it wasn't a fair race because you used magic."

"Did not."

"Did too."

"Children, behave," Nana called.

I crossed my arms and glared at Dimitri. "You always want to win. You're just jealous because I'm getting faster than you."

"Only because you're half faerie," he taunted. "You're not a real Mohiri."

Nana stood and started toward us. "Dima, that is not nice."

Tears burned my eyes. "I am so."

"Jeremy said real Mohiri don't have magic."

"Jeremy is stupid and mean, and so are you," I yelled and shoved him.

He shoved me back. "You're stupid."

My body grew hot, and I started to cry. Dimitri had never said such cruel things to me before, and it made my belly hurt.

"You're mean." I slapped water at him. "I hate you."

The water hit Dimitri with a burst of white light. He flew into the air and plunged head first into the water.

"Dima!" I screamed at the spot where he'd gone under.

Someone blurred past me and dived into the water. Nana's head broke the surface, and she swam toward me holding Dimitri's limp body.

Shouts came from behind me, but all I could do was stare at Dimitri's pale face and closed eyes as Nana carried him to the dock. Mommy ran down the steps from the house and lifted Dimitri from Nana's arms. She laid him on the dock and lowered her head to his. Coldness spread through me at the fear on her face when she shook her head at Nana. She started breathing into his mouth, and Nana pressed down on his chest.

Daddy and Papa Mikhail ran down to the dock, and they all hovered over Dimitri, who still wasn't moving. I wanted to go to them, but my body was so heavy I couldn't walk. Everything around me seemed to sparkle, and I couldn't hear over the ringing in my ears.

Mommy disappeared, and when she came back, Eldeorin was with her. He touched Dimitri's face and said something to Mommy, who nodded. Everyone watched as he laid his hands on Dimitri's head, and a blue glow surrounded my brother.

I'm sorry, Dima. Please, wake up. Please, please, please. *I couldn't see them anymore through my tears, and I'd never been more scared or alone in my life. I shivered, and my teeth chattered, but I still couldn't move.*

Strong arms swept me up and cradled me against a warm chest. "Daddy's here, solnyshko."

I curled into him, seeking warmth and safety, but for the first time, there was no comfort in his arms.

"Are you hurt?" he asked tenderly.

I shook my head, and he walked to the dock where Nana and Papa waited for us. I looked around frantically for Dimitri, but he and Mommy were gone.

"Mommy took Dimitri to the house," Nana said. "Eldeorin is taking good care of him."

Daddy carried me inside and upstairs to their room. I felt like I was in a dream while Nana put me in the bath and dressed me in my pajamas. She laid me in the middle of Mommy and Daddy's bed and pulled the covers over me. The whole time, I wanted to ask if Dimitri was okay, but I was too afraid to speak.

Mommy and Daddy came in with Eldeorin, and they talked in low voices while

Eldeorin touched my face and blue light came from his fingers. He asked me a question, and I didn't know if I answered him. All I could think about was Dimitri and remember his colorless face when he lay on the dock.

"Where's Dima? Is he going to die?" I whispered, and all the adults stopped talking.

Mommy sat on the bed and pulled me into her arms. "Dima is in his bed, and he's going to be okay."

Her voice was calm and reassuring, but I could feel her tremble. Mommy was never afraid, and knowing she was scared now terrified me. I lifted my head to look at Daddy and saw his worried face before he smiled to hide it.

I pulled out of Mommy's arms. "I want to see him."

"He's asleep," Daddy said.

"I don't care." I scrambled off the big bed. "I want to see him."

Mommy and Daddy looked at Eldeorin, and then Daddy picked me up. He carried me downstairs to the bedroom I shared with Dimitri. Papa was sitting in a chair by Dimitri's bed, and he looked as worried as Daddy.

I stared past Papa at Dimitri, who was dressed in his pajamas with the covers pulled up to his chest. He looked like he was asleep, but he was surrounded by a blue glow. I pointed at him. "What's that?"

Mommy walked over to stand beside Dimitri's bed. "That is Eldeorin's magic. Dima is sick, and Eldeorin put him in a special sleep so he can get better."

Daddy put me down, and I ran to Dimitri, who was so still he looked like one of my dolls. I reached over to touch his cold hand, and the blue glow surrounded my hand, too.

"It's gone," I cried. I could always feel his Mori when we touched, but it wasn't there anymore.

"What's gone?" Mommy asked.

"His Mori." I clasped his hand and wailed, "I killed Dima's Mori."

Mommy knelt and wrapped her arms around me. "No, baby. Dima's Mori is sleeping too so it can get better. It's not gone."

I buried my face in her neck. "You promise?"

She rubbed my back. "I promise."

"Why don't we go and let Dima sleep?" Daddy said softly. "We can come back and check on him later."

"No. I want to stay with him," I pleaded. "I won't wake him up."

Eldeorin spoke up. "They have a connection. It might be beneficial if she is near."

"We will both stay," Mommy said. Everyone else left, and she sat in the chair Papa had used.

I sat on her lap, watching Dimitri's face as he slept. The need to be closer to him *grew, and I slipped out of her arms to sit on his bed. I held his hand even though doing it made my Mori sad because it couldn't find his.*

I'm sorry, Dima. Please, wake up. *I gripped his hand tighter, trying as hard as I could to feel his Mori. I wished I could help him. Mommy had taught me how to heal sick birds and rabbits, but she said my magic would hurt demons.*

I bit my lip and cried quietly so Mommy couldn't hear me. Dimitri was right. I wasn't a real Mohiri. If I was normal like him, I wouldn't have magic, and I couldn't hurt him. Now he was sick, and it was all my fault. I wished I'd never been born with magic.

As if it knew what I was thinking, my magic shifted inside me. I'd always loved its warmth and felt soothed by its presence, but now it scared me. Go away! *I shouted in my head as I pushed it down. It resisted, but I pushed and pushed until only a faint echo of it was left. The fight made me so tired I couldn't keep my eyes open.*

I lay down beside Dimitri with an arm across him. I promise I'll never hurt you again.

Dimitri slept for four days. When he finally woke up, I was a real Mohiri, just like him.

4

____

"You actually killed a vampire?" Naomi stared at me with wide eyes the next morning after I finished recounting my adventures with Eldeorin.

"*Without* a sword," Dimitri said. I'd told him about it when I got home last night, and he couldn't wait to tell our friends today.

Sean whistled. "Fecking cool."

"A baby vampire," I clarified. "She didn't know how to fight, and I had the pipe for a weapon."

Kai laid an arm across my shoulders. "Wish I'd been there to see it."

"I can't believe you got to fight Gulaks *and* a vampire." Anna eyed me with envy. "I can't wait to see some in person."

"Then today's your lucky day." Gavin walked up to where all the trainees had gathered in our usual spot outside the training wing door. "A small team is going to Boise on a job tonight, and the seniors get to go along."

A thrill went through me. It wasn't unheard of for trainees to go on small local jobs in their last year, but not much happened in Boise anymore unless a concert or event drew vampires there. It was too close to Westhorne, and there were much bigger cities to hunt in.

"Are you serious?" Kai asked as Luis said, "No way."

Unhappy muttering erupted among the junior trainees, and Jamar asked, "Why are they the only ones who get to go?"

Gavin raised a hand for silence. "They get to go because they are seniors. Your turn will come."

Sean's face flushed with excitement. "Is it vampires?"

"Gulaks," Gavin replied. "A gang of them have moved in and set up shop there, and the team is going to clear them out."

"They must be pretty stupid Gulaks to choose Boise," Kai said.

Gavin smiled. "They are most likely young Gulaks trying to break out on their own. They're either ignorant about our presence or too arrogant to care."

"Or both," I quipped.

He laughed. "Meet the team at the garages at eight o'clock. Now, let's get to work."

"Gavin," called my mother. I looked past him to see her jogging toward us.

He smiled at her. "Good morning, Sara."

"I was wondering if I could borrow your students for half an hour or so," she said when she reached us. "We received an unexpected delivery for the menagerie, and I need some help getting them into the cages."

"What are they?" I asked. Of all the creatures I'd seen come and go from the menagerie, there wasn't one Mom couldn't handle on her own.

She turned to me. "Paluks – about three dozen of them."

A murmur went through our group. Paluks were a cousin to wild boars, with the addition of fangs and venom, which caused paralysis and hallucinations. They were found only in a region of northern Mongolia, and I had no idea why anyone would bring them to the US. Adult Paluks were vicious when provoked, and they were easily five hundred pounds.

"How are we going to fit three dozen Paluks into the menagerie?" Dimitri asked.

Mom smiled. "These are piglets."

Anna placed a hand over her heart. "Piglets? Aw! I want to help."

"Me too," I said, along with everyone else.

Gavin chuckled. "I can't compete with piglets. Let's go."

I walked beside my mother as we crossed the grounds. "Where did you find the piglets?"

"The LA command center got a tip about a black-market operation that had a truckload arriving tonight from Calgary. The informant gave us the route, and one of our teams was able to intercept them in Idaho Falls."

Anna joined us. "Why would someone want paluk piglets?"

Mom's lips flattened. "They want them for their organs."

"Their organs?" Anna and I said together.

Mom nodded grimly. "Young Paluks produce an enzyme that can reverse the signs of ageing on the skin. The enzyme can't be replicated so you need to eat the raw organs to get it."

My stomach rolled. "Ew. People actually do that?"

"Some humans will do anything to keep their youthful appearance," Gavin said from behind us.

"And some will pay anything for it," Mom added. "We've learned the buyers lined up for this shipment were willing to pay six figures for one piglet."

I released a breath. "That's insane."

"It's a new operation, and we're aware of it now, so we'll do everything we can to stop it," Mom said. "We've already alerted the Mongolian government, and they don't take kindly to black market smugglers."

We approached the two-story, rectangular stone building, which served as the menagerie. A cattle trailer had been backed up near the entrance, and a warrior I didn't know stood beside the trailer.

As we neared the trailer, we could hear little grunts and squeals coming from inside. I ran the last few yards and jumped up onto the wheel well to peer through the slats. The volume inside increased, but all I could make out was a mass of wriggling black, hairy bodies.

"There's no way to herd that many, so we'll have to carry them from the truck to the cages," Mom called over the noise. She glanced up at the overcast sky. "It's going to rain any minute, so this might get a little dirty."

Sean pulled up his sleeves. "What's a little dirt?"

"That's the spirit. I'll make sure the cages are ready, and then we'll begin," Mom said and disappeared into the building with Gavin.

Anna walked over to stand below me. "What do they look like?"

I jumped down. "Like little black pigs from what I can see."

"Let's have a look." Sean put a foot on the back bumper and grabbed the bars on one of the doors to pull himself up. The door moved.

"Wait," Dimitri called. "The door's not –"

Sean yelled as the door swung open under his weight.

"– locked," Dimitri finished lamely, a second before the first piglet leaped from the truck and took off as fast as its little legs could carry it.

"Catch it," Naomi shouted as a wave of Paluks spilled from the truck. Sean tried to shut the door, but he jumped back when a few of the piglets squealed in pain.

The only word to describe what happened next was pandemonium. Shouts rang out, and people ran after the piglets, which had scattered in every direction. As if on cue, the sky opened up and pelted us with fat raindrops.

Anna and I chased two of the escaping Paluks into the woods, and it surprised me how fast they were on their stubby little legs. Luckily, we were faster. I caught mine by the back leg and lifted the squealing creature into my arms. He was covered in prickly black hair, which tickled my arms, and his two tiny lower tusks gave him an adorable underbite. His black button eyes were so wide the whites were visible.

"It's okay, little guy," I crooned. He quieted, but I could feel his little heart thumping wildly. The poor thing was terrified.

"Ow! Stop that," Anna yelled behind me.

I turned to see her with one arm wrapped around a squirming piglet and her other hand sporting a small bite mark. I went over and took the piglet from her, nestling it under my other arm, where it immediately calmed.

Anna gaped at me, and I shrugged. "Animals like me."

We jogged back to the grounds. The first sight that greeted us was Mom walking toward the menagerie like the Pied Piper with at least a dozen Paluks trotting happily after her. Everywhere else though, it was chaos as people ran through the pouring rain trying to round up the rest of the creatures.

I paused to watch Victoria and Elsie, who were so focused on their quarry they didn't see each other until they collided. The girls went down, and the piglets scrambled away, causing Anna to erupt in a fit of giggles. She sank down to sit on the wet grass, laughing uproariously.

"Get up, you idiot," I said, but she only laughed harder.

"Was she bitten?" Mom called.

I walked over to her and set my piglets on the ground with hers. "Yes."

Mom sighed. "The piglets aren't dangerous, but we've learned their bite can still affect us. She's the third one."

I scanned the grounds until my gaze found Sean and Luis, who were rolling around laughing on the grass near the manor. "Will they be okay?" I asked Mom.

"Yes. The venom will wear off after a few hours and it has no lasting effects." She pointed a thumb over her shoulder. "I think the others could use your help though."

I looked past her at Dimitri, Naomi, and Kai, each struggling to carry two wriggling piglets. Not far from them, Gavin, Jamar, and Teresa tried to herd eight or ten piglets without much success.

Gavin's group looked like it needed the most help, so I set off in a run toward them. Halfway there, I had to leap over a piglet with Elsie in hot pursuit shouting curses at it. I was laughing when I reached Gavin, earning a suspicious look from him.

"I'm fine." I grabbed up two of the piglets and ran back to the menagerie. Depositing them inside, I swiped rain from my eyes and went back for more, earning a grateful smile from my trainer.

"Feel free to help us," Dimitri called when I passed them a second time. He adjusted his hold on his piglets. "Stop squirming."

"You're doing great," I shouted over my shoulder.

I was on my third trip when Kai yelled and dropped the two Paluks he carried. The piglets hit the ground and sped away like their tiny tails were on fire. Kai ran after them, but the pair split up with one headed toward the manor and the other going straight for the river.

Veering in the direction of the river, I yelled, "I'll get this one."

I flew across the grounds, rapidly closing the distance between me and the fleeing piglet. A few yards from the riverbank, the piglet froze like a petrified rabbit staring down a fox. I skidded to a stop in time to see Hugo stalking toward us, his hungry eyes fixed on the creature.

"Hugo, no." I put up a hand. "Sit."

The hellhound gave me a baleful look and sat.

"Good boy." I glanced around for Woolf but didn't spot him. Sending up a silent prayer he wasn't somewhere snacking on a paluk, I inched toward the piglet three feet away.

The sound of running feet stopped me, and I looked around to see a red-faced Elsie chasing her piglet in my direction. She leaned down to grab it, and the wet creature slipped through her fingers. "Come back here, you little bugger," she shouted.

Snickering, I turned back to my own piglet, and my gaze swept over Ronan emerging from the woods farther up the riverbank. In his arms were two squirming piglets that squealed as if he was trying to eat them. I guessed I wasn't the only one who didn't like him.

The noise frightened my piglet out of its frozen state, and it shot forward. Moving too fast to stop, it lost its footing and fell over the end of the bank.

"Shit." I ran to the edge in time to see the little black body tumble down the muddy slope and into the water. In seconds, the current grabbed it and carried it away.

I slid down to the rocky shore and kicked off my boots. Catching a glimpse of the piglet through the rain, I dived into the river and swam after it. The current was strong, and I used it to help me reach the terrified paluk. The poor thing was so exhausted it didn't struggle when I caught it and hugged it to me with one arm.

"Let's get you back with the others," I said.

Swimming against the current with one hand was a waste of energy, so I let the river carry me to a shallow section a dozen yards downstream. I thought someone shouted my name, but it was drowned out by the roar of the river.

My feet had barely touched bottom when I heard a splash behind me. I gasped and sucked in water when an arm wrapped around my middle, lifting me off my feet and towing me toward the shore.

Coughing, I tried to pull away from my would-be rescuer, but he didn't release his iron grip on me until we were only knee-deep in water. The second his arm loosened around me, I spun and thumped my palm against his chest. "What the hell are you –?"

The words died on my lips when I looked up into Ronan's wild hazel eyes. His hands gripped my shoulders, and the heat of his touch flooded me despite the pouring rain. There was something almost primal in the way he stared at me, making my breath quicken and my chest flutter.

My Mori growled. At first, I thought I'd imagined it because I'd never experienced anything like it. It came again, and this time, it was unmistakable. *What the hell?*

Ronan's nostrils flared. "Are you insane? You could have drowned."

"I was fine until you came along." I pushed against him, but I might as well shove a boulder.

"You were not fine." His eyes blazed. "The current had you, and you are no match for this river."

I stiffened at his tone, the same one he used with me in class, and I poked him hard in the chest. "The current did *not* have me. I let it carry me."

"That is not how it looked to me."

"Then look again." I thrust the piglet at him. Startled, he released me to take it. I ran and dived into the river, swimming against the current to the other side with powerful strokes. I reached the far bank and swam back upstream to where I'd left my boots.

Hoots and clapping greeted me, and I smiled up at Dimitri and Kai standing on top of the bank. I wanted to ignore Ronan, who had walked up to stand on the rocks beside my boots, but the squealing piglet under his arm made it impossible. Taking the creature from him, I bent to pull on my boots. The paluk quieted, but it didn't stop squirming until I put a few feet between Ronan and me.

"Dani's half fish," Dimitri told Ronan, laughing. "If you ever fall into a river, she's the one you want to jump in after you."

Adjusting my hold on the piglet, I climbed the slippery bank, which proved to be more challenging than the river. I didn't look in Ronan's direction, but I was keenly aware of him watching me, judging me. A few feet from the top, Kai stretched out his hand, and I took it, letting him pull me up.

My ponytail had come loose, and I pushed wet hair off my face before I remembered my hands were covered in mud from the climb. Kai's smirk was enough to tell me what I looked like.

"What on earth happened to you?" Mom called, hurrying toward us.

Dimitri guffawed. "Dani jumped in the river to save a piglet, and Ronan went in to save her."

"Did he?" She laughed as her eyes shifted to something behind me. "You must be Ronan. Welcome to Westhorne."

"Thank you," he replied in a polite tone I'd never heard him use.

Mom walked over to him with her hand outstretched. "I'm Sara, Dani and Dimitri's mother."

Ronan took her hand, and for a few seconds, the two of them stared at each other. Her back was to me, but I saw his eyes widen. Sometimes, when she used her magic, traces of it remained around her like an aura. I wondered if she'd shocked him like I had in our first class.

She came back and took the piglet from me. Holding him up so they were nose to snout, she said, "You've had an exciting day, haven't you? Let's get you back with your brothers and sisters."

She tucked him under her chin and reached out to wipe a glob of mud from my cheek. "I'll take care of this little one. You go home and clean up."

"What about the rest of the Paluks?" I asked.

"We have a few stragglers left to round up, but I think we can manage the rest without you." She looped her arm through mine, and we walked toward the menagerie.

"Mom, what just happened with Ronan?" I asked when we were out of earshot.

After a brief pause, she said, "That was nothing. Sometimes, I forget not everyone who comes here is familiar with my magic."

"Did you shock him?"

She laughed softly. "You could say that."

We neared the menagerie and met Gavin and Anna on their way to the manor. She was still giggling and went into another fit of laughter when she saw me.

I looked down at my muddy clothes and realized I'd gotten off easy. I had a feeling Anna wasn't going to be laughing when the effects of the venom wore off.

"I'm taking her to the medical ward," Gavin told us. To me he said, "I'll see you after you get cleaned up."

"Thanks for your help," Mom said as we passed them. She stopped at the door to the menagerie. "I hear you're going to Boise tonight on a job. Stay safe, and have fun."

"We will." In all the excitement, I'd completely forgotten about tonight. The warriors probably wouldn't let us fight the Gulaks, but at least, we'd be close to the action. I picked up my pace. Soon, anticipation for the Boise job pushed all thoughts of the encounter with Ronan out of my head.

Dimitri and I ate dinner with our friends in the dining hall that evening, and then the six seniors hung out in one of the common rooms. Thankfully, Anna and Sean had recovered from their paluk bites, and the healers had cleared them to go to Boise. The rest would have felt terrible if they'd had to miss out on this.

When it was time to go, we exited the building through the door in the training wing, shoving each other playfully. We hurried to the garages, where three warriors were loading gear bags into the back of two large SUVs.

My excitement dimmed when Ronan came around the side of one of the vehicles. I should have known one of our trainers would accompany us, but why couldn't it be Gavin?

When I recognized the two red-haired warriors by the other SUV, my mood brightened, and I headed straight for them.

Niall turned at my approach, and his eyes widened. "There is no way our little Dani is a senior already."

"Lord, help us all." His twin brother Seamus put his hands together in mock prayer.

"Ha-ha." I hugged them. "I'm not Mom."

Seamus snorted. "Time will tell."

Seamus and Niall had lived at Westhorne until six years ago when they'd started traveling between Westhorne and command centers all over the country. I missed seeing them every day and hearing their stories about Mom when she was my age. My favorite was the one where she and Aunt Jordan locked them in Alex's old cage at the menagerie the night they snuck away from Westhorne. Niall said it had taken two showers to get the stench of wyvern dung off him.

Dimitri and Kai joined us, and the five of us climbed into the SUV. I glanced over at our friends, who were getting into the other vehicle with Ronan and Claire. Claire was great, but I doubted Ronan was much of a conversationalist. It should make for an interesting drive to Boise.

During the trip, Seamus and Niall entertained us with stories about some of the jobs they had done since we last saw them. Before I knew it, we were pulling into the parking lot of an out-of-business tattoo parlor, and the other SUV parked beside us.

Seamus pointed to an old pawnshop next door. "The Gulaks are in there."

I pressed my face to my window. The three-story building had no exterior lights on, but the light spilling through the cracks in the boarded-up windows told us someone was there.

We got out, and the trainees stood back while the warriors donned their gear and weapons. A nervous thrill went through me as Claire strapped on her sword. One day soon, this would be me preparing for a job.

Ever since my first day of training, it had been drilled into me that a warrior's life is dangerous. Until last night, I'd never truly grasped the reality of fighting vampires and demons. It was messy and heart-pounding, and you had to think fast or your next move could be your last one.

Claire tied her blonde hair into a ponytail. "There are eight Gulaks we know of. So far, they only go out late at night, which means they should all be inside now. Seamus and Niall, you have the front. Ronan and I will take the back."

Sean raised a hand. "What do you want us to do?"

She looked at our eager faces. "Three of you will come in with us. The other three will hang back until we've secured the building."

Sean's face fell, and I knew my expression mirrored his. "Why can't we all go?" he asked.

"Too many bodies will get in the way," Claire said. "Smaller teams work with more precision."

Seamus opened the back of our SUV and lifted out a weapons bag. "Don't worry. There'll be plenty to see and do after we take the building. There's a lot more to our job than the fighting."

"Who gets to go?" Dimitri asked Claire.

She tipped her head in Ronan's direction. "This is a training exercise for you, so I'm going to let your trainer decide."

My shoulders slumped, and any hope I had of going dissipated like a wisp of smoke in the wind.

"Dimitri, Kai, and Naomi," Ronan said without hesitation as he sheathed his sword.

"Yes." Kai said under his breath. He shot me an apologetic look and mouthed, *"Sorry."*

I smiled to let him know it was okay. Disappointment burned in my gut, but I couldn't fault Ronan for choosing the top three of our group. Besides, I had gotten to fight two Gulaks last night.

Once the three of them were armed, we walked to the rear of the tattoo parlor. Anna, Sean, and I stayed there while the rest moved toward the pawnshop. The buildings backed up to a wooded area, which divided it from a neighborhood on the other side. I could make out some of the house lights through the trees.

"How long do you think it will take?" Anna whispered as we watched the team split up to assume their positions. Dimitri went with Seamus and Niall while Kai and Naomi went with Claire and Ronan.

"They have to clear three floors and a basement," I said, mentally doing the calculations. "I'd say ten minutes depending on how well the Gulaks fight back."

Sean groaned. "This sucks."

Anna pointed at Claire's group, which had gained access to the rear door. "There they go."

We held our collective breath and watched the two warriors file inside followed by Kai and Naomi. The door shut quietly behind them, and a full minute passed before the first muted Gulak bellow reached us. The fight had begun.

The night filled with thumps, yells, and the sounds of breaking glass. I wanted so much to be in the middle of the action, fighting beside Dimitri and my friends. Sean was right. This sucked.

Movement at the back of the building caught my eye, and I focused on a small shape running around the far corner. They stumbled and fell to their hands and knees then scrambled to their feet as if the devil was after them.

"Is that a child?" Sean asked as Anna said, "It's a little girl."

The girl sped in our direction, her long golden hair streaming behind her. It wasn't until she had almost reached our building that she noticed us standing there. She let out a terrified whimper and veered away, but I caught her.

"Let me go." She twisted and clawed at me like a feral cat, her sharp nails leaving four thin slashes on the back of my hand.

"Ow." I pulled her against me and pinned her arms with mine. She struggled to break free, but I was too strong.

"Whoa." Sean gaped at the girl. "She's a werecougar."

I turned her to see her face, which was half-covered in golden fur. Tiny canine fangs protruded from her gums, and her irises flashed between green and amber. Her terrified eyes filled with tears, which spilled down her cheeks. She wore a dirty pink top with a torn frill at the bottom, jeans, and one pink sneaker. The sock on her other foot was covered in dirt and twigs.

"It's okay," I told her in my most reassuring voice. I knelt so I was at eye level with her. "What's your name?"

She wiped her runny nose with the back of her hand. "Sofie Burke."

"You're safe with us, Sofie. The Gulaks won't hurt you anymore," I said gently.

The girl let out a broken sob and threw her thin arms around my neck. I patted her back and murmured soothing words to her. The poor little thing couldn't be more than ten years old, and judging by her smell, she'd been held captive for several days. Imagining the Gulaks selling a child into slavery or worse made me want to storm into the pawnshop and take them all out myself.

"Lilly!" She let go of me and stood back, her face in human form. "They're going to take her away."

I pointed at the pawnshop. "Our friends are in there now getting all the Gulaks. They won't let anyone take Lilly away."

Sofie frowned and shook her head. "Lilly's not in there. She's over there." She raised a trembling hand toward the houses on the other side of the woods. "The bad men are going to leave with her. We need to hurry."

I stood and met Anna's and Sean's shocked eyes. "We have to do something."

"We have to wait for the others," Anna said, and Sean nodded in agreement.

"No," Sofie cried. She grabbed my hand and tried to tug me toward the trees. "They'll be gone soon. I need to save Lilly."

I pressed my lips together. My training told me to wait for the warriors, but my gut said we needed to act now before it was too late. If Sofie was right, even a few minutes could mean the difference in saving her friend.

"How many men are there?" I asked her.

She stopped pulling on my arm to look up at me. "Three. There were four of them, but one left this morning."

I felt for the knife I carried on my hip. "Do they have weapons like guns or knives?"

"Yes."

"Dani, what are you doing?" Sean asked warily.

I faced him and Anna. "I'm going to check it out and see if I can help Sofie's friend. If not, I'll figure out how to stall the men long enough for Claire and the others to come."

Anna shook her head. "Are you crazy? You can't go over there alone."

"Then one of you come with me. The other can wait here and let the warriors know where we are." I took Sofie's hand and turned toward the trees.

"I'll go," Sean said in resignation. He came over and picked up Sofie, who squirmed until he told her it would be faster since she was missing a shoe.

"Wait," Anna whisper-yelled. "What house do I send them to?"

I paused and looked at Sofie, who said, "It's white with a blue door and a white fence. There's a pool in the backyard."

"Let's hope there's only one white house with a blue door," Anna said as we entered the woods.

"How did you get away from the men?" I asked Sofie as we crossed the wooded area.

"They locked us in cages in the basement when we got there yesterday. The man who came down with dinner tonight forgot to lock my cage, but I couldn't get Lilly's door open. I listened at the top of the stairs and heard them talk about leaving soon, so I climbed out a window and ran into the woods." Her voice broke. "I didn't want to leave Lilly, but I had to get help."

"You did the right thing," Sean said.

We reached the other side of the woods and walked along the back of the quiet neighborhood until Sofie pointed at a white ranch-style house. A pool, which looked like it hadn't been cleaned in a week, took up most of the small backyard surrounded by a white five-foot privacy fence.

I left Sean and Sofie near the fence and crept through the neighboring yard to see the front of the house. A white cargo van and an SUV were parked in the driveway, and two raised male voices came from the other side of the vehicles.

"I told you hours ago to gas up the van," one of them said. "We're already running late."

"I had other things to take care of," the second man shot back.

One of the men strode into view. He was tall and muscled with buzzed hair and wearing jeans and a black T-shirt. He yanked open the van's driver side door and got in.

"Pack up," he said to the other man as he shut the door. "We're leaving as soon as I get back."

I hurried to Sean and Sofie and told them what I'd seen. "Sofie, where is the window you used to get out?"

"There." She pointed a finger at the back of the house, and I followed it to a tiny basement window.

"Shit," Sean muttered. "No way are we going to fit through that."

I studied the window. "You won't, but I might."

"Dani –" he started to argue as I grabbed the top of the fence and vaulted over it.

5

"Call Anna and tell her where we are," I whispered as I headed for the house. The yard had no cover, but it was unlit, and I was counting on the men being too preoccupied with packing to look out the windows. I ran around the pool and reached the open basement window without one of them sending up an alarm.

The window was smaller than I'd thought, and I had to remove my jacket and knife belt to squeeze through. Grabbing my knife, I lowered myself to the floor of a laundry room, careful not to knock over the stepladder Sofie had used to escape.

Footsteps sounded overhead, but the basement was quiet. I peeked out into a large rec room with tile floors and recessed ceiling lights. The room had a large television, two couches, and some cardio equipment in one corner. It looked like a normal family room – except for the pair of cages in the middle.

I crept closer. The cages were big enough to hold a Great Dane, but the dull gleam of the bars told me they were made of silver, which was toxic to demons and shifters. One cage was empty. Inside the second one, a small shape huddled in the center. My hands curled into fists, and I had to remind myself this was no time to let my emotions take over. There'd be time to vent after I got the little girl out of here.

A child's sob came from the cage when I reached it. I crouched and whispered, "Lilly?"

The girl raised her head and stared at me with wide terrified eyes. Like

Sofie, she was golden-haired and green-eyed, and her cherubic cheeks put her at only six or seven years old. She tried to back away, but she couldn't get near the bars.

"It's okay." I raised my hands. "My name is Dani, and I came with Sofie."

"Sofie?" Hope lit up her eyes.

I smiled. "She's outside with my friend, waiting for you. I'm going to get you out of here."

Lilly sniffled. "The door won't open."

"I'll take care of that." I did a quick search of the basement and found a small work area with bins of tools and other stuff. Selecting two pieces of stiff wire, I returned to Lilly. I fashioned a rudimentary tension wrench from one piece of wire and went to work on the lock. All trainees learned how to pick locks, but I never thought I'd be using the skill so soon. I made a mental note to carry a pick set on me after this.

The lock clicked just as the door at the top of the basement stairs opened. I put a finger to my lips to silence Lilly, and I hid under the stairs as a man descended them. He was muscled and only slightly smaller than the man I'd seen by the van, and he wore a shoulder holster, which held a SIG-Sauer.

My mind raced. As soon as he saw the empty cage, he would raise the alarm, and I couldn't let that happen. One armed man I could handle with the element of surprise on my side. Two armed men was a different story.

I tensed as he reached the bottom and walked into view of the cages. I crept up behind him as he stopped and stared at the empty one.

"What the –?"

I attacked, wrapping my arm around his neck in a sleeper hold. He grabbed my arm, attempting to pull it away, but I held tightly. When that didn't work, he tried to headbutt me and twist in different directions. The man was strong and a decent fighter, but his movements became sluggish from lack of oxygen, and he went limp in my arms.

I dragged him out of sight under the stairs, disarmed him, and hurried back to Lilly. If he'd come down here to get the girls, it wouldn't be long before his friend wondered where he was.

"Is he dead?" Lilly whispered.

"No. He's sleeping." Opening the cage door, I helped her out, careful to keep her from touching the silver bars.

A car door slammed outside. *Shit.* The other man was back with the van. We needed to get out of here.

I picked up Lilly and carried her to the laundry room, where I hoisted her to the open window. "Sofie is with my friend Sean outside the fence at the back of the yard. Run to them as fast and as quietly as you can."

She climbed out and stared back at me. "What about you?"

"I'm right behind you. Go."

She took off running as a man's voice called from the top of the stairs. "Wesley, what's taking so long?"

I gripped the window frame and pulled myself up. The opening looked a lot smaller from this side, and I barely managed to squeeze my shoulders through when boots pounded on the stairs.

"They're gone," the man shouted from the other room.

I braced my hands on either side of the window and pushed with all my strength. My body inched forward slowly, too slowly.

Hands grabbed one of my feet and yanked hard. "Oh, no, you don't," the man snarled.

I kicked out blindly with my free leg as I held onto the window to stop him from pulling me back inside. The first two kicks met air, but the third one connected with his face.

He grunted in pain but didn't loosen his grip on my foot. I kicked again, and this time, I struck him square in the chest. He flew backward and struck the wall. A string of loud curses followed as he shouted for someone named Cole.

A fresh wave of adrenaline surged in me, and I used it to pull my body through the window. I lay face-down on the grass for a few seconds, panting more from the close call than the exertion.

The sound of running footsteps drove me to my feet. The other man was coming around the corner of the house.

I looked for Lilly and found her at the back fence where Sean was reaching down to lift her over. I took off in a sprint with a single purpose – stop the man from reaching Sean and the girls.

I dove at the man and tackled him, our momentum taking us to the edge of the pool and over. The moment the cold water closed over my head, I released him.

The man broke the surface behind me, and I spun, ready to fight him. I accidentally sucked in water when I came face-to-face with a scowling Ronan. A leaf was plastered to his cheek, and for a second, I could swear his eyes flashed gold. His glare made me wish I had tackled the armed man instead.

"We have to stop meeting like this," I joked awkwardly, and his scowl deepened.

Deciding it would be prudent to put some distance between us, I swam to the side of the pool. Lights came on in the yard as a hand reached down to help me out of the water. I took it and looked up at Sean's grinning face.

"You have all the fun," he said when I stood next to him.

I shivered in the brisk night air. "I can push you in if that will make you feel better."

He backed away with his hands up. "No, thanks."

"Where are Sofie and Lilly?" I peered around him at the fence and saw Anna staring back at me over the top. Her eyes widened when Ronan climbed out of the pool behind me, and she pretended to swoon.

"They're with Anna," Sean said. "What happened in there?"

I started to give him a quick rundown, but I was interrupted when a hand appeared in front of me, holding my coat. "Put this on," Ronan ordered.

Taking the coat, I turned to thank him, and my brain seemed to short-circuit. The wet fabric of his gray T-shirt clung to his muscular body, outlining his broad shoulders and the contours of his chest, abdomen, and arms. Swallowing, I lifted my gaze to his. Droplets of water accentuated his cheekbones and strong jawline and added fullness to his eyelashes.

My fingers twitched with the insane urge to run them through his wet hair. It jolted me to my senses, and I mumbled a thank you as I slipped into the coat.

He walked away without another word. I guessed I hadn't done anything to improve his opinion of me.

Sean smirked at me. "Sweet tackle, but next time, you might want to check that you're taking down one of the bad guys first."

"Ha-ha." I spun and stalked toward the house. The back door was open, and I spotted Ronan talking to Seamus, so I assumed there was no longer a threat. I walked into the kitchen, which opened into the living room. The big man I assumed was Cole was unconscious and bound with zip ties. On another chair sat a man with a bloody face and a broken nose. He must be the one I'd fought as I escaped from the basement.

"Where's the third guy?" I asked, interrupting the warriors' conversation.

Seamus gave me a questioning look. "I only found those two."

I went to the basement door, but Ronan put out an arm to stop me. "He could be armed. I'll go."

I tried to push past him, but his arm was like a steel rod. "He's probably still out cold, and I took his weapons."

Surprise flickered in Ronan's eyes, but he didn't let me pass. He turned and went down to the basement.

"He's under the stairs," I called after him.

Seamus barked out a laugh and handed me a towel he'd grabbed from the bathroom. "Nothing like your mom, huh?"

I rolled my eyes at him as I towel-dried my dripping hair. I'd fought a couple of human men. When Mom was my age, she'd snuck away from West-horne to track down a Master, whom she'd killed.

Ronan appeared at the top of the stairs with the unconscious man slung over his shoulder. Our gazes met, and for a second, I thought I saw admiration in his eyes. I dismissed it as the trick of the light.

"Nice work, Dani," Seamus said when Ronan laid the man on the living room floor and proceeded to bind his wrists and ankles.

Ronan stood and surveyed our three captives before he turned to me. "You should have waited for us."

I opened my mouth to argue that it would have been too late if I'd waited, but his next words made me forget what I was going to say.

"But you did well."

"Um, thanks," I said, ridiculously pleased by his praise.

He looked at Seamus. "Do we know who they are or what they were up to?"

Seamus's smile faded. "The two I checked had wallets with cash in them but no IDs. Judging by their weapons and gear, I'd say they're hired mercs."

"Hired by whom?" Ronan looked at the bloodied man who was the only one awake. The man stared back with a stony expression.

"Why would someone hire mercenaries to kidnap two werecougar children?" I asked.

"Good question." Ronan folded his arms across his chest. "Werecougars are very protective of their young. Did the children tell you where and how they were taken?"

"There wasn't time. I'll go ask them." I left the house and ran over to stand beside Sean. On the other side of the fence, Sofie and Lilly huddled together wearing Sean and Anna's coats. Sofie looked less frightened now, but Lilly clung to the older girl with her face hidden against Sofie's side. They looked so tiny and frail my anger at the men began to boil again.

I smiled. "Hey there. Are you girls okay?"

"I want Mommy and Daddy," Lilly wailed in a muffled voice.

"We're going to get you home as soon as we can." I looked at Sofie. "Where do you live?"

Her face lit up. "Wintree."

"Is that in Idaho?" Anna asked.

"It's in Nevada." Sofie rubbed Lilly's back. "It's a pretty small place. Mom takes us shopping in Carson City."

"Is Wintree a werecougar town, or do humans live there, too?" I asked her. Most werecougar prides lived apart from humans, which made me wonder how mercenaries could have gotten close to the girls. The men in the house didn't exactly blend in.

"Mostly werecougars but a few humans live there, too." She fell silent for a moment as if she could read my thoughts. "I was supposed to watch out for Lilly, but I couldn't stop the bad men from taking us."

Anna put an arm around the girls. "That's not your fault. I'm a lot bigger than you, and they would have gotten me, too."

"Not Dani." Lilly lifted her head for the first time. "She made the bad man go to sleep."

Sean chuckled. "You're right. They'd have to be stupid to mess with Dani."

"Sofie, can you tell us where you were when the men took you?" I asked.

She gave a shaky nod. "There's a creek behind our house. We play in it sometimes after school until Mom calls us in for dinner. That's where we were when they came. I tried to run away, but something stung me, and I fell down. When I woke up, we were tied up in a van."

Sean, Anna, and I shared a look. Tranquilizers? Who the hell were these guys?

"Did they say anything about why they took you?" I pressed gently. I didn't want to make her relive the experience, but we needed to get the information while her memories were fresh.

Lilly spoke up. "One of them yelled because they were supposed to get a boy. He was scary."

Sofie hugged her sister closer. "The man said they would get paid less because they were supposed to bring a boy and a girl"–her face scrunched as she searched for the word–"specimen."

My stomach lurched, but I tried not to react. A glance at Anna and Sean told me they were doing the same. The girls were traumatized enough without us adding to it.

"Do you want to call your parents, or would you rather we do it for you?" I searched my pockets for my phone. Not finding it, I looked at Sean who held up his.

Sofie reached for the phone and pulled her hand back. "Can you call them?"

"I'll do it," Sean said to me. "I think Ronan wants to talk to you."

I looked toward the house where Ronan and Seamus stood outside watching us. I told Sofie and Lilly I'd be back soon and returned to the house to relate the girls' story to the warriors.

"This was no crime of opportunity," Ronan said in a hard voice. "It took surveillance and planning to carry it off."

Seamus's grim expression looked foreign on his usually cheerful face.

"Black market traffickers don't often use the word specimen unless they are selling to a very specific kind of buyer."

"You mean the kind of people who buy body parts and stuff like troll bile?" I asked in a low voice.

Ronan's eyebrows rose.

"When my mom was a teenager, she sold troll bile on the black market to buy exotic medicines for her friend Remy. He used them to heal people," I said. "I don't think they ever bought body parts, though."

Ronan looked at me like I'd sprouted a horn in the center of my forehead. Sometimes, I forgot how different my mother was, especially to people who didn't know her.

"Mom didn't steal the troll bile. Remy's a troll, and he gave it to her," I tried to explain when he kept staring at me.

Seamus laughed and came to my rescue. "As crazy as it sounds, it's true."

We went into the house. I looked over at the bound men and met the furious eyes of the man I'd kicked in the face. What made a person become a mercenary who steals children for money? How did he live with himself knowing the horrors those children suffered? A person who would do that was capable of anything.

A thought struck me, and I spun back to Ronan and Seamus. "Do you think there's a connection between this and the disappearances my dad is investigating?"

"Those are all demons," Seamus said thoughtfully. "But the people behind it could be escalating to other species. We'll see what our people get out of these men."

Sean entered the kitchen wearing a harried expression. "We contacted Sofie and Lilly's parents. Their father threatened to skin me if anything happened to his girls, and that was after I put Sofie on the phone to explain I wasn't the one who took them."

"Most shifters are mistrustful of outsiders," Ronan said, sounding like he had firsthand experience with them. "Some werewolf packs have begun integrating with humans, but for the most part, shifters stick with their own kind."

Sean grimaced. "I don't want to be around when those parents get here. Speaking of which, they want to know where to pick up the girls."

"Westhorne," I said before anyone else could speak. "We can't keep them here or take them to a hotel after what they've been through. Mom can heal Sofie's cuts and bruises and clean them up."

Seamus nodded in approval. "Sara is the best person to talk to the parents. She has a way with shifters."

Ronan shot him a strange look but said nothing. Surely, he knew about my mother's abilities, unless he really had been living in the wild for years.

"I'll let them know," Sean said as he turned to leave.

I followed him to search for my phone, which had fallen out of my coat pocket. I found it in the grass beside the basement window and read a bunch of texts from Dimitri and Kai.

Dimitri: **Seamus and Ronan just ran out of here. What did you do? jk**

Dimitri: **Seriously. Where are you?**

Kai: **Are you ok? Claire said you guys ran into trouble.**

Dimitri: **Did you really save some werecougar kids? Cool!**

Kai: **You took out a bunch of armed mercs???**

Kai: **My girlfriend is a badass!**

Smiling, I texted them back that I was okay, and I would fill them in later.

Seamus came out to tell us he was staying here to wait for the backup team. Claire and Niall were busy with the Gulak job, which left Ronan to take Sofie and Lilly to Westhorne. Lilly promptly announced she wasn't leaving without me, so I agreed to go with them. I was relieved when Anna said she'd come, too, which saved me from having to carry a non-conversation with Ronan for the hour-long drive.

I called my mother to let her know what was going on. As I knew she would, she said to bring the girls to our house instead of the manor. It was cozier and a lot less intimidating.

Ronan left and returned five minutes later with one of the SUVs. I got into the back with Sofie and Lilly, and Anna was more than happy to ride up front with Ronan. She tried multiple times in the first thirty minutes to draw him into conversation, but all she got out of him were a few one-word responses. For the second half of the drive, the only sound in the vehicle was Lilly's tiny snores as she slept with her head resting against me.

When we got to Westhorne, Ronan dropped off Anna at the manor before he drove the girls and me to the lake. Mom was waiting outside for us, and she ran over to help the girls out of the SUV. It took them less than a minute to get over their fear of someone new. Mom held out her arms to Lilly, and the little girl ran into them like they'd known each other forever.

I turned to thank Ronan and saw him watching Mom take the girls' hands and lead them to the house. "Everyone loves my mother," I said lightly. "Well, everyone but vampires."

Ronan's expression was unreadable as he looked at me over the hood. We were alone for the first time since we met in the woods, and I was at a loss for words. He was the only male I'd ever met who made me feel like an awkward thirteen-year-old.

To say we'd gotten off to a rocky start was an understatement. Tonight, he'd praised my performance for the first time, and I felt I owed him something in return.

"I'm sorry for knocking you into the brook that day in the woods...and for tackling you tonight." My fingers twisted the hem of my coat, and I began to babble. "I guess I should also apologize for zapping you in our first training class. I swear it was an accident and not because I don't like you or anything." I clamped my lips together. *Shut up, Dani.*

"Good. I would hate to see what you'd do if you didn't like me."

At first, I thought he was serious, until one corner of his mouth twitched. I was so taken off guard I couldn't think of a response.

"Good night, Dani." Ronan got into the SUV and drove away. I stayed where I was, watching him until his taillights disappeared.

———

I flicked off the television in the common room and checked the time on my phone. "It's ten o'clock. I should get home before Dad comes looking for me."

"I'll walk you home." Kai stood and reached out a hand to me.

Laughing, I took his hand and stood. "You can walk me to the woods. Hugo and Woolf are probably there waiting for me."

He shook his head. "I've been at Westhorne for five years, and I still can't believe you guys live with a pair of hellhounds."

"Most people have that reaction," I said as we left the common room and walked through the main hall to the entrance. The door in the training wing was closer to the woods, but I liked the walk across the grounds.

Outside, there was a chill in the air. Soon, the leaves would change color, and winter would be here.

I looked up at the manor as we walked, not surprised to see light coming from Grandfather's office. He seemed to be working all the time now. In the week since we'd rescued Sofie and Lilly, four more demons had been reported missing, and someone had tried to snatch a werecougar boy from a family in Oregon. The would-be kidnappers got away, but Grandfather believed they worked for whomever had hired the mercs to snatch the girls. If these incidents were connected to the missing demons, the people behind them were escalating and getting bolder.

An interrogation of the mercs revealed they were hired and paid anonymously to deliver the girls to North Dakota. We captured them before their mystery employer could give them the location. They had no knowledge of the other kidnappings. We knew they weren't lying because Mom's hacker friend David was also an Emote. He could read a person's aura and tell if they were being truthful.

Mom had spent the last week visiting every werecougar pride and family she could find to spread the word about the potential threat. Unlike werewolves who lived in packs, there were werecougar families who chose to live apart from a pride, which made them more vulnerable.

"There he goes for his nightly stroll," Kai said, pulling me from my thoughts.

"Who?"

He pointed toward the river, where a figure walked along the bank. "Ronan. I think he goes out to patrol every night."

"That sounds like something he'd do." I thought about my first impression of Ronan in the woods and the little I'd learned about him since. Dad said Ronan preferred to work alone and usually went months without checking in with anyone. Someone like that was used to watching their own back and wouldn't trust anyone but himself with his safety.

His solitary lifestyle also explained his lack of conversational skills and his blunt, no-nonsense style of training. He didn't waste a minute of his classes on anything other than training, and he was nothing short of brutally honest when giving feedback.

At least, he was no longer singling me out for his harshest criticism. He didn't go easy on me, but his voice had less of an edge to it. I'd even gotten the only nod of approval from him in an agility exercise, which had surprised me so much I almost let go of the rope I was climbing.

We reached the edge of the trees, and I smiled when I spotted Woolf lying on the road. His tail thumped the ground when I leaned down to scratch his head.

Kai tugged me into his arms and kissed me. He was a great kisser, and I wrapped my arms around his neck to pull him closer.

The sound of someone clearing their throat right behind me had us jumping apart like we'd been burned. I spun to find Eldeorin wearing an amused expression.

I glared at him. "Do you mind?"

He gave Kai an appreciative look, which would have made me blush. "I apologize for intruding on your fun."

"You don't look sorry." I eyed him warily. "What are you doing here in the middle of the night?"

"It's hardly the middle of the night, and it's time for your next lesson."

A tiny thrill shot through me, but I took a small step backward. "Mom and Dad are expecting me home soon."

"I let Sara know I was coming for you." His mouth quirked. "We decided she should tell your father."

I hadn't been there when Mom informed Dad about my training with Eldeorin, but I knew he wasn't happy about it. For her part, she hadn't been surprised at all when I told her about my first lesson with Eldeorin.

"Oh," was all I could think of to say.

"Then let's be off, shall we?"

I raised my hand to hold him off, but Eldeorin's fingers wrapped around my wrist, and Westhorne disappeared.

Seconds later, we were standing in a small parking lot behind a two-story black brick building, and the quiet of home was replaced with the sounds of a noisy city.

I whirled on Eldeorin. "You could have let me say goodbye to Kai."

He shook his head. "I have never understood this need people have to always announce their departure."

"It's good manners." I looked around. "Where are we?"

"Visiting a friend of mine before we begin training." He looked me over. "First, however, we need to do something about your clothes."

"What's wrong with my clothes?" I demanded. I looked down at my jeans and sweater...only to discover I was no longer wearing them. In their place was a porcelain blue satin slip dress and matching shoes with three-inch heels.

Eldeorin nodded. "Perfect."

"For what?" I asked suspiciously.

He smiled. "You'll see. Shall we?" Looping his arm through mine, he led me to the door and rapped softly on it.

Music spilled from inside as the heavy metal door swung open to reveal a glowering seven-foot-tall ogre with a buzz cut, a massive chest, and arms the size of tree limbs. He gave a slight nod in greeting when he saw us.

"Good evening, Lorne," Eldeorin said with easy familiarity.

"Evening, Mr. Eldeorin." Lorne stepped to one side, and we ducked under the arm holding the door for us.

I knew where we were the moment I saw the people on the dance floor. There was only one place I'd heard of where demons mingled with faeries, shifters, and humans. We were at Blue Nyx, a Los Angeles night club owned by a succubus named Adele.

I stared like a voyeur at the dancers as they moved against their partners in an erotic display. Although they shared the dance floor, the demons and faeries kept a safe distance between them.

The deeper we walked into the club, the more the sensual music flowed around me, until my heart seemed to match the hypnotic beat. The melody was a soft caress against my skin, filling me with the urge to lose myself among the undulating dancers.

Eldeorin's hand touched my cheek, and I jolted back to awareness. It felt like I'd been released from the influence of a potent drug. Disoriented, I looked at him. "What was that?"

"That was succubus magic. It's why all these people come here."

"They like being controlled by it?" I asked in disbelief.

He turned me to face the dancers. "It's not control. Adele's magic merely removes their inhibitions and increases their arousal. In exchange, she feeds off their sexual energy. They know this, and they submit to it freely."

A small shudder went through me when I realized how close I'd come to joining them. To each their own, but I had no desire to let a succubus feed off me.

I watched the dancers. "How can faeries fall under the thrall of a succubus? Aren't they immune to demon magic?"

Eldeorin laughed softly. "Faeries are immune, and we have no sexual inhibitions. We enjoy it when everyone else loses theirs." He led me away from the dance floor. "Once you free your magic, you will be immune to it as well."

We walked over to a long bar where Eldeorin signaled to one of the bartenders. "*Glaen* for my young friend and me."

The woman reached under the bar and lifted out a bottle of luminescent, milky liquid. She poured some into two small glasses and placed them in front of us.

I looked at my glass but didn't touch it. Mom kept some of the Fae drink at the house for Eldeorin, but she never drank it herself because she'd gotten a bit drunk the first time she tried it. Why would Eldeorin want me to drink it?

I looked over at him. "I thought we were here for training."

"We are." He picked up his glass. "First, we will enjoy some of Adele's fine spirits and hospitality."

"I don't understand."

"You will." He tipped his glass to me and took a drink. "Go ahead. I would not allow you to do something that would harm you."

I opened my mouth to argue, but instead, I raised the glass to my lips. I *was* curious about Glaen, and it smelled heavenly, like a bouquet of spring wildflowers and honey fresh from the hive.

I took a cautious sip and went still as flavors exploded in my mouth. I tasted fresh peaches and cream, lavender, jasmine, honey, and something else I didn't know. The second sip sent warmth through me from my fingers to my toes. I took a deeper drink and knew what pure bliss was.

"Another?" Eldeorin asked.

Looking down at my glass, I was shocked to find it empty. I did a self-check. My body felt pleasantly warm and light, but my mental focus was clear. It was nothing compared to the effect Adele's magic had on me.

I nodded at the bartender, who stood across from me with the bottle of glaen. She refilled my glass, and I smiled my thanks. I took a sip and set the glass on the bar, determined to go slower with this one.

Angling my body toward Eldeorin, I asked a question, which had been on my mind since we arrived. "How does a faerie become friends with a succubus? Aren't demons and faeries mortal enemies?"

He gave me an amused look. "An interesting question from someone who is half Fae and has a demon inside."

"That's not the same. I was born this way, and it's not like my Mori and I are two separate people like you and Adele."

"You both have emotions, do you not?" He tipped his hand toward me. "Do you and your demon hate each other?"

I rolled my eyes. "That's like me asking you if you hate your heart. My Mori is just as much a part of me, and its emotions are my emotions."

"Does it not fear your Fae magic?" he asked.

"Of course, not." I paused because it wasn't entirely true. "When I was little, my Mori was afraid a few times when I got upset and had an outburst. Mom taught me how to shield it from my magic even when I was upset, and it was never afraid again."

He nodded thoughtfully. "So, it comes naturally to you to protect your demon from your magic."

"Yes." I lifted my glass and discovered it was empty again. I didn't even remember drinking it.

Eldeorin motioned for the bartender to refill our glasses. This time, I didn't hesitate to take a drink from mine. Aside from feeling relaxed and care-free, I was totally in control. Glaen must not affect me like it did Mom.

"And you shield your demon by suppressing your magic," he said after a minute.

"I did that to protect Dimitri, not me."

His expression said he'd already known that, so why was he asking me these questions? I frowned, trying to remember how we'd started this conversation.

An ogre, not the one who had greeted us at the door, came over and leaned down to say something to Eldeorin. He left, and Eldeorin looked at me. "There is something I must attend to. I will be back in a few minutes."

"Okay."

I sipped my drink. The warmth in my body had drawn back from my limbs and gathered somewhere deep within me. I looked inside myself and saw a soft glow near my core. How strange? I made a mental note to ask Eldeorin if this was normal when drinking glaen.

Putting my back to the bar. I watched the people around me. It was fascinating to see demons conversing openly with humans, and faeries interacting with werewolves as if it was a natural occurrence. I wished all races could get along like this outside of Blue Nyx.

My eyes met those of a blond male whose features were too perfect to be human. He smiled and walked over to me. When he got within a few feet of me, his brows drew together in confusion.

"Forgive me. I thought..." He stared at me like he was trying to work out a difficult puzzle. "I mean no offense, but what are you?"

A laugh bubbled from me. "What do you think I am?"

He took another step toward me. "I thought you were human until I saw you were drinking glaen. I can sense you are Fae, but I also sense the presence of a demon. That is not possible."

I set down my drink. "You've heard of Sara Grey?"

"No."

That surprised me. I'd thought all faeries knew about my mother because she was the first Fae/demon hybrid. I gave him the condensed version of how my mother came to be born half undine and half Mohiri, and she passed it to me. The faerie, who said his name was Cieran, listened with rapt attention.

"I knew Blue Nyx would be interesting, but I never expected to meet someone like you." He leaned against the bar and ordered a glass of glaen. "Would you like another?"

"I think she has had enough," Eldeorin said.

"Eldeorin." Cieran straightened. "I did not know Dani was with you."

The way he said it left no doubt he thought Eldeorin and I were a couple. I giggled at the very idea of it. "We're here together, but we're not *together*. He's my godfather, which practically makes him my uncle. And he's my teacher."

"Danielle is under my protection," Eldeorin clarified.

The other faerie dipped his head in deference. "I apologize for the misunderstanding."

"No worries," I said cheerfully. "I enjoyed talking to you."

Cieran smiled at me. "I enjoyed it as well, and I hope I see you again." He gave Eldeorin another quick nod and walked away.

"He was nice." I met Eldeorin's gaze. "Are we leaving now?"

He took my empty glass and laid it on the bar. "How do you feel?"

"I feel great. Mom said she got drunk on glaen, but I don't think it affects me at all." Something niggled the back of my mind, some question I meant to ask him, but I couldn't think of what it was. It must not be that important.

He took my hand and laid it on his arm. He was such a gentleman. "Come. We are going to see my friend Adele."

"Really?" I went with him eagerly. "I've never met a succubus. I hear they are very beautiful. Do I look nice enough?"

Eldeorin said something I couldn't quite make out. It sounded like "Three might have been too much."

We ascended a winding staircase to the second floor where more people milled about near the rail overlooking the dance floor. I thought I caught a glimpse of naked bodies on a corner couch, but Eldeorin turned me in the other direction before I could take a second look.

We stopped at a closed door. Another ogre stood guard outside. How many ogres did she have working here? She must have a whole...tribe...er... clan? What did you call a group of ogres anyway? I made a note to ask Eldeorin later.

"She is expecting me," Eldeorin said to the ogre, who nodded and stepped aside to let us pass.

We entered a large office with a wall of windows looking out over the club. There were couches along two sides, and at the end of the room was a lovely ornate desk with the most beautiful woman I had ever seen sitting behind it. Her long blonde hair was arranged atop her head and held there by diamond barrettes, showing off the delicate column of her throat and her flawless skin.

She smiled and stood, revealing a formfitting red dress, which clung to her like a second skin. "Eldeorin, it's been too long. I was so delighted when Lorne told me you were here." She looked at me, and her smile reached her violet eyes. "And who might this be? I remember the last time you brought a young lady to my office to meet me. I believe you called her your cousin."

Eldeorin laughed. "This one is also my cousin. I'd like you to meet Danielle, Sara's daughter."

Adele's violet eyes widened, and she came around the desk. "Sara and Nikolas's daughter. Of course. Madeline told me she had grandchildren."

Madeline was my maternal grandmother. She and my mother were estranged for many years, but they had reconciled when Dimitri and I were born. She lived in Australia now, and we usually saw her once a year.

Adele reached out a hand to touch my cheek. "I see so much of Nikolas in you."

The familiar way she said Dad's name made my hackles rise. The warm glow inside me pulsed, spitting out tiny sparks that crackled on my skin like static electricity.

Adele jerked her hand away and took a step back. "I see you are more like your mother than your father."

"I'm so sorry. I didn't mean to do that." I looked to Eldeorin for help. Instead of the disapproval I expected to see, he wore a satisfied smile. He guided me over to sit on one of the couches, and Adele took the one across from us. She didn't look angry, so I relaxed again.

"Danielle is my student," Eldeorin told her. "She does not yet have a full grasp on her magic."

Adele arched perfect eyebrows. "And you brought her to a club full of demons."

"I placed a ward on her to prevent an accident." He leaned back and crossed his legs, looking right at home. "I hear you have been having a vampire problem."

I perked up. "I thought vampires couldn't enter this club."

"They can't." Adele's expression turned hard. "There are two of them who lurk nearby waiting for people to come and go. I hired a hunter, but so far, this pair has been adept at evading him."

"What about the Mohiri?" I asked. Los Angeles had its own command center so they should be able to help.

Adele got up and went to a sideboard to pour herself a glass of amber liquid. "I can send for glaen if you would like a drink."

Eldeorin declined for both of us, and she took her seat again. "To answer your question, I have alerted the local Mohiri, but LA is a big city, and there has been a significant increase in vampire activity over the last few years. Not to mention the recent demon disappearances."

I leaned forward. "You know about that?"

"Not much happens in my city I don't know about." She put the glass to her mouth and drank half the contents. "My club is well-known, and I do not like the idea of someone snatching my patrons after they leave here. I've added more security, but there is nothing I can do once people leave the premises."

"Have any demons been taken after they leave here?" I asked.

She shook her head. "Not to my knowledge."

Eldeorin unfolded his legs and stood. "Adele, it's been lovely to see you, as always. I believe it is time for Danielle's training."

I shot to my feet. "Does this mean you'll finally tell me why we're here?"

"Patience." He and Adele said their goodbyes, and we left. Excitement built in my chest as we descended the stairs, and I paid the dancers little notice this time as we walked past them.

Lorne opened the back door for us and bid us good night. I hadn't known ogres could be so courteous. They were known for their strength and their tempers.

Outside, we walked to the edge of the parking lot and stopped. Eldeorin closed his eyes and appeared to be concentrating on something. Whatever he was doing caused my skin to tingle and made the hairs stand up on my arms.

"What was that?" I asked when he opened his eyes.

"I sent out my magic to find any vampires in the vicinity."

My mouth fell open. "Faeries can do that?" Mom's vampire radar let her sense when vampires were close, but she couldn't send it out like he had.

"Only older and stronger faeries can do it because it requires a great deal of magic." He reached for my hand. "There are at least two vampires one street over. Shall we?"

The world blurred, and we materialized on the roof of a four-story parking garage. Looking around, I caught a glimpse of Blue Nyx between two buildings. It was so close. I walked to the edge of the roof to check out the busy street below and caught sight of two young women in short dresses walking in the direction of the club.

Eldeorin sent out his magic again and smiled. "The vampires are inside this parking garage. They are likely the pair Adele told us about."

A bolt of excitement shot through me. "Are we going in after them?"

"Not we, you."

"You're crazy." I backed up a step. He had lost his mind. "I could barely fight that female vampire last time. I can't take on two of them. I don't even have a sword."

He sighed. "We have so much work to do. First, you must learn to stop thinking like a Mohiri."

"I *am* a Mohiri." I crossed my arms. I was proud of who and what I was.

"You are also Fae and, like it or not, it is your dominant side." He raised a hand when I opened my mouth to argue. "The Mohiri are valiant warriors, and their demon gives them strength and speed. However, there is a reason demons fear us more than anything. We are more powerful, and our magic is lethal to them. The oldest, strongest vampire alive would be no match for

Sara, and she is only half Fae. When you learn to wield your magic, you will need no Mohiri weapon to defeat any demon."

He spoke without arrogance, and I knew he was right about Mom. But I wasn't her. How did I make him see that?

Stepping closer, he placed his hands on my shoulders. "Tell me you cannot feel your magic at this very moment, waiting to be set free."

"I..." I faltered and thought about the warm glow deep inside me.

"You asked why I wanted you to drink glaen. I had a theory that consuming it would help unlock your magic, and I was right. I can sense your magic more strongly now." He smiled. "You are ready."

I swallowed dryly, even as my excitement grew. He wouldn't lie to me about something like that. Had the glaen really freed my magic?

There was no time to ponder the question before we were standing on the ground floor near the entrance. Eldeorin released me. "I will be with you but hidden."

I waved at my short dress and heels. "I'm wearing this?"

He smiled. "You are also the bait."

"Great." I straightened my shoulders, took a fortifying breath, and walked toward the ramp to the second level.

I hadn't been in many parking garages, so I'd never realized how quiet and eerie they were at night. This one was well lit, but there were many shadowed corners and vehicles someone could hide behind. I didn't try to be quiet, and the click of my heels echoed off the gray concrete walls. The deeper I went, the more muted the street sounds and the more alone I felt.

It wasn't easy to behave like an unsuspecting human when every cell in my body was on alert. Something fluttered behind me, and I whirled, expecting an attack, only to see a pigeon flying past. I almost laughed out loud. If a vampire was watching me now, he definitely didn't see me as a threat.

I was nearing the elevator on the second floor when I shivered and rubbed my arms. I took several more steps before realization set in. The cold I felt was not in the air around me, but inside me.

I stopped walking as a different kind of chill slithered down my spine.

6

"Hello?" I called, and it took less work than I wanted to admit to make my voice quiver. "Is anyone there?"

A teenage boy walked out from behind a blue van – or he had been a teenager when he was made into a vampire. He was my height with short brown hair, a round, youthful face, and a guileless expression. Wearing blue jeans, sneakers, and a black T-shirt bearing the name of an old band named Metallica, he looked like a normal sixteen-year-old boy.

I felt a moment of sadness for the teenager, whose life had been stolen from him, but the icy lump in my chest reminded me this was no longer a boy.

"You okay, Miss?" he asked in a boyish voice, which would never deepen with adulthood.

I made myself visibly relax and giggled like I'd had a little too much alcohol. "Yes. These places always make me jumpy at night."

He smiled. "I can walk you to your car if you want."

"Would you?" I asked, settling into the pretense.

"Sure. I'm just waiting for my friend." He walked casually toward me. "I'm Eddie, by the way."

"Not to be nosy, but aren't you a little young to be out in this part of town at night," I asked as I called to my magic, something I hadn't done since I was five. The glow expanded, but it didn't flow to my hands like it used to.

"We're having a late dinner." He was less than ten feet away now, close enough for me to see the hunger in his eyes. I tried to hide my panic as I called to my magic again. It began to move this time, but not fast enough.

Eddie stopped abruptly and sniffed the air. "What is that?"

Heat slowly spread to my chest. I needed more time. "I don't smell anything."

"It smells delicious." He smacked his lips, and his brown eyes darkened until they were black. They focused on me and widened. "It's you."

"It must be my new perfume." I wriggled my fingers as if it would entice my reluctant magic toward them.

He inhaled deeply through his nose. "I've never smelled anything like you."

"I –" I broke off when fangs sprouted from his gums where his canines had been.

"Oops." He grinned, but the fangs turned it into more of a sneer.

I schooled my face to remain calm, but I couldn't stop my heart from racing. *Come on,* I pleaded with the glow, which had stalled in my chest. What if Eldeorin was wrong? What if I couldn't do this?

Eddie's smile faltered, and he stared at me in confusion.

Bluff, said a voice inside me, which sounded a lot like Ronan's when he barked orders at me in class. If this wasn't bad enough, I had to think of him?

"I guess this is the part where I'm supposed to scream and run," I said as I stepped out of my shoes.

"Yeah," Eddie replied dumbly, his gaze dropping to my bare feet.

I asked the first question I could think of. "How long have you been a vampire?"

"Huh?" His eyes met mine again. "Three years."

This time it was the voice of my old trainer Callum in my head reciting facts. *In their first year, vampires are no stronger than a new warrior. Two-year-olds are stronger than you but not faster. It's when they reach three years that they start to surpass you in speed. That's when your training will save your life.*

I was pretty sure Callum had been referring to our weapons training because what warrior would be idiotic enough to go after a vampire unarmed?

Me, that's who.

The vampire charged me. I ducked, rolled, and popped up behind him to deliver a kick to the center of his back, which sent him stumbling away from me. The move made my dress slide up and I silently cursed Eldeorin for making me wear the stupid thing.

He whirled to face me, the confusion in his eyes replaced by excitement. "So, you want to play?"

I backed up until my legs touched the bumper of a car. My whole body was coiled as tightly as a spring, and my eyes frantically searched for a weapon.

He came at me, moving faster than the female vampire I'd fought in the alley. I jumped up and backward, onto the hood of a silver Mercedes, and out of reach of his slashing claws.

I hopped to the roof and leaped to the next car amid the sound of ripping fabric. I didn't need to look down at my dress to know it was torn up one side.

"Stop playing around, and kill him," said Eldeorin's disembodied voice, which I was sure only I could hear.

"With what, harsh words?" I retorted as I ran along the tops of the cars with Eddie in pursuit.

The vampire caught up to me near the end of the line. Claws raked my calf as I jumped into the air to grab one of the metal pipes connected to the sprinkler system. I swung my body out and over him, landing in a crouch a dozen feet away.

He spun toward me. I couldn't outrun him in here so my only option was to stand my ground and fight. And hope Eldeorin intervened before I got my throat ripped out.

I had forgotten the icy knot under my breastbone. It grew larger, and I didn't realize what it meant until a whisper of sound came from behind me.

An arm wrapped around my middle, and another encircled my neck. I fought to break free, but my attacker was too strong. My heart hammered my ribs so hard it hurt, and blood roared in my ears.

"Need some help?" asked an amused male voice, which sounded even younger than Eddie's.

Eddie laughed. "Just having some fun. You know it makes them taste better."

"Hmmm. This one already smells so good." The vampire behind me sniffed my neck, and it was all I could do not to gag on the stench of decaying meat clinging to him.

Eddie started toward us. "I get first dibs, Tony. I'll save you some."

"Ah, man. Let me have one little taste first," Tony wheedled. He nuzzled the side of my neck. My body went rigid, and the air was so thick and warm I couldn't breathe.

Eddie's angry gaze moved from his friend to me, and his eyes bulged. He froze mid step and stared at me, his voice coming out as a squeak. "Tony..."

The scrape of fangs against my neck jolted me like a shot of adrenaline to the heart. I raised my hands and pressed them against the sides of the vampire's head to push him away, and an explosion went off in my chest.

White hot flames raced along my arms to my hands, which felt like they were welded to his head. I didn't think I could let go if I tried.

Tony screamed and called his friend's name, but Eddie was backing away from us, his face a mask of fear. A burst of brilliant white light lit up the garage and made Eddie cower with an arm over his eyes.

The smell of scorched flesh stung my nostrils, and snowflakes fluttered in the air around me. Dazed, I reached out a hand and caught one. Not snow, ash.

I turned slowly and blinked several times, trying to make sense of what I was seeing. On the concrete floor lay a jean-clad corpse, which might have once belonged to a teenage boy. I'd never know for sure because it was headless. All that remained above the shoulders was a charred stump where his neck had been.

I looked back at Eddie and met his terrified eyes. His gaze dropped to what was left of his friend, and then he spun and fled. I started after him and skidded to a stop when a blast of light came out of nowhere and struck him square in the back. He jerked like he'd been hit by lightning before he vanished with a small pop.

A beaming Eldeorin appeared. "Incredible. That turned out even better than I expected."

"I'm glad I could entertain you." I tried to brush ash off my arms and only succeeding in smearing it. My feet were filthy, and my dress looked like it belonged on the set of a post-apocalyptic movie.

"When you were in the womb, I sensed you were powerful," he went on, ignoring my retort. "Tonight, you showed you are already stronger than Sara was before her liannan. Once we set your magic free, it will be magnificent."

I stopped trying to clean myself and frowned at him. "What do you mean? You said the glaen freed my magic."

Eldeorin waved a hand, and I was back in my own clothes. "I was not entirely honest with you about that. The glaen did nothing more than take away your fear of your magic. The rest was all you."

"What?" I shouted. "You sent me in here to face two vampires, and you had no idea if I could even use my magic? One of them almost bit me."

"But he didn't because you used your magic to kill him."

I put my hands on my hips. "I didn't use it. When I tried to call my magic, it wouldn't come. I have no idea what the hell happened."

He pointed at the headless corpse on the floor. "What happened is you unlocked your magic, and its natural response was to destroy the threat to you."

I searched for the glow inside me, but it was no longer there, leaving behind an emptiness I hadn't felt in many years. "It's gone."

"It is where it has always been, behind the walls you built around it." He flicked his hand, and the vampire's body disappeared. "Tonight, we proved you can release your magic when you stop fearing it. You must learn to lose your fear of it."

He came over and looped his arm through mine. "Do not look so glum, Danielle. It only gets better from here."

"Thanks for helping out tonight," Mom said as we finished feeding the last bunch of Paluks the next evening.

"No problem." I closed the cage door and smiled at the happy piglets that looked much healthier after a week under her care. They were almost ready for the trip back to Mongolia.

"So," she gave me an expectant look. "Are you going to tell me about last night?"

I took my time wiping my hands on a rag. "I figured Eldeorin would fill you in."

She laughed. "You and I both know he won't do that. I trust him with your safety, but I remember my own lessons with him all too well."

"You promise you won't overreact...or tell Dad?"

She gave me a searching look and motioned toward the office. "Something tells me I'm going to need to sit down for this."

"It's not that bad, really," I said, following her. "It's just that you know how Dad is when it comes to Eldeorin."

Once we were seated, I related the events of the previous night. I might have glossed over a few parts – such as the length of my dress – but she heard enough to have a clear picture of what happened. When I finished, she wore a pensive expression. I couldn't tell if she was angry or reliving her own experiences with Eldeorin.

"We most definitely won't be telling your father about this," she said with a wry smile. "I'm not sure what would upset him more, the vampires or you going to Blue Nyx."

"He won't be mad if we keep it from him?" I asked, relieved she was taking it well.

She lifted a shoulder. "He doesn't like it, but I trust Eldeorin, and that is enough for him. Your father saw what I went through during and after my liannan, and he would do anything to save you from that. He might not like Eldeorin, but he will always be grateful to him for saving my life."

I relaxed in my chair. She was the one person in the world who could relate to my experiences with Eldeorin.

"Eldeorin's methods are unorthodox and a bit extreme, but he knows what he's doing. Only he would think of using glaen to ease your fear. It never even occurred to me it might help." She narrowed her eyes at me. "Not that I approve of you drinking alcohol."

I laughed. "Oh, I know. I've heard enough from you and Dad about the effects of human alcohol on faeries to never try it."

"Good." She pursed her lips. "Now, tell me more about the glow and how it felt when your magic killed the vampire."

I noticed she didn't say "when you killed the vampire." She got it when I told her I hadn't been controlling my magic, and that made me feel a lot better.

We spent the next half hour talking about it. Mom didn't push me for information. She let me tell her what I was comfortable sharing and mentioned some of her own experiences. I could tell she was excited about this new development, but she didn't suggest I try using my magic with her. She was letting me do this at my own pace.

"It's getting late, and I think we're done here for tonight." Mom stood and reached for her leather satchel hanging on a hook. Her phone rang, and she hurried to answer it. "Hi, Margot."

Margot was a healer who helped care for the orphans Mom worked with. If she was calling this late, it had to be urgent.

"I'll be there right away," Mom said. She hung up and looked at me. "Ariana is having another episode."

Ariana was one of her more difficult cases. Most orphans Mom helped were younger than ten, but Ariana was sixteen. She had spent the last three years in a mental hospital, diagnosed with acute schizophrenia, until our people found her two months ago. Before my mother began healing orphans, someone like Ariana would have spent her life in a special home for Mohiri like her.

"Go. I'll see you tomorrow morning," I said.

She hugged me and hurried out. I reached over to turn off the light and paused when my phone vibrated with an incoming text from Summer.

He asked me out!

I sat and wrote back. **When? How? I need details!**

The bubble appeared as she typed. We talked or texted every day, so I knew she had run into her mystery guy Damon a bunch of times around campus. They'd flirted, and he'd hinted about going on a date, but nothing more. Yesterday, she'd said she was giving him another two days, and then she was asking him out.

Sydney and I were at the dining hall and he came over to sit with us. We joked about the food and he asked if I liked Thai food. I said yes and he asked if I wanted to go to a new restaurant near campus tomorrow night. EEP!

I smiled. **I'll expect a full report.**

Of course! She sent me a sleepy emoji. **Off to bed. Talk tomorrow.**

Pocketing my phone, I turned off the lights and left. It was a cool night, and the full moon cast a soft blue light over the grounds. I loved nights like this, and I stood with my face upturned to the starry sky.

The clash of metal drew my attention to the arena, a square stone building with a domed roof to the left of the menagerie. Light came from its tall narrow windows, and the door was slightly ajar. Warriors liked to duel there, and it was a real treat when Dad and Grandfather Tristan participated in the fun.

I walked over and pushed the door wider to see inside. A short hallway led to the main room, and from here, I saw Grandfather sparring with another warrior. His opponent met him thrust for thrust, and I assumed it was Dad until they shifted positions and the other warrior came into view. It was Ronan.

Grandfather moved with the lethal grace of a samurai. Ronan moved with the smooth agility of a jungle cat. Muscles rippled beneath his blue T-shirt, and his tanned arms could have been sculpted from stone. But it was his powerful aura of raw strength and the fierce intensity on his face that made my pulse skip. I knew I was staring, but it was impossible to look away from him.

The match ended, and I couldn't tell who had won. Grandfather smiled and said something to Ronan, but all I heard was the rumble of their voices. I waited to see if they would start again, and I was surprised when another warrior walked over to join them. She had dark hair tied back in a ponytail, and she also carried a sword. I didn't recognize her, but there were always people coming and going from Westhorne.

Ronan said something, and the female warrior laughed and placed her hand on his arm. Out of nowhere, a surge of something hot and ugly tore through me, and I rocked back on my heels. I stared at her. I was *not* jealous. I didn't even like Ronan, *and* I had a boyfriend.

Thinking of Kai made my stomach twist. We weren't in a serious relationship, but I felt guilty, like I'd cheated on him somehow.

As if he sensed someone watching him, Ronan looked my way. When our gazes met, I expected to see annoyance at the intrusion, and I was completely taken off guard by the warmth in his eyes. I knew it had nothing to do with me, but it didn't stop my stomach from doing a little somersault. It also didn't stop a part of me from wishing the look *was* meant for me.

Grandfather said something, drawing Ronan back to their conversation. The second his head turned away, I bolted. I reached the woods and kept running because I needed to put as much distance as possible between me and whatever the hell had just happened.

The woods were quiet with patches of moonlight to light the way. I weaved swiftly through the trees, trying to outrun the strange, unsettling emotions chasing me.

When I heard the splash of water over rocks, I slowed and turned toward the sound. A minute later, I emerged from the trees into a narrow grassy area, which sloped down to the river. Here, large rocks had formed a deep, natural pool separate from the faster flowing water. On either side of the pool, huge boulders stood like guardians of this tranquil hidden place. It was one of my favorite places to go when I needed to think.

The water sparkled invitingly in the moonlight, and I wasted no time stripping off my clothes. I dived into the cold water and floated there, letting it wash away all my negative thoughts. The leaves had begun to turn, and soon it would be too cold for swimming. I loved autumn, but I missed this during the long winter months. Westhorne's indoor pool was nice, but nothing compared to this.

The river worked its magic on me, and I felt better when I got out. I shivered as I wrung water from my hair and dressed, but I wasn't ready to leave yet. I walked around to the other side of the largest boulder and climbed up to lie on the wide flat top staring at the moon. It was a great spot to soak up the sun on a warm day, and I imagined the sun's heat warming me now.

My body jerked, and I opened my eyes, blinking at the inky sky. I hadn't meant to fall asleep, and the position of the moon told me I'd been out for at least an hour. I grimaced. Mom and Dad were used to my nighttime strolls, but they didn't like me staying out too late, especially when I had training in the morning.

I was about to sit up when I heard movement below. Peering over the edge, I nearly gasped out loud when I saw a large brown werewolf standing beside the river. I scanned the area, but the wolf appeared to be alone and oblivious to my presence.

What was a werewolf doing out here? Years ago, Grandfather had issued an open invitation to all the packs in the country, but only members of the

Maine pack had taken him up on it. Could this be a lone wolf? I hoped not. It was a sad, lonely existence for a wolf without a pack.

The wolf dived into the water and came up with a large trout in its mouth. Shaking water from its thick fur, it sat on its haunches and devoured the trout in a few bites. It licked its chops and sat facing the river for a long moment.

Should I announce my presence? It felt rude to let the wolf believe they were alone, but at the same time, I knew nothing about them. Not all werewolves were friendly like my friends in the Maine pack. Some could be downright hostile and still carried old hatred and resentment of the Mohiri. But one of those wolves wouldn't come near a Mohiri stronghold, would they?

The wolf stood and stretched and began to shrink. I'd seen werewolves shift many times, but it wasn't until this one stood on their hind legs I realized what was happening. The coarse hair receded, and a human form took shape. Their back was to me, but there was no mistaking this was a male.

I knew I should look away, but I couldn't stop my eyes from traveling over the broad shoulders, the muscled back tapering down to a narrow waist, the hard buttocks, and the sinewy thighs. I used to crush on a few of the boys in Summer's pack, but not one of them had looked like him. He was the picture of male perfection, and I couldn't help wishing he would turn around so I could see if his front was as beautiful as his back.

He dived into the water and disappeared, coming up on the other side of the pool. This was the perfect time for me to sneak away, but my fascination with the strange wolf kept me where I was. He swam a few laps and emerged from the water, giving me a tantalizing view of well-defined pecs and chiseled abs.

I averted my gaze from his lower half, but not before I saw enough to set my face aflame and send a small tingle of pleasure through me. It was quickly followed by shame. I lowered my head and squeezed my eyes shut. What was wrong with me tonight? First, I was jealous over Ronan of all people, and now I was ogling this stranger like a total creep.

I needed to get out of here. The only problem was werewolves had heightened senses, too. Even if he didn't hear or see me leave, he might smell me. I heaved a silent sigh. Why didn't I reveal myself the moment he showed up and be on my way? Any interaction now was going to be all kinds of awkward and embarrassing. Unless he left first. He'd had his meal and a swim, so he might be ready to move on.

Lifting my head, I peered over the edge until his upper body came into view. At that moment, he tilted his head up toward the moon, and I couldn't stop the gasp that slipped from me.

It can't be.

His head swiveled in my direction, and I stared into surprised hazel eyes. I don't know who was more shocked – me or Ronan.

Ronan was a werewolf? No, it wasn't possible. I sensed his Mori the day we met and again in class. He was Mohiri, I was sure of it.

He was also a werewolf. It was hard to wrap my head around it, but I'd seen him shift with my own eyes.

Seconds ticked by, or maybe it was minutes. Neither of us spoke, and I had no idea what to say if I could find my tongue. His jaw tightened, and I waited for his justifiable anger at me for spying on him. But the emotion that crossed his face wasn't anger. If he were anyone else, I'd say he looked almost vulnerable, but the Ronan I knew was anything but that.

Moonlight glistened on his wet shoulders, reminding me he was naked. Werewolves didn't care about nudity, but he was my trainer. How was I ever going to face him in class again?

I rolled to my feet and jumped off the other side of the boulder. The second my feet touched the ground, I ran as if he was going to give chase. I didn't slow until I reached the lake.

My mind swirled as I walked around the lake toward my house. I thought about every time I'd seen Ronan since his arrival at Westhorne, and I wondered if I'd missed some sign he was part werewolf. There was nothing except... I remembered the times his eyes seemed to turn more gold than hazel, and I'd thought it was a trick of the light.

Ronan is a werewolf. Maybe if I said it to myself enough times, it would sink in. He was a werewolf, but he was also Mohiri. Did he have a pack somewhere, or was he the only one of his kind? The second thought brought with it a pang of sadness.

I stopped walking abruptly and turned my head toward the mountains. From far off in the distance came the mournful howl of a lone wolf.

7

———————

"What's up with you today?" Dimitri whispered to me as we walked to our table at lunch the next day.

I laid my tray on the table and pulled out my chair. "I'm fine."

He snorted and took the chair beside me. "You know that means 'I'm not fine, but I don't want to talk about it.'"

"Then stop trying to get me to talk about it." I stabbed a few of my cheese fries with my fork and lifted them to my mouth.

"So, there is something wrong," he persisted. "Is it Ronan?"

I nearly choked on my mouthful of food. "Why would you say that?"

Dimitri cut into his steak. "Because he's been the cause of most of your bad moods since he got here. And you avoided him like the plague in class this morning. I thought things were better with him this week."

"They are. I'm just having an off day, okay?"

He blew out a breath. "Okay, but you will tell me if he starts giving you a hard time again?"

"I will." I smiled at my plate. Technically, I was two minutes older than Dimitri, but ever since he got bigger than me, he'd assumed the protective older brother role. Sometimes, it annoyed me, but I knew we would always have each other's back.

Kai joined us and pulled out the chair on my other side. He was followed by Naomi, Luis, Anna, and Sean. The rest of our friends took the table next to ours and half a dozen conversations sprung up. Usually, I participated, but today I was content to listen.

"Who's she?" Anna asked.

I looked up from my plate at the female warrior walking to the food counter. She was the one I'd seen at the arena last night.

"Her name is Abigail," Naomi said. "She works in Vegas with Mom and Dad." Naomi's parents ran the command center in Las Vegas and split their time between Westhorne and there.

Abigail's hair hung loosely around her shoulders today, softening her face and making her even more beautiful. She had friendly eyes and an easy smile as she carried her tray to a table two down from ours.

I resumed eating until Elsie said, "Score one for the new girl." I followed everyone's gazes to Abigail's table where she had been joined by Ronan and Gavin. Heat crept up my neck as it had every time I'd seen Ronan today.

Abigail smiled and said something to them. Gavin took the seat across from her, and Ronan sat beside her, facing us. My plate suddenly became interesting, although I'd lost my appetite and could only play with my food.

Kai said something to me. I lifted my head, and my eyes skimmed over Ronan's face to find him looking my way. My traitorous belly gave a little flutter. Once again, his expression was impossible to read, and I couldn't tell if he was angry with me or worried I would blurt his secret to everyone. I wouldn't, but he didn't know that.

I turned my head toward Kai, whose expression changed to one of concern. "You look a bit flushed. Are you okay?"

"Yes. I just remembered I was going to help Mom in the menagerie over lunch." I stood and pushed back my chair. "I'll see you in class."

Picking up my tray, I carried it to the busing station, which took me past Ronan's table. I could feel his eyes on me, but I stared straight ahead. I dropped off my tray and escaped the dining hall as fast as I could go without breaking into a run.

I did go to the menagerie, but Mom wasn't there. I spent the remainder of my lunchtime watching the Paluks and reading a book on my phone.

The afternoon classes were a repeat of the morning. I tried to interact with Ronan as little as possible, and the few times our eyes met, I quickly looked away. I was wound tight by the time training was over. I usually went for a run in the woods to let off steam, but I was afraid of running into Ronan there.

Dimitri went off to do whatever he did these days when we weren't in class, so I headed home alone. Mom caught up to me on the road to the lake, and we were greeted by Hugo and Woolf, who flanked her like bodyguards. They loved Dimitri and me, but there was never any question about who their master was.

She scratched Hugo's head. "The Paluks are being picked up tonight. I could use your help with them again."

"Sure."

"What's wrong? You look upset." She sent the hellhounds away and slipped an arm around my waist. "Did you and Kai have a fight?"

"No. Kai and I are great," I answered automatically, but I wasn't so sure anymore. It was something I'd deliberately put off thinking about since last night. How could I have these confusing feelings around Ronan if I cared about Kai?

Mom hugged my waist. "Is it Ronan?"

"What?" I came to a stop. "Why would you ask that?"

She chuckled. "I'm not blind. I saw the tension between you and him at the river last week. I asked Dimitri, and he said Ronan was hard on you at first, but things have gotten better."

"Oh." I resumed walking. "It's not that."

"You know you can tell me anything," she prodded softly.

I stared at the ground for a long moment, and the words burst from me. "Ronan's a werewolf." Mom said nothing so I went on. "He's a werewolf and a Mohiri."

"He told you?" she asked without a hint of surprise.

I spun to face her. "You knew?"

"Your grandfather told me before Ronan arrived."

"Does Dad know?" I asked.

"Yes."

"Why didn't you tell us?" I asked although I already knew the answer.

She pressed her lips together in reproach. "If Ronan wants the trainees to know, he will tell you. Which brings me to the following questions. How do you know what he is, and why does it bother you? You love werewolves."

"I don't care if he's a werewolf. It's how I found out that bothers me."

Mom watched me expectantly, and I couldn't meet her eyes. "I don't want you to be disappointed in me."

She took one of my hands between both of hers. "You could never disappoint me."

Tears pricked my eyes. The next thing I knew, I was telling her everything that had happened at the pool. Well, almost everything. My mother did not need to hear about my – um – appreciation of his naked body, trainer or not.

"I can't even look at him now," I said when I finished. "How am I supposed to train with him?"

She gave me one of her reassuring mom smiles. "You were wrong to watch him when he thought he was alone, but it's not like you followed him there to spy on him. I would have been shocked, too, to see a strange were-wolf in our woods, only to discover he was someone I believed was full Mohiri."

"Have you ever heard of a Mohiri/werewolf hybrid?" I asked. "How is that even possible?"

"How is a Mohiri/Fae hybrid possible?" she countered. "Before me, no one could even conceive of it. Yet, here we are."

I mulled it over. "Do you think he's the only one of his kind?"

"The Mohiri have been around for thousands of years. I wouldn't be surprised to learn there are others, maybe even different hybrids."

We walked in silence for a few minutes until another thought came to me. "Werewolves live in packs. What does that mean for someone who is half werewolf?"

"I don't know," she said quietly.

Werewolf packs shared a special connection through their Alpha. Would a half werewolf be able to feel that, and what would it mean if they couldn't?

It was too much to ponder, so I turned my thoughts to my immediate problem. "What should I do?"

"What do you want to do?" she asked.

I made a face. "Move to Mongolia with the Paluks."

She laughed warmly. "How about something a little less dramatic?"

"I know I should apologize, but I have no idea how to do it. He's not the most approachable person on a good day, and I'm sure I'm the last person he wants to talk to now."

Mom patted my arm. "Give it a few days. You're embarrassed, and he's probably wondering if you are going to share his secret with the others."

"I wouldn't do that. I mean, I told you, but I wouldn't tell anyone else, not even Dimitri."

"I know," she said as our house came into view. "And once Ronan knows that, I believe no other apology will be necessary."

I let out a huge breath. "You think so?"

"Yes."

I smiled for what felt like the first time today. "I hope you're right. I don't think I'd like Mongolia."

"What about this one?" Summer walked in front of the camera, wearing jeans and a red cowl neck top.

I put a hand to my chin. "Almost, but not quite."

She pulled the top over her head. "How about that blue one you picked out for me this summer?"

"That's a nice one. Try it."

She tossed the top onto her bed and went to her small closet, humming a nameless tune. Summer loved music, and if she couldn't hear it, she made up her own melody. Her parents should have called her Sunny instead of Summer because it perfectly described her personality.

"Why haven't I seen a photo of this mystery man?" I asked as she dug through her clothes.

Her laugh was muffled. "I couldn't exactly pull out my phone and snap his picture. I'll get one tonight."

"Good because I'm dying to see if he's as hot as you say he is."

"Oh, Damon's that and more," said a new voice. A smiling brunette appeared in front of the camera and gave me a finger wave. "Hey, Dani."

I waved back. "Hi, Sydney."

Summer's roommate looked at her. "Are you still trying to decide what to wear tonight?"

"Darn it." Summer turned to frown at me. "I think that top is in my laundry bag."

Sydney walked out of sight. "I told you to wear my green dress. It will look amazing on you."

She returned and held up a cute fern green wrap dress. "What do you think, Dani?"

"I love it. Her brown boots would look great with that."

"That's what I told her." Sydney thrust the dress at Summer. "Wear this, and Damon will be asking for a second date before the appetizers arrive."

Summer took the dress from her. "Thanks."

"Anytime." Sydney retrieved two books from her bed. "I'm off to my study group." She shot a grin at Summer. "I won't wait up for you."

"I like your roommate," I said after the door closed.

Summer pulled off her jeans. "Me too. I was lucky to be paired with her." She put on the dress and spun in a slow circle. "What do you think?"

I gave a little clap. "It's perfect."

She grabbed her tall brown boots and bent to slip them on. "You haven't mentioned Ronan today. Did he leave?"

"I don't mention him every day." An image of Ronan at the pool flashed through my mind for what had to be the hundredth time. I desperately wanted to tell her about that, but my mother was right. It wasn't my secret to tell.

Summer snorted. "Yeah, you do. If you weren't always venting about him, I'd say you have a crush on your new trainer."

I sputtered a laugh. "A crush on Ronan? Have you heard what I've said about him?"

"Yes, and you know what they say. There's a fine line between love and hate." She straightened and tossed back her hair. "How do I look?"

I crossed my hands over my heart. "If I wasn't straight, I'd want to date you."

"Aww," she cooed, and we snickered at each other.

Her eyes widened, and she hurried toward the phone. "He just texted. He'll be here in five minutes, and I still need to touch up my makeup."

"Go. But you better call me as soon as you get home. I want to hear all about it."

"I will." She blew me a kiss, her face glowing with excitement. "Later, Bestie."

"Have fun," I said as she reached for her phone. "I'll be waiting."

"We're going to be late," Dimitri sang in a teasing voice as we walked to the manor the following morning.

I glanced up from my phone to see he was a dozen yards ahead of me. I held up a finger and finished typing my text. **Do you need bail money? That's the only excuse I'll accept for you not calling me last night.**

Tucking my phone in my pocket, I caught up to him. "Sorry. I was texting Summer."

He snorted. "Talking ten times a day is not enough for you two?"

"We don't talk ten times a day. Nine times at the most."

"And what is *so* important you have to text her this early?" he asked.

"She had a date last night, and she didn't call me when she got home." I realized how silly that must sound to him. "She said she would call."

He grinned. "A college girl goes on a date and doesn't call her best friend after? I'm guessing our girl Summer got a little dessert after dinner."

"Shut up." I lifted my hand to smack his arm and let it drop back to my side. What if he was right? Summer had joked a few times about college hookups, and she was gaga over this guy Damon.

Dimitri nudged me with his shoulder. "Stop worrying, and let the girl have a little fun."

"You're right."

"I'm always right." He picked up his pace. Turning, he jogged backward and said, "Race you."

I laughed and ran after him. "You really are a sucker for punishment, aren't you?"

Morning classes with Ronan were as awkward and uncomfortable as the previous day. My friends had started to notice and shot me curious looks, but no one came out and asked what was up. By the time lunch rolled around, Mongolia was beginning to look pretty good.

Phones weren't allowed during training, so I had to wait until lunch to read Summer's texts – only there weren't any. I stared at the screen, and the niggling feeling from earlier grew into real worry. This wasn't like Summer. Something was wrong.

Instead of following the others to the dining hall, I went in search of my father. I found him in the security center with Dax. They appeared to be having a serious conversation, but they stopped and smiled when I came in.

"Dad," I said, and his smile fell away.

He met me halfway across the room. "What is it?"

"It's Summer. I haven't heard from her since yesterday." I held up my phone. "She was supposed to call me last night, but she didn't, and she's not answering my texts today. Is there any way we can check on her to see if she's okay?"

I waited for him to smile and assure me there was nothing to worry about. When his expression became serious and he exchanged a look with Dax, a tiny knot of apprehension formed in my gut.

"What?" I looked between them in alarm. "Do you know something about Summer?"

"No," Dad said as we walked over to where Dax sat in front of a bank of monitors. "When did you last talk to her?"

"Yesterday around six-thirty. She was getting ready for a date."

"Who do we have in Boston now?" Dad asked Dax.

Dax brought up a map of the country on one of his monitors. He hit a few keyboard buttons, and it zoomed in on Boston where three green dots showed the location of our safehouses there. When he clicked each dot, a box appeared with the names of the warriors stationed at them.

"Denis's, Rachel's, and Paulette's teams," he said. "You want me to call Paulette."

Dad nodded, and Dax hit another button. Ten seconds later, a female voice came from the speaker on his desk. "Paulette here."

"Paulette, it's Nikolas," Dad said. "Are you free?"

"Until tonight. What's up?" she answered.

Dad looked at me as he spoke. "I need someone to check in on a student at Northeastern. Her name is Summer Kelly, and she's a member of the Maine pack."

"I'm not far from the university now," Paulette said. "What am I checking for?"

"Summer is Dani's friend, and Dani hasn't heard from her since yesterday," Dad told her. "They talk every day, so Dani is worried about her."

"Do you know what residence she's in? And do you have her class schedule?" Paulette asked.

I spoke up. "Hi, Paulette, it's Dani." I gave her Summer's phone number and dorm room. I had her class schedule saved on my phone, and I sent it to Dax to forward to Paulette. She didn't ask for a photo of Summer, but I sent one anyway.

"Got it," Paulette said a moment later. "I'll call you back in thirty."

She hung up, and I sat on a chair to wait. Knowing we had someone on the campus looking for Summer made the knot in my stomach loosen. Paulette would call back soon and say she'd found Summer in one of her classes. Summer would tell me she didn't call because she'd lost her phone or she forgot to charge it last night. She *was* terrible at remembering to do that, and she sometimes left Post-it notes on her nightstand to remind her.

Summer was okay, and I had overreacted. Maybe I was subconsciously projecting my anxiety about Ronan onto her to distract me from the real problem. She would get a kick out of it when she heard I'd asked Dad to send a warrior to check on her.

The phone rang, startling me, and I stood as Paulette's voice came over the line. "No one answered at her dorm room, and she's not in the class she has now according to her schedule."

I sucked in air, and Dad laid a hand on my shoulder.

"You want me to go back to her dorm?" Paulette asked, and I knew she was asking if we wanted her to pick the lock and go inside.

Dad didn't hesitate. "Yes. And bring in anyone who is free on your team to search the campus."

"Will do. I'll get back to you after I check her room," Paulette said.

Dad's mouth formed a grim line, and neither he nor Dax said anything. I caught another look between them, and the knot became a cold lump of fear in my gut.

"What are you not telling me?" I demanded.

Dad looked at me, and what I saw on his face was not the warm reassurance I was hoping for. His eyes were troubled, and I couldn't remember the last time I'd seen him like this.

"Roland called us an hour ago," Dad said. "He learned this morning a young male wolf from the Montana pack has been missing for five days."

I felt the blood leave my face. "What?"

Dad held up a hand. "There is no reason to believe it has anything to do with Summer. She's on the other side of the country, and we don't know yet if she is missing."

I wanted so much to believe him, but his expression after Paulette's call told me he did suspect a connection. My father did not believe in coincidences, and his intuition was one of the things that made him a great warrior.

Paulette called back fifteen minutes later. "No sign of trouble in the dorm room, but I did find her backpack and books. She could have dropped them off at any time today, though."

"What now?" I asked no one in particular.

"I found her roommate's class schedule, and I'm going to track her down and see if she can tell us anything," Paulette said. "Dani, is there anything you can think of that might help? Friends she mentioned, places she likes to hang out, a boyfriend."

My mouth went dry. "She had a date last night."

"A date with whom?" Paulette asked.

"His name is Damon, and she met him on campus a few weeks ago." I thought back on our conversations about him. "She said he's an engineering student there."

Dad pulled over a chair to sit beside me. "Did she tell you where they were going on their date?"

I nodded. "A Thai place. She didn't say the name, but it's close to the university."

"There shouldn't be many Thai restaurants nearby," Paulette said almost to herself. "This is good, Dani. I'll check it out after I talk to her roommate. Meanwhile, I shared her photo with the team, and they are going to search the campus. She had to leave a trail somewhere."

"Her student ID," I blurted. "She needs her ID to access her dorm. The university must log that somewhere."

Dad smiled. "Good thinking, Dani. Dax?"

"On it." Dax started typing. "This will take a few minutes."

"See if you can track her phone, too," Dad said. I hadn't thought about doing that, and it gave me renewed hope.

Dax brought up a window on another screen. "I'll do that first. It's quicker." A minute later, he said, "No luck with the phone. It must be turned off."

"Let me know what you find with the student ID," Paulette said. "Don't worry, Dani. If she's here, we'll find her."

"If she's here." Paulette's words echoed in my mind as Dad thanked her and

ended the call. What if they couldn't find her? I didn't want to consider that outcome.

Summer, where are you?

"It's time to call Roland," Dad said, pulling me from my thoughts. "Someone there might know where Summer is. And her parents need to be informed."

I felt sick as he made the call. Uncle Roland answered, sounding surprised to hear from Dad again so soon. Dad wasted no time getting straight to the reason for the call.

Uncle Roland's voice went from congenial to hard by the time we had brought him up to speed, but he softened it when he spoke directly to me.

"Summer talks to you more than anyone else, Dani. Is there anything you can think of that you haven't told us about this man she was dating?"

"They weren't dating. She ran into him around campus, at the library and dining hall, places like that. They flirted, but he didn't ask her out until two days ago." I racked my brain for any little thing that could help. "Her roommate, Sydney, met him. Summer was with her a few of the times she saw Damon."

Dad pulled out his phone and sent off a text. "I let Paulette know so she can ask the roommate about him."

The door opened, and Mom hurried in. Dad must have told her about Summer through their bond. She took one look at our faces and said, "You haven't found her."

Dad shook his head. "Not yet. We have Roland on the phone now."

Mom came over to stand beside me. "Is Peter with you?"

"Pete and Shannon are in Portland. Emma is on the phone with them now." Uncle Roland let out a heavy sigh. "It'll kill them if anything happens to her."

"Don't even think that," Mom told him in a firm voice. "We're going to find her."

The phone beeped. Dax looked at the display and said, "It's Paulette."

"Conference her in," Dad told him, and it felt like every one of us held our breath as we waited for her to join. He let her know Uncle Roland was on the call, and she responded with, "Good," before she let us know what she'd found.

"The roommate doesn't think Summer came back to the dorm last night. She took something to help her sleep, so she said it's possible Summer came in without waking her and left early. But Summer borrowed a dress from her, and it hasn't been returned."

Uncle Roland swore, and Mom put a hand to her mouth. It felt like

Paulette had reached through the phone and punched me in the stomach.

Paulette continued. "Sydney gave me a good description of Damon, but she never got his last name. He didn't set off any red flags with her. She said he was clearly pursuing Summer, but he wasn't aggressive about it." She paused. "That's all I have so far. I'm headed out to find this Thai restaurant."

"Thanks, Paulette," Dad said.

Uncle Roland spoke up. "Peter and Shannon left Portland to drive to Boston. If anyone can pick up Summer's scent, it's them."

"Can you let them know I'll meet them there?" Mom asked.

Dad leaned closer to the phone. "We'll use every resource we have, and we won't stop until she's found."

The confidence and authority in his voice gave me hope for the first time today. We had more money, technology, and connections than the FBI and CIA combined. If Damon had taken Summer, he had no idea what he was up against.

"Thank you." Uncle Roland's voice was rough with suppressed emotion.

"You and Peter are family," Dad told him.

"And family takes care of each other." Mom's eyes were bright with tears. Uncle Roland and Uncle Peter had been her best friends since they were kids, and she couldn't stand to see the people she loved in distress.

Uncle Roland cleared his throat. "I'm going to get my best trackers together. If Pete doesn't find her, we'll scour the whole state if we need to."

They ended the call, and I turned to Mom. "I want to go with you."

She shook her head. "We don't know who or what we are dealing with. It's best if you stay here."

"Summer is my best friend." I fought the lump trying to form in my throat. "I can't stay home while she's in trouble."

"Boston is no place for a young Mohiri," Dad said in a firm tone I knew well. "We have three teams in the city because vampire activity is increasing there."

"But I would be with Mom."

Mom placed her hand against my cheek. "I don't know what I'll have to do. I won't risk leaving you unprotected even for a minute."

I stared into her eyes, identical to mine. "If I had my magic, you'd let me go, wouldn't you?"

A few seconds ticked by before she said, "I don't know."

I wanted to argue that it wouldn't be any more dangerous than my last lesson with Eldeorin, but I couldn't say that in front of Dad. He was able to sleep at night only because he didn't know exactly what my lessons entailed.

"We will find her." Mom kissed my forehead. "I'll see you soon."

She kissed Dad and vanished.

"Got it," Dax announced. Dad and I crowded around his chair to see the text file displayed on his screen. All I could make out were columns of numbers and datetime stamps.

Dax pointed to a number in the first column. "I had to find her student ID number first. This is hers. The second column of numbers is the building where the ID was scanned, and the third column shows the exact time and date."

His finger moved down the rows to the last one. "According to this, the last time her ID was scanned was at 3:47 p.m. yesterday."

My heart sank. "That's around the time she got back to her dorm from her last class."

Dad picked up his phone. "I'll let the others know."

A small blue couch sat against one wall. I sank onto it and pulled my knees up to my chest as fear and guilt assailed me. I should have known something was wrong when Summer didn't call last night. If I had come to my father twelve hours ago, we might have found her by now.

Forty agonizing minutes passed before Mom called. She and Paulette had found the Thai place, and the hostess recognized Summer's photo. She and Damon had been there for dinner, and the time on their credit card receipt was 8:02 p.m. The question was where did they go when they left the restaurant?

"I think we need to bring David and Kelvan in on this," Mom said. "No one is faster at gaining access to city traffic cams and the university security cameras than them. No offense, Dax."

He grinned. "None taken."

While Dad called David, I retreated to the couch and read every text from Summer over the last two weeks. I thought back to our calls and tried to think of any tiny detail I'd overlooked that could be important. There was nothing.

An hour and a half later, Mom called again, and the second I heard her voice, I knew it was bad news. Dad did, too. He put an arm around my shoulders when I walked over to where he stood by the phone.

"I'm with Peter and Shannon. They picked up Summer's scent at the Thai restaurant and followed it to a parking lot down the street. We found her phone; it was smashed to pieces." Mom drew in a ragged breath.

My body went cold. *No.*

"There were several drops of blood near the phone. It's Summer's."

8

"David, what did you find?" Dad asked the man on Dax's central monitor.

David Ito, a fortysomething Japanese man, sat in a room full of computer equipment. His round glasses reflected his screen, hiding the faint gold ring inside his irises that identified him as an Emote.

"We searched the college security recordings for the days and places Dani said Summer encountered Damon, and we were able to capture a decent image of him," David said. "Kelvan ran it through his face recognition software, and he got a hit."

I held my breath as a slightly grainy headshot of a dark-haired man appeared in the corner of the screen. He appeared to be in his early twenties.

"Meet Damon Webb aka Andrew Ried aka Richard Hill. His real name is Reese Meyer, he's twenty-six, originally from Miami, and he's wanted in four states for grand larceny, computer fraud, wire fraud, and a host of other crimes." A collage of photos replaced the first one. Each one showed Reese Meyer with a different woman, all older than him. "Meyer likes to get to know rich women and swindle them out of large sums of money."

"A con artist." I studied the photos. "What would someone who targets wealthy women want with Summer? She's on a scholarship and far from rich."

David nodded. "Good question. Also, he's never been charged with a violent crime that we know of. Kidnapping is not a part of his M.O."

"Were you able to get anything from cameras near the Thai restaurant?" Dad asked.

"We located two security cameras between the restaurant and the parking lot, and both show the couple walking along the street." David pulled up a video clip, which clearly showed Summer and Reese. She was smiling and happy.

"There's a traffic light camera near the parking lot," David said. "We're working on getting access to that now."

Dad rested his hand on the back of my chair. "Thanks, David. Send over everything you have on him in the meantime."

"Will do. Talk soon."

The screen went dark, and Dad turned to me. I knew what he was going to say, and I crossed my arms. "I'm staying."

It had been two hours since Mom called with the news about Summer's phone, and I was doing everything I could to not think about those drops of blood they'd found. If I couldn't be out there looking for her, I needed to be here at the center of the search.

His expression softened with understanding. "Do you want to help us go through the information on Meyers David is sending over?"

"Yes." I would spend all day and night on it if it would lead us to Summer.

Dax set me up at one of the many computers in the room, and soon I was poring over arrest reports, school records, family history, social media pages, and even medical records. David and Kelvan were nothing if not thorough. A second batch of documents came over an hour after the first one, and it contained old phone records, credit card and bank statements, and the logins for two email accounts.

I had gone through a quarter of it when my phone vibrated with an incoming text. My heart leapt before I remembered it couldn't be Summer.

The text was from Dimitri. **Where are you? Why did you skip classes after lunch?**

In security with Dad. Summer is missing, I wrote back.

A second after I sent the text, I got one from Kai. **You OK?** I began to type what I'd told Dimitri. Instead, I said, **With Dad. I'm OK.**

I stared at my phone after I sent my reply. Why hadn't I told Kai about Summer? He was my boyfriend, and he'd want to be here for me. I wanted that, too, didn't I?

Setting my phone on the desk, I went back to work and focused on the last person to see Summer before she disappeared. Finding her was all that mattered.

I jumped when someone waved a hand in front of my face, and I looked up at Dimitri. The concern in his eyes was almost enough to free the dam of emotions I was holding back.

"Sorry. I said your name a few times." He pulled over a chair and sat next to me. "What happened to Summer?"

I filled him in on what we knew so far and watched his expression change from shocked to angry to worried. Summer was his friend, too.

He looked at the arrest report I had up on the monitor. "Need some help?"

"Yes." I pointed at the workstation next to mine. "Ask Dax to set you up there, and I'll share what I have with you."

There were no windows in the control room, and it was easy to lose track of time as Dimitri and I carefully went through everything we had on Reese Meyer. The man had built up a long resume of crime for someone who was only twenty-six. How he'd managed to stay out of prison so far was a mystery to me.

When Dad said we should go eat dinner, I refused to leave, and Dimitri said he was staying with me. Dad had the kitchen send food for all of us, and we ate at the small round conference table. Then it was back to sifting through the life of the con man who had kidnapped my best friend. If I could only figure out his reason for targeting Summer, it might tell us where to look for her.

"Let's go, you two." Dad reached around me and turned off my monitor.

"I'm not done." I reached for the power button. "There's still so much to go through."

His hand blocked mine. "It's almost 1:00 a.m., and the only thing keeping you awake is your stubbornness."

I opened my mouth, and a yawn came out. "But Summer –"

"We are not going to stop the search if you go get some sleep." He took my hands and pulled me to my feet. "You won't be any help to her if you fall asleep at the computer."

He had a point, but it killed me to leave. I wasn't surprised to find Grandfather waiting for us in the hallway. He drove us to the lake in one of the SUVs and wrapped me in one of his warm hugs when we got out. "We'll find her," was all he said.

Even though I was tired, I slept fitfully and woke feeling like I'd barely closed my eyes. I ate a quick breakfast, told Dimitri I was skipping classes again, and ran to the manor.

I could tell something had happened the second I entered the security center. Mom was there deep in conversation with Dad, Grandfather, and Claire while Dax clicked away at his keyboard. They were so caught up in their discussion they didn't hear me come in.

I hurried over to them. "What is it? Did we get a lead on Summer?"

Mom turned to me, looking like she'd gotten less sleep than I'd managed. "We just received word two werecougars went missing yesterday."

"Not Sofie and Lilly?" I put a hand to my throat.

"No. These were two nineteen-year-olds from Oregon." She let out a defeated sigh. "I tried to spread the warning to all werecougars about the girls' kidnapping, but I couldn't reach them all."

Dad placed a hand on her back. "You did everything you could. This is not your fault."

She gave a halfhearted nod. "I'll visit them and see if they will accept our help looking for their teenagers. Then I'm meeting with the Alpha of the Montana pack about their missing wolf. They are one of the less welcoming packs, but I healed one of their pups a few years ago, so they have agreed to talk to me."

"You think those disappearances are connected to Summer, don't you?" The dread twisting my stomach told me the answer. There was no way two werecougars and two werewolves going missing in one week were not related.

It was Grandfather who answered. "The timing suggests they could have been taken by the same people, but we won't know for sure until we learn more about the other disappearances."

If the people who hired the men to kidnap Sofie and Lilly were responsible for taking those Oregon werecougars, they could have Summer, too. I thought about the cage I had rescued Lilly from, and I suddenly found it hard to breathe. Summer could be alone and terrified in a cage like that at this very moment.

Picking up where I'd left off last night, I scoured the documents with renewed urgency. There had to be something here to lead us to Summer.

Hours later, Dad laid a hand on my shoulder. I looked up at him with eyes bleary from lack of sleep and staring at the monitor.

His brows drew together. "Did you sleep at all last night?"

"A little," I admitted.

He spun my chair toward him and pointed at the door. "You're going to eat lunch and get some rest. I don't want to see you back here until after dinner. And you are back in training tomorrow."

"But –"

"No argument." He tugged me up and gently shoved me to the door. "Go outside. Get some fresh air."

When my father issued an order, there was no refusing him. I left the security center and exited the building by the main entrance to wander aimlessly across the lawn. The sun was too bright after hours in the windowless room, so I entered the woods and let the earthy scents envelop me.

Images of Summer trapped in a cage played over and over in my head, filling me with helpless rage. I ran, but no matter how fast I moved, I couldn't outrun my anger and frustration.

I stopped and fell to my knees on a damp mossy patch, not caring about the wetness seeping into my jeans. Tilting my face up to the canopy of branches, I blinked away stinging tears. I didn't want to cry. I wanted to rage. I wanted to scream, to hit something, to do *anything* but wait around for news. No one said it out loud, but I knew the more time that passed, the smaller our chances of finding her.

Summer needed me, and I was useless to her. I wasn't a warrior like Dad, and I couldn't travel like Mom or do the things she could do. A bitter laugh slipped out. I couldn't even use my own magic. For the first time since I was five, I needed it, and I had no idea how to summon it.

Closing my eyes, I looked deep within myself, but I saw no trace of the glow, which had been there at Blue Nyx. I couldn't even sense my magic. Eldeorin said I had locked it away. If that was so, I should be able to unlock it. The problem was I didn't even know where to look for it.

I thought back to that night, recalling how it felt when I drank the glaen. I'd felt warm and light and carefree. I was anything but carefree now, and no amount of pretending would change it.

But there was something else that could. I stood and started toward home, my pace increasing with every step. The voice of doubt in my head told me this was a bad idea, but it was drowned out by Mom's voice telling us about the drops of blood next to Summer's destroyed phone.

Our house was empty, except for the imps and Brontë. Dimitri was in class, and Mom had left this morning to visit the werecougars and the Montana pack. Dad was most likely still in the security center overseeing the search for Summer.

I opened the cabinet door above the refrigerator and took down the bottle of glaen. Setting it on the counter, I found a glass approximately the same size as the one I'd had at Blue Nyx and put it next to the bottle.

A squeak drew my gaze to the imps standing on the coffee table and watching me with interest. I held up the bottle and shook my head. "No, you can't have some. This stuff is for faeries only. It's poison for demons. You understand?"

Their eyes rounded, and they nodded. I was sure Mom had told them not to touch the glaen, but I wanted to reinforce it. Imps would eat anything, and telling them not to touch something often made them more curious about it.

I opened the bottle and poured some of the milky liquid into the glass.

When I lifted the glass and caught a whiff of the aroma, my mouth watered at the memory of my first taste.

"For Summer," I said and downed the whole glass.

A pleasant warmth spread through me. I licked a drop off my lip and smiled at the imps. "One down."

After the second glass, my body felt so light I thought I would float up to the ceiling.

When I finished the third glass, the worry and fear smothering me since yesterday melted away.

"That should do it." I put the glass down and waited for the glow to begin. A few minutes passed, and nothing happened.

I tapped my lips with a finger and stared at the glass. Maybe it *was* smaller than the one at the bar. To be sure, I poured another glass and drank it. Then I waited, and waited, and waited.

"Where is the glow?" I asked.

The imps chattered among themselves. Orville threw up his arms and shrugged.

I pressed my lips together as I returned the bottle to the cabinet and rinsed my glass. What was I doing wrong? Maybe this glaen wasn't as strong as the stuff at the club. Or maybe it hadn't been the glaen at all. Eldeorin must have done something to me and he lied about the glaen removing my fear and releasing my magic.

I crossed my arms and huffed. "I drank half Mom's glaen for nothing."

Eliot, Orwell, and Verne crossed their arms and squeaked in solidarity.

I checked the time on my phone. Dad had ordered me to stay out of the security center until after dinner. They were serving dinner in the dining hall now.

Hugo and Woolf were waiting outside when I left the house. They ran up to me, sniffed, and backed away. I guessed they didn't like the smell of glaen. They accompanied me as far as the grounds, but stayed six feet away from me for the entire walk.

My stomach rumbled as I crossed the lawn, and I tried to remember the last time I ate. Was it breakfast? Maybe I should grab some dinner first.

I entered the building and followed the murmur of voices and the clink of silverware to the dining hall. I went straight to the serving tables and filled a plate with a thick slice of prime rib, rosemary roasted potatoes, and a buttered roll. For almost two days, I'd had no appetite, and I was ravenous.

"Dani," Dimitri called when I turned to find a table. He was sitting at our usual table with Kai and our other friends. I waved and started toward them.

Halfway across the room, a dizzy spell hit me, and I stopped to wait for it to pass. This was what I got for going too long without eating. I looked down at my tray and swayed. *Whoa.*

"Dani?"

Dimitri's voice sounded hollow, but I was distracted by the heat suffusing me. It was like I'd submerged my body in a bath that was a little too hot. My skin prickled and itched, and sweat broke out on my forehead.

I stared at my arms, fascinated by the blue static crawling over my skin. My hair crackled with it, and I remembered the times I would rub a balloon on my head to make it stick out everywhere. The memory made me snort a laugh.

"Stay back."

I lifted my head at Dimitri's shout and saw him grabbing Kai, who was moving toward me. The look of alarm on my brother's face penetrated the haze around me. Something must be wrong. I turned my head to the left and right but could see nothing but people still seated and staring at me.

I felt it then, the glow at my core, only it wasn't building slowly like it had the first time. It was growing brighter and hotter by the second and already spreading outward. My body hummed like a live wire as electricity rolled beneath my skin and sparks flew from my fingers.

Kai was fifteen feet away from me when Dimitri caught him by the arm. At the same time, a tendril of my magic shot out toward them and snapped the air like a whip. It didn't come close to them, but it was enough to make everyone in the room back away from me.

Someone behind me shouted my name. I turned toward the door as my father entered the room. He said something to me, but I couldn't make out the words over the roaring in my ears.

He took a step toward me. I dropped my tray of food and put up my hands. "No. I can't control it."

The memory of my magic attacking the vampire in the parking garage replayed in my head. Mom's glaen *had* worked, and the presence of so many Mori demons must have triggered my magic. A few people close to the door were able to get out of the room, but the rest were trapped in here with me. If one of them moved, my magic would lash out, and this time it might reach its target.

Ronan appeared in the doorway behind my father. He and Dad spoke, and he left. Was he going to get Mom? No, she wasn't at Westhorne.

A minute later, Dad moved aside as a werewolf ran into the room. Ronan came straight for me, ignoring my shouts for him to stay back. I barely had time to register my magic didn't attack him before he pounced.

I went down under his large body with no time to brace myself for the impact. One of his paws protected my head from the floor, but the rest of me wasn't so lucky. The wind was knocked out of me, and I gasped for air, which was impossible with a three-hundred-pound werewolf on top of me. I was going to suffocate if he didn't move soon.

He must have realized my distress because he lifted his body a few inches so I could breathe. Once I was no longer in danger of dying, I pushed at his chest to get him off me. He wouldn't budge.

His fur crackled with static from our contact. Other than that, he seemed immune to the magic churning inside me like a tornado. His wolf had to be shielding his Mori from me. In fact, I couldn't sense his Mori at all.

I wasn't sure how many minutes passed until he stood and backed away from me. I stayed on my back, staring at the ceiling and taking in deep breaths until the magic receded enough for the roaring in my ears to go away.

The effort it took to sit up left me shaking and lightheaded. The room was empty except for me and the werewolf sitting on his haunches a few feet away quietly watching me. If Ronan's human face was hard to read, in wolf form it was impossible.

"You covered me so everyone could get out," I said weakly.

He nodded once.

I let out a weighty sigh. "I'm sorry."

His eyes widened, and I imagined he'd be raising his eyebrows if he were in human form.

"I'm sorry you had to shift and give away your secret." I drew my knees up and wrapped my arms around them. "And I'm sorry about what happened the other night at the pool. I know I should have apologized before now, but I was too embarrassed about it."

A few days ago, I would have blushed admitting that to him. Oddly, I felt no embarrassment at all now. Could the glaen be responsible for it, or was it because it was easier to talk to him in his wolf form?

"I want you to know I didn't follow you there. That's one of my favorite spots, and I go there often. I was up on the boulder when you arrived, and I should have left, but I was so surprised to see a werewolf in our woods. Then you shifted, and I was even more surprised to see it was you."

I smiled ruefully. "I know that's no excuse. I invaded your privacy, and that was wrong, but I wouldn't have told anyone about you. Well, I did tell my mother, but no one can keep a secret like her. She told me she already knew what you are."

Ronan gave another nod. I relaxed, astonished by how at ease I was with him like this.

The moonlight hadn't done his wolf justice. He was bigger than a lot of wolves. His size reminded me of Uncle Roland. His fur was a warm brown with golden highlights from a lot of time outdoors, and his amber eyes were softer than the hazel ones I was used to seeing.

My phone rang, startling me. Reaching behind me, I pulled it from my back pocket and grimaced when I saw who it was. I had some explaining to do, and I was not looking forward to it.

"Dani, are you okay?" Dad asked before I could say a word. His worry-laden voice made me feel even worse about what I'd done.

"Yes. We both are." My voice cracked a little, and I hoped he didn't notice.

He exhaled loudly and murmured something in Russian. "What happened? Is it safe for me to come in?"

"No." My magic had subsided, but not nearly enough for me to trust it around him. "I'll explain it to you when I come out."

His brief silence told me he wasn't happy with either answer. "I'm going to open the door enough to throw Ronan's clothes inside. Come find me when you can leave the room."

"I will." The call ended, and the door opened a few inches. Ronan turned his head to look that way as his clothes landed on the floor and the door shut again.

Ronan gave me another questioning look, and I shook my head. "It's not safe yet, but you don't have to stay. I'm okay to be here alone."

He didn't get up, and I looked down to hide my relief. I had no idea why his presence comforted me when I'd avoided him for days, but I'd think about that when I wasn't so out of sorts.

"I guess you're wondering what the hell happened here." I rested my chin on my knees. "It's a long story."

He lowered his head to the floor and watched me expectantly.

I blew out a breath. "I'm going to have to start at the beginning."

And so, I found myself sitting on the dining hall floor, spilling my life story to Ronan. I kept it to the relevant stuff about what I was, what happened when I was five, and Eldeorin's training to help me free my magic and prepare for my liannan. Then I told him about Summer and my desperation to help her, which led me to drinking the glaen this afternoon. The rest, he'd witnessed himself.

"I don't know what happened. Maybe I drank too much or too fast and nothing happened until I was around all the Mori. Or maybe Eldeorin used magic on me the first time and didn't tell me. Either way, it was a monumentally stupid thing to try on my own, and I'm so glad no one got hurt."

"Anyway, that's the whole story." I rubbed my face with both hands and let out a pained laugh. "My screwup probably hasn't done anything to improve your opinion of me, but thank you for jumping in to keep everyone safe. And for staying to make sure I was okay."

I straightened my legs and stood. I was a little shaky, but otherwise, I felt like myself again. The warm glow was no more than a pale glimmer, which was fading fast. I went to the nearest table and sat. "It's safe now. You don't have to stay any longer."

Ronan got up and walked over to his clothes. He looked back at me, and I turned on the chair to face the other direction. Listening to him shift, I could not help but remember him standing gloriously naked in the moonlight like some pagan god. A different kind of warmth flooded me, and I forced myself to think of anything else – such as what Mom would say when she learned what I'd done.

I waited for the sound of the door opening, and I was surprised when he pulled out the chair beside me. He was the only person I knew who moved as quietly as I did. I stared at my clasped hands, unable to meet his eyes now that he was back in human form. What if he didn't accept my apology, and he was angry at me? The possibility bothered me a lot more than I cared to admit.

We sat like that for several minutes. He was the first to break the silence.

"I don't care if the people here know what I am. It's not a secret, and it was my choice to reveal it to them. You have nothing to apologize for."

"But the other night –"

"– was not your fault," he finished for me. "It was my mistake to assume no one would be out there late at night."

I pulled my bottom lip between my teeth. He was being gracious and uncharacteristically nice, and I wasn't sure what to say.

"And I do not have a low opinion of you."

That had me turning my head to shoot him a disbelieving look. "Since day one you've criticized me more than anyone else in training. I may not be on the same level as Dimitri or Kai or Naomi, but I'm still a damn good fighter."

"Yes, you are."

"I know I didn't make a good first impression the day we met, but that's no reason to..." I paused when his words registered. "What?"

"I do push you harder than the others," he admitted. "Because you hold yourself back."

My jaw tightened. "I do not."

He nodded. "You don't do it consciously, but I saw it the first time you fought me in class. Some of the other trainees have better swordsmanship, but none of them match your speed or agility. I've seen you demonstrate superior hand-to-hand combat several times when you forgot you aren't supposed to be the best in class."

"That...that's ridiculous," I sputtered.

"Is it?" He leaned in slightly and dipped his head so we were at the same eye level. "Less than a minute ago, you said you aren't on the same level as them. I don't know if someone told you that or you came up with it on your own, but you started to believe it. I'm going to push you until you recognize your potential to be as good or better than every other trainee here. And –"

A knock at the door interrupted him before he could finish. "Dani, Ronan, is everything okay in there?" Grandfather called.

Ronan pushed back his chair and stood, and I felt a prick of disappointment. I wanted to know what he'd planned to say.

He leaned down, startling me, and spoke into my ear. "And anyone who would jump in front of a wyvern to protect it might be a little mad, but she does not lack courage."

He walked to the door, and I stayed where I was as a smile spread across my face.

9

———————

"Dani, how could you have done something so reckless?" Mom demanded as she paced our living room two hours later. "What were you thinking?"

"I don't know," I said miserably from my seat on the couch. "I was upset about Summer, and I thought if I had my magic, I could help search for her."

"Why didn't you wait for your mother to get home?" asked Dad, who sat in the chair across from me.

"I didn't think it would hurt anything to try the glaen again," I said honestly. "It didn't affect me like that the first time."

His eyes hardened. He didn't know what took place during my sessions with Eldeorin, and hearing I drank glaen with my faerie mentor was not sitting well with him.

As if he'd heard me thinking about him, Eldeorin appeared in the kitchen. Mom had called for him as soon as she learned what happened, but he must not have considered it an urgent matter.

He took in the three of us and smiled. "A family meeting? Wonderful."

"Not wonderful." Mom spun to glare at him. "Do you want to know what my daughter did today?"

Eldeorin's curious gaze slid to me and back to Mom. "I couldn't possibly guess. May I have a hint?"

Dad's hands gripped the arms of his chair. Mom looked his way, and he eased his hold. I didn't need to hear her to know she'd spoken to him through their bond and asked him to stay calm.

Mom put her hands on her hips. "Glaen. How is that for a hint?"

"Is that so?" he replied as if he couldn't see what the fuss was about. "She is eighteen. Is she not old enough to drink?"

"One glass, yes. Half a bottle, no." She stalked over and wagged a finger at him. "And what do you think happened next? Take a wild guess."

Eldeorin's eyes widened. He looked at me, and his mouth curved into a delighted smile. "You used your magic again."

"She did not *use* it," Mom ground out. "It went haywire in a room full of people, and she had no control over it. We're lucky no one was killed."

I blanched. I had been worried about hurting someone, not killing them. I thought about Dimitri and Dad, and all the other people I'd put at risk, and I felt sick.

Mom continued to berate him. "This is on you for putting the idea into her head."

"I can see why this was upsetting, but you are looking at this wrong," he said. "Dani *wanted* to use her magic, and she attempted it without any persuasion on my part. The results were less than ideal, but this was an important step forward for her."

Mom looked at me with a thoughtful expression. "I'm happy she is making progress, but this raises an issue we didn't consider. We expected her magic to come back gradually, not in huge bursts. It's like when I went through liannan. I wasn't used to so much magic, and I couldn't control it around Nikolas. Dani is surrounded by Mohiri here. We can't risk her losing control of her magic."

"It will only get worse as liannan nears," Eldeorin said, and Mom's expression told me she was thinking about that time in her life.

"What should we do?" she asked him.

"I could take her to live at one of my homes as I did with you."

"NO," Mom and Dad said at the same time.

Eldeorin's smirk told me he'd made the offer to get a reaction from my father. Mom saw it, too, and scowled at him.

"I can place a ward around her to contain her magic until she has full control," he said. "She will still be able to use her magic without posing a risk to the other Mori."

Mom visibly relaxed. "Yes. That will work."

"This ward will only hold until she enters liannan," he warned as he came over to me and motioned for me to stand. A quick wave of his hands on either side of me and it was done.

"Why didn't the glaen work like it did the first time?" I asked him.

One corner of his mouth turned up. "Well, for one, you weren't supposed to consume half a bottle."

"I drank the same amount I had...that night." I'd almost said "at Blue Nyx," which would have made Dad burst a blood vessel. "Nothing happened, so I drank another glass to be sure. That didn't work either, so I thought you must have done something in addition to the glaen."

His eyes glittered with amusement. "Did you drink it slowly?"

"Not exactly," I answered, starting to suspect where he was going with these questions.

"And then what did you do?" he asked.

"I walked to the manor for dinner."

He nodded as if it all made sense. "Next time, sip it slowly and give it time to work on you. And stay away from places with a lot of demons until you learn to control your magic. The ward will prevent you from harming them, but it won't help you control your magic."

"I will."

"Keep practicing, and I will return soon for our next lesson." He turned to my mother. "I am pleased with Danielle's progress. She is going to have missteps and complications in her situation, but she is strong, and she has us to guide her."

Mom smiled for the first time since she came home. "Thank you, Eldeorin."

"You will not thank me when you get my bill," he joked and vanished.

I sank down to the couch again, and Mom came over to sit beside me. I rested my head on her shoulder and closed my eyes.

"Is it safe to come out now?" Dimitri called. He had gone to his room to escape the fallout the minute we walked in the door.

"Yes," Mom and I called back.

He sauntered into the living room, looked at each of us, and plopped down in the other armchair. "On a scale of one to ten, how much trouble is she in?"

"She's not in trouble," Dad said. "We're just glad you two are okay."

"Thanks to Ronan, which, by the way, is going to the top of my list of things I never saw coming." Dimitri leaned forward and rested his elbows on his knees. "Are we going to talk about the tiny fact that our trainer is half werewolf?"

"Our trainer is half werewolf," I said with a deadpan expression.

"Ha-ha. I don't know how you can be so blasé about it." He looked at our parents. "Did you know?"

Mom nodded, and Dad said, "Yes."

"*Okay,*" Dimitri mouthed. "Putting aside the fact most werewolves don't like us, how is it biologically possible for him to have a Mori and a wolf inside him?"

It was the same question I'd asked Mom a few days ago. She gave him the same answer, adding, "We live in a world where a race of people is born with a demon inside, where faeries exist, and people can shift into werewolves. Anything is possible."

Dimitri looked at me. "You and Ronan were in there for over an hour. What did you talk about? Did he tell you anything about his family or where he's from?"

I hadn't been able to stop thinking about my mostly one-sided conversation with Ronan since I left the dining hall. I kept replaying the things he'd said to me and wishing Grandfather had waited another half hour. I didn't know how I felt about any of it, except I didn't want to share it with anyone, even my twin.

"He couldn't shift with my magic acting up, so he was in wolf form for most of it. When he was able to shift, we talked about training until Grandfather came in."

Dimitri fell back against the cushion. "Training? He could be the only Mohiri/werewolf hybrid in existence and all you talked about was *training*?"

I pretended to scowl. "I was a little preoccupied at the time."

"One thing's for sure. Training is going to be interesting tomorrow," Dimitri said.

I remembered Dad had ordered me back to class tomorrow. I didn't know what to expect from Ronan. Would he treat me differently, or would he still be the hard trainer I could never please?

My phone vibrated, and I knew who it was. Kai had texted me twice since the incident to check on me, and I hadn't replied to him yet. A month ago, I was giddy when I got a text from him. I didn't know when exactly it happened, but I didn't feel that excitement anymore. It wasn't anything he'd done; he was a great boyfriend. It was me; I had changed. And I knew what I had to do. Not tonight, though. This I had to do in person.

Dad let me go back to the security center after our family talk, but he made it clear I had to leave at eleven. When I tried to argue, he told me those were his final terms. I discovered there wasn't much for me to do because he and Dax had gone through the rest of the documents on Reese Meyer. I ended up hanging out on the couch with a book, afraid to leave and miss some news about Summer.

An hour after I got there, David's voice pulled me from my thoughts. Setting the book aside, I went to stand next to Dad to hear what they were talking about.

"The deposit was made this morning at a branch in Philadelphia. And we got this." David put up a video clip, which showed the main entrance to a bank. The door opened, and a man came out. The video froze, and I easily recognized Reese Meyer's face.

I moved closer. "Are we able to track him from the bank?"

"Why do you think your grandfather pays us so well?" David flashed a grin at me. "Watch and learn."

A series of pictures appeared on the screen, each one of Meyers as he traveled down several streets and got into a cab. More pictures came up, showing him getting out of the cab and going into a hotel.

"He's checked in under his Richard Hill alias," David said.

"Great work." Dad looked at Dax. "Can you get someone from the Philly unit on the line?"

A warrior named Terrence came on the phone, and Dad told him what he needed done. Terrence said he'd call back within the hour. I didn't know if I could wait that long to find out what that bastard had done to Summer.

I was chewing my fingernails by the time a video call came in from Terrence. He flashed a big smile at us. "We picked up that package for you. Nikolas."

The camera panned around a basement and stopped on a hooded man dressed in sleep pants and an undershirt, with his arms and legs zip-tied to a chair. A warrior stood behind him, and another one went over to pull the hood off the bound man's head.

This Reese Meyer was not the suave smiling man from his photos. His dark hair stuck out in all directions, his face was mottled and tear-streaked, and his eyes were red. He looked around wildly at the armed warriors. "Who are you? What do you want?"

"Information," Dad told him.

Reese's eyes darted around until they spotted the camera. "What information? This is a big mistake. You have the wrong man."

Dad crossed his arms. "Perhaps we should talk to Damon Webb, instead."

The man paled and went still.

"I'm going to ask you some questions," Dad said in an icy voice I'd never heard. "How honestly you answer them will decide whether or not you see tomorrow."

Reese dropped his head and let out a sob. I knew my father was bluffing, yet a little shiver ran down my spine.

Dad cut right to the chase. "Three nights ago in Boston, you went to dinner with a college student named Summer Kelly. After dinner, you left the restaurant and walked a block to the parking lot where you'd left your car. Miss Kelly has not been seen or heard from since. What happened to her in that parking lot?"

I couldn't breathe as I waited for Reese's answer. I wanted to know where Summer was, and I was terrified to learn what fate she'd met at his hands.

Reese wore an expression of wide-eyed innocence when he lifted his head to look at the camera. "Nothing happened to her. I drove her back to her dorm, and that was the last time I saw her."

"You are not being honest, Mr. Meyer," Dad said slowly, reminding Reese of his earlier threat. "We know this because the traffic camera next to the parking lot shows you alone in your car after you pulled out of the lot. Would you care to revise your answer?"

Reese swallowed convulsively. "Okay. We argued, and she said she was walking home. She was fine when I left her. I swear."

Dad's voice was dangerously calm. "We found Miss Kelly's phone in the parking lot along with some of her blood. We know you were involved in her disappearance. This is your final chance to answer my question truthfully."

Off camera came the unmistakable sound of a sword sliding from a scabbard. Reese's eyes bulged, and he started to babble. "They said the drug would knock her out, but she woke up when they were putting her in the van. She went crazy, clawing and growling like an animal. They had to tase her twice...and they wrapped a silver chain around her arms and legs. Then they loaded her into their van and left."

I saw red for the first time in my life. "You son of a –"

Dad put a hand over my mouth and shook his head at me. He signaled for Dax to mute the mic and released me. "You need to let me do the talking. I know what you're feeling, but you can't show emotion in an interrogation. Do you understand?"

I nodded stiffly. He gave me a quick hug and turned back to the monitor. "Who took her, and why did they want her?"

"I don't know who they were." Reese's voice had become more of a whine. "And they didn't say why they wanted her."

"You spent weeks gaining this girl's trust so you could deliver her to these people, and you have no idea why and for who?" Dad asked with a lot more control than I had.

"They said they wouldn't hurt her," Reese said weakly.

"That is not what I asked you," Dad barked, and Reese flinched like he'd been struck.

Reese began to cry again. "I swear I don't know who they are. A woman I know asked me if I wanted to make some easy cash. All I had to do was flirt with this college girl and get her to go out with me. She told me when and where and to get out of Boston as soon as it was done."

My jaw hurt from clenching my teeth, and I was trembling from the effort to keep quiet. When we found the people behind this, I was going to make them wish they had never heard her name. No one, not even my father, was going to stop me.

Dad put an arm around my shoulders and hugged me to his side. He looked at the monitor and said, "And you're positive this woman didn't tell you why they wanted the girl?"

"She said I didn't need to know that." Reese hiccupped. "That's everything. I swear."

I stiffened as a fresh wave of anger burned through me. He'd lured Summer into a trap so she could be taken captive by God only knew, and he had no idea what they would do to her.

"That is not everything," Dad said. "I want the name of this woman and descriptions of the people you gave the girl to. I want to know every communication you had about this job and how you received your payment."

I wasn't surprised when Reese immediately gave up his friend to save his own ass. Her name was Iris Morgan, and she lived in Chicago. He didn't know her home address, but he happily offered up her P.O. box number and location.

He described the three men in the van, who sounded like hired mercenaries like the ones who had taken Sofie and Lilly. He and Iris Morgan hadn't talked much, and it had all been done using burner phones. One of the men in the van had handed him an envelope full of cash as payment.

When it was clear Reese had nothing more of value to tell us, Terrence turned the camera back to himself. "What do you want us to do with our charming guest? You know dismemberment and disposal cost extra."

Behind him, Reese moaned and started to blubber. One of the other warriors made a sound of disgust. "Ah, hell, Terrence. I am not cleaning up urine."

"The FBI wants him," Dad said. "Turn him over to them, and let them decide what to do with him."

"You got it."

The called ended, and I sagged against my father. He put both arms around me and rubbed my back.

"I should not have let you listen to that," he said roughly. "It was too hard for you."

"No. I'm glad I heard it firsthand." I stepped back and wiped my eyes with my sleeve. "They had silver chains. They took her because she's a werewolf."

"Yes."

"It's the same people who took the werecougars and the werewolf from Montana, isn't it?" I could no longer deny the truth staring me in the face.

He hesitated a few seconds, and I could see he was thinking of a gentle way to confirm my suspicion. "I believe it is."

My throat went dry, making it hard to swallow. "Do you think they are the ones behind all the demon disappearances?"

"I think it's highly probable." He rubbed his jaw. "The demons are vanishing without a trace and with no physical evidence left behind, which points to a professional job. The werecougar girls were taken by trained mercenaries, and based on Reese's description, the men in the van were mercenaries. Someone with deep pockets and the resources to hide their trail is behind all of this."

I hugged my middle, suddenly cold, and afraid to ask the question haunting me since Summer disappeared. What reason would someone have to go through this much trouble to kidnap shifters and demons? They had nothing in common other than being nonhuman. The most likely answer was some wealthy person creating a private collection. I shuddered at the thought of Summer locked up in a menagerie for the entertainment of some millionaire.

"What do we do now?" I asked.

"Now we locate Iris Morgan." Dad pointed to two of Dax's monitors, where he was already running searches. "That is most likely an alias, but we can trace the owner of the PO box. We'll ask David to look into her as well. Between him and Dax, we'll find her."

Dax nodded without taking his eyes off his monitor. "It's impossible to go completely off the grid unless you live in the wilderness and have zero contact with the outside world. No matter how clever people think they are, they always leave something behind."

I looked at my father. "What can I do?"

"I know you don't want to hear it, but there's nothing else you can do. Train, work on your magic, be with your friends."

"I can't act as if everything is normal," I said.

"No one expects you to." He gently gripped my upper arms. "Take tomorrow off if you need to. And then you take the anger you're feeling and channel it into your training with the knowledge we will employ every resource we have to bring Summer home. We won't stop until she's found."

I forced a smile. "I know you won't."

He exhaled heavily. "I need to call Roland and Peter and tell them what we've learned. You go on home."

"Okay." I wanted to stay, but my long day was finally catching up with me. The call he was about to make was going to be a hard one, and the last thing any of them needed was to worry about me. I kissed his cheek and left.

A light rain had started, and it picked up as I walked toward the woods. The weather suited my mood, and I didn't care if I would be drenched by the time I got home.

Someone stepped out of the woods near the river. Shielding my eyes, I watched Ronan walk along the bank, as uncaring about the rain as I was. I wondered if he was returning from another trip to the river pool and if he thought about that night as much as I did.

I replayed our conversation in the dining hall. He'd shown me a different side of him, and it was impossible to dislike him after that. I wasn't sure exactly how I felt, and the more I got to know him, the more of an enigma he became.

Ronan paused and looked my way, and I realized I was staring at him. I gave an awkward wave and hurried toward the woods.

"Tell me again why I have to get into the lake." I asked as I dipped a toe into the lake the following afternoon.

"Because you are half undine and water is the perfect medium for you," my mother said. "I think you can use the water's magic to help you control your magic."

I looked over my shoulder at her. "I only drank one glass of glaen. Is that enough?"

"How do you feel?" she asked.

"Warm and tingly." I swished the water with my toe. "But not too warm to know this water is freezing."

Mom laughed. "You remind me of myself the first time Aine told me to get into the lake. We were in this very spot. That was the day I learned I could control water."

I waded into the water. "Let's hope I follow in your footsteps."

This morning, I'd decided to skip training again and spend the day with Mom instead. First, we went to the menagerie to care for the newest inhabitants; three wyvern hatchlings seized during a raid in Texas. The wyverns were no more than a month old and had tiny nubs where their wings would be someday. They were about a foot tall and so stinking cute when they hissed and tiny wisps of smoke came from their snouts. Fortunately, wyverns couldn't produce fire until adolescence. By then, they would be on the way to their new home at the training facility in Argentina.

During lunch, I'd asked if Mom would help me with my magic, which brought us here. I was afraid to do it alone even with the ward Eldeorin put on me.

"Stop there," she called when the water was up to my knees. "Now sit facing me."

I made a face. "Is that necessary?"

"Yes," she answered, clearly enjoying this.

I obeyed, and the water came almost to my chest. Pulling my legs up, I wrapped my arms around them as if that would warm me up.

"Can you feel your magic yet?" she asked.

"No."

She walked to the water's edge. "I want you to think back to what your magic felt like after you drank glaen at Blue Nyx but before you saw the vampires."

Closing my eyes, I imagined the warm glow deep inside me. It was easier than I thought it would be.

"Now try to summon it," she said.

I tried over and over, but it was like reaching for a hologram. Frustrated, I gave up and opened my eyes. "I can't."

"That's okay. Let's try this instead. Think of your magic, but this time picture what it would look like in the water. Watch." She crouched and touched the water with the tip of one finger. Instantly, a sparkly golden cloud formed around her finger, and a vague long-ago memory surfaced of me doing the same thing.

I did as she said and remembered the glow again. I imagined the glow was in the water instead of inside me. In my mind's eye, the glow spread out and surrounded me.

"Dani, open your eyes," Mom said softly.

Her smile was the first thing I saw. She pointed at the water, and I looked down.

"Wow." The water around me didn't just sparkle. It was filled with a white glow extending at least four feet in every direction. I cupped my hand and scooped up some water. Looking closer, I saw the glow was created by thousands of tiny individual sparks of light.

"How did I call the water's magic without my own?" I dipped my hand to let the water fall back into the lake.

Mom stood. "You can't completely lock your magic away. It's as much a part of you as your Mori is. You opened yourself to the magic in the lake, and it responded because it recognizes the magic in you."

I moved my hand through the water, awed by the way the sparkles followed it. They began to cling to me until my submerged parts were surrounded by a soft white glow, and I no longer felt cold.

I met my mother's proud gaze. "I think I remember doing this when I was little."

"You used to love playing with water magic. Your favorite trick was to create –"

"– waterspouts!" I said as an image formed in my mind of two tiny waterspouts dancing around each other.

Her eyes took on a faraway look, and she smiled. "By the time you were five, you could already control water better than I did at seventeen."

"Only because I had you to teach me from the time I could walk." I swirled the water with a finger, trying to create a whirlpool. "If you'd known Aine when you were little, you probably could have created blizzards by the time you were seventeen."

Another memory surfaced. "Do you remember the time you froze the lake so we could skate?"

She grinned. "Grandma Madeline gave you and Dimitri ice skates for Christmas, but the lake hadn't completely frozen over yet. You were too impatient to wait until January."

"We spent the whole afternoon on the lake. That was one of my favorite Christmases." I thought about Mom and Dad teaching Dimitri and me to skate. Uncle Chris and Aunt Beth had been there with two-year-old Grace, and at dusk, Mom made it snow only on the lake.

"It was a fun day." She clapped her hands. "But back to your lesson."

Buoyed by the happy memory and the effects of the glaen, I looked down at the glowing water. "What do I do now?"

"Focus on the feel of the water magic. It's essentially the same as yours, only weaker." She leaned down and held her hand a few inches above the surface of the water. The water beneath her hand began to sparkle, and a tiny column of magic rose to touch her. "Call to the water magic, and let it try to draw yours out."

I placed my hands on my knees and closed my eyes again. I thought about the water magic and how warm it was against my skin. When I concentrated harder, I realized that under the warmth was the faintest tingle of electricity. I called to it like I would my own magic until I felt it moving under my skin. Mom was right; it wasn't nearly as strong as mine.

I was so focused on feeling the water magic I didn't notice the glow at first. Slowly, I became aware of the heat building at my center and tendrils of energy reaching out in every direction. Elation filled me as the two magics connected and merged, and I felt whole for the first time in many years.

Opening my eyes, I swirled my hand in the water. The sparkles followed my hand, and I moved faster and faster until it created a tiny whirlpool. It was as if a long unused part of me had woken up, and it knew what I wanted to do before I did. I lifted my hand, and the water rose with it. Holding my hand palm down, I envisioned the water spinning faster until a waterspout rose two feet into the air.

A wave of exhaustion came out of nowhere, and my hand felt like it was attached to the end of an elastic band stretched too tightly. I let it drop back into the water as my magic receded, and the glow shrunk to nothing more than a tiny ember, which flickered and went out.

"I couldn't hold it," I said between pants. "I don't understand. It lasted for almost an hour yesterday."

Mom sat on a large rock. "Yesterday, you weren't controlling it, which is why it behaved like that. Today, you drank only one glass of glaen, and you were channeling your magic to move water. Plus, you are out of practice."

I stood and was surprised when my legs wobbled. Leaving the water, I joined her on the rock. A breeze made me shiver until she laid a hand on my arm. My clothes dried instantly, and warmth flooded me.

"Thanks."

She reached up to tuck my hair behind my shoulder. "You did so well, Dani, even better than I hoped for on your first try. Eldeorin and Aine will be pleased."

"Why didn't he start me off doing something like this instead of throwing vampires at me?" I asked.

She chuckled. "Eldeorin doesn't believe in half measures, and as powerful as he is, he doesn't think like an elemental. Once you said you wanted to regain control of your magic, I had a feeling being in the water would help you."

"You were right." I gazed out at the glassy surface of the lake. "Should I go again?"

"That's enough for today. We'll pick it up there tomorrow *after* your training."

"Okay." I did need to get back to training, if only to work off all the negative energy I'd been holding in. I missed my friends, too, although they were sure to pepper me with questions after my little incident yesterday.

Mom stood. "I have a session in thirty minutes. Do you want to walk to the manor with me?"

"I'm going there this evening, so I think I'll hang out here until dinner." I was a bit drained from practice, but I didn't want her worrying about me and deciding we should take it slower.

"To see Kai," she asked with a knowing smile.

"Yes."

She gave me a quick hug. "I'll bring some dessert for after dinner. You've earned it."

I stayed on the rock when she left to walk to the manor. She could have transported there in a second, but she liked walking. Hugo and Woolf bounded from the trees and took their places on either side of her. They loved to protect her, and she would never deny them that pleasure.

My good mood dampened when I thought about why I was going to see Kai tonight. It was time for the talk I had been putting off, and I dreaded it. I liked Kai, and it wasn't fair to string him along. I stood with a sigh. Why did doing the right thing have to be so hard?

***

"Is it someone else?" Kai asked quietly.

"No." I stared up at the lights of the manor from our seat in the gazebo. A face came unbidden to my mind, and I pushed it away. I had no idea where that had come from or why it caused a tiny stab of guilt.

Kai gave me a halfhearted smile. "It's not you, it's me."

"As cliché as that is, it's true. I'm dealing with a lot, and I don't exactly make good girlfriend material these days. We hardly see each other anymore as it is."

His shoulders drooped. "I felt you pulling away this week, and I hoped it was temporary."

"I'm sorry, Kai," I said roughly.

"I know." He reached over and took my hand. "You don't need to apologize for your feelings. I saw what happened to you in the dining hall, and I heard about your friend Summer. I hope they find her soon."

My throat tightened. "Me, too."

"Are you okay?" he asked. "That was pretty intense yesterday."

I grimaced. "I put on quite a show, didn't I?"

He leaned forward. "What happened? All Dimitri would tell us was it was fixed and you were alright."

"Let's just say I attempted something to free my magic, and it worked a little too well. It didn't hurt me, and Eldeorin put a ward on me so it won't happen again."

"I'm glad you're okay." He broke into a grin. "Of course, that was *nothing* compared to Ronan shifting into a werewolf. Never saw that one coming."

I thought about my shock the night I discovered what Ronan was. "Me either."

"Do you think Tristan knew?"

"Yes. My parents knew about it, too." I plucked at a loose thread on my sleeve. "Did Ronan say anything about it in class today?"

Kai snorted a laugh. "Not a word. He came in, and it was business as usual."

"That sounds like him." Ronan hadn't said anything to me about it yesterday either. I had so many questions. Where was he from? Which one of his parents was the werewolf? What was it like to have a Mori and a wolf inside? Did silver hurt him? Dimitri had tried to get Mom and Dad to tell us, but he'd had no luck.

"Are you coming back to training tomorrow?" Kai asked.

I nodded. "I have to if I plan to be a warrior next year."

Standing, he held out a hand to me and tugged me to my feet. "You will, and you'll be a great one."

"Because it's in my blood," I joked as we left the gazebo. I'd lost count of how many times someone had told me that.

"Because you're you," he said. "Sometimes, when I watch you in training, I wonder if you pretend not to be better than the rest of us to save our egos."

"Why on earth would you say that?" His words were so close to what Ronan had told me. It was strange the two of them had mentioned it within a day of each other.

I was floored when he said, "It's the way you move. We're all great fighters, but you make it look effortless. Naomi said once you remind her of a lethal ballerina, and that stuck with me."

I let out a short laugh. "Trust me; I am not protecting anyone's ego, especially Dimitri's. But thank you for saying that."

We reached the manor, and I said, "Thanks for being so nice about everything. We're still friends?"

"Always." He waved at the door. "Are you coming in? I think the others are watching movies in the common room."

"Next time." I felt weird about the two of us joining our friends when we'd just broken up. It wouldn't feel as awkward in training tomorrow.

"Want me to walk you home?"

"I'm good." I leaned in and kissed his cheek. "Night, Kai."

"See you tomorrow," he said and turned to go in.

I started in the direction of home but changed course and went to sit on the riverbank. Lying back on the grass, I stared at the stars and tried to unwind my jumbled emotions. I was glad Kai had taken it well, but I was also a little sad it was over. He was my first boyfriend, and we'd had a lot of fun together.

I threw an arm over my eyes. What was wrong with me? I was thinking about boyfriends while Summer could be going through all kinds of horrors. At the very least, she was a captive. At the worst... I tried not to think about what that could be.

The only thing that allowed me to sleep at night was knowing my father was personally heading up the search for her. Working with David and Kelvan, he would turn over every rock and follow every trail to figure out who had taken her. No one was better than the two hackers, which was why they worked exclusively for us and were well compensated for it.

I pulled my arm back to look at the stars, but some of them were missing. I squeezed my eyes shut and opened them again. They focused, not on the stars, but on the dark shape blotting them out.

I rolled away and came to my feet with my knife in hand. Heart racing, I glared at Ronan more out of embarrassment than annoyance. "Are you trying to get stabbed?"

His eyebrows rose. "Are you expecting an attack at Westhorne?"

"No. Sorry." I sheathed my knife. "Out for your nightly walk?"

"I prefer to run."

"I like to run, too," I said, and then I realized he meant running as a wolf. He started toward the woods, and I fell in step beside him. A few days ago, I would have walked in the other direction. "How far do you go?"

If he didn't want my company, he didn't show it. "Five miles or so. I try to stay out of the wyvern's territory."

Was that amusement in his voice? I slanted a look at him, but I couldn't make out his expression from this angle.

"His name is Alex, and that's probably a good idea. Alex leaves people alone, but anything on four legs is fair game – except for the hellhounds. Not even Alex will mess with them."

When Ronan didn't respond, I explained how we had a wyvern living in the mountains. "I think he stays because of my mother. He saved her life again after the attack on Westhorne. She and my father were in the woods surrounded by vampires. Alex swooped in, killed two vampires, and flew away with her."

That got a reaction. Ronan turned his head to look at me, and I laughed at the incredulity on his face. "It's all true. Mom has that effect on animals, even grouchy wyverns. They're drawn to her. How do you think we came to have two hellhounds?"

"And you have this ability, too?" he asked as if he had discovered the answer to a confusing puzzle.

I made a so-so gesture. "Yes, but it's nothing compared to hers, at least, not since I suppressed my magic. You're wondering if that's why I was with Alex the day we met."

"It did baffle me," he admitted.

I grinned. "Now you know."

We stopped at the edge of the woods, and I was taken aback by a sudden reluctance to part ways with him. What was up with me lately? I needed to ask Mom if releasing my magic could mess with my emotions. It was the only explanation that made sense.

"I better go so you can shift." I took a step toward the trees, and his voice stopped me.

"You shouldn't be in the forest alone at night. I will walk you home."

Laughing, I turned to him. "I am home, and this is my backyard. I know every inch of these woods, and this way is faster than taking the road." At his skeptical look, I said, "I'll be halfway to my house by the time you undress and shift."

He made a sound between a grunt and a laugh.

"Good night," I said lightly and entered the woods. I didn't wait for his response before I set out at a run, picking up speed when my vision adjusted to the deeper darkness. The familiar rush of adrenaline filled me, the unbridled joy of moving as swiftly and freely as the wind through the trees.

The crack of a twig and a soft chuff told me I was no longer alone. My breath quickened, and my surroundings became more vibrant as the competitor in me awakened. "Race you to the lake," I called and put on an extra burst of speed.

I used to run with Summer and my other werewolf friends in the Knolls, but it hadn't filled me with the exhilaration I felt racing side-by-side with Ronan. We weaved fluidly through trees and over obstacles as if we shared a consciousness, and all my heavy thoughts and worries fell behind me. Even my Mori fluttered in excitement.

When the lights of my house peeked through the trees, I pushed myself even harder, determined to win. It wasn't enough. Ronan sprinted past me, reaching the lake a full three seconds ahead of me.

Stopping beside him in a small clearing by the water, I tried to control my breathing so he wouldn't see how winded I was. "I let you win this time."

Ronan snorted, and I was tempted to push him into the lake until I thought of all the ways he could get payback in training.

He headed back into the woods to continue his run. I waited until he was almost out of sight to say, "See you in class tomorrow."

His reply was a short guttural bark as the forest swallowed him up.

10

———

"Dani, you're up," Claire called as Dimitri jogged around the corner of the large barn wearing a self-satisfied grin.

Cheers went up for Dimitri as Kai patted my back. "Good luck."

I shot him a smile and went to join Claire. We walked over to the base of a thirty-foot tower with a small platform near the top. A thick rope dangled from the platform to the ground.

"You remember the instructions I gave you earlier?" she asked.

"Yes."

"Good." She held up a stop watch. "Go."

I gripped the rope with both hands, locked it around my feet, and began to climb. After running, climbing was my best activity, and I reached the top in less than fifteen seconds.

Standing on the platform, I had a clear view of the obstacle course and the surrounding farmland. The forty-acre property in Butler Falls had been a dairy farm until it closed two years ago. Grandfather bought it this summer to use as an additional training location. The townspeople thought West-horne was an eccentric private school, so they didn't question our need for an outdoor exercise facility.

A narrow balance beam connected my platform to another one twenty feet away. I sped across the beam and stopped briefly on the platform to study the next obstacle. At the other end of a rope bridge hung a life-size dummy blocking access to the next platform. A red target was painted on the dummy's chest, and three throwing knives lay at my feet.

The dummy jerked and started toward me on a pulley system above the bridge. I snatched up a knife, aimed, and threw it. The blade sank into the dummy's shoulder, but the dummy kept coming. *Crap.* I had to hit the target before the dummy reached me, or I was out.

I grabbed the second knife. Taking a breath, I lined up my aim and threw the knife at the dummy, which was already halfway across the bridge. The knife hit the center of the red target.

Yes.

For a second, nothing happened. Then the dummy swung back to its starting position. I ran across the bridge and leaped at the pole beside it. I slid down the pole to the ground and found myself in a walled structure. On the ground was a fencing foil. I picked it up and continued through the only door into a room with another door on the opposite wall.

No sooner had I entered the room when a hooded, masked figure in dark clothes stepped in front of me, holding a foil. Like the dummy, he had a red target over his heart.

My opponent raised his foil in a brisk salute. I repeated the gesture and launched into an attack. He deftly parried my thrust, but he didn't make a counterattack. I realized the goal was for me to land a strike to the target, not for him to hit back.

I attacked again, and he blocked it with a circular sweep of his foil. I followed it with a series of rapid lunges and feints, but he expertly blocked every move.

It took half a minute of sparring with him to know whose face was under the mask. Since that day in the dining hall, things had changed between Ronan and me in training. I'd taken his comments about me holding myself back to heart, and I worked hard to be as good as he said I was. The more I improved, the more he pushed me, but I no longer mistook his criticism for dislike. I soaked up everything he said to us and closely watched his demonstrations to improve my own technique. I'd know his swordplay anywhere.

Although I worked with him every day in class, neither of us mentioned our run two weeks ago. Or the six times we'd run together since then. If I wanted a running partner, I waited for him at the edge of the woods when he went for his nightly run. No words were exchanged. I smiled a hello at him and set out, and a minute later, his wolf caught up to me. We always parted ways at the lake, but I wished we could run like that for hours.

If I was honest with myself, our shared love of running wasn't the only reason I enjoyed those nights so much. Although he was all business in class, a camaraderie had developed between us. I didn't know if it was because of our talk or our nighttime runs, but the more time we spent together, the more I looked forward to the next time.

Despite all that, Ronan wasn't making this obstacle easy for me. I was very aware of the ticking clock as he blocked every one of my attacks. I remembered one of our classes when he'd shown me several ways to adjust my technique when fighting a larger person. His words that day came back to me. *"It's a natural reaction to underestimate a smaller opponent. That flaw is another weapon you can use against them."*

I feinted a strike to his chest and went for his stomach. As I expected, Ronan anticipated the move. What he wasn't expecting was for me to stumble. He paused for a second, but it was all I needed to slip through his defenses and press the tip of my foil to the target on his chest.

"Gotcha," I whispered, stepping back.

He gave a slight head shake, and I pictured his eyebrows rising. Ronan was one of those people who could speak volumes without uttering a word – when he wasn't wearing his stoic face. He raised his foil and saluted me. Then he stepped aside to let me pass.

Dropping my foil, I ran through the doorway. I smiled in glee at the twenty-foot climbing wall and grabbed the first handhold. Scaling a wall was as easy as climbing a tree, and in thirty seconds I was over the top and sliding down a net to the ground.

In front of me was a shipping container with a padlocked door. Gavin had warned us there could be locks in our exercise today, so we'd all remembered our pick sets. I took my case from my pocket and went to work on the heavy-duty padlock. After two attempts, the lock clicked and the bolt opened.

I tossed the lock aside and opened the door. Inside the shed, a dummy lay on the floor. I snickered at the sign on the dummy's shirt, which read RESCUE ME. Hoisting the heavy dummy over my shoulders in a fireman's hold, I left the shed and ran around it to the other side where Claire waited for me behind the barn.

She clicked the button on her stopwatch and gave me a nod of approval. "Good job, Dani."

"What's my time?" I dropped the dummy at her feet and tried to look at the stopwatch.

Claire laughed, holding it out of my reach. "You'll find out when the exercise is over."

I gave her my best pout and ran around the barn to where my friends hooted and clapped for me. Gavin called for Kai, and we slapped hands as he passed me.

"Damn, girl," said Victoria, who'd already had her turn. "Did you fly over the course?"

I shrugged, grinning at her. I had noticed an improvement in my speed and coordination since I'd started racing Ronan, but I wasn't telling *her* that. It all came down to how much time I'd lost fencing with him and picking the lock. Overall, I felt great about my performance in the exercise.

The mood was light and playful as my friends and I joked around and speculated about who had been the fastest. We weren't supposed to discuss the course until everyone had gone through it, so a few of us hinted at difficult obstacles that didn't exist. By the time Elsie went last, she expected to dodge flying knives and swing on a rope across a pit of flames.

I hadn't realized how much I needed this until now. Summer had been missing for over three weeks, and the last lead we had was dead, literally. We had tracked down Reese's friend Iris Morgan in Chicago, only to discover her body had been pulled out of Lake Michigan three days after Reese's interrogation. Whoever had hired her was leaving behind no witnesses and wiping out any connection to them.

Elsie finished the course, giving us dark looks for misleading her. A few minutes later, Ronan, Gavin, and Claire appeared from behind the barn and walked over to us. We quieted as we waited for our times.

Gavin looked at the phone in his hand. "The fastest time was three minutes and eleven seconds."

"Wow," Sean said in a low voice. "Guess that rules out me."

"And me," said a few others.

"And the winner is..." Gavin did a dramatic pause. "Dani."

I had expected him to call Dimitri's name. I didn't register what he said until Dimitri whooped and grabbed me in a one-armed hug.

"Way to go, Sis."

Claire waved her stopwatch. "Impressive, Dani."

Naomi said something to me. I started to turn my head in her direction when Ronan said, "Well done."

My gaze flew to him. He wasn't smiling like Gavin and Claire, but there was a flicker of admiration in his eyes I hadn't seen before. He tipped his head at me, and my chest swelled like he'd sung my praises. I was on such a high I paid little attention to Gavin as he called out everyone else's times.

When it was time to go, Naomi and Luis sidled up next to me, and she murmured, "Well done, Dani. I don't think I've ever heard Ronan say that to anyone."

"Me either," said Luis.

We walked to the vehicles, and I went to the six motorcycles parked beside the SUVs. One of the perks of being a senior was being allowed to ride our motorcycles to town if we were accompanied by a warrior. Dimitri and I got our bikes on our sixteenth birthday. He'd chosen a Ducati, and I'd gone with a Kawasaki. I'd wanted red, but I got a black one because it didn't stand out as much.

We donned our jackets and helmets and mounted our bikes as the other trainees piled into the three SUVs driven by Ronan, Claire, and Gavin. Claire took the lead with the seniors following her and the last two vehicles taking up the rear.

"I wish they'd let us ride ahead," Dimitri grumbled over my helmet speaker as our caravan stopped at the last intersection in town.

"Maybe if they didn't know you so well, they would," I retorted. His love of driving fast was no secret to anyone at Westhorne.

Sean's voice cut in. "Way to go, Dimitri."

"Hey," Dimitri protested, and we all laughed.

The light changed. Dimitri was ahead of me, and I gave him a slight lead before I followed him through the three-way intersection.

"Dani, watch out," Kai shouted.

I turned my head to the left, and everything seemed to happen in slow motion. I saw the large blue pickup run the red light, and I hit the gas, but it was too late. The truck slammed into the rear of my bike.

The force of the impact whipped me around and sent me through the wooden guard rail. I saw the deep ditch below me, and the only thing I could do was jump free of my motorcycle in the air.

I hit the rocky embankment on my feet, but my ankle twisted painfully, and I went down. My helmet protected my head as I tumbled, but my body took a beating on the rocks. I landed hard on my right side, and a sharp pain in my chest stole my breath. I'd never broken a rib, but I was pretty sure I'd just made up for it.

I rolled onto my back, and searing pain arced through me. My chest felt like it was on fire, and I couldn't catch my breath. People shouted from a long way off as darkness crept across my vision.

Someone opened my visor and touched my face. I jerked involuntarily as my body thrummed with electricity, which sent my heart racing. *My magic.* I'd freed it somehow, and it was going to hurt someone.

The warm touch disappeared, and a wave of anguish threatened to suffocate me. My Mori was in pain. Was I dying?

The hand returned, and an image of a snarling wolf flashed behind my eyes. Someone said my name, but they were drowned out by a low growl from my Mori before it began to flutter wildly.

"Dani," the voice said again. "Can you hear me?"

I cracked my eyes, and a blurry face swam in my vision. I tried to speak, but all that came out was a moan.

"That's it. Open your eyes," he ordered.

I obeyed, and Ronan's face came into focus. He wore a strange expression somewhere between relief and shock. I must look worse than I felt.

"Dani," cried another voice. Dimitri's anxious face appeared above me followed by Gavin's.

"Where does it hurt?" Ronan asked me. His expression was back to normal, except for his eyes, and his voice sounded off, strained.

"Chest...ribs," I mumbled.

He unzipped my jacket and pulled up my top to examine me. When he felt along my right side, I gasped in pain.

"Can you move your arms and legs?" he asked, and I did.

I gritted my teeth. "Ankle."

Gavin handed Ronan a small metal cylinder, and I knew what was coming. I opened my mouth dutifully and let him place the awful green paste on my tongue. I tried in vain to swallow it before its dry, bitter taste filled my mouth.

The only thing good about gunna paste was how fast it worked. Numbness spread through my body, dulling the pain and allowing me to take in a full breath. I let out a sigh.

Ronan looked as relieved as I felt. "You have two – maybe three – broken ribs. We need to bind them before we can get you out of here."

"Okay," I croaked. My mouth and throat were dry from the gunna paste.

He grabbed the back of his black T-shirt and yanked it over his head. I could only stare at his muscular shoulders and chest as he tore the shirt into strips and tied them together. If the gunna paste hadn't made me forget my pain, this sight would have.

Dimitri and Gavin got on either side of me and carefully lifted me into a sitting position. Was it my imagination, or did Ronan's jaw tighten when he glanced at Gavin?

Ronan eased my helmet off my head and set it on the ground. I caught a glimpse of the scuffs and small dents on the surface and realized I'd gotten off easy with a few broken ribs.

He reached inside my jacket and began wrapping the makeshift binding snugly around my chest. When he leaned in close enough for me to smell the subtle fragrance of musk, woods, and sun-warmed earth on his skin, I wanted to press my lips to his throat and taste him.

Taste him? What the hell had gotten into me?

He finished binding my ribs and straightened. "How does that feel?"

I cleared my throat. "Good."

A frown marred his brow. "Are you sure? You look flushed." He reached over to check the tightness of the binding. Satisfied, he slipped one arm under my knees and the other around my back.

"What are you doing?" I asked breathlessly.

"You can't climb with your injuries." He stood with me in his arms and started up the steep embankment as sure-footed as a mountain goat.

My friends lined the guardrail, watching us, and a few of the girls were slack-jawed at the sight of a shirtless Ronan. Out of nowhere, anger flared in me, and I almost yelled at them to look somewhere else. Could you sustain a concussion while wearing a helmet?

Kai met us at the top and held out his arms. "I can take her."

Ronan's chest rumbled against my cheek. "No." He carried me to one of the SUVs and set me on the front passenger seat.

Dimitri followed us and helped me fasten my seat belt while Ronan spoke to Claire. "You scared the shit out of me," he said shakily.

"Sorry." It had happened so fast there'd been no time to be scared. If it had been him in the crash, I would have been terrified.

He studied my face. "Are you still in pain?"

"No."

He didn't look convinced. "Your Mori feels weird."

"Probably because it was in an accident," I teased. As twins, our Mori shared a special connection. If one of us was upset or in pain, the other could sense it when we touched.

Ronan got behind the wheel, and Victoria and Elsie climbed into the back. Elsie leaned forward and put a hand on my shoulder. "You okay?"

I rested my head against the seat. "A little dinged up but I'll live."

Ronan was stone-faced as he started the SUV, and he said nothing during the drive home. I had no idea what to make of his sudden mood change, but I was still too disoriented to think about it. My Mori was out of sorts, too, excited one minute and confused in the next. And it kept shivering, if that was the right word for it.

My parents and grandfather were waiting for us on the steps when we pulled up to the front entrance. Dad opened my door and reached around me to unhook my seat belt. He lifted me out, and Mom fussed over me as he carried me into the manor.

"We'll see you later, Dani," Victoria said in the main hall.

"Later," I called when Dad headed for the east wing.

We entered the medical ward, where two healers were waiting for us.

They took me into an exam room, did a few scans, and concluded I did indeed have three broken ribs and a severely sprained ankle.

The gunna paste had started to wear off, and I grunted in pain when a healer named Cora wrapped my sprained ankle. She gave me an injection, and in no time, I was pleasantly warm and pain free.

"Does she need to stay here overnight?" Mom asked.

"I don't think that's necessary," Cora said. "She can go home as long as she takes it easy tomorrow and comes back for a follow-up."

My Mori was still acting weird, but I didn't mention it because they might change their minds about letting me go home. It had stopped shivering, but it felt agitated. Hopefully, it would be better after a good night's rest.

Mom helped me into fresh clothes she had brought from home, and Dad came in to carefully pick me up. Dimitri was waiting for us in the main room.

"It wasn't enough you blew us all away in the obstacle course," he teased. "You just had to get all the attention today."

I wrinkled my nose. "You're welcome to it any time."

Dad smiled proudly. "First place. That's my girl."

"She was twenty seconds faster than the second-place time," Dimitri said, opening the door for us. "Are you sure she can't do that Fae travelling thing yet?"

"Har-har." I stroked my chin. "And who came in second? I can't remember."

He laughed, and Mom said, "At least, we know she is feeling better."

Dad had an SUV parked out front, and he settled me in the back before they all got in. I didn't see Ronan, and I was surprised to feel a twinge of disappointment. It wasn't like I expected him to wait around, but a small part of me had hoped he would.

"Does anyone know what happened to the truck driver who hit me?" I asked during the drive home. "Was he hurt?"

"He was fine. The sheriff took him in for reckless driving," Mom replied. "Claire said he was fifteen, and only had a driver's permit."

Dad's eyes met mine in the rearview mirror. "You were both very lucky. If you hadn't moved in time, he would have hit you instead of the back of your motorcycle. And if he'd hit a human, they might not have survived that crash."

I shivered at the thought of how much worse it could have been. "How's my bike?"

"In worst shape than you," Dimitri said. "It's going to need some work."

Dad shook his head. "Don't worry about the bike. We'll get you a new one."

At home, Mom made me eat something even though I said I wasn't hungry. "Your body needs fuel to heal itself," she reminded me.

Grandfather showed up after dinner, and he and I played chess at the dining room table with Eliot, Orwell, and Verne looking on. Every time I captured one of Grandfather's pieces, the imps squeaked and did a little victory dance.

By nine o'clock, I was yawning, and Dad ordered me to bed. Although I was tired, I lay in bed staring at the ceiling feeling antsy and jittery. Something felt different, but I didn't know what. The more I tried to figure it out, the more anxious I became.

I threw off the covers and sat up, careful of my ribs. Using the wall for support, I hobbled over to the large chair beside the window overlooking the lake. I sank down in the chair with a sigh and propped my leg on the small ottoman. I couldn't remember ever being restricted like this by an injury, and it was getting old fast.

I stared at the lake and the woods beyond it with longing. If it wasn't for my injuries, I'd be out there at this moment, running off my restlessness. I imagined meeting up with Ronan and racing with him until exhaustion forced me to stop. I'd sprawl on the grass, and he'd lie beside me. His arms would wrap around me, holding me against his warm body as the forest sounds lulled us to sleep.

A sound from the bathroom jarred me out of the daydream. I put a hand to my heated face and shifted in the chair. It wasn't the first time I'd thought about Ronan since we started spending time together, but none of my imaginings had ever been this vivid.

I returned my gaze to the lake, and my breath caught. Was that...? I sharpened my vision until I could easily make out the outline of a wolf standing on the other side of the lake. *Ronan.* It was as if my imagination had conjured him in real life.

What was he doing here? He didn't move, and I began to wonder if I was imagining him. After an hour, he turned away and melted into the trees.

I stayed where I was for another thirty minutes, but if he was out there, I couldn't see him. I didn't know why, but seeing him had eased my anxiety. When I went back to bed, I fell asleep not long after my head hit the pillow.

I wish I could say I woke up the next morning refreshed and rested. If anything, I felt worse than I had the previous night. My ribs and ankle were mostly healed, but I was moody and on edge from the moment I got out of bed. I snapped at Dimitri when he took too long in the bathroom, and I immediately felt so bad I almost teared up.

"Are you still in pain?" Mom asked when I left my room.

"No." I poured a glass of water and sat on one of the stools at the counter. When she continued casting worried glances at me, I said, "I didn't sleep well."

Appeased, she walked over to the refrigerator. "What would you like for breakfast?"

"I'm not hungry." At her frown, I said, "I'll get something later."

"Okay." She gave me another searching look and picked up her messenger bag. "Take it easy today. I'll be back at noon to see how you're doing."

I tapped a fingernail against the side of my glass. "I'm not five, Mom. You don't need to check on me."

She smiled. "I'll bring you a hamburger with the works. Do you want cheese fries with it?"

I scowled at my glass. She knew I couldn't say no to cheese fries. "Yes."

I spent half the morning wandering around the house, unable to stay in one place for long. I tried reading and watching a movie, but nothing held my interest.

Thinking I could channel my restless energy into something useful, I went down to the lake to practice my magic. I had been working on it every day with Mom. Two days ago, I'd finally managed to summon my magic without drinking glaen first. I still couldn't use it long without getting tired, but I was making progress.

Today, I couldn't focus enough to summon anything, not even the water magic. After numerous attempts, I slapped the water in frustration and stomped out of the lake.

"You're trying too hard," said Mom, whom I hadn't realized was there. "Remember, your magic is an extension of you and should come naturally."

"I know that." I stuffed my feet into the shoes I'd left on the shore. I knew I was being a brat, but I couldn't seem to adopt a better attitude today.

As I walked up to the house, she met me and blocked my path. "You haven't been yourself since last night. Is it the accident? Do you want to talk about it?"

I pinned my arms against my stomach as tears burned the back of my throat. "I don't know what it is. I don't like feeling weak. Maybe that's it."

"That could be it, but you are anything but weak." She held up a basket. "I brought lunch."

My mouth watered at the delicious smells wafting toward me. I hadn't eaten yet today, but I wouldn't tell her that.

We went inside, and she unpacked the basket. She had brought burgers and enough cheese fries to feed a hungry sumo wrestler. I dug in, but halfway through my burger, my appetite disappeared. When I tried to take another bite, my stomach rebelled, and I put the burger down.

"I'll finish this later," I said when Mom gave me a questioning look.

She got up and came over to place her hand against my forehead. I pushed it away with a forced laugh. "I don't have a fever, Mom. I'm just not that hungry."

"You barely touched your fries. You're not feeling well, and you're trying to hide it from me."

She took my hand. The next thing I knew we were standing in the medical ward at the manor where I spent the next ninety minutes being examined and answering a hundred questions about how I felt. She wouldn't take me home until the healers assured her they could find nothing physically wrong with me.

Mom decided to stay home with me despite my protests I was okay. By dinnertime, I was starting to wonder if that was true. The restlessness of the night before had returned, and I became distraught to the point of being on the verge of tears. Dad held me and pleaded with me to tell him what was wrong. I couldn't answer because I didn't know why I felt this way.

"If it's not physical, it has to be your magic," Mom said. "I'm sending for Eldeorin."

No sooner had she said it than my Mori fluttered crazily. A second later, a knock came at the door.

Dimitri went to answer it, and when he returned, Ronan was with him. The moment I saw Ronan, calm washed over me like a warm summer rain.

Ronan wore an expression I'd never seen on him. He looked unsettled. When his eyes locked with mine, I felt longing so fierce it brought me to my feet.

He broke our gaze to look at my parents. "Sara, Nikolas, would you mind if I speak to Dani alone?"

Dad stood and put his arm around me. His body was tense, but I was too overwhelmed by emotions to understand why. Mom must have read his thoughts over their bond because her eyes widened, and she put a hand to her mouth. I looked between her and Ronan, trying to make sense of what was going on. The only person who looked as confused as I felt was Dimitri.

Mom recovered first. "We can leave, or you two can go out to the deck."

"The deck," Ronan and I said together.

I stepped away from Dad and walked to the door, which opened to the deck. Dimitri brought me my jacket, and his brows knitted in confusion. He wasn't the only one wondering what was going on.

Our deck was three-tiered and lit by strings of lights all the way down to the dock. Sensing a need for privacy, I led Ronan down to the bottom deck and sat on a sofa, which would soon be stored away for winter. He chose to stand with his back to the water, his hands gripping the rail behind him.

"How have you been feeling since the accident?" he asked. He'd come to see how I was doing?

"I'm mostly healed. The healers said it will take a day or two."

"That's good." He shifted his weight. "Other than your physical condition, how do you feel?"

The question caught me off guard, and I said the first word that came to mind. "Strange."

"Strange how?"

"I don't feel like myself. I go from being upset to snapping people's heads off." I rubbed my hands on my thighs. "I'm starting to wonder if I'm going crazy."

He raked one of his hands through his hair. "Do you know when it started?"

"Last night," I said then caught myself. "Actually, I started feeling weird after the accident, but it didn't get bad until last night." I studied his face. "Do you know what's wrong with me?"

Ronan blew out a breath and walked over to where I sat. When he squatted in front of me, my heart started to beat faster. He reached out and took my hands in his.

I jumped when a mild electric current shot up my arms. It spread through me until my body vibrated with energy. I lifted my eyes to his, and something shifted inside me like a flower opening to the sun. From the depths of my mind came a single word, which would change my life forever.

Solmi.

11

For several heartbeats, I didn't know what had happened. All I could feel was the pure joy radiating from my Mori. Underneath it, a new awareness blossomed.

I stared at Ronan as understanding dawned. In his eyes, I saw a storm of emotions like the ones coursing through me. Somehow, knowing he was as shaken and overwhelmed as I was kept me from being swept away by it.

I opened and closed my mouth a few times, but I couldn't form the words. What did you say to the person you'd just learned was your mate?

His throat bobbed. "It happened after the accident – or that's when it started. My Mori reacted to you, but yours didn't respond, so I thought I imagined it. I tried to shake it off, but it only got stronger."

My memories of the moments immediately after the crash were foggy, but I remembered his voice and seeing his face when I opened my eyes. There was something else that slipped away whenever I reached for it, but it felt more like a dream than a memory. One thing I hadn't forgotten was how disoriented and upset my Mori had been.

"The only thing I can come up with is your Mori was in shock from the accident, and it somehow prevented it from recognizing mine." His fingers tightened reflexively. "I think yours knew something was wrong, which made it confused and agitated. What you've been feeling are your Mori's emotions."

I needed only to remember how I'd felt when he arrived to know he was right. My Mori calmed because it sensed its mate, but it didn't know it until Ronan and I touched again.

Ronan – my mate.

I drew in a shaky breath. "We've touched dozens of times in training, and nothing happened. Why now?"

Ronan released my hands and sat on the sofa with me. "I don't know. To be honest, I thought being what I am made it impossible for me to bond, and there was no one like me I could ask about it. I wasn't sure I had bonded until I walked into the house and saw you."

I stared out at the lake. "You were here by the lake last night."

He nodded. "Did that upset you?"

"No. I couldn't sleep, and I think it helped." I adjusted my position so I was facing him with my legs tucked under me.

He angled his body toward me, and we looked at each other. I had seen him almost every day for over a month, but I was looking at him now through new eyes. In this moment, he wasn't my trainer or my running companion. Of all the Mori demons in the world, Ronan's was the one my Mori recognized as its mate.

My head was still spinning, and this all felt too surreal. Some people, like my father, went many years without finding their mate. Other people, like my mother, bonded young. I hadn't thought much about it because it always felt like something that would take place years into my future.

"What happens now?" I asked, hating how young and uncertain I sounded.

Ronan's gaze didn't waver. "What do you want to happen?"

The question caught me off guard. He'd had a whole day to process this, and I expected him to have already made up his mind about what he wanted to do. He had never intended to stay long at Westhorne, and his future did not include a mate. He'd said as much a few minutes ago.

I wouldn't delude myself about any feelings he might have for me. Running with me a few times a week was one thing. It was another thing to spend the rest of his life with me.

I didn't have to examine my feelings for him to know they were more than friendly, but not enough to commit my life to someone I knew so little about. I also didn't want to say goodbye to him.

"I understand if you want to end it here," he said quietly when I took too long to answer. "This is life-changing, and it's okay if you're not ready for it."

I swallowed dryly. "Can we...? Do we have to decide now?"

His eyes softened. "No."

I smiled, but he wasn't finished.

"There's something I need to tell you." He glanced away, and when his eyes returned to me, they were serious again. "I'm safe from your magic when

I shift because my wolf shields my Mori. It's like my Mori is dormant when I'm in wolf form, which means it can't sense another Mori."

"I thought that was the case," I said, not sure where he was going with this.

He hesitated to speak as if he was trying to formulate the right words. "My wolf doesn't know my Mori has bonded with yours, so it doesn't recognize you as our mate.

I deflated when the meaning of his words sank in. "Your wolf hasn't imprinted on me."

"No." Ronan scrubbed a hand over his face. "I don't know if it can imprint. A lone werewolf without a pack can't imprint, but I'm also not a full wolf, so I don't know if it applies to me."

"I understand." I looked down at my hands so he couldn't see how much his words affected me.

"That doesn't mean it won't happen," he said. "When you told me about the effect you and your mother have on animals, I thought it was why I'm drawn to you. But if that was the case, I would feel the same pull toward your mother. I don't."

Warmth invaded my chest, and I lifted my head. "You are?"

"Since the day you yelled at me for rescuing you from the river," he said with a teasing note in his voice.

I blinked in surprise. That had happened only a week after he arrived at Westhorne. Until our conversation in the dining hall, I'd been sure he didn't even like me.

"My wolf likes you and enjoys running with you, but I don't know if it will go beyond that," he admitted. "But I am willing to find out if you are."

"I am." It was far from a declaration of love, but it ignited a spark of hope inside me. Summer told me Uncle Roland's wolf imprinted on Aunt Emma because he spent a lot of time with her in his wolf form. Maybe the same could be true for us.

He smiled and glanced up at the house. "First, I must speak to your parents."

A rock landed in my stomach. Mom *might* be okay with this, but Dad wasn't going to take it well. I was his little girl. He'd probably have a hard time with it if I was fifty.

"Your father will not scare me off," Ronan said as if I'd voiced my fear aloud. "I believe he already knows about our bond."

"What? How?" I swung my legs off the sofa and sat up straight.

"He is perceptive, and he saw how we reacted to each other when I arrived. A bonded male can see signs others will not."

I remembered wondering why my father was angry at Ronan. It meant Mom knew, too. Did Dimitri? Soon all of Westhorne would know, including my friends. I pictured their shocked faces and everyone watching us together. How could Ronan and I be ourselves and get to know each other living under a microscope?

"Do you mind if we keep this between us and my family for now? And my grandfather?" I asked. "I think it will be easier that way."

"We will do whatever is more comfortable for you." He stood. "It might be best if I spoke to your parents alone, your father in particular."

"Oh. You're probably right." I let my arms hang at my sides, unsure of what to do next. Were we supposed to hug? Kiss? My heart thumped. Why hadn't anyone ever told me the etiquette for bonding?

Ronan stepped toward me and placed his hands on my arms. He leaned in and pressed a featherlight kiss to my forehead. "I will see you tomorrow."

The tender gesture was so unexpected I forgot to reply until he was halfway up the steps. I sank down on the sofa and stared blankly at the lake as shock rolled over me again. I was bonded to Ronan. *Ronan.*

I loved the story of how my parents met, especially when Dad described the moment he had bonded with Mom. I had only seen the romantic side of it. I'd had no idea how complicated and emotional and all-consuming it was.

I walked down to the dock and paced back and forth before I sat cross-legged listening to water lap softly against the wood. That was where my mother found me. She sat beside me and waited for me to speak.

"At least, we know I'm not sick or dying," I said in an attempt at humor. "How is Dad handling it?"

She played with my hair. "Like a father who's realized he is no longer the most important male in his daughter's life. He'll need a few days – or weeks – to come to terms with it."

I sighed. "And you?"

"I'm happy as long as you are happy," she said. "Ronan told us you are going to get to know each other better before you decide what to do. Is that what you want?"

I answered without hesitation. "Yes."

Her hand stopped. "Was there something between you and Ronan before you bonded?"

"No, at least, not what you think." I turned my head to look at her. "I've been spending time with him outside of training, but there's nothing romantic about it. We run together."

Her eyebrows shot up. "You run?"

"Remember the night I broke up with Kai? I was on my way home, and I met Ronan going for his nightly run. He shifted, and we ran to the lake. We've done it a few times since, but that's it. We don't even talk. I think he wishes he had a pack to run with."

Compassion softened her eyes. "I forget sometimes he is as much a wolf as a Mohiri."

I stared at the lake again. "And a wolf has to imprint on his mate."

"Dani…"

"He doesn't know if he can imprint without a pack," I said around the tightness in my throat. "But he never expected his Mori to bond either."

Mom put an arm around me, and I turned into her embrace. She stroked my hair, and I rested my head on her shoulder.

"You have feelings for him," she said.

I nodded.

She inhaled deeply and let it out. "If he doesn't imprint, he might decide to leave. The more time you spend together the more painful it will be to break the bond. You're willing to take that risk?"

"Yes." I knew a wolf could imprint on someone the male cared about because it had happened to Uncle Roland and Aunt Emma. The question was *could* Ronan imprint?

I pulled away from her and stood when I heard footsteps above us. Looking up, I met my father's eyes as he descended the steps. His mouth was set in a straight line, but his eyes were tender when he reached us. I bit my lip waiting for him to speak.

He enveloped me in a tender hug. "It's okay to say no if you aren't ready for this."

"I know. Ronan said the same thing."

Dad held me at arm's reach and searched my face. I didn't know what he was looking for, but he must have found it. "I don't know if *I'm* ready for this, but nothing is more important to me than your happiness."

I hugged him tightly around the waist. Until that moment, I hadn't realized how much I needed to hear those words from him.

"Are you guys going to tell me what is going on?" Dimitri called from the doorway.

I pulled away from Dad. "I want to tell him alone."

"Go on. We'll be up soon."

I ran lightly up the stairs. At the top, I looked back and saw my parents exchange a loving kiss. That could be Ronan and me someday.

"What's with the goofy look on your face?" Dimitri asked.

I smiled and pushed him into the house. "Come on. I'll tell you all about it."

The next day, Ronan and I learned it was harder than we'd thought to keep our bond a secret. I couldn't stop staring at him in class, which didn't go unnoticed by the other girls, who shot me sly looks. It didn't help that my Mori kept doing the whole fluttery thing that apparently happened whenever its mate was nearby.

Ronan had more experience with hiding his emotions, but a few times he slipped, and I caught him scowling when one of the male trainees touched me during an exercise. Once, when Sean pinned me under him, Ronan looked ready to throw him off me. Dimitri saw it and asked Ronan a question to distract him. By noon, I was convinced my father had superhuman self-control to have hidden his bond from everyone for so long.

At lunch, all my friends could talk about was the accident, and the girls spent a large part of the conversation gushing over Ronan.

"When he stripped off his shirt to bandage you, my lady bits melted." Elsie pretended to swoon, earning eye rolls from the boys at the table.

"And then he picked you up and carried you." Victoria leaned across the table to whisper, "What was it like?"

Dimitri scoffed. "She had three broken ribs. How do you think it felt?"

I shot him a grateful look. He'd had my back all day, and I wasn't sure I could have done this without him.

Elsie made a sound of appreciation, and I looked up to see Ronan over by the serving tables. I tapped my foot in irritation. When he turned to find a table, she did it again, and I'd had enough.

"Remember when Celine stepped in for Gavin last fall and all the boys were drooling over her?" I asked Elsie. "You told them to stop objectifying her. You're doing the exact same thing with Ronan."

"No. I'm just..." She looked around our table. The other girls said nothing, but a few of the boys nodded. Her cheeks turned pink. "You're right. Sorry."

I felt bad for calling her out, but I was one more *Mmmm* away from elbowing her. We'd been friends a long time, and the last thing I wanted was to start a fight with her over it.

I picked up my water glass to take a drink, and my eyes locked with Ronan's. He sat on the far side of the room with Gavin, but even from that distance, his gaze set off butterflies in my stomach.

Dimitri nudged my foot with his, drawing my attention to him. He gave me a look that said Ronan and I were about to set tongues wagging if we didn't cool it. I mouthed *"Thanks"* at him and kept my eyes off the other side of the room for the remainder of lunch. I was careful for the rest of our classes and avoided looking at Ronan unless I had to.

That night, I waited for Ronan near the woods. Though we hadn't arranged it, I knew he'd be there like he had all the other times. Normally, we didn't talk, but this was my first opportunity to be alone with him today.

"Hi." I smiled, hoping I didn't look as awkward as I felt.

He stopped two feet away from me. "Hi."

All day, I'd thought of things I wanted to tell him and questions to ask, and I forgot every single one of them. This was starting off well.

"I was going to call you, and I realized I don't have your number," I said in a rush. "Do you have a phone?"

"Yes." He took one from his back pocket and gave it to me. I stared at it until he said, "Put your number in it."

I picked up a note of laughter in his voice, and it occurred to me I'd never heard him laugh. There was so much I didn't know about him.

I entered my name and number into his phone and handed it back to him. Seconds later, my phone vibrated in my pocket. I checked it and saw a text from him. All it said was **Hi.** I hid a wry smile as I saved him to my contacts. He still wasn't much for conversation. Getting to know him would be fun.

"We should probably do more than running." I blushed at how that sounded and hurriedly said, "We should talk."

The corner of his mouth twitched. "We should."

"If you and I start eating together, it'll raise too many questions. We could eat in your cabin, but someone is bound to see me coming or going from there. I didn't realize until today how little privacy there is at Westhorne. It was never an issue growing up at the lake."

Ronan nodded. "I'm used to being alone, so it's been an adjustment for me, too."

He said it casually, but my heart constricted at his admission. He was a wolf without a pack and the only one of his kind he knew of. I had my mother to guide me and the love of a large extended family. I couldn't imagine being on my own without them. How isolated and lonely that life would be.

"I guess we could go to town or go for a walk in the woods," I mused.

"The pool," he said, taking me by surprise. "Meet me there tomorrow evening."

I immediately thought about the last time we were at the pool, and I hoped his night vision wasn't good enough to see my flushed face. "What time?"

He thought for a moment. "Six."

"Okay." A thrill went through me, and my body vibrated with nervous energy. "Do you want to run tonight?"

"Yes." He waved for me to enter the woods ahead of him. "I will give you a good head start."

I glared at him in feigned indignation. "In your dreams. I go slow so you can keep up."

He didn't reply as he followed me into the trees, and I had a feeling he was going to make me eat those words. That didn't mean I had to make it easy for him.

I glanced back to find him already reaching for the hem of his shirt. Adrenaline surged through me, and I took off. It wasn't long until he closed in, and I dug into my reserves for more speed. I pulled ahead, and I had about ten seconds to celebrate my pending victory when a blur of brown fur blew past me.

When I reached our usual spot near the end of the lake, he was taking a leisurely drink. He lifted his head, and his amber eyes said, "What took you so long?"

I folded my arms. "You've been holding back this whole time."

He chuffed a few times.

"Are you laughing at me?" I narrowed my eyes. "I think I liked you better when you were grumpy Ronan."

He snorted and walked past me so closely his fur brushed my arm. I turned, and he stopped at the edge of the clearing to look back at me over his shoulder.

"Good night," I called softly, already looking forward to tomorrow evening and our first date.

I glanced at my phone for the fifth time, and my shoulders sagged. I had been at the pool for fifteen minutes, and there was no sign of Ronan. He hadn't called or texted, and he didn't strike me as someone who would bail without a word. Five more minutes and I was going home.

Five minutes later, I swallowed back my disappointment and stood. There must be a good reason why he hadn't shown up. He'd seemed so sincere last night when he asked me to meet him here.

"I'm sorry I'm late," said a voice from behind me.

I spun to face Ronan, who stood a few yards away. He held a small cooler and a blanket, and he looked more than a little frustrated.

"Gavin stopped me to talk when I went to the dining hall for our food," he said as he closed the distance between us. "I didn't have my phone on me to send you a message."

I smiled. "It's okay."

He set the cooler on the ground and spread out the blanket. My smile grew. He had planned a picnic for us.

We sat, and he produced a small battery-powered lantern, which he placed on the blanket. He opened the cooler and took out a basket of cold fried chicken, potato salad, and bottles of water.

I picked up a drumstick. "How did you know this is my favorite picnic meal?"

Ronan set out plates, forks, and napkins. "I asked your mother."

My hand stopped halfway to my mouth. "My mother?" I hadn't told anyone I was meeting him tonight. This was all so new, and it felt strange talking about it around my parents.

"She also said I should bring these." He reached into the cooler and held up a container of chocolate fudge brownies. His teasing smile turned my insides to warm goo and caused me to drop the drumstick in my lap.

"She knows me so well," I managed to say. I tried for an air of nonchalance as I picked up the piece of chicken, but the glint of mischief in his eyes told me I'd failed miserably. I cleared my throat. "This is perfect."

We ate in companionable silence for a few minutes, serenaded by the night sounds of the woods. The babble of water over rocks was a soothing background music for the crickets, frogs, and the calls of a whip-poor-will.

I glanced over at Ronan, who looked more relaxed than I'd ever seen him. Wiping my mouth with a napkin, I said, "You know my story. Will you tell me yours?"

He nodded. "I was born at Bogdan Castle and spent my early childhood there. It's a Romanian stronghold in the foothills of the Carpathian Mountains."

Romania. That explained his accent.

"My mother, Elinor, was born in England, but her family moved to Bogdan Castle when she was young. She grew up there and stayed after she became a warrior. My father's pack lived in the mountains, and she met him one day when she was out on patrol. He was caught in a bear trap, and she freed him."

An edge crept into his voice when he mentioned his father's pack, but he went on as if he hadn't realized it. "They struck up a friendship, and they soon fell in love even though they knew they could never be together."

"Because a Mohiri and werewolf couple was forbidden?" I asked when he stopped for a swig of water.

"In Romania, Mohiri and werewolves are more tolerant of each other than they are here, but they keep to their own kind." His voice hardened slightly again. "My father, Dorin, was the son of the Alpha and next in line to succeed his father."

"Oh," I murmured. Werewolf packs would not tolerate their future Alpha taking a mate who was not a member of their pack, even if he imprinted on her. Uncle Roland and Aunt Emma were the exception.

Ronan continued. "The only way they could have been together was for him to step aside and let someone else become Alpha or for him to leave his pack altogether. The first option is impossible for a wolf with Alpha blood, and his loyalty to the pack came before anything else. It was his duty to take a werewolf mate one day and produce strong offspring to continue his line.

"My mother's pregnancy came as a shock to them because they thought only mated Mohiri females could conceive. They knew Mohiri males could father children with humans, but they had no idea a female can become pregnant when the father is not Mohiri.

"My mother raised me at the stronghold, and I went for monthly visits with my father. Dorin was good to me, and I had friends in the village, but the rest of the pack never let me forget I wasn't one of them. They didn't abuse me, but I knew from a young age I would never be fully accepted into the pack."

His voice was even, but I caught a fleeting glimpse of pain in his eyes. An ache started in my chest for the little boy who'd had to learn such a cruel lesson so young. His father's pack might not have physically hurt him, but there was more than one kind of abuse.

Ronan stared at the river. "When I was five, my father imprinted and took a mate, and their first child was born a year later. My visits became shorter and less frequent. When I was eight, I overheard him arguing with his mate, Sonia, one day. She said it would confuse their son to have me around. I was his first born, but their son Dragos would be his successor. It wasn't until years later I understood the real reason she wanted me gone."

The ache in my chest had moved to my throat, making it hard to swallow. "You have alpha blood."

He looked at me and nodded slowly. "Sonia was afraid I might challenge Dragos one day. It didn't matter I was a half breed. I was older and stronger, and she did not want to risk me taking that role from her son."

"What happened then?" I asked though I had a good idea what was coming.

"I stopped going to visit my father shortly after that. He started coming to see me once a month, but eventually his visits became less frequent. The last time I saw him was on my tenth birthday."

His tone held no bitterness, only acceptance and sadness I wasn't sure he was aware he still carried. I wanted to touch him, but I was afraid he'd mistake my gesture for pity. I twisted my napkin in my hands to keep from reaching for him.

When Dorin bowed to his mate's will, he hadn't only deprived his son of a father. He had taken away Ronan's pack, condemning a child – *his* child – to the life of a lone wolf. That was not the action of a strong leader or a father. It was the behavior of a weak male who didn't deserve a son like Ronan. I sincerely hoped Sonia had made his life miserable.

I plucked a blade of grass and twirled it between my fingers. "You said you spent your early childhood at Bogdan Castle. Did you and your mother leave when you were ten?"

"We stayed for two more years because my grandparents were there," he said. "I think my mother secretly hoped Dorin would change his mind and want to resume a relationship with me. When she finally accepted it wasn't going to happen, she moved us to her childhood home in England. We lived at Hadan Castle until I finished training."

"Is your mother still in England? Do you see her often?" I couldn't believe she would want to return to Romania after what she and Ronan had suffered there.

"She bonded a year after I left home, and she and her mate, Edward, live in Italy now."

"And your father's pack?" I asked hesitantly.

Ronan shook his head. "I haven't spoken to Dorin or anyone in his pack since I left Romania. He would be fifty now."

I did a double take. Fifty? That would make Ronan... "How old are you?"

"I'm thirty."

My mouth fell open, and I snapped it shut. I'd believed him older than that because he was such an experienced warrior.

He pointed at my plate. "You have barely touched your meal."

I picked up my fork and waved it at him. "You haven't touched yours either."

We started eating again. In between bites, I asked, "When did you come to the US? Where do you live?" Last night, he'd said he was used to being alone, which ruled out a stronghold.

"Eight years ago." He reached for another piece of chicken. "I have a place in Montana, and I go there when I'm not on the road. I enjoy being outdoors, and I will sometimes take to the wild and live off the land for months."

"Ah." That explained his appearance the day we met. I'd thought he was a wild mountain man before I'd mistaken him for one of my mother's patients.

"When Tristan asked me to come to Westhorne, I didn't know it had a strong connection to a werewolf pack," he said. "That is unusual."

I smiled. "There is nothing normal about my family."

"As I have discovered. Your mother grew up with the Maine Pack?"

"Yes." After the way his own pack had treated him, he was no doubt wondering how a Mohiri had come to live among the biggest and strongest pack in the country. As we finished our meal, I told him what I knew about Mom's childhood in Maine, her friendship with Uncle Roland and Uncle Peter, and how she and Dad met.

"We've visited New Hastings every summer for as long as I can remember. Uncle Roland and Uncle Peter used to come here every year too, until Uncle Roland became the Alpha and Uncle Peter became the lead Beta wolf. Mom said they have too many responsibilities to spend a lot of time away from the pack. They try to visit every other year now."

"Is that where you learned to run with werewolves?" Ronan asked as he opened the container of brownies and held it out for me.

Laughing, I took one. "You noticed that, huh?"

"The only other person I know who does it is my mother," he said. "She used to run with me after Dorin stopped visiting. I...have missed that."

His admission brought another stab of pain for the little boy who had lost his pack. I almost said he'd never have to be alone again, but I couldn't make that promise until we both agreed not to break the bond.

Solmi. A wave of distress came from my Mori. It did it every time I thought about Ronan and I severing our bond.

"Have you ever thought about joining another pack?" I asked, needing to shift the direction of my thoughts. "I've heard some lone wolves find a new pack."

Ronan gave me a rueful look. "No Alpha will accept an alpha male into his pack and risk a challenge."

"It's so unfair." I tossed my napkin onto the blanket.

"It's not personal." He gathered our dishes and the leftover food and put it into the cooler.

I harrumphed. "You are too nice."

The corners of his eyes creased. "That is one thing I have never been called."

"Not by your trainees." Grinning, I got up and went to the pool to wash my hands, which were sticky from the two brownies I'd eaten. I wiped my hands on my pants as I walked back to the blanket where Ronan lay on his side, propped up on his arm.

"You know what would make this picnic perfect?" I asked.

His lips curved into a small teasing smile, which sent my heart into a gallop. I forgot what I was going to say until he raised his eyebrows inquisitively.

"A run," I said at last.

He stood. "Another race?"

I wagged a finger at him. "One of these days, you'll be the one chasing me."

His only response was a smirk as he kicked off his boots.

12

———————

"Are you sure?" Mom said as I walked into the living room three days later. She was looking at her phone, and she raised a finger for me to wait.

Kelvan's voice came from the phone. "Yes."

She pressed her lips together and stood. "Send me a link. I want to see it."

Curious, I followed her to the kitchen where her laptop sat on the island. She propped her phone on the counter and opened the laptop.

I leaned in to see the Vrell demon on the screen. "Hi, Kelvan. How's Nala?"

"Hi, Dani. Nala is well." Kelvan smiled and waved back, and I glimpsed the two tiny horns almost hidden by his brown curls. He reached down and lifted a fluffy gray tabby, which had been sleeping on his lap. The cat opened its eyes, yawned, and went back to sleep.

I glanced over at the laptop where Mom had opened a chat window with him. She clicked a link he'd sent, and it opened a browser window on a message board thread. Her breath hissed from between her teeth, and I saw why when I read the post over her shoulder.

SEEKING FOY. Substantial reward for credible info. Money no object.

"Is that...?" I trailed off as Mom scrolled through the thread, reading the responses. Most of them mocked the original poster for their ridiculous request. Others, though, were more serious. It wasn't until we neared the end of the thread that my eyes went wide.

There used to be someone in Maine, but that had to be twenty years ago.

Do you know if they're still around?

Meet me in a private room.

Mom finished the thread and looked at Kelvan, who had been quiet the whole time. "You saw this post on more than one site?"

"Four so far. I'm still running a search." He stroked his cat's head. "This is the only one that's gotten some traction."

She tapped her fingers on the counter. "I need to make a call. Can you let me know if you find anything else?"

"I will." He said goodbye and ended the call.

"Are they talking about you?" I asked as Mom opened her contacts on her phone.

"Yes." She put the phone to her ear, and a few seconds later, she said, "Malloy, we need to talk."

Tom Malloy was the middleman Mom had gone through to sell troll bile on the black market twenty years ago. Troll bile could cure incurable diseases and extend life, hence its nickname FOY or fountain of youth. It was also virtually impossible to obtain.

I gave up trying to follow Mom's one-sided conversation with him and waited for her to finish the call. Her face was grim when she set her phone down five minutes later.

"What did he say?" I asked when she didn't speak immediately.

Her eyes were troubled when she looked at me. "He used to get inquiries about troll bile years ago. He always responded he never knew the real identity of the person who sold him the bile. His story is they disappeared twenty years ago, and he thinks they must have been killed by a troll."

It was a plausible story and one Mom had paid him a lot to use. Troll bile could only come from a live troll, and they were the most reclusive and deadliest creatures on the planet. It was impossible for anyone to corroborate the story.

I searched her face. "Then why do you look worried?"

She let out a harsh breath. "Malloy told me there was renewed interest a few months ago. They tracked him down through an old business contact and offered him half a million dollars to give up his source, but he stuck to our cover story."

My jaw dropped. "He didn't think that was important enough to let you know about?"

"He never heard from them again, so he assumed it was a one-off. And it's not unusual for black market buyers to spend that kind of money when they want something bad enough. I once used a red diamond to buy something."

She stared at the message board thread still open on her laptop. "This is too much of a coincidence. I think it's the same people who contacted him. Malloy does, too, and he's going to disappear for a while."

"Even if Malloy gave them a name, he never knew your real identity," I said. "And if they somehow managed to trace it back to you, everyone in New Hastings thinks you disappeared or ran away when you were seventeen. It only backs up his story."

Mom rubbed her mouth. "It's not me I'm worried about. I need to go see Remy."

"Can I come?" I clasped my hands together and bounced on my feet. "I haven't seen him in ages."

The tightness around her mouth and eyes softened. "I think you've earned a reward after all the hard work you've been putting in."

She sent a quick text to Dad and looped her arm through mine. In a blink, we were standing in a cave looking out at the Atlantic. The cave, which was half the size of my bedroom, was in the side of a treacherous one-hundred-foot cliff south of New Hastings. Unless you knew the cave was there, it was not visible from above or below, and it had been Mom and Remy's secret childhood hangout.

Mom went to the back of the cave and picked up a rock sitting on a narrow ledge. She used the rock to draw a symbol on the wall while whispering a few guttural words. It was essentially the troll version of a text message.

"He should be here soon." Replacing the rock, she turned toward me and stopped. She walked to a spot two feet from the message she'd written and reached out. Her hand seemed to disappear into the wall and reappear a few seconds later.

Smiling to herself, she joined me again. Her face took on a faraway expression as she looked down at the foaming waves battering the base of the cliff far below.

"What the hell was that?" I asked when she said nothing. "Did you just put your hand through the rock?"

A small laugh slipped from her, and she motioned for me to follow her to the back wall. Taking my hand, she placed it where hers had been a minute ago. It wasn't until I touched the wall that I felt a small gap hidden behind a lip of rock. The opening was hardly wide enough for my fingers to slip inside and touch a piece of coarse cloth.

"What is it?" I asked when I withdrew my hand.

She reached into the hole and lifted out a bundle wrapped in brown cloth. Unfolding the cloth, she revealed three small vials of yellowish-brown liquid.

"No way."

"I don't think I ever told you where Remy and I used to hide the bile until I needed it to buy something." She picked up one of the vials and handed it to me. "No one knew this cave was here, and even if someone found it, they'd never find the bile. Remy created a ward to hide the crevice, and only someone with Fae magic can access it."

My mouth worked, and I stared at the vial in my hand. "This is troll bile?" I whispered.

She laughed again. "Three ounces if I remember correctly. And you don't need to whisper here."

I gave the vial back to her. "It's been here all this time?"

"I didn't need it, and neither did Remy." She wrapped the vials again and returned the bundle to its hiding place. "I forgot about it until today."

"I knew troll bile existed, but it never felt real until now," I said as we walked back to the cave entrance. "You never did tell me whose idea it was to sell it on the black market."

"My idea," said a voice from behind us.

We turned to face Remy. Thin and gray-skinned, he had shaggy gray-brown hair and large violet eyes. He smiled broadly, showing off his sharp teeth, and the effect was kind of terrifying if you didn't know him.

Mom hugged him. When they released each other, he looked at me. "You bring little one to visit."

"She's not so little anymore," Mom said. "Dani will soon be a warrior."

Remy gave me an appraising look. "Warrior like father. Healer like mother. Strong magic."

"Eldeorin thinks Dani's magic will be stronger than mine after liannan," Mom said proudly.

"You bring her to learn healing ways?" Remy asked.

"No." She grew serious. "I came to tell you someone is looking for troll bile, and they've been asking around about me. They don't know my identity, but they know I was in Maine when I sold it."

His expression didn't change. "Humans not find us. You not worry."

She wrung her hands. "We underestimated them the last time, and they found your little cousins. I'll never forgive myself if what I did back then leads someone to you again. Please, warn your clan, and tell the young ones to stay close to home."

The last time Mom sold troll bile, it led a dangerous man to the trolls, and three of Remy's little cousins, who had snuck out of the clan, were taken. Mom found out where they were in time to rescue them. She still blamed herself for putting them in danger.

The fierce look in Remy's eyes made the hair on the back of my neck stand up. "I warn clan."

"Thank you." Her shoulders relaxed. "Could you also pass along a warning to your other friends?"

"Why warn friends?" he asked confused.

"Over the last few months, demons have been disappearing around the country," she said. "Now some werewolves and werecougars are missing. I haven't heard of any others, but this new interest in troll bile has me worried."

My mind went back to something she'd said a minute ago. "Do you think the people who took Summer and the others could be the same ones looking for troll bile?"

It was Remy who answered first. "Bile cure humans. What if people think demons have cure, too?"

"How would demons cure humans?" I put a hand over my mouth as acid burned the back of my throat. He meant there might be something inside the demons that could be a cure – like paluk organs being eaten to reverse skin aging. And if the same people had taken the shifters...

The cave grew dark. The next thing I knew, Mom was in front of me with her hands framing my face.

"Breathe through your nose," she said in her calm, gentle voice. "That's it, Dani, nice and slow."

I blinked as her face came back into focus. "What happened?"

She let go of me. "Just a little hyperventilation. You're okay."

"I've never done that before." I leaned against the wall, a little lightheaded.

"After all you've been through in the last few weeks, I'm not surprised." She went to Remy and came back holding a silver cup. "Drink this."

I took the cup and peered at the clear liquid. "Is it water?"

"Yes. It's from an underground troll spring, and it will make you feel better."

I tipped the cup back and drank it down. It tasted like normal spring water, but by the time I finished, I felt as rejuvenated as I did after a run through the woods.

"We have no proof the people who have Summer also want the troll bile," Mom said. "The post on the message board brought back some bad memories and made me nervous for Remy."

I gripped the cup tightly. "But it's possible."

"Yes," she admitted. "Anything is possible."

Mom and Remy talked for a few minutes, and then she said we needed to get back. She wanted to check in with Dad, and she had a session with one of her patients in half an hour.

Dad was at home when we got there. Mom filled him in on what Kelvan had found and told him Remy's theory about a possible connection between the troll bile posts and the disappearances.

"Kelvan's going to stay on it and let us know if anything else pops up," she said. "I want to monitor it even if it has nothing to do with your investigation."

Dad agreed. "The timing does seem suspicious."

My phone vibrated, and my mood immediately improved when I saw a text from Ronan. We saw each other every evening, and one of the highlights of my day was when I got his text asking me to meet him.

Will be late tonight. See you at eight?

As if I would say no. Smiling, I wrote back, **See you then.**

"Where are we going?" I asked a week and a half later as we drove through the gates. I practically bounced in my seat because this was our first date away from Westhorne. Until now, we had only met in the woods and at my house. There weren't a lot of places to meet secretly at the stronghold.

Ronan cast an amused glance in my direction. He hadn't told me anything except to meet him at the garage at noon. It was Saturday, so there were no classes, which meant we had the whole afternoon to ourselves.

"Boise," he said at last.

"Really?" I couldn't have sounded more excited if he'd said we were going to Disney. "Where in Boise?"

He shrugged. "I thought we would drive around and see what appeals to us."

"That sounds like fun." I settled back happily in my seat, and we talked about things to do in Boise.

"Can I ask you something?" I said during a brief lull in the conversation.

"You can ask me anything."

I turned slightly in my seat to face him. "That day I first met you in the woods, you ran so fast. And when you fight you move a lot faster than my aunt who is ten years older. Is it because of your wolf?"

He smiled at the mention of that day. "Yes, but I wasn't always fast. It took me years to learn how to tap into my wolf's strength and my Mori's strength at the same time. And I can't do it when I'm in my wolf form."

"Because your Mori is dormant then," I said.

"Yes."

I fell quiet at the reminder he couldn't sense my Mori in his wolf form. I ran with his wolf every night, and sometimes, we sat together for a while in our little spot at the lake. He was affectionate and playful, but he showed no signs of imprinting on me.

"You're fast, too. I've seen young warriors who couldn't catch you in a foot race," he said.

"One of the perks of being half Fae," I joked. "Speed, stealth, and the ability to kill vampires with a touch. I'm still working on the last one."

He looked over at me. "You've fought more than one?"

"A few," I said reluctantly. I'd told him about the vampire in the alley, but not about the two in the parking garage or the one after that. Eldeorin had taken me for two more sessions since the night we went to Blue Nyx. During the last session I'd killed a young vampire with my magic, but it was far from a perfect kill.

Ronan turned his attention back to the road. "When?"

"During some of my lessons with Eldeorin," I said before I noticed Ronan's tight jaw. Mom had told me this would happen. Males felt the bond more strongly, and it made them overly protective.

I reached over and touched the hand gripping the gear shift. "Eldeorin trained my mother in the same way, and she made him my godfather. Do you think she would have done that or let me go off with him now if she didn't have complete trust in him?"

Ronan's grip eased a little, and I continued. "He is always with me during a lesson, and he is so powerful he can incinerate a vampire from a hundred feet away." I wasn't sure if the last part was accurate, but it worked to make Ronan relax.

I moved the conversation to safer topics for the rest of the drive. We drove around for a quarter of an hour until I spotted a colorful billboard. "Look. There's a carnival in town. I've never been to one."

"I haven't either," he said. That didn't surprise me, given his aversion to crowds.

"We don't have to go if you want to do something else," I said, but he was already changing direction.

The carnival wasn't hard to find, and the parking lot was almost full. When we opened the doors to get out, we were greeted by the din of music, shouts, and mechanical rides. As we walked to the fairground, I was assailed by dozens of different smells, half of them unpleasant. Sometimes, I wished I could turn off my sense of smell.

We strolled through the game booths and food carts, and stopped at a booth where people fired arrows with blunt Velcro tips at moving targets painted like ducks. I paid the booth operator, who handed me a bow and five arrows and explained the rules. Three hits for a small prize and four for a medium prize.

"What do I get for all five?" I asked.

The lanky young man smirked and pointed at the large stuffed animals lining the top of the booth. "You feeling lucky?"

I positioned myself and nocked an arrow. "Yeah."

The bow was plastic and too light, but at this distance, I'd have to be blind to miss. I drew the bow and released the arrow, which struck the first target.

"Nice shooting," said the man, who still wore his cocky smile.

I glanced at Ronan standing off to the side with his arms folded across his chest. He gave me a little shake of his head, and I flashed him a grin as I reached for my second arrow.

When arrows two and three hit their marks, the operator's expression changed to one of surprise. Arrow four brought cheers from the half dozen people waiting for their turns.

I nocked the last arrow and looked up at the hanging stuffed animals. My eyes lit on one, and I smiled at the operator. "I'll take the wolf," I said as I aimed and fired.

My little audience cheered like I had won a gold medal. The operator eyed me suspiciously as he reached up to unhook the gray wolf.

"Thanks." I hugged the wolf and stepped aside for the next player.

A little girl tugged at the sleeve of the teenage boy next to her. "Can I have a wolf, too, Kenny?"

He ruffled her hair. "I'm not that good."

I walked over to them and held out the wolf to her. "I think he wants to go home with you."

"Really? You don't want him?" She took the stuffed toy and clutched it to her chest.

I cast a look over my shoulder at Ronan. "I have my own wolf."

Heat flared in his eyes as I returned to him. He took my hand and laced our fingers together with a possessiveness that made my Mori flutter wildly.

After we stopped at a few more game booths, we rode the Ferris wheel. I took a selfie of us at the top and realized it was our first photo together. When I looked at the picture, I wondered how anyone at Westhorne could not see the connection between us. Our smiles were warm and affectionate, and the chemistry between us was almost palpable. A person would have to be blind not to see I was half in love with Ronan already.

"What do you want to do now?" he asked when we got off the Ferris wheel.

I pointed at some food stands. "We can't come to a carnival and not eat carnival food."

We spent the next hour stuffing ourselves with cheese fries, corn dogs, and churros. After that, we tried the fun house, bumper cars, and a few more games. It was the most fun I'd had in ages, but by the time the sun set, I was ready to leave.

"I don't want this day to end," I said as we walked across the fairground in the direction of the parking lot.

Ronan's hand squeezed mine. "It's not over yet."

"Oh, really?" I said playfully. "What else do you have planned –"

I stopped so fast a man behind us almost ran into me. Putting a hand over the cold knot in my chest, I looked into Ronan's questioning eyes.

"What's wrong?" he asked, stepping closer to me.

"Vampire," I whispered.

Ronan knew about my ability to sense vampires. His pupils dilated, and he pulled me against him. "Where?"

"I don't know." I turned in a circle, scanning the crowd and wishing my radar was as good as my mother's. She could not only pinpoint the vampire's location, she could sense how many there were. "I can't tell unless we get closer to it."

The look he gave me said that was not the answer he wanted to hear. He didn't want me getting anywhere near a vampire, but he didn't have much of a choice. We had to find it before it killed one of these humans.

We walked in a wide circle until the cold in my chest grew more intense, telling me we were close. It was Ronan who spotted a dark-haired male in his late teens leading a teenage girl through the gap between two booths.

Ronan turned to me. "Stay here."

"I want to go with you."

He shook his head firmly. "We don't know how old or strong he is. It'll be better if I go after him alone."

"Okay," I said reluctantly. I wanted to argue, but it would waste time the girl didn't have. "Be careful."

Watching Ronan go after a vampire alone and armed with nothing but a knife was one of the hardest things I had ever done. My body was rigid with fear, and I stared at the spot where he disappeared as the seconds ticked by with agonizing slowness.

I was so focused on watching for him I almost didn't notice the cold blooming in my chest again. I searched the crowd and caught sight of a brunette in her late teens approaching the space between the booths. She paused and looked around furtively before she slipped inside.

Oh, hell no. I reached inside my jacket for my knife as I speed-walked to the gap. Taking a breath, I gripped the knife and silently followed the vampire.

13

Behind the row of booths was a large cluster of RVs and eighteen-wheelers. It was darker back here, but some of the RVs had lights on. I had a moment of panic when I didn't see Ronan, until I spotted the brunette walking between an RV and a semi.

The sounds of a fight reached me when I neared the RV. I peeked around the corner, and my Mori growled. A lump of fear lodged in my throat at the sight of Ronan deflecting a strike from the male vampire's clawed hand. The vampire was a lot faster than the ones I'd fought, but Ronan matched it in speed.

My gaze shifted to the female vampire. She had flattened herself against the side of the RV, and she was inching toward the fight. If she was as old as the male, Ronan would be in trouble. I had to do something.

I looked down at my knife. In my hands, it wasn't going to be much use against an older vampire. I had only one weapon that might level the playing field.

I summoned my magic, and the reassuring warmth filled me until I felt the electricity moving under my skin. Stepping back, I tapped my blade against the back of the RV and waited.

The female vampire did not make me wait long. She came around the corner and stopped when she saw me. Her eyes dropped to the knife in my hand, and a slow smile spread across her face.

"You want to play, little girl?" she taunted, even though I had at least two inches on her.

I didn't answer, afraid I couldn't keep my voice from quivering. Facing a vampire alone without Eldeorin was scarier than I'd thought it would be.

Someone hit the side of the RV as the fight between Ronan and the male vampire intensified. It jolted me from my fear and reminded me what was at stake.

The female took a step toward me. "I'm afraid your friend is a little too busy to help you."

I backed up, watching her movements and trying to figure out how old she was. Even if she was half as old as the male, she would be too fast for me to fend off with a knife.

She frowned. "Are you mute?"

I shook my head. She glanced at my knife again, and I caught a flicker of uncertainty in her eyes. Maybe I could stall her long enough for Ronan to kill the other vampire.

She moved so fast I was against the back of the RV with her hand around my throat before I knew what was happening. Her other hand held my wrist in an iron grip.

My magic pulsed. She hissed and let me go. I lifted my knife, but she smacked it out of my hand.

"I don't know what that was, but you smell…" She swallowed convulsively, and her fangs extended as her eyes turned feverish with blood lust.

I brought my hand up a second before she struck. My palm hit her chest as her teeth grazed my throat.

Magic exploded from my hand. The vampire's body spasmed, and she staggered back from me. I went after her with both hands, and she began to jerk like a marionette on strings, her mouth frozen in a silent scream.

She collapsed to the ground, but the ice beneath my ribcage told me she was still alive. I looked around for my knife and spotted it behind the rear wheel of the RV.

Her claws dug into my ankle as I bent to get the knife. I sucked in air at the stabbing pain and grabbed her hand. She let out a garbled scream, but I didn't let go until my other hand closed around the handle of the knife.

I spun and found her writhing on the ground, clutching a charred stump where her hand used to be. I moved in to finish her off as Ronan sped around the corner of the RV like a man possessed. He was on the vampire and driving his blade into her heart before I reached her.

He stood and stepped over the dead vampire to pull me into his arms. His body was rigid, and his vicelike embrace threatened to suffocate me. "I felt you, but I couldn't get to you," he said hoarsely.

I thumped his back. "Can't breathe."

He loosened his hold but didn't let go of me. "Why didn't you stay where it was safe?"

"I saw the female vampire following you, and I couldn't let her ambush you," I said. "She was sneaking up on you when I got here."

"So, you decided to take on a vampire twice your age?" he asked. I couldn't tell if it was anger or incredulity in his voice.

I stiffened. "Yes, and I'd do it again. In case you didn't notice, I was about to finish her off."

"I noticed." Ronan lifted his head, and I met his eyes, which looked more golden than hazel. Whatever he planned to say was forgotten when his gaze dropped to my mouth. Breathless with excitement, I parted my lips in a silent invitation. His head lowered, and all I could think about was how much I wanted to feel his mouth on mine.

A door opened, spilling laughter into the night. Ronan and I turned our heads at the same time toward the other end of the line of RVs where an outside light had come on.

We broke apart as if the moment between us had never happened. He gripped the female vampire's collar and dragged her to where the male lay. I ran to the teenage girl, who was motionless on the ground. There were bloody bite marks on her throat, but she was breathing.

"She's alive but unconscious," I whispered. "He bit her."

Ronan nodded as he took out his phone and called it in. We had one team working the Boise area, and two of the warriors were already on the way here to patrol the carnival.

I stayed with the girl while he stowed the bodies in the back of the semi in case someone came upon us. It wasn't long until two female warriors arrived. I remembered seeing them at Westhorne a few times, but I didn't know them.

One of the warriors, who said her name was Juliette, handed me a tube of gunna paste, and I squeezed some into the girl's mouth. She started to come around immediately and tried to spit it out, but I held her mouth closed until she swallowed. The medicine quickly went to work on her, and she relaxed.

Fifteen minutes later, the rest of the team showed up to take over the cleanup. One of them produced a syringe and gave the girl a dose of gorum, a drug to modify her short-term memory. She would forget what happened here and never have to relive the horror of the attack.

I helped Juliette clean up the girl while Ronan assisted the others in removing the bodies. Aside from the bite, which was already healing thanks to the gunna paste, she had no other visible injuries. Juliette told me she would see the girl got back to whomever had come to the carnival with her.

Ronan and I decided to call it a night, and we were quieter on the drive home. Though neither of us mentioned the almost-kiss, I sensed a shift in our relationship. I saw it when he looked at me as we got into the SUV, and I felt it in the way he held my hand during the drive.

"Thank you for today," I said when he walked me to my door. "I had fun."

He wrapped me in his arms. "I did, too, but let's try it without the vampires next time."

I gave a breathy laugh. "I'm up for that."

He kissed my forehead as he always did, but this time, he lingered longer than usual. It got harder for me every time I said goodbye to him. Tonight, I wasn't the only one reluctant to go.

The door swung open to reveal my father's worried face. Ronan had insisted I call my parents from Boise so they heard about the incident from me instead of someone else. I'd played it down as much as I could, but Dad was anxious about my "first" vampire encounter. He had no idea this had been my fifth vampire, and I had no intention of telling him.

I smiled at him as Ronan and I separated. "I'm fine, Dad. Not a scratch on me."

My father looked at Ronan, who nodded. "She handled herself well. She would have killed the vampire without my help, and I'm sorry I took the kill from her."

A warm, pleasant sensation spread through me at his praise and the pride in my father's eyes. I did feel good about what I'd done, and Eldeorin would be delighted when he heard about me incapacitating an older vampire.

"Is it true?" Dimitri came up behind Dad. "Did you guys kill vampires at a carnival in Boise?"

"Yes," I said, and he gave me a playful scowl.

"You have all the fun." He threw an arm over Dad's shoulder. "What do you say to a trip to the carnival? It could be a great training exercise for me."

Dad laughed. "I doubt we'll find more vampires at this one. I'm surprised we found two there."

Dimitri's dejected expression gave way to a smirk. "Mom said you called her a disaster magnet when you met her. Maybe Dani inherited that from her, too."

I shook my head at Ronan's inquisitive look. "Ignore him."

"No, I might be onto something," Dimitri said, grinning. "The Boise team can go a week without trouble. The last two times you went to Boise, you ran into armed mercenaries and vampires."

I lifted a shoulder. "I'm just lucky I guess."

Ronan made a noise, and I gave him a sidelong smile. "Look at it this way. Life will never be dull."

I dropped my backpack on the ground and gazed at the crystal-clear lake. Its surface was so calm it reflected a mirror image of the snow-capped mountains rising around it and the puffy white clouds in the blue sky. The crisp air was thinner up here, and it carried the scent of pine and the promise of snow in the next day or so.

"We'll make camp here," Dad called. "Find your partner, and set up."

Turning away from the lake, I scanned our group of hikers and located Naomi, who was already unpacking the tent she and I were sharing. I grabbed my pack and went to help her. In minutes, we had the tent up and our stuff stored inside.

I surveyed the eight tents forming a semi-circle around the firepit Dad had started to dig. His and Dimitri's tent was on one end, and he'd directed me to set up mine beside theirs. The rest of the trainee tents were pitched on our other side with Ronan and Gavin's tents on the opposite end.

I rolled my eyes. My father might be a clever tactician in battle, but I saw right through his plan to keep my sleeping bag as far from Ronan's as possible. Almost three weeks had passed since Ronan and I bonded. Dad seemed to have come to terms with it, but he was nowhere near ready for what would inevitably happen.

I caught sight of Ronan breaking up a large branch for firewood, and I watched him until Dimitri walked by and cleared his throat. It was getting harder and harder to keep the bond a secret. Ronan and I spent time together whenever we could, and it felt like I'd known him my whole life.

Aside from our near kiss over a week ago, he had kept our relationship almost platonic, to my eternal frustration. The lack of physical intimacy hadn't stopped our feelings from growing deeper. I was head over heels in love with him, and I believed he felt the same way about me. He didn't come out and say it, but I knew he was holding back because his wolf still hadn't imprinted on me.

I turned with an audible sigh and went to help Dad. This had been our thing since our first camping trip. Dimitri and Mom gathered firewood while Dad and I built the firepit. Then we would take our fishing gear and catch dinner in whatever river or lake we were camped beside.

He and I worked quietly and efficiently. When we finished surrounding the pit with rocks, I laid the tinder and kindling so it was ready for our campfire tonight.

"Better than yours, Dad," Dimitri joked as he dropped an armload of firewood nearby.

"Of course, it is." Dad ruffled my hair like I was still ten years old.

Dimitri brushed off his hands. "We'll need a good fire for the big trout I'm catching for my dinner."

"Oooh, that sounds like a challenge." I nudged Dad with my shoulder. "Be gentle when you annihilate him."

Dad laughed. "You're not going to accept the challenge?"

"I'm relying on you guys to catch my dinner. The girls and I are going exploring." I pointed at a ridge above us. "There are supposed to be some caves up there and an amazing view."

He studied the mountain. "Take your radios, and be back by dark."

"Better take a flare, too, just in case," Dimitri said.

We made a face at each other. The chances of running into anything more dangerous than a mountain lion up here were slim. If we couldn't fight off a cougar, we might as well go back to junior training.

Naomi waved to me, and I walked over to where she stood by our tent with Anna and Teresa. I grabbed the small hiking pack from my backpack and stuffed my water bottle inside along with a radio, a small flashlight, and my phone. We had no cellular service up here, but I wanted to get some photos for Mom. She couldn't leave her patients to come with us this time.

Victoria and Elsie joined us, and we set out. I couldn't resist casting a last look around for Ronan, and I spotted him disappearing into the woods farther along the lakeshore. I pictured him shifting and running through the trees, and I wished I was with him. This was only a three-day trip, but I already missed being able to go off alone with him.

A colorful carpet of fallen leaves crunched under our feet as we entered the woods and began our ascent. The slope grew steeper as we climbed until we had to hold onto the skeletal branches to pull us up. The higher we went, the colder the air got, causing our breaths to come out in steamy puffs.

It took us twenty minutes to reach the ridge. From this vantage point, we had a sweeping view of the entire lake and the surrounding plateau. The woods were a canvas of rich colors from the thick evergreens to the blanket of red and gold leaves on the ground. The turquoise lake glittered like diamonds in the sun, and the figures standing on the shore looked no bigger than ants.

Naomi uncapped her water bottle. "Now this was worth the climb."

"Totally." I took out my phone and snapped a few panoramic photos. I scanned our surroundings and pointed to a rock formation a hundred yards away. "I think the first cave is behind that."

"Lead the way." Anna waved for me to go ahead of them.

I made my way along the wide ledge and around the outcropping where I was greeted by an icy blast of air. Tufts of yellow grass grew among the rocks, and there were patches of snow and ice that made the path a little treacherous. I walked another dozen yards, and the terrain leveled into a small grassy area strewn with a few large rocks. On the other end, the way was blocked by a pile of boulders and smaller rocks deposited by an old rock slide. To my right, the ground sloped upward, and twenty feet above me was a dark crevice.

"Found it," I called over my shoulder. I waited for the others to catch up before I climbed to the cave entrance. It was wide enough for a large man to fit through, and after a few feet it expanded into a cavern no more than fifteen feet across with a tunnel at the other end.

I took out my flashlight, expecting it to be dark inside the cave, but there were smaller crevices that let in light. It was enough to make out the streaks of mineral in the walls along with something that looked like quartz. Light came from the tunnel as well, indicating another opening down there.

"Cool," said Anna as she entered the cave behind me. Her voice echoed through the cave and down the tunnel.

The others filed in. Teresa sniffed the air and wrinkled her nose. "What's that smell?"

"Bat guano," Anna answered. From somewhere in the tunnel came a chirp and the flutter of leathery wings.

Elsie made a face. "Ugh."

"If you say you're afraid of bats, I'm going to need to reevaluate our friendship," Anna told her.

"I am not scared of bats." Elsie took off her gloves and rooted in her pack. She pulled out a stocking cap and tugged it down over her hair. "I don't want to have to wash guano from my hair when we get back. I don't know about you, but I didn't pack shampoo for this trip."

Everyone snickered, but we all covered our heads with caps and hoods. I was hoping to sneak a few minutes with Ronan later, and stinking of bat dung wouldn't exactly set a romantic mood.

Anna led the way into the narrow tunnel, which curved downward. A few small slits in the rock let in enough light to guide us. We walked for two minutes and came to a branch in the tunnel. The right side went farther into the mountain, and the left led to a smaller cavern lit by an entrance large enough for us to exit through.

"Right or left?" Anna asked.

I checked my watch. "Left. There's another cave I'd like to check out before we head back."

"Left it is." She ducked through the opening and entered the cavern.

I followed her and grinned when I saw the low ceiling. I was the only one who didn't have to stoop.

I peered through the cave entrance and discovered it opened to the same grassy area but on the other side of the rock slide. We'd have to go back through this cave to return to camp.

"Damn it," Elsie muttered. "I lost one of my gloves. It must be in the first cave."

"You can get it on the way back," I said.

She turned to the tunnel. "I might need it. Give me a few minutes to run back and get it." She disappeared through the opening, and we could hear her footsteps as she hurried up the tunnel.

I stepped outside, and I had to shield my eyes from the sun after the dim cave interior. Finding a rock to sit on, I took out my water bottle and drank. The others did the same while we waited for Elsie to return.

A tickle of awareness at the back of my neck was my first warning we were no longer alone. I leaped to my feet and spun to face a huge tawny cougar standing beside a boulder thirty feet away. Piercing amber eyes locked with mine, and I was startled by the intelligence gleaming in them. I knew this was no ordinary cougar before the cat curled back its upper lip to reveal four-inch fangs.

Someone gasped behind me as a second werecougar appeared atop the boulder. One by one, more cougars walked into view until eight of them faced us. They watched us with narrowed eyes, their muscles bunched as if they were about to spring at any second. Werecougars were aggressive by nature, but they didn't normally provoke a fight unless they felt threatened.

"What do you want?" I asked in a loud clear voice. A group this large had to be a hunting party, and they went after large prey such as elk and deer, which they were unlikely to find up here.

None of them moved except the two baring their fangs at us. If they thought that would intimidate us, they were in for a disappointment. Werecougars derided anyone who showed them fear or weakness, so the only way to handle this was to match their aggressive stance.

I crossed my arms. "I'm not a mind reader. Tell us why you're here or leave."

Several pairs of eyes dropped to the knife on my hip, which was now visible to them. The cougar on the boulder jumped down to the other side, and seconds later, a girl no older than me with strawberry blonde hair walked out, her breast bared and her lower half hidden behind her friends.

The girl's mouth twisted into a sneer. "We will ask the questions."

"Fine. Go ahead," I said since I was apparently the unofficial spokesperson of my group.

She stared at me for a moment, clearly surprised by my response. "What are you and your friends doing here?"

I looked down at my hiking clothes and held my arms out from my sides. "We're hiking. What does it look like we're doing?"

"Few humans come up here this time of year, and those that do are not armed." Her eyes moved over us. "And they do not know what we are. You did as soon as you saw us, which tells me only one thing. You were looking for us."

"Bzzt! Wrong on all counts." I held up my hand and began ticking off each finger. "First of all, we are Mohiri, not human. Second, we are hardly armed to the teeth. Third, even a moron knows normal cougars don't travel in groups or have fangs that big."

A ripple went through the werecougars, and the girl spat. "We've heard of you demons. You call yourselves protectors of humans, but all you want is to rule over everyone."

I scoffed. "This is getting us nowhere. Why don't you tell us what you want, and go on your way?"

She folded her arms over her breasts. "We will leave, but we are taking you with us."

"And why would you want to do that?" I let my hands rest on my hips, my right one within reach of my knife.

Her teeth gnashed. "My brother Felix and his girlfriend Lena were kidnapped last month, and now we find Mohiri sneaking around our terri-tory, no doubt to spy on us. We will take you to our elders, and they will decide what to do with you."

Their presence and aggression suddenly made sense. Mom had told us the Oregon werecougars were riled up since the kidnapping, and I didn't blame them. That didn't mean my friends and I would meekly become captives ourselves.

"I'm sorry about your brother, but we had nothing to do with that," I said in a softer tone. "My best friend was kidnapped, too, and we have been doing everything we can to find her and the other people taken."

She scoffed. "A nice story. You expect us to believe someone kidnapped one of the mighty Mohiri?"

"She's not Mohiri. She's a werewolf." I choked a little on the last word and covered it with a cough.

The werecougars moved restlessly, and the smallest one looked back at the girl. For a moment, she wore an expression of vulnerable uncertainty, but her face hardened again. "You can tell your story to the elders and see if they believe you."

"And what will your elders say when I tell them we aren't even in your territory?" I asked. "You're from Oregon, and this is Idaho."

She faltered and said, "We are close enough to it. No more talking. You will lay down your weapons and come with us now."

"I don't think so." Anna strode over to stand beside me.

Naomi appeared on my other side. Victoria and Teresa took up positions next to her. I wondered briefly where Elsie was, but I forgot about it when all but the smallest werecougar spread out in a circle around us.

"Defensive positions," Naomi ordered.

The five of us drew our knives and moved into a circle with our backs to each other. I still faced the girl, who appeared less confident than she had a minute ago. The look in her eyes said she wouldn't back down now and lose face in front of her friends. I didn't want to fight them, but I would to protect my friends and me.

"You are outnumbered, and your knives are no match for us," she said loudly. "This is your last chance to surrender."

None of us responded. She and I were locked in a stare down until she broke it to shift back to her cougar form. For a long moment, no one moved.

There was a rush of movement behind me, but I didn't take my eyes off the cougars. Naomi lunged, and a werecougar let out a pained yowl.

Two cougars ran at Anna and me. I waited until mine was about to pounce, and then I slashed my blade, nicking both of his front legs. I didn't want to kill them, only make them give up and leave.

Hot pain scored my cheek when one of his claws made contact. His wide eyes told me he hadn't meant to hurt me, and I felt bad when he limped away.

"Stop this," I shouted at the leader who hadn't moved yet. "We don't want to hurt you."

For a second, I thought she was going to listen to me. My heart sank when she screamed and came at me. Her enraged eyes and snarling mouth told me she meant to do more than take me down. The cougar I'd injured tried to cut her off, but she leaped over him and closed the distance between us.

"Dani!" Anna yelled, but I blocked out everything except the charging cougar.

She pounced, her claws aiming for my throat. At the last second, I dropped to my knees, and she sailed over me. I was back on my feet in a second and whirled to make sure none of my friends were hurt by her attack. Naomi and Anna had pulled Teresa and Victoria out of the way just in time.

The female cougar spun and roared. My stomach twisted at the realization she wasn't going to stop until someone made her stop.

"Felicity, no," shouted a boy.

She leaped at me. Expecting me to kneel again, she swiped a paw beneath her. I jumped to the side, and her fur brushed my face as she flew past.

Something hit the ground hard behind me. I whirled and nearly fell over the cougar lying on her side, the hilt of a knife protruding from her chest.

"No!" someone screamed, and a naked girl no older than fourteen sank to her knees beside the fallen cougar. Her strawberry blonde hair and features were too like the leader's for them not to be siblings. "You killed her," she wailed.

I thought she was talking to me until Naomi said, "I was aiming for her shoulder. I only wanted to stop her from hurting Dani."

The girl grabbed the knife and pulled it free before I could stop her. Blood gushed from the cut and soaked the grass beneath. Unzipping my coat, I yanked it off and wadded it up to press against the wound. The cougar's chest rose and fell in short rapid pants, and soon my coat was soaked with blood.

"Please, don't die, Felicity," sobbed the girl cradling the cougar's head on her lap. She raised her tear-streaked face to look at me with terrified eyes. "You have to help my sister. Please."

I stared helplessly at the cougar, whose breaths were growing weaker. We were in the middle of nowhere, and she was mortally wounded. Even if I called Dad on the radio, she'd be dead by the time he got here.

Blood dripped from between my fingers. I threw the drenched coat aside and pressed my hands over the wound. Beneath them, the cougar's damaged heart beat weakly as it struggled to pump oxygen through her.

An image floated up from the depths of my memory of two tiny hands holding a small brown furry body between them. The hands began to glow, causing the animal's body to jerk. I closed my eyes, trying to hold onto the memory. I didn't know why, but it was crucial I did not let it go.

"What is that?" cried a male. "What is she doing to her?"

"Stop her," someone else yelled.

Anna's voice came from somewhere close by. "Dani, can you hear me?" followed by Naomi's frantic shout. "Anna, no. Don't touch her."

I grunted in pain. It felt like my hands were submerged in water too hot to bear. I forced my eyes open and stared at them, expecting to see red blistered skin.

My hands were glowing. Not only my hands, but my arms were bathed in brilliant white light all the way to my shoulders. Magic pulsed from deep within me, coursing through me with purpose like a river seeking the ocean. It pooled in my hands as if blocked by a dam, and if it didn't find release soon, it would erupt from me.

The memory of the furry brown animal resurfaced, and this time I saw it was a kit fox, its fur matted with blood. Magic flowed from the small hands into the animal, and I followed its path, watching as the healing fire knit torn tissue and muscle back together.

Something moved under my hands. I opened my eyes again and saw I was no longer glowing. The cougar's chest rose and fell in deep steady breaths, and her eyes fluttered open. I lifted my hands to see bloody fur but no trace of the knife wound.

The cougar lifted her head, and her eyes met mine. She dropped her head back to her sister's lap and released a shuddering breath.

"Felicity?" The girl looked at me. "Is she going to be okay?"

"She is going to be fine," said my father. He sat on his haunches beside me. "Dani?"

I turned my head toward him, and for a second, his face swam out of focus. My vision cleared, and I looked into his worried gray eyes. "Dad? You're here."

He cupped my chin. "How do you feel? Are you hurt?"

"I'm a little tired. That's all." I shivered and hugged myself against the cold.

"I'm not surprised," Dad said as he removed his coat and put it on me like I was a little girl again.

I tried to stand, but my legs wobbled. He stood and helped me up, holding me steady until the world stopped spinning. I leaned against him and noticed, for the first time, how quiet it was. I looked at the faces around me and found them all staring at me.

The other werecougars had shifted into four boys and two girls and stood together behind Felicity and her sister. The teenagers, who obviously cared little about their state of undress, watched me with a mix of shock and fear. The only one of them not looking at me was the younger girl, who was focused on her sister.

My friends, who knew about my magic, stared with eyes full of wonder. They had never witnessed me heal something because I hadn't done it since I was five.

Gavin stood behind the girls along with Elsie. She held up her radio, and I understood how my father and the others had found us. She had seen the werecougars surround us, and she'd gone back through the cave to radio for help. I shot her a grateful smile.

Felicity flicked her tail and tried to stand, but all she managed to do was roll onto her stomach. I stepped away from my father to help her, but two of the boys beat me to it. They gently lifted her to her feet and stood on either side to support her until she was steady enough to stand on her own.

The younger girl stood and wiped her wet cheeks with the backs of her hands. She offered me a watery smile. "Thank you."

"Dani!" Dimitri emerged from the cave entrance with Kai at his heels. They ran over to me, and Dimitri pulled me into a fierce hug. Releasing me, he looked down at my clothes. "Elsie said you were attacked by werecougars, and Dad and Gavin took off. I had no idea if you were okay."

"Everyone is fine." I looked past him at the cave entrance, about to ask where Ronan was, when I remembered seeing him going off alone in the woods.

Kai's gaze swept over me, and he whistled. "What the hell happened to you?"

"I'll tell you guys about it later," I said in a tired voice, aware of the werecougars watching. They were the ones outnumbered now, and they were most likely wondering what we were going to do with them. They had attacked us, and Felicity had tried to kill me in a fit of rage. If not for Naomi, I would have been forced to take her down. I felt like I should say something to them, but I had no idea what.

A red-haired boy stepped forward. "We're sorry. Felicity's been really upset since Felix and Lena disappeared. I know it's no excuse, but...I wanted you to know." His eyes flitted nervously to Dad. "I understand if you want to punish us, but please let Fanny go. She's only thirteen, and she didn't take part in the fight."

Felicity's sister straightened her back. "Stop treating me like a little kid."

Dad rubbed the back of his neck. "No one is punishing –"

His words were interrupted by a low growl.

Dimitri paled, and I followed his gaze to the cave. Ronan stood in front of the entrance, his jaw clenched so hard the tendons in his neck stood out. His eyes were coal black, and his nostrils flared with each breath. A vein throbbed in his temple, and muscles bulged in his arms and thighs.

"Ronan," I breathed, and my chest expanded at the sight of him. At the same time, my Mori cried, *Solmi.*

"What is that?" the werecougar boy asked.

Ronan's eyes shifted from me to the boy, and wolf claws extended from his fingertips. He growled and comprehension slammed into me. I jumped in front of the boy and put my hands out as Ronan stalked toward him.

"Ronan, no."

14

"Gavin," Dad shouted as he ran past me.

The two of them grabbed Ronan by the arms and held him back. They were seasoned warriors and stronger than he was, but he was driven by rage. He roared and dragged them forward several feet before they forced him to his knees.

Everyone backed away as far as the area would allow them, leaving me facing Ronan. With the boy gone from his sight, his black eyes locked on me, and he went still.

I walked to him, my eyes never leaving his. Kneeling in front of him, I placed my hands on either side of his face. "I'm not hurt, Ronan," I said softly as my thumbs stroked his cheeks. "I need you to come back to me."

He trembled as he fought his demon for control. I didn't know how long we stayed like that as color slowly returned to his eyes. A shudder went through him, and the tension drained from his body.

I smiled. "Hi."

"Hi," he said roughly.

His breath caressed my lips, and I rubbed them together, remembering the last time we had been this close. In his eyes, I saw he was thinking about it, too.

I leaned in and brushed my lips tentatively against his. Ronan gave a little intake of breath, and the seconds seemed to stretch into hours until his mouth opened to mine. The kiss was slow and lingering as we explored each other's mouths for the first time.

His arms wrapped around me, creating a warm cocoon where no one else existed in the world but us. Our mouths separated. I pressed my face against his warm throat and closed my eyes, content to stay in his arms like this forever.

"Dani," Ronan said.

"Hmmm," I murmured. I raised my head and discovered he was sitting on the ground with me on his lap. When did that happen?

"I'm sorry if I frightened you," he said in a husky whisper. "I heard you were attacked, and when I saw all the blood, I lost control."

I touched the curve of his jaw. "I could never be afraid of you."

His eyes searched mine, and his smile made me want to kiss him again, not that I needed much urging. I tried to hide my disappointment when he stood and lowered me to my feet.

I took a step back and looked for my father – but he wasn't there. I swiveled my head from one side to the other, stunned to discover there wasn't another soul here besides us. How had they all left so quickly and without me realizing it?

"Where is everyone?" I asked.

"They left an hour ago."

"What?" I turned in a full circle and shivered. "An hour ago?"

Ronan tugged the sides of Dad's coat together and zipped it up. "You fell asleep, and I didn't want to wake you. Your father told me what you did. He said it tired you."

"It did, but I'm fine now. Was Felicity okay?"

"Yes, thanks to you." He glanced at the darkening sky. "We should get back to camp before your father comes looking for you again."

I laughed, suddenly buoyant. Ronan and I no longer needed to hide our bond from everyone. The air seemed fresher and the world brighter despite the approaching twilight.

It wasn't until we started our descent I realized Ronan and I had shared our first kiss in front of all my friends...and my *father*. When we got back to the campsite, I would not be surprised to find my dad had moved Ronan's tent to the other side of the lake.

During the hike down, I told him what I remembered of the healing. The whole thing had felt like a waking dream, and I didn't know how I'd done it. It was as if reliving my memory of healing the fox had made me subconsciously do the same for the werecougar. Mom might be able to explain it, and I was excited to tell her about it.

It was almost dark when we reached the bottom. Voices and the aroma of roasting trout greeted us as we neared the campsite, but everyone quieted when they saw us. Dad gave me a questioning look, and I smiled to assure him I was okay.

I felt eyes on me when I walked alone to the lake to wash my face and hands, and when I went to my tent for a change of clothes. I'd expected stares after what they had witnessed, but I wished they would say something.

When I emerged from the tent and saw most of my friends sitting and standing together off to one side of the fire, I walked over to them. Bonding was deeply personal, and I didn't owe them an explanation about why I'd kept it a secret, but I wanted to get it all out in the open.

They watched me approach with a mix of fascination and confusion. The only one who avoided my gaze was Kai. I hoped it was due to awkwardness and not because he was hurt.

"It happened the day of my accident," I said without preamble. "Trust me; I was a lot more shocked than you are now."

Everyone smiled, and Sean chuckled. I gave them a condensed version of how it happened. Some of the girls felt bad about the way they'd talked about Ronan, but I brushed it off. They never would have done it if they'd known about the bond.

When I finished, Victoria gave me a sly smile. "Now that everyone knows, are you going to move into Ronan's tent?"

Dimitri snorted behind me. "Not unless you want to see steam coming out of Dad's ears."

The boys snickered, but Kai was more subdued than usual. As normal conversation resumed around us, I motioned for him to walk a few feet away with me.

"Was he the reason we broke up?" he asked quietly with a hint of sadness in his voice.

"I didn't lie when I told you there was no one else, but I think my Mori sensed Ronan was my mate before we bonded," I said honestly. "I was drawn to him but not romantically if that makes sense."

He nodded. "That's how it was for my parents. My dad said they didn't even like each other when they met, but they kept finding reasons to be around each other."

"Looking back, I can see that now." My gaze sought out Ronan and found him alone on the other side of the fire. Now that we were no longer hiding our relationship, it wouldn't raise any eyebrows if I joined him.

Dad called for us to come and eat a few minutes later. I took two plates and went to sit with Ronan. We didn't say much as we ate, and I liked that neither of us felt the need to fill the silence with conversation.

After dinner, some of the boys got it into their heads we should see which trainee could run the fastest around the lake. I decided to sit it out, and Dimitri gleefully cracked his knuckles as he joined the others.

When the temperature began to drop, I moved closer to Ronan, who seemed not to notice the cold. Wordlessly, he shifted positions so he was sitting behind me with my back pressed to his front and his arms around me. I watched the races and ignored all the curious looks cast our way. I couldn't remember ever feeling as content and happy as I did in that moment.

"Thanksgiving is in three weeks," I said. "Will you spend it with my family?"

Ronan took so long to answer I wondered if he had fallen asleep. "Yes."

I smiled and rested my head against his chest. "I should warn you my family goes all out for the holidays, and there'll be at least a dozen of us there."

He chuckled. "I think I can survive it."

"Also, Mom told me to ask you to come to dinner at our house this week." I twisted to look at him. "If you want to."

"I would like that." In the light of the camp fire, his eyes were twin blazes that warmed me down to my toes. My gaze dropped to his mouth, and my pulse sped up. The memory of our kiss lingered on my lips, and I ached to repeat it. If not for my father sitting ten feet away, I would give into the impulse to pull his head down and kiss him again.

Ronan's intake of breath said he knew exactly what I was thinking, and he wanted it, too. Instead of acting on it, he tugged me back against him so I was facing the lake again. It was difficult to concentrate on anything else after that, and not even the mountain temperatures could extinguish the fire he had started inside me.

***

"Are we late?" Dad called as he entered the house three days later.

My Mori stirred, and I looked up from setting the table to see Ronan behind my father. His eyes met mine, and warmth unfurled in my belly, something that also happened with increasing frequency whenever I was around him.

"You're just in time." Mom carried a sliced beef roast from the kitchen and set it on the table beside the bowls of mashed potatoes, roasted vegetables, gravy, and dinner rolls.

"Great. I'm starving." Dimitri swooped in from the living room and reached for the roast, but Mom swatted his hand away.

She gave Ronan a welcoming smile. "We're so glad you could join us. Come sit."

Within a minute, we were all seated around the table and filling our plates with food. I sat beside Ronan, and every time his arm brushed against mine, a little thrill went through me.

We hadn't kissed since we were on the mountain, and I craved the feel of his lips against mine. The heated looks he gave me at times told me he wanted more, too, and I wondered how long we could hold out against this growing need for each other.

Conversation at the table was light, and I noticed Ronan didn't say much. He'd hadn't grown up in a close family setting, and it struck me he wasn't used to this. I began to worry he was uncomfortable, and I searched for a way to make him feel more at home.

"I visited the Oregon werecougar pride today," Mom said. "I met Felicity, and I couldn't tell she had ever been seriously wounded. Her parents asked me to pass along their gratitude and their apology. They also wanted you to know she and her friends are being disciplined for their actions."

"She shouldn't have attacked us, but I don't blame her for overreacting," I said as I buttered a roll. "I'd feel the same way if one of you were taken like her brother."

I looked at my father. "Any new leads?" They'd hit nothing but dead ends lately, but he'd said you never knew when you'd turn over a rock and find something.

"We do have one lead but not about the disappearances." He laid down his fork. "Kelvan found the identity of the person who posted about troll bile on the message boards."

Mom's gasp was audible. "You didn't tell me that."

"I only learned it two hours ago."

I nearly came out of my chair. "Who is it? Do you think they know where Summer is?"

"Her name is Mariana Tate, and she lives in Montreal. She's an oncology nurse, married with one child, and she has no criminal record."

"An oncology nurse?" Mom mused. "Is it possible she's looking for troll bile to help a patient?"

Dad nodded. "It's possible, but they'd have to be wealthy to pay the kind of money she's offering. David dug around and found something interesting. Mariana's daughter has Type One diabetes, and five years ago, she participated in a trial for a new diabetes drug called Nexovir, which stimulates the pancreas to produce insulin. It's the closest thing there is to a cure. The girl was very sick, and the drug saved her life."

I frowned. "What does a diabetes drug have to do with missing shifters and demons?"

"I'm getting there," he said. "Nexovir was created by a company called Caladrius Pharmaceuticals. Caladrius was relatively unknown before they announced their new diabetes drug. The company is now estimated to be worth twenty billion dollars."

Dimitri whistled. "Wow."

I sat up straighter. "Wait. Isn't Julian Cross the CEO of Caladrius?"

"Who is Julian Cross?" Ronan asked.

"He's this millionaire who hangs out with all the celebrities," I said. "He's everywhere on social media and the celebrity gossip sites."

Mom helped herself to more vegetables. "If the drug is a cure for diabetes, why would Mariana be looking for troll bile?"

A gleam entered my father's eyes. "That is where this gets interesting. There is an unsubstantiated rumor Caladrius is working on a new drug to treat neurodegenerative diseases... specifically Alzheimer's."

Mom's fork clattered against her plate. When she and Remy sold his bile on the black market, someone had traced it back to her, and they'd tried to capture three of Remy's little cousins. The man behind it was in the early stages of Alzheimer's, and he'd heard troll bile would stop the disease.

"Why is that significant?" Ronan asked.

Mom explained, and he stared at us like he was waiting for someone to yell "gotcha." I'd told him once she had sold troll bile, but he must have thought I was pulling his leg.

"A drug that could stop Alzheimer's would be worth billions," Dimitri said.

Dad crossed his arms. "And there are people who would do anything for that."

I shivered. "You said whoever was taking demons and shifters has the money and resources to hide their trail. Caladrius could do that."

"Yes." His gaze met mine. "We don't know if Caladrius is responsible for the disappearances, but their connection to Mariana Tate and the troll bile is no coincidence. I asked David and Kelvan to focus on them and see what they can turn up."

"And if they find something?" I asked.

"Then we'll send someone into their lab. If Caladrius is clever enough to cover their tracks, they can hide evidence from government inspections."

The thought of Summer in a cold sterile lab made my dinner want to come back up. I was about to excuse myself when Ronan put his hand on my leg under the table. His warm touch was enough to settle my roiling stomach.

Mom must have seen my distress too because she abruptly turned the conversation to a different topic. "Ronan, Tristan told me you spent part of your childhood at Hadan Castle where he grew up."

Ronan's hand didn't move from my leg. "Yes. I did my training there."

"Dad trained there, too," Dimitri said as he went back for another scoop of mashed potatoes. "And Grandfather."

Mom smiled at Dad. "Hadan Castle makes great warriors."

"Westhorne does, too." Ronan gave my leg a light squeeze and removed his hand. I didn't know if the tingle traveling up my spine was from pride or something else. Maybe both.

"You have a home in Montana, is that right?" Mom asked Ronan.

"Yes. I have a cabin in the Boulder Mountains," he said.

My fork paused halfway to my mouth. I knew he lived in Montana, but it hadn't occurred to me to ask him where his cabin was. The Boulder Mountains were less than a six-hour drive from Westhorne, and we'd gone there on two of our annual camping trips.

Dimitri chuckled. "There you go, Dani." He looked at Ronan. "Dani used to bug Dad to build a cabin in the mountains. She wanted us to live there half the year."

Ronan's curious gaze settled on me. He knew I loved the outdoors, but there was a lot we still hadn't discussed – such as where we would live. Did he think I expected him to live at Westhorne because my family was here? He preferred the quiet of the mountains, and I'd never ask him to give up his home for me.

Dad and Ronan talked about fishing in Montana while Dimitri and I cleared away the meal and Mom served dessert. I kept darting glances at Ronan and Dad, happy to see them conversing so easily. Ronan looked comfortable with my family, and Dad seemed to have finally come to terms with everything.

After dinner, Ronan and I left my house to go for a walk. Instead of going into the woods like usual, I headed for the road to the manor.

"We spend most of our time together outdoors," I said. "I think it's time we do something different."

He fell in beside me. "Like what?"

I grinned at his wary tone. "Nothing drastic. Let's start with watching a movie. Or we could play a game. Do you like chess?"

"I have never played, but you can teach me," he replied, sounding more relaxed. "We could have done that at your house."

I shot him a sideways look. "With my family hovering nearby? No."

"It will be more crowded at the manor."

"That's why we are going to your place," I said. "There are chess boards in the cabins."

I waited for him to argue against it. He hadn't invited me to his cabin yet, and I couldn't help but wonder why. It could be because he wasn't used to having someone else in his space. I hoped it was that and nothing more.

When he didn't respond, I smiled to myself. He was a private person, but he was slowly opening himself to me. I used to think I could only be with someone who was outgoing like me, but it turned out I preferred the strong silent type.

A cold breeze nipped at my face, and the fresh clean air was heavy with moisture. I inhaled deeply and let it out. "It's going to snow. Before we know it, it'll be time to dig out the skis."

"You like the snow," he said amused.

I grinned. "How can you tell?"

We neared the edge of the grounds as the first fat snowflakes floated around us. We stopped walking and stood under the canopy of branches, watching the snow thicken and stick to the trees and grass. A tranquil hush fell over the grounds, and the only sound was the muted roar of the river. The first snow of the year was always magical.

I left the trees and turned my face up to the falling snow. "Is there anything better than this?"

Ronan didn't answer, and I turned to find him watching me. My heart gave a little flutter at his tender expression.

"You are not dressed for this weather," he scolded lightly. "We should head back. The snow is getting heavier, and your parents will wonder where you are."

Laughing, I walked backward. "If I go home now, they'll wonder what is wrong with me. Besides, this snow is not going to last long. I want to enjoy it while I can."

He caught up to me, and we strolled around the grounds. The manor was lit up, but we seemed to be the only ones outside. I couldn't understand how anyone could stay inside on a night like this.

To my disappointment, the snow began to slow sooner than I expected. The fluffy white flakes became a flurry of wet snow as we circled the manor, and it quickly turned to icy raindrops.

We sprinted for his cabin as the rain began to pelt us, and we fell inside laughing. I pushed dripping hair out of my eyes and smiled ruefully at him. "I guess I'm not as good at predicting the weather as I thought I was."

The corners of his eyes creased, and he reached up to remove some hair plastered to my face. My breath faltered when his warm fingers brushed my cold cheek. I took a step toward him, putting us so close I could feel his body heat.

His voice was husky when he said, "I will get you a towel."

"Mm-hmm," I murmured, mesmerized by the water clinging to his dark eyelashes.

Ronan's lips parted slightly, and my stomach quivered as the air in the room became charged with electricity. His head dipped until our mouths were only inches apart. I was a powder keg waiting for a spark to set me off.

I stared into his eyes and saw raw desire in them. I needed to kiss him more than I needed air, but I wanted him to make the first move this time.

A drop of water ran down my face to my upper lip, and I licked it away. Ronan's pupils dilated as gold bled into his irises. His hands framed my face as his mouth came down on mine.

If our first kiss had been a gentle exploration, this one was a dam bursting open. Weeks of pent-up emotion and need poured out, threatening to sweep us away. His mouth was hungry and possessive, and my lips parted eagerly for his demanding tongue. Dizzy from the force of the kiss, I clung to his shoulders as he stoked the fire in my blood until I thought I would combust.

Without breaking the kiss, I pulled off my coat. It wasn't enough. I shoved his coat off his broad shoulders, and he released me long enough to let it fall to the floor with mine.

I slid my hands beneath the bottom of his shirt and felt him tremble as I ran them over the contours of his hard abdomen. He pulled me against him and deepened the kiss until my legs threatened to give out.

I don't remember how we got to the couch. One minute we were standing by the door, and the next, I was straddling him on the couch and yanking his shirt off over his head. I pushed him back against the cushion to claim his mouth again.

"I love you," I whispered against his lips.

Ronan made a sound deep in his chest, and cool air touched my skin when my shirt followed his. I arched my back as his mouth blazed a trail down my throat to the top of my bra. His fingers went to the clasp at the front, and I leaned back to allow him access.

Lost in the haze of desire, it took several seconds to realize his hands had stilled. He bent his head and rested it against my chest as his arms hung loosely around my waist. I ran my fingers through his wet hair, and a shudder went through him. Confusion and doubt crept in as the seconds ticked by. Was he trying to slow us down because we were going too fast, or was it something else?

"Ronan?" I asked hesitantly.

He released a ragged breath and tipped his head back to look up at me. The worry and self-recrimination in his eyes sent a shaft of pain through my chest.

"I can't... We have to stop," he said.

My throat constricted, and I slid off him. I sat with my back against the armrest and folded my arms across my breasts. "Did I do something wrong?"

"No." His answer was so forceful I almost jumped. He turned so he was facing me, and his burning gaze held mine. "You are everything I could ask for."

I swallowed. "Then why?"

He dragged his fingers through his hair. "You know why. It's the same reason I've kept my distance all this time."

"Your wolf." It came out as a hoarse whisper.

"Yes." He picked up my shirt, which had landed on the back of the couch, and expelled a harsh breath when he saw two of the top buttons were missing. Handing it to me, he stood and disappeared into the bedroom. By the time he returned with a towel and a sweater, I had donned my torn shirt.

Wordlessly, I took the towel and dried my hair, using my fingers to comb it. I pulled the thick sweater on over my shirt, catching myself before I buried my nose in the soft wool to inhale his scent.

I looked up to see he was fully dressed again. My eyes followed him as he went to the door and cracked it. When he turned back to me, his shuttered expression made an icy thread curl in my stomach.

"The rain has slowed. We should get you home," he said.

Standing on shaky legs, I walked over to pick up my coat. "I can walk home by myself." It made no sense for him to walk to the lake and back again in the rain.

He retrieved his own coat. "I want to walk with you."

I didn't argue, and we left his cabin. The rain had become a light drizzle, and the thin layer of snow was gone, causing an inexplicable swell of sadness in me.

Ronan's warm hand found my cold one inside the too long sweater sleeve, and he laced our fingers together. The gesture was sweet and comforting, but it couldn't dispel the feeling something had changed between us tonight.

Neither of us spoke until my house came into view. Ronan stopped us at the end of the road and faced me. "My wolf needs to hunt, so I'm going into the mountains tomorrow."

"When will you be back?" I asked, trying to keep my voice even. Werewolves needed to hunt at least once a month, but he hadn't mentioned his trip until now. It seemed very sudden, and I worried that what had happened at his cabin was the reason for it.

"Sunday, Monday at the latest." He drew me close and wrapped me in his warm embrace. "We haven't been apart more than a day since we bonded. Two or three days away might help my wolf."

"Absence makes the wolf grow fonder," I joked humorlessly.

He kissed the top of my head, and his arms tightened around me for a few seconds before he released me. "I'll see you soon."

My throat closed up. "Be safe out there."

The rain picked up again as he walked away, but I stayed rooted to the spot until Ronan was out of sight. A chill settled over me, and a troubling question began to play on repeat in my head. What would happen upon his return if this absence *didn't* make his wolf grow fonder?

15

"Uncle Chris!" I ran to the blond warrior getting out of an SUV in front of the house across from ours. He straightened in time to catch me when I threw myself at him.

"Oof. If you get any faster, you'll bowl me over next time." Laughing, he squeezed me tightly and set me on my feet.

Aunt Beth came around the SUV with her arms spread. "Do I get one, too?"

I hugged her as Grace opened the back door and slid out. At fifteen, Grace was only an inch shy of my height. She was a carbon copy of her mother, except for the two dimples she had inherited from her father. Her dimples were the bane of her existence. Everyone thought they were adorable, and Grace would rather be called a hag than adorable.

"Hey, Grace." I smiled at her and got a sulky scowl in return. She muttered a hello, grabbed her backpack off the seat, and stomped toward their house.

I shot Aunt Beth a questioning look, and she chuckled. "Grace is a little upset because she had to leave her boyfriend when we came back to the US."

"Boyfriend," Uncle Chris grumbled as he opened the cargo door. "She's too young for that. She needs to focus on her training."

Aunt Beth watched Grace enter the house. "She will now that she's home. She won't say it, but she missed you and Dimitri."

"Does this mean you guys are home for good?" I asked hopefully.

"Not quite." Aunt Beth picked up a small suitcase. "We're here through the holidays, and then we're going to run the New York command center for a year. Grace is staying at Westhorne to train."

My eyes widened. "You're letting her stay in the house alone?"

Uncle Chris laughed. "We said she can have a room in the trainee wing until we come back."

"Ah." Grace had been begging her parents to let her stay at the manor since she started training three years ago. My friends had a lot of fun in the training wing, but I'd take our house at the lake over the manor any day.

I grabbed one of their suitcases and walked with them to their house. It was similar in style to ours and a lot neater because they had been away a lot the last few years. Our home had a more lived-in feel.

"How are you?" Aunt Beth asked after we deposited the bags in the living. Her expression told me she wasn't asking about training. After word got out about my bond with Ronan, it hadn't taken long for everyone we knew to hear about it.

"I'm great." I ignored the doubt gnawing at me since I last saw Ronan three days ago. I missed him more than I thought was possible, and I'd feel better when he got back today.

Her kind gray eyes searched mine. "Are you sure? I remember how confusing it was for me when Chris and I bonded."

"I love him," I said simply.

She gave my hand a squeeze. "And that is all that matters."

"Knock, knock," called my mother as she entered the house. Aunt Beth let out a little squeal, and they hugged each other like they were still teenagers.

As soon as the reunion was over, they launched in to a conversation about Thanksgiving, which was a few days away. I left them discussing side dishes and returned to our house where I'd forgotten my phone when the SUV pulled up. My heart leapt when I saw a missed call and a text from Ronan. He was home, and he wanted to see me tonight.

The hours seemed to stretch on forever. Uncle Chris, Aunt Beth, and Grace came over for dinner, but I was too distracted to pay attention to the conversation. When a knock came at the door at eight o'clock, I practically ran to answer it, earning a teasing jibe from Dimitri.

Ronan smiled when he saw me, but he looked tired. I grabbed my coat and gloves, and we set out toward the manor. When he clasped my hand in his, I felt lighter than I had in days.

"Was the hunting good?" I asked.

"Yes. There are plenty of elk, deer, and moose in the mountains this time of year."

He fell quiet again in his usual manner, and we didn't say much else until we reached the main grounds. Instead of taking the long way around as we had a few nights ago, we went directly to his cabin. The closer we got, the more I thought about how heated things had been between us the last time I was here. I was hoping for a repeat soon, but for tonight, I was happy just to be with him again.

It was chilly inside his cabin, and his duffle bag still sat beside the door where he'd dropped it when he arrived. He turned up the thermostat with an apology. "I should have set this before I went to your place."

"It's okay." I smiled at him and went to sit on the couch.

Ronan came into the living room and went to stand by one of the windows facing the manor. He stared out for a long moment and turned to face me with a tortured expression that stole my breath. A vice started to tighten around my chest as he began to speak.

"My wolf hasn't imprinted on you," he said thickly. "I hoped this trip would help, but it hasn't."

I clenched my hands together. "It needs more time."

"We've been together almost every day since we bonded, and you spent half those times with my wolf. We were running together for two weeks before we bonded."

"Some wolves take longer to imprint." My voice cracked, and I swallowed.

His eyes seemed to lose their light. "You've been around werewolves your whole life. You know another wolf would have imprinted by now."

My body felt like it was encased in ice. "What are you saying?"

He drew in a deep breath. "My wolf can't or won't imprint on you."

"I don't care." I stood and went to him. "I love you, and I know you love me, too. There are lots of unmated couples, and we can be like them."

He shook his head. "None of those couples are bonded, and if one of them did bond with a potential mate, they could break it without anyone getting hurt. When a wolf imprints, it is forever. If my wolf one day imprinted on another female, I could never be with you again."

I started to speak, and he cut me off. "My mother loved my father, even when he imprinted on another and took a mate. She thought she hid it from me, but I saw how much she suffered." He cupped my cheek. "If I stay here, we will give in and complete the bond. You'll be trapped with someone who might never fully be yours, and it will eventually destroy you."

I laid my hand over his. "I'm willing to risk it."

"I'm not," he said, his words slicing through my heart like a blade. "I can't do that to you. I'd die before I hurt you like that."

"You're hurting me now."

His hand trembled. "And I hate myself for it. I was too selfish and weak to leave when I should have, and I would give anything to carry this pain for you. I deserve nothing less."

Tears scalded my cheeks. Ronan pulled me into his arms and buried his face in my hair. "Someday, the pain will end, and you will be happy again." He held me for a long moment as sobs wracked my body. He kissed my forehead and whispered, *"Inima mea îți va aparține mereu."*

He released me, and it felt as if there was no warmth left in the world. For a heartbeat, I thought he would reach for me again and tell me he couldn't leave me.

When he walked away from me, it was all I could do to not splinter into a million pieces. He stopped at the door to pick up his duffle bag, and I realized why he hadn't unpacked it. Even as he reached for the door handle, I held out the tiniest hope he wouldn't go through with it.

Don't say it. Please, don't say it.

He looked back at me. His eyes were wet and reflected the agony threatening to swallow me. When he spoke, his voice was like gravel. "Forgive me, Dani. I have to break our bond."

My Mori roared. Excruciating pain tore through me as if invisible hands had punched through my ribs and were ripping me in two. Ronan walked out, and I sank to my knees. I gasped for air, but he'd taken all the air in the room with him.

The edges of my vision grew dark. My Mori was a wild beast slamming against the bars of its cage to free itself and go after its mate. It would be so easy to give in to it and let it take control. I could fade into oblivion, free from this agony.

I released my hold, and the demon surged forward. Pressure built inside my head as the demon's consciousness became the dominant one. At the back of my mind, a chasm opened, and I floated toward it.

My body seized as magic burst from deep within my core. It poured from me, encasing me in a bubble so bright I saw it through my eyelids. The bubble closed in, and my raging Mori shrank away from the magic, getting smaller and smaller until it was forced to relinquish its control of my body.

I hugged my knees tightly to my chest and rocked back and forth. No matter how small I made myself, there was no escape from the merciless waves of pain slamming into me.

"Dani, can you hear me?"

The voice was hollow and dreamlike. I tried to focus on it, but my Mori's agonized wails drowned it out.

"I think she's in shock," said the voice again. It sounded like my mother.

Hands gripped either side of my head. "Look at me, *Sladkaya*. Please."

I forced my eyes open, and my father's face floated before me. For the first time, I saw fear in his eyes.

"Daddy," I gasped. "It hurts... It hurts so much."

"I know, baby." He gathered me in his arms. I curled into him, but the solace I'd always found in his embrace was gone.

He stood and carried me outside. I kept my eyes closed, but I heard grandfather's voice and the sound of an idling vehicle. My father got into the back, cradling me, and I slid back into my private hell.

I roused when the vehicle stopped, and my father carried me into the house. He laid me on my bed, and I curled into a fetal position. My heart felt like it was tethered to Ronan, and with each step he took away from me, it was slowly being torn from my chest. Every breath was torturous, and the constant flood of anguish from my Mori was more than I could bear. Hugging myself, I moaned, "Make it stop. Please, make it stop."

I floated on an ocean of pain where time didn't exist. Sometimes, I heard far away voices, but I was alone here with my Mori, neither of us able to offer comfort to the other.

"Danielle." Eldeorin's voice echoed in the vastness. "I cannot take away your pain, but I can offer you a reprieve from it."

"Yes," I begged, willing to do anything to escape it, if only temporarily.

A hand touched my forehead, and warmth spread through me. It was followed by blessed numbness as the world receded into nothing. Ronan's haunted eyes were the last thing I saw as I sank into oblivion.

My warm cocoon opened, and my weightless body floated free. I tried to fight the current taking me away, but it carried me slowly upward toward a murky light. Muffled sounds reached me as I neared the surface, and an ache started in my chest. The higher I rose, the sharper the pain became as a steel band tightened around me.

I opened my eyes with a gasp. A hand hovered above my face, and it moved away to reveal Eldeorin leaning over me.

"Welcome back," he said without his usual humor. "How do you feel?"

All at once, the pain came flooding back. I rolled onto my side away from him and shook with silent sobs.

He laid a gentle hand on my shoulder. "I am sorry, Danielle. I wish I had the power to end your suffering."

His footsteps left the room. From the hallway, my mother said, "Thank you, Eldeorin."

"I don't think it was long enough," he replied. "Perhaps I should put her into a longer sleep."

Yes, I thought as my grandfather said, "Sleep will only delay the inevitable. This is not a physical injury that will heal on its own. Dani must endure the pain, as cruel as it sounds, to get through this. Time is the only thing that will help her now."

I squeezed my eyes shut. How could anyone endure this?

"Dani."

I turned my head to look at Dimitri, who stood in the bathroom doorway. His jaw was covered in several days' growth of beard, and his eyes were tired and dull.

Wiping my eyes with my sleeve, I rolled over to face him. "Hi," I croaked.

He walked over and sat on the edge of the bed. I held out a hand to him at the same time he reached for me. We clasped them tightly together and stared at each other for a long moment, neither of us knowing what to say.

"How long was I asleep?" I asked. My voice was scratchy from disuse.

"Five days."

I swallowed dryly and looked past him at the trees outside the window. It had been five days since I'd seen and touched Ronan. Five days since he'd walked away from me forever. The pain in my chest intensified, and I rubbed the spot over my heart.

"Do you want to talk about it?" Dimitri asked hoarsely.

I didn't think I would ever be able to talk about it, but I said, "It's too soon."

He gave me a wan smile. "I'm here when you're ready."

Mom came into the room. She looked as tired as Dimitri, but her eyes brightened when she saw us together. "I'm going to make you some lunch. Do you want to eat in here?"

"I'm not hungry." The thought of food made my stomach churn.

Her brow furrowed. "You haven't eaten in five days. You need to eat."

"Later." I let go of Dimitri's hand and pushed up to a sitting position. "What I need is some fresh air. I think I'll go for a walk."

Dimitri stood. "Do you want me to go with you?"

I wanted to be alone, but his earnest expression made it impossible to tell him that. "Yes."

Mom made me dress in warm clothes, and I saw why when I stepped outside. A couple of inches of snow lay on the ground, and the temperature hovered above freezing.

Dimitri and I walked around the lake because Mom didn't want me to go far. He filled me in on what I'd missed while I was asleep. Thanksgiving had come and gone, but no one at the lake had felt like celebrating it. The manor had its usual holiday meal, and grandfather had brought food here afterward.

No one trained during the week of Thanksgiving, and Dimitri hadn't talked to any of our friends. He didn't say it, but everyone at Westhorne had to know by now. I didn't ask who was taking Ronan's place as trainer, and Dimitri didn't offer it. We avoided any mention of Ronan.

I ate in my room that night, and for the next week. My family meant well, but it was too hard being around them when they fussed over me and watched me like I would break at any second. During the days, I walked in the woods, alone or with Hugo and Woolf. I stayed close to home at first, but as the days passed, I ventured out farther and farther.

Pain was my constant companion, even in sleep. It followed me into my dreams and waited for me when I awoke. There was no escape from it, and it never let me forget what I'd lost.

Two weeks after Ronan's departure, I agreed to help Mom in the menagerie. I hadn't come within a quarter of a mile of the manor since that night, but she'd gotten two more wyvern hatchlings even younger than the first three. They had to be hand-fed five times a day, and she couldn't manage it alone with her schedule.

I finished the noon feeding and started to leave the menagerie when voices came from outside. Not wanting to encounter anyone, I stayed back, waiting for them to pass. They came closer, and I recognized Grandfather and Gavin's voices.

"Callum agreed to cut his trip short," Grandfather said. "He'll be here next week."

"Have you heard from him?" Gavin asked.

I held my breath because something in his voice said he wasn't referring to Callum.

"Not since the day he left. He was planning to head up north to Alaska. He said he would stay there until it was over."

I stumbled back from the door and doubled over like I'd been punched in the gut. It took a few minutes to catch my breath, and by that time, Grandfather and Gavin were gone. I left the menagerie, ran into the woods, and didn't stop.

I ran with no destination in mind. It didn't matter where I went because I could never outrun the pain. Thoughts of Ronan invaded my mind, and I tried to push them away, but he was everywhere in these woods. The place that used to bring me so much happiness had become a graveyard of memories.

Exhaustion eventually forced me to slow my brutal pace. Resting my hands on my knees, I looked around at my surroundings until I spotted a few familiar landmarks. I was almost eight miles from home in the rocky terrain at the base of the mountain. There were fewer trees here, and a hundred yards from me, the ground inclined sharply.

I hadn't come this far since... An image of a bearded vagrant with wild hair and eyes came unbidden to my mind, and I breathed through the stabbing pain accompanying it.

Straightening, I resumed walking, desperate to find a place free of him. Two hundred feet above me was a ledge and a small cave, which was little more than a deep indentation in the rock. I hadn't been to the ledge in ages, so I'd find no memories of him there.

I trudged through knee-deep snow, breathing heavily at the effort. It took longer than usual to reach the ledge, and I was out of breath when I plopped down and dangled my legs over the edge.

The snow-covered valley was laid out below me. Half a mile away, a herd of mule deer stood beside a small lake, and farther away, I could make out a black bear foraging before it started hibernation. In summer, the valley was alive with sound, but the snow muted everything today.

I inhaled deeply and waited for the joy that always came when I saw our valley like this, but I felt nothing except the pain I'd brought with me. My eyes brimmed and spilled over, and I wondered vaguely how I could have any tears left. I'd cried enough in the last week to last a lifetime.

It started to snow, and the wind picked up, whipping my hair into my face. The snow became a squall obscuring everything below me, and I felt like I was the last person left on earth. I knew I should go back down, but I couldn't summon the will to move.

I pictured Ronan's wolf running through the vast Alaskan wilderness and replayed Grandfather's words. Ronan intended to stay there until our bond dissolved. Did he feel the same soul-deep pain, or was he spared in his wolf form? I wouldn't wish this agony on anyone, least of all him.

A blast of icy wind rocked me. Shivering violently, I pulled my numb legs up and looked behind me at the cave. It wasn't much, but it would provide some protection from the wind.

I started to back up when I glimpsed something through the swirling snow. I squinted but saw nothing. A few seconds later, it was there again, a dark shape in the sky. I stared at it as it grew larger until I was able to make out two long wings.

I should have been worried a wyvern was coming straight at me, probably mistaking me for prey, but I was too miserable to care. Alex landed on the ledge, folded his leathery wings, and sat close enough for me to feel the heat radiating off him.

"H-hi, Alex." I shivered hard, and my teeth chattered. Even with his warm body pressed against my side, I was too exposed to the bitter wind and snow.

He moved and flexed his wings. I was too cold and tired to react when he wrapped one wing around me, enveloping me in warmth. I tucked my legs in and leaned against his scaly side. It took several minutes for his heat to penetrate my numb body.

"He's gone, Alex," I whispered. "I'll never see him again."

It was the first time I'd uttered the words, and the finality in them sent fresh tears coursing down my cheeks. I cried until I was spent and too exhausted to lift my head.

I jerked awake. Disoriented, it took a moment to remember where I was. Alex's wing was still around me, but he was shifting restlessly, which had to be what woke me. Peering around his wing, I saw it was almost dark and the storm had ended. I needed to get home. My family had no idea where I was, and they were probably worried to death.

"Daaanniiii."

I lifted part of Alex's wing and leaned forward to look at the ground far below. A lone figure stood on top of a boulder silhouetted against the snow.

"I'm here," I called.

My mother tipped back her head to look up at us. In the next second, she was standing beside me on the ledge. I prepared for a scolding, but she knelt and pulled me into her arms.

"I'm sorry, Mom. I didn't mean to stay out so long."

"I'm just glad you're okay." She released me and smiled at my companion. "Thank you, Alex."

He cocked his head at her. Standing, he shook out his wings and took flight. Within seconds, he disappeared into the darkness.

"I knew you were still coming out here to see him," Mom scolded lightly.

"He's alone, and he doesn't have any friends."

She shook her head. "Male wyverns are solitary creatures. The only time they go near another of their kind is to mate."

I glanced at the dark sky. "Alex isn't like other wyverns. You know that."

Laughing, she said, "Yes, but we probably shouldn't tell your father about your friendship."

"How did you find me anyway?" She could sense Fae magic, but only when it was close. The valley was too big for her to search, unless she knew I had come out here.

"You set off a perimeter sensor, and Dax told me one of the drones saw you running this way." She stood and held out a hand to me. "I understand your need to be alone, but promise you'll take your phone and let us know where you're going next time."

I let her help me up. "I will."

"I won't pretend to know what you're going through," she said in a gentler voice. "But you can talk to me about anything."

"I know."

She stepped closer to me. "Are you ready to go home, or do you need more time?"

I look down at the valley cloaked in darkness. I could stay here all night, and it wouldn't change anything or make me hurt less. The only thing that could was a thousand miles away in Alaska.

I looped my arm through hers. "Let's go home."

16

———————

I scrolled through the hundreds of photos and videos of Summer on my phone. In some of them she was alone, and in others she was with me. There were a few of us with Dimitri, her brother Caleb, and her cousins. In every photo, Summer's green eyes sparkled and her face glowed with happiness.

I stopped on the last one of the two of us, arms around each other's shoulders, taken near Portland Head lighthouse in Cape Elizabeth this summer. It had been the last day of our visit to Maine, and we'd decided to visit every lighthouse from Portland to Portsmouth. If I'd known that day it would be the last time I hugged my best friend, I would have held on to her for dear life.

My fingers absently began scrolling to the most recent photos. I stopped before I got to any of Ronan and closed the app. I hadn't been able to look at them since he left. I should delete them because they'd only cause me more pain, but I couldn't bring myself to do it.

I stared blindly at the screen for a long moment and laid my phone on the table. From my chair beside the tall window, I had a wide view of the grounds between the manor and the river. Movement drew my gaze to two figures running across the lawn covered in a fresh layer of snow. Naomi bent and grabbed a handful of snow, which she formed into a ball and threw at Luis. He ducked but another snowball came from behind him to hit him in the back of the head.

Victoria and Elsie came into view, and all three girls launched a snowball attack on Luis. I couldn't hear them, but their expressions told me they were laughing. It was two days to Christmas Eve, and everyone was in a holiday spirit. Tomorrow, most of my friends would go home to spend the holidays with their families.

I sank back in my chair and buried my nose in the soft wool sweater I wore. Fresh pain lanced my heart, and my Mori whispered, *Solmi.* At the same time, I was strangely comforted by his familiar scent. I knew holding onto his sweater wasn't healthy, but like the photos, I couldn't get rid of it.

The library door opened, and a feminine voice said, "So, this is where Sara used to hide out."

My head whipped around, and I stared at the blonde warrior in the doorway. I sprung out of my chair and ran to her. "Aunt Jordan."

She caught me in a fierce hug and held me at arm's reach to look at me. Her eyebrows pulled down, and she pressed her lips together. "You look like shit. I got here just in time."

"Thanks." I scowled at her. "I thought you and Uncle Hamid were spending the holidays in Japan."

"Change of plans." She stepped back and spun slowly to take in the whole room. "You know, I think this is the first time I've come up here." Her nose scrunched. "It's so dark and old-fashioned. It reminds me of that Jane Eyre movie I watched with your mom ages ago. I can see why she liked this room."

"You've been waiting for two years to train with Daigo again. Did he cancel?" Daigo Matsui was a legendary Mohiri samurai warrior, whom she had trained under in the past. She'd told me the wait to see him was years long, and when Daigo called, you went.

She shrugged. "I felt a need to come home and see my favorite goddaughter."

Tears stung my eyes, and I blinked them away.

"You know what you need?" She didn't wait for me to answer. "You need a good sparring session, and who better to spar with than me?"

"I don't feel like it right now." I returned to my chair by the window.

She came over and sat on the edge of the table. "Listen, Kiddo. I know you're in a lot of pain, and I'm not going to try to tell you how to cope with it. I don't think anyone who hasn't been in your shoes can do that. But the way I see it, you're going to hurt whether you hide up here or train. Wouldn't you rather be doing something?"

I stared blindly out the window and pressed my fist to my chest. Over the last three weeks the pain had dulled to a sharp ache, which drained my energy and made it hard to get out of bed most days. I hadn't returned to training, and I had little interest in the things I used to enjoy. Even running held no joy for me anymore. I hated this shell of myself I had become, but I could see no way back to the person I used to be.

Aunt Jordan laid a hand over mine. "Give it a try. If it's too much, we'll stop."

I bit my lip. "I don't want to go to the training wing."

"Me either." She smiled at me. "Come on. I know the perfect place."

Hesitantly, I stood and grabbed my coat from the back of the chair. I followed her downstairs to the main hall where she told me to wait for a minute. She ran up to the apartment she was using and returned with two swords, one of which she handed to me.

"You're letting me use one of your swords?" Reverently, I gripped the handle and slid the katana from its scabbard. The flawless blade gleamed, and intricate silver ornaments were woven under the handle's blue silk wrapping. If Aunt Jordan was obsessive about one thing, it was her swords. She had a whole collection she kept in immaculate condition, and she never allowed anyone else to use them.

"Of course, not." She fingered the handle of the sword she held. "I'm letting you use *your* sword."

"Mine?" My jaw dropped, and I stared first at the katana and then at her.

She grinned. "It was supposed to be your graduation gift, but I couldn't wait that long to give it to you."

"It's the most beautiful sword I've ever held."

"I knew you'd like it." She pointed toward the main entrance. "Want to go try it out?"

I slid the sword back into its scabbard. "Yes."

If my answer was a bit lackluster, she pretended not to notice. We left the manor and walked in the direction of the arena while she told me about their last job hunting a Rageon demon in the Sahara. Rageon demons had ten-inch claws, diamond hard scales, and they grew up to thirty feet long.

"Did you get it?" I asked.

"What do you think?" She pulled out her phone and showed me photos of her standing beside the body of a massive red serpentine demon. "There's a woman in Yemen who is making me armor from some of the scales. You'd need a rocket launcher to penetrate it."

I didn't ask why she needed armor that strong. Aunt Jordan loved weapons, and she practically had her own armory at their home in Cairo.

We entered the arena and walked to the main room lit only by the light coming in through the windows. The bleacher-style seats on three sides of the room could accommodate every person at Westhorne, and the wood floor was polished to a high shine.

Aunt Jordan drew her sword and laid the scabbard on one of the seats. She walked to the center of the floor and gave me an expectant look.

I left my coat and scabbard on a seat. Pausing, I took off the sweater, too, before I joined her. I hadn't picked up a sword in over a month, and I was out of practice. This was the longest I'd ever gone without using one since I started training.

I got within four feet of her when she feinted a strike to my right side. She immediately changed direction with a horizontal strike on my other side. She had tricked me with this move in the past, and I brought my sword down in time to deflect hers.

Her mouth curved into a wicked smile. "That was to make sure you were paying attention."

I sliced my new sword through the air a few times to learn the feel of it. Dad let Dimitri and me use his swords sometimes, but they were not as light as this one. The handle fit better against my palm, and the sword felt like an extension of my arm.

"Ready to show me what you learned since the last time I kicked your ass?" she teased.

I lunged, thrusting my blade at her chest. She easily sidestepped and parried my strike with her blade. Then she countered with a horizontal strike. I ducked under the strike, and she came back, swiping her blade low. Jumping over it, I brought the flat side of my blade down to rest on her shoulder.

She straightened with a wide grin. "Damn, you're fast. I was going to slow down for you, but I don't think I need to."

The tiny spark of pleasure flaring in my chest felt foreign. I couldn't remember the last time I had known anything but pain.

"Now that we've had a little warm-up." She brought her sword up in a salute. "Let's see what else you can do."

We circled each other like two mountain lions preparing for a fight. My gaze locked with hers as we moved in careful deliberation, and the world outside our circle fell away.

She struck fast, and I blocked it. A rapid series of strikes followed, and I parried them all as she kept me on the defensive. As soon as I saw an opening, I attacked, but she blocked me effortlessly. Our blades locked, and we stood face-to-face for several seconds before she gave me a taunting smile and stepped back.

"Not bad. Now stop holding back, and show me what you really have," she ordered.

I gritted my teeth at a memory of Ronan using almost those same words with me. Anger surged beneath my breastbone, and I went on the offensive. The only sound in the arena was the clang of metal as our blades met again and again.

I was no match for her, but we weren't playing to win. I poured my grief and rage into it until I couldn't tell the tears from the sweat rolling down my face. When she finally stepped back, I stood with my chest heaving and my sword arm hanging limp at my side. I lifted my head to look at her and was met by a wide smile.

"Now *that* is how my godchild does it." She looked at something behind me. "She gets it from me."

Turning, I was surprised to discover we were no longer alone. Sometime during our match, my father and Uncle Hamid had come in and taken seats near the door. Dad's eyes, which had been filled with worry for so long, held a mix of pride and hope.

"It was the sword," I mumbled, holding it up.

Aunt Jordan came to stand beside me. "It's the warrior, not the weapon, who wins the battle. Tristan told me that once, so you know it's true."

Uncle Hamid nodded. "She is right. It takes more than a great sword to hold your own against Jordan for an hour."

"Stop. You're going to make me blush." She put a hand to her cheek as we walked over to them.

"Good to see you, Jordan," Dad said. "How long are you two staying?"

"Three weeks or until the rest of the Council discovers we didn't go to Japan as we intended." She sheathed her sword. "They weren't happy when we told them we'd be gone for six months."

Uncle Hamid smiled at her. "Jordan reminded them there were plenty of other warriors who would be happy to work for them."

My gut tightened at the adoring look he gave her, and I averted my eyes so I couldn't see what I would never have.

Shame filled me. I could not expect people to hide their love for each other because it made me sad.

Dad chuckled and stood. "I'm sure Tristan will cover for you as long as he can."

"We heard about your investigation," Aunt Jordan said as we left the arena. "Let us know if we can help while we're here."

Dad shot her a grateful look. "I'll take you up on that."

"How are Peter and Shannon holding up?" she asked as we walked toward the lake. It was late afternoon, and already the light was fading.

"As well as can be expected," Dad said. "It's hard for them to stand back while we search for Summer, but they don't have our resources and technology. They know we'll do everything in our power to find her."

Aunt Jordan nodded somberly. "Where are you in the investigation?"

"We're looking at Caladrius Pharmaceuticals and their CEO, but so far, they are clean. Too clean. No one gets to where they are without having some secrets to hide."

"Have you sent someone inside?" Uncle Hamid asked.

"Yes, and everything appears to be above board so far. But my gut tells me we're on the right track. I asked the lab at Valstrom to reverse-engineer the drugs Caladrius has developed. I want to know if there's anything in the drugs they didn't disclose to the FDA."

I shivered, but not from the cold. Ever since Dad had first mentioned his suspicions about Caladrius, I'd tried not to think about the implications. If they were experimenting on demons to create drugs, they would have no qualms about expanding their research to shifters and other creatures.

Aunt Jordan's mouth formed an O. "What will you do if Valstrom finds what you're looking for?"

I looked over at my father. It was a good question. Most humans we apprehended were collectors or those working on the black market. We turned those people over to the government, which had created a covert agency to handle such situations. Caladrius was a high-profile company, and Julian Cross had reached A-list celebrity status. Any whiff of a government investigation into him or his company would be all over the news, and we could not let the public learn about the existence of demons and shifters.

Dad's lips thinned. "Any illegal research is being done elsewhere. We can't show our hand until we find that lab, or we risk them moving it to another location. Tristan and the rest of the Council are deciding the best course of action for handling the public aspect when we make our move."

"I'm going with you," I said in a hard voice. "I know you're going to say it's too dangerous, but if Caladrius has Summer, I want to be there for her. And if she's gone, I need to..."

"You will be there. I promise," he said.

"If you're going to join a strike team, you'll need to be ready," Aunt Jordan threw an arm over my shoulders. "I'm going to teach you everything I know."

"I can't do it," I cried, letting my hands fall to my sides.

My mother, who stood ten feet away on the frozen lake, gave me one of her ever-patient smiles. "You're trying to force it. Feel for the magic, and let it come naturally."

I made a half-hearted attempt. "I can't feel anything."

It was a lie. The truth was I felt too much. Too much anguish, too much loneliness, too much pain. Grandfather said a bond transcended the physical and emotional planes beyond the understanding of our oldest scholars. It wasn't merely a connection between two Mori but a link between two souls. Severing this link caused a soul-deep wound, which could only heal when the bond dissolved. The stronger the bond, the deeper the pain and the longer it took to fade.

I had learned to live with the constant feeling that a hand was crushing my heart, but it was one thing to function physically and another to perform mental tasks as if the pain wasn't there.

Aside from the time my magic acted on its own to stop my Mori from taking control, I hadn't been able to summon it since Ronan left. It wasn't like before when I had locked it away out of fear. I wanted to use it, but I couldn't see beyond the pain. Mom and Eldeorin had left me alone to give me space, but when I started training with Aunt Jordan two weeks ago, Mom decided it was time to practice my magic again.

"How long are we going to keep trying this?" I asked, defeated.

"Until you stop trying and do it," said a new voice.

I spun to face Eldeorin, who watched me with a determined expression, which filled me with unease. He walked over to stand beside my mother and fixed me with a stern look. "We have made allowances because you suffered a traumatic event, but it is time you resume your training."

"A traumatic event?" I bit out. "You say it like it's past tense, like it's not something I live with every minute of every day."

"Eldeorin," Mom admonished.

"You, Cousin, more than anyone, know what will happen to her when liannan comes. And it will come whether she wants it or not." To me he said, "I am truly sorry you are suffering. If I could take away your pain or delay liannan, I would. I cannot do either of those things, so you have no choice but to push through this."

Mom's eyes shimmered with tears. "He's right, Dani. I know you feel alone in this, but Eldeorin and I will help you through it."

I didn't know if they could help me, but I didn't want to be like this anymore. I set my shoulders. "How?"

Eldeorin walked over to me and motioned for my mother to join us. "Sara, demonstrate how you summon and use the snow's magic."

Mom picked up a handful of powdery snow and held it on her palm. The snow began to sparkle and swirl to form a perfect rotating column roughly six inches high. I'd seen her do this on a larger scale, but the ease with which she controlled water magic still awed me.

"Dani, can you see the snow's magic?" Eldeorin asked.

"Yes."

He put a hand on my back and moved us closer. "Do you see her magic controlling it?"

I focused on the sparkles until I saw the hundreds of threads connecting them to her hand. The threads were so fine they were almost invisible.

"I see it," I said.

Taking my hand, he held it so the tips of my fingers touched the column. The snow moved around my fingers, but the column remained intact. "Do you feel the magic?"

"All I feel is cold –" My fingertips tingled, and the cold receded. They began to sparkle like they were covered in glitter. "I feel it."

"Good." Eldeorin released my hand and stood by Mom, facing me. "Now, let the magic coax yours out."

I thought back to the first day I stood in the lake and called the water magic to me. I focused on how it had felt, the warmth and the tiniest prickle of electricity. My hand grew warm, and the tingle in my fingers spread up my arm.

A memory of Ronan's warm hand encasing mine flitted through my mind, and the vice around my chest tightened. I gasped at the sharp stab of pain, and the magic receded.

"What happened?" Eldeorin asked.

I didn't answer. I called to the magic again, and it moved up my arm. This time, I forced my mind to think about something else. I brought up an image of Julian Cross and thought about how likely it was he had taken Summer. Anger flared and spread through me like a wildfire. It grew hotter and hotter until I thought it could melt the snow around us.

"Dani," Mom and Eldeorin said together.

I blinked, and their faces came into focus. Mom looked a little concerned, but Eldeorin was smiling. I shifted my weight, and water sloshed. Looking down, I stared at the half-inch-deep puddle of water around my feet.

"I would call that a success," Eldeorin said. "Do it again. This time, I want you to take the snow from Sara without melting it or the ice."

I tried it without blocking the pain, but it was only a repeat of my first try. When I used the anger, I almost melted a hole in the ice. Anger helped me focus on something other than the pain, but it also took away my ability to control my magic. I finally understood what Aine and Mom meant when they said our magic was connected deeply to our emotions.

What I needed was to find a balance between the two. Anger was okay, but I had to temper it so I could control it and not let it control me. I lost count of the number of attempts I made, and twice Mom had to refreeze the ice beneath me.

Finally, it happened. I held my glowing hand palm up and pulled on the threads connecting my magic to the snow's magic. At first, nothing happened. Mom relinquished her hold on the magic, and the column of snow moved to my hand.

Eldeorin clapped. "Very good."

At the sound, the column collapsed on my hand. "Damn it. I can't keep my focus."

Mom beamed at me. "You'll get there. You got through the hardest part."

"Should I keep doing it?" I was a little wrung out emotionally, but I didn't want to admit it to them.

"Let's add some variety to keep it fun," Eldeorin said. "We know you can melt ice, but can you make ice?"

Mom demonstrated while explaining how to draw energy from water. She went as slow as possible so I could watch the transfer of energy and see the water molecules form crystalline structures.

It didn't require half as many attempts to make ice now that I knew how to summon my magic again. After I'd done it a few times, we switched to creating steam and fog. Mom made it rain, but that was beyond my abilities.

"There is water everywhere, and where there is water, there is magic you can control and manipulate." Eldeorin pointed at the snow on the ground. "You don't need to see water to know it's there. Send out your magic to call to it, and you will find it."

He flicked a finger, and a claw-foot tub appeared on the ice a few yards away. "Can you lift that and bring it to you?"

"Using the magic in the ice?" I asked, trying to figure out how that would work.

"Using the water magic in the air," he replied. At my *are you kidding* look, he said, "It is about to snow, so the moisture in the air has increased. That will make it easier for you."

"Let me show you." Mom held out a hand. "It's the same as calling the magic in the snow and ice. You connect with it and tell it where to go. In this case, you tell it to surround the object you want to move. Then you move it wherever you want it to go."

The tub rose a foot in the air and floated toward us. She lowered her hand and set the tub down three feet from us. This close, I saw the soft glow covering the entire surface of the tub.

Mom looked at Eldeorin. "She should start with something lighter."

He thought for a moment and nodded. The tub disappeared, and in its place was a small metal jug.

Following her instructions, I discovered it was a lot easier to call magic to me than to send it somewhere else. It took a few minutes to get the magic to do my bidding and adhere itself to the jug. I couldn't lift the jug, but I managed to slide it six inches across the ice.

Clapping came from the shore, and Aunt Jordan called, "Nice job, Dani."

"She is right," Eldeorin said. "That was quite good for your first attempt to move something other than water."

"You made a lot of progress today," Mom said as we started toward the shore.

Eldeorin didn't say anything else until we reached Aunt Jordan. "Before I leave, I would like you to try moving another object. Something smaller."

"Like what?" I asked.

He produced a single white pearl and held it on his palm. "Take this pearl from me and give it to Jordan."

Aunt Jordan simpered at him. "For me? You shouldn't have."

It was much easier to pick up the pearl. I floated it to her and dropped it in her outstretched hand.

"That was perfect, Dani," Mom said.

Eldeorin nodded. "It was. Did you feel like you were in full control of your power?"

"Yes. Did I pass your test?"

He smiled widely. "You passed two tests. You moved the pearl, and you used your magic near a Mori demon without losing control."

"Because you put a ward on me to stop that from happening," I reminded him.

"I removed the ward before we walked over here," he said casually.

"What?" I yelled. "I could have killed her."

He fluttered a hand dismissively. "I would not have let you harm her. The world is too interesting with her in it."

"Thanks," Aunt Jordan said dryly.

"Does that mean I no longer need the ward?" I asked.

"We will see how you do after a few more sessions," he said. "But it might be wise to leave it on you until you go through liannan."

I tucked my hands into my coat pockets. "Will it stop me from losing control of my magic during liannan?" I still wasn't convinced I would go through liannan. Mom went through hers when she was a year younger than

I was now. She'd started showing signs of it a few months before it came. I hadn't seen one indication it was near.

He shook his head. "It will stop your magic from having accidental outbursts, but it won't help your control when you deliberately use your magic. That you will learn from practice."

Mom laid a hand on my back. "I think that's enough for today. We'll pick it up again tomorrow."

Eldeorin gave me an approving look. "You did well today. I will see you tomorrow."

He disappeared, and Aunt Jordan shook her head. "He hasn't changed at all."

"I doubt he ever will," Mom said with a laugh.

"Did you come to train?" I asked Aunt Jordan. I was more tired than usual from the magic session, but I wouldn't pass up a chance to work with her. She pushed me hard, and it helped me channel the pain for a little while every day.

Her mouth turned down. "Yes, but I also bring unhappy news. The Council has evidence of an active Lilin in Berlin, and they need us there."

My shoulders slumped. I knew she and Uncle Hamid couldn't stay here indefinitely, but I'd hoped for a few more weeks with them.

"When do you leave?" Mom asked.

"Tomorrow morning." Aunt Jordan offered me a rueful smile. "We'll have to make the most of our session today. It might be a few months until I can get back here."

I managed a semblance of a smile. "It gives me time to practice everything you taught me. Next time we spar, I'll kick *your* ass."

"Them's fighting words." She mussed my hair playfully. "Let's go train while I can still beat you. I have a feeling it won't be nearly as easy next time."

"Damn it, Brontë." Dimitri's raised voice came through the open door of our shared bathroom. He strode into my room and held up a mangled object, which used to be a pair of snow goggles. "These were brand new. I never even got the chance to use them."

"I told you not to keep them in your room." I ran a soft cloth slowly along the length of my sword's blade to wipe away excess oil.

He huffed and tossed the destroyed goggles into the bathroom garbage can. "I'll need to order a new pair for the trip."

I held my blade up to the light to examine it. "Better buy two pairs just in case."

"Probably a good idea." He walked over to sit on my bed. "The others asked me if you're coming to Colorado with us."

"Did you tell them I'm not?" I started on the other side of the blade.

"No, because I'm hoping you'll change your mind."

My gaze flitted to him. "I won't."

"You haven't talked to any of them since..." He seemed be searching for the right words to finish the sentence and abandoned it. "They miss you."

I dipped my head and pretended to focus on my task. I missed them too, but I wasn't the same person they knew before my life shattered. I'd spent the last two months trying to put it back together, but some of the pieces were missing, and I didn't know if I could ever get them back.

"*I* miss you," he said quietly.

"I'm right here," I said without looking up.

"No, you're not." The catch in his voice made my throat hurt. "We used to be able to talk about anything, but we barely talk at all anymore. I haven't heard you laugh in so long I've forgotten what it sounds like."

Tossing down the cloth, I slid the sword into its scabbard. "I haven't felt like laughing lately."

He fell silent for a long moment. "I'm not trying to tell you how to feel. I'm asking you to talk to me and tell me what you're feeling."

"What do you want to hear?" I laid the sword on my desk and stood. "Should I tell you the best part of my day is the few seconds between when I wake up and when I remember he's gone? Do you want to know how it is to live every day waiting for the pain to end, while not wanting it to end because when it does the bond will be gone forever?"

I hadn't seen Dimitri cry since we were little, but he looked like he wanted to after my outburst. I went to sit on the foot of the bed. "It's not that I don't want to talk to you, Dima. I don't want you to feel what you're feeling now. I wish I hadn't said anything."

He cleared his throat. "I'm glad you did. I –" He looked past me at the doorway, and I knew by his expression one of our parents was there.

"Dani, we'll need to put off practice until tomorrow," Mom said, her voice giving no hint of how much she'd heard. "One of the Seattle teams found an orphan, and they requested my help with him. I'm not sure what time I'll get back."

I twisted my upper body to face her. "I hope he's okay."

"Me too." She lingered in the doorway for a moment and turned away.

An awkward silence fell over the room until Dimitri's phone rang. He went to answer it and came back a minute later. "I forgot I promised Grace I'd help her with her footwork."

"How's she doing?" I felt a twinge of guilt. I hardly saw her these days except for the times she came to dinner. She'd told me she was having a blast living at the manor.

He smiled. "You know Grace. She's already threatening to sneak into the bedroom of anyone who calls her Dimples and shave their heads while they sleep."

"She'll do it, too."

"They've all started locking their doors." Dimitri snickered. "Should I tell them there's no lock she can't pick?"

I placed my sword on its wall mount. "It won't matter. If Grace wants in, she'll get in."

His phone vibrated, and he looked at the screen. "I better go before she decides I'll look better with a buzz cut. I'll see you later."

After he left, the house was so quiet I heard one of the imps snoring in the living room. I opened my laptop and typed Julian Cross's name into a search engine, not surprised by the thousands of results. I clicked on the first one, which opened to a photo spread from a celebrity charity event two days ago. There were several photos of Cross on the red carpet with his arm around the waist of a beautiful brunette. Wearing a tuxedo and a playful, boyish smile, he looked more like a millionaire playboy than the CEO of a pharmaceutical company.

I enlarged one of the photos. Was this the face of a man capable of kidnapping and experimenting on people? We still hadn't found proof Caladrius was responsible for the disappearances, but Dad believed it was only a matter of time until we made the connection. I wished I could help with the investigation, but all I could do was wait.

"Enjoy it while you can," I said to the smiling face on the screen. "If you've hurt her, I won't rest until you pay."

The air was so frigid it almost took my breath away, and every exhale created a billowing cloud of steam. The woods, heavily laden with snow, were still and silent but for the languid murmur of the river. Standing beside the pool in the dead of night, it was easy to imagine I was the only person in this ghostly world.

The clouds moved, and for a moment, the pool was bathed in silver moonlight. It brought back a memory of another moonlit night, and I closed my eyes to will it away. Why was I here? I hadn't visited this place since Ronan left. I'd been a fool to think I was ready to come back.

I turned away from the pool, weighed down with a soul-deep weariness. I was so tired of feeling this way. He wasn't coming back. I accepted that, and I needed to move on with my life.

Snow scrunched quietly under my boots as I started home. My conversation with Dimitri that afternoon replayed in my head, and I couldn't stop hearing the sadness in his voice when he said he missed me. Wrapped up in my pain, it was easy to forget others were hurting, too. In shutting him out, I had been unintentionally punishing him for my suffering.

A low rustle snapped me out of my thoughts, and I froze midstride. I knew every sound in these woods, and that had not come from an animal.

I was not alone.

I swung my gaze in the direction of the noise and saw the outline of a figure six feet away. It blended in so well with the trees and snow it would be invisible to anyone without enhanced vision.

The tiniest movement to the left of the figure alerted me to the presence of a second person. All my senses heightened as my hand inched toward the knife at my waist.

17

I knew two things with absolute certainty. These were not Mohiri, and they did not want anyone to know they were here.

My mind raced. I was less than a mile from the lake. How had they gotten this close to Westhorne? More importantly, how the hell had they gotten past our perimeter security?

A whisper of sound came from behind me. I dove to the side, rolled, and came back up in a fighting stance four feet from where I'd been standing.

Nothing moved, but I could now make out four distinct shapes wearing white camouflage. At least one held a handgun painted to match their outfit.

"Who are you, and what are you doing here?" I demanded.

None of them spoke or moved.

My ears picked up a faint murmur from one of the people on the left, and I focused on it. It was too low to make out, but if I had to guess, I'd say it was a voice coming from an earpiece. Warriors kept theirs on a low volume because some hostiles such as vampires could hear as well as they did.

I rested my hand on the handle of my knife. "You are trespassing on private property, which I guess you know since you four are dressed in camouflage from head to toe."

In the silence, it was easy to hear the small intakes of breath. One of the people on the left moved, and the radio went silent as he stepped out in front of me. He wore a balaclava, which matched his outfit and showed only his eyes.

"Impressive," said a deep male voice. "How do you know there are four of us?"

I kept my eyes on him while tracking the other three in my peripheral. "You haven't answered my question?"

"We're on a training op. I wasn't aware we had entered private land," the man said.

"Oh yeah? What kind of training op?" I asked. "Are you with the Air Force or the Marines?"

"I'm afraid that's classified." He put his hands on his hips and moved his fingers in a subtle signal to the others. "Isn't it late for you to be out in the woods alone?"

"Not really." Every muscle in my body tensed as adrenaline pumped through me. The rational part of me said I should run home and raise the alarm. These humans could not catch me.

NO, said a part of me that had spent the last two months suffocating under a mountain of pain. It had been pent up too long, and now it simmered with fury. I didn't know what these people were up to, but it was nothing good. They dared to come into my home, to pose a threat to my family. The thought made blood pound in my ears.

For several seconds, we stared at each other. The five of us leaped into action at the same time. The leader charged me, and I sidestepped his tackle. Spinning, I landed a kick against the side of his knee and heard a crack as he went down.

Two more of the men rushed me. I evaded one, but the other managed to snake an arm around my waist. I whipped my head back and was rewarded with the satisfying crunch of his nose. He loosened his grip on me, and I slipped away from him.

I turned in time to see the third man come at me again, now with a knife in his hand. I grabbed his knife arm and twisted it upward sharply, sending the weapon flying away from us. I shoved him and delivered an uppercut punch to his jaw. He staggered, and I backed away out of his reach.

"Stop," commanded a different voice.

I looked at the last man, who stood with his legs apart and his gun pointed straight at me. I was fast, but I couldn't outrun a bullet, and this close he would not miss. My father might be almost impervious to bullets, but I wasn't.

"Kneel on the ground with your hands over your head," the man ordered. "We're going to secure you until we're done here. Behave and you'll see the next sunrise."

I didn't move. "What are you after?"

"On your knees," he said with more force.

I stared him down. "If you pull that trigger, there'll be dozens of armed and very pissed off people here in minutes. If *you* want to see the next sunrise, I suggest you and your friends run away as fast as you can." I didn't tell him my father would catch them before they got halfway to the perimeter.

"I said –" The man stared at something behind me, and his eyes widened in horror.

A demonic growl raised the hair on the back of my neck, and I turned my head to see the glowing red eyes of the hellhound standing less than ten feet away. I nearly sighed in relief as Woolf stepped from the trees, a menacing shape against the snowy background. All the men, except the one with the gun, froze.

"What the hell is that?" He swung his gun toward Woolf, who snarled, showing off his gleaming white fangs.

"That is a hellhound, and he isn't too happy about the gun in his face. I'd lower it if I were you." I scanned the trees for Hugo. They never went anywhere without each other.

Woolf walked slowly toward me, and the man backed up. "Call him off, or I'll shoot."

"I can't. He won't back off as long as I'm in danger."

Woolf reached my side, and I put a hand on his back. His hackles were raised, and his muscles were bunched, ready to attack.

He whipped his head toward the other men. One of them had a bloody balaclava and held a gun. The three men were focused on us, so none of them saw a second pair of red eyes glowing in the darkness behind them.

The man with the bloody balaclava trained his gun on us. A warning growl rumbled from deep within Woolf's chest, and he moved to put himself between them and me.

The crack of gunshots split the air and echoed through the woods. Woolf jerked and made a sound between a cry and a howl. Before my mind could register he had been shot, Hugo burst from the trees.

All I saw was fur and fangs as the two hellhounds pounced. A man's scream became a gurgle, which ended in a snap. Another gunshot rang out, followed by more screams and the sickening sound of ripping flesh.

As quickly as it had begun, it was over, and I was left standing in the aftermath of a bloodbath. My stomach roiled at the scene around me. Two of the bodies had their throats ripped out, and a third lay with his intestines spilling out into the snow. Swallowing down bile, I looked for the fourth man and found him crumpled in a heap a dozen feet from the others like a toy tossed aside by a dog. His head was twisted at a grotesque angle, and one of his arms ended in a bloody stump below the elbow.

I staggered a few feet away from the bodies and threw up. Wiping my mouth, I went back to the hellhounds, who looked like they had bathed in blood. Hugo stood beside Woolf, who sat on his haunches calmly licking his paws. I decided to wait until they were no longer covered in gore to hug them.

"Dani," shouted my father from a distance. "Dani, where are you?"

"I'm here," I called.

A minute later, he sped toward me. He came up short when he saw the bloody carnage. "*Iisus Khristos.*" He ran to me. "Are you hurt?"

"I'm okay," I reassured him. "Not a scratch on me."

He pulled me into his arms. "I heard those gunshots, and when I checked your room, you weren't there. It scared the hell out of me."

"I'm sorry," I mumbled against his shirt.

"Can you tell me what happened?" he asked.

Before I could answer, Grandfather arrived. He took one look at the scene and hurried over to us.

"She's okay," Dad told him.

"What happened here?" Grandfather looked around at the corpses. "Who are they?"

Dad let me go. "A better question is what were they doing here."

"They didn't say." I avoided looking at the bodies while I told them about my encounter with the four men. "I should have tried to use my magic to stop them or run for help instead of confronting them. If I had, they wouldn't be dead."

"This is not your fault," Dad said. "These men snuck onto our land with weapons and attacked you. Hugo and Woolf protected you in the only way they know how."

"You said one of them was speaking on a radio? That means there are more of them either on our land or close by." Grandfather took out his phone and called Dax to apprise him of the situation and to request drones and two teams to sweep the entire valley.

"I'm going to take Dani home. I'll be back," Dad said to Grandfather, who bent to search the nearest body.

I shook my head vehemently. "I'm staying. They're dead, and I'm safe with you and Grandfather."

Dad handed me his phone. "Call Dimitri, and let him know you're okay. He wasn't happy when I made him stay behind."

I called Dimitri and filled him in as Dad and Grandfather went through the pockets and packs of the dead men. They found nothing but weapons and gear until they searched the man I assumed was the leader.

Dad took a device from one of the pockets and held it up for Grandfather to see. "Could be a signal jammer. It would explain how they got past the sensors."

Grandfather took it and studied it. "This is advanced tech, better than what the intelligence agencies use."

"It had to be to disable Dax's sensors. We'll need to upgrade our security," Dad said as he resumed searching the body. He reached into an inner pocket and pulled out a touch screen storage device with a cracked screen. "I'll see what Dax can do with it."

He stood. "No identification on any of them. They look like military or ex-military."

"The military has no reason to infiltrate Westhorne," Grandfather said. "I'll make some calls. If they are ex-military, their biometrics will be in the system."

Dad looked at me. "There's not much else we can do here. Let's get you home."

I didn't argue this time. Hugo and Woolf followed us home and lay down outside the door. I rubbed their heads and told them how brave they were before I went inside where Dimitri waited for us.

I went to shower, leaving Dad to answer Dimitri's questions. I grimaced at my reflection in the bathroom mirror because I was covered in blood spray. Stripping, I tossed my clothes in a heap to be thrown away and stepped under the hot water. I couldn't stop thinking about what happened. What were those men looking for? If I hadn't come upon them, would they have gotten what they were after?

Mom was sitting on my bed when I left the bathroom. She had planned to stay in Seattle overnight, so Dad must have called her.

"You didn't have to come home," I said even though I was glad she was here.

"Someone attacked you. Do you think I could have slept after hearing that?"

I went into my closet to change into warm pajamas and sat on my desk chair to towel dry my hair.

"Do you want to talk about it?" she asked.

I let the towel drop to my lap. "I know I'll see a lot of death when I'm a warrior. I've already killed vampires. But it's different when you see humans die, especially like that."

Our primary purpose as warriors was to protect humanity. Even when the enemy was a human, we tried to capture instead of kill, and we turned them over to the proper authorities. I wished that had been the case tonight.

Mom patted the bed, and I went to sit beside her. She put an arm around me and rested her head against mine. "Sometimes, I wish you and Dimitri would stay young and never have to see the ugliness in the world."

"I guess the ugliness will find you no matter where you are. I just never thought it could reach us here." I lifted my head to look at her. "What do you think they were after?"

"I have no idea," she said softly. "It's 2:00 a.m. Get some sleep. Hopefully, we'll know more in the morning."

She stood and pulled back the covers for me. I got into bed, and she tucked me in like she used to when I was little.

"I don't know if I can sleep," I said when she straightened.

"Do you want me to help you sleep?" she asked.

"How?"

"Eldeorin has been teaching me." She laid a hand on my cheek. Within seconds, my eyelids grew heavy, and I yawned. The last thing I remembered was her light kiss on my forehead as I drifted off to sleep.

I stared at my mother and father. "You want to send me to Russia?"

"No." Mom smiled at me across the table the following evening. "We thought you might like to visit your grandparents and have a change of scenery. You could finish your training at Miroslav if you want, and Eldeorin and I will come there to continue your practice sessions."

I exchanged a look with Dimitri, who appeared to be as surprised by their suggestion as I was.

"This is because of what happened last night, isn't it?" I asked. "Those men weren't after me. They told me as much."

Mom shook her head. "We had already planned to talk to you about it."

As much as I loved spending time with Nana and Papa, I couldn't leave the country now. Any day, we could get a break in the investigation, and I had to be here when it happened. Dad had promised I would go with them, and that wouldn't happen if I was halfway around the world.

"I can't leave, not until we find Summer."

Dad released a breath. "We know how important that is to you, but we can't stand back and watch you suffer like this anymore."

I gripped the edge of the table. "Going to Russia won't make the bond go away faster."

"No, but being away from Westhorne might make it easier for you," Mom said.

I swallowed. "You mean being away from everything that reminds me of him?"

"Yes." She got up and came around the table to sit beside me. "You've shut yourself off from your friends, and you don't go to the manor anymore. You can't even go to training because it reminds you of him. The house, the lake, and the woods are the only places you go now."

"A fresh place with new faces will give you more freedom," Dad said. "If you don't want to leave the country, there are plenty of other strongholds you can go to. Longstone is only a few hours away."

I considered it. The Oregon compound wasn't a military stronghold like Westhorne. It resembled a small enclosed town where everyone had their own houses. It was a nice place with lots of woods and lakes to explore. It was unlikely anyone at Longstone knew about my situation, so there would be no curious stares or pitying looks.

Mom laid a hand on my arm. "You could also stay with the pack for a while if it's not too hard for you. They would love to see you."

I shook my head quickly. I loved the pack and the Knolls, but I couldn't bear to be there without Summer.

"There's another option." Dad looked at Mom, and at her nod, he said, "Chris and Beth suggested you stay with them at the New York command center. It's more restrictive than a stronghold, but they have state-of-the-art facilities, and you can continue your training under them."

Interest sparked in me for the first time since we began this conversation. New York was a vibrant, noisy city, and it couldn't be more different from Westhorne if it tried. The warriors there were too busy with their jobs to pay attention to a visiting trainee. That alone might be worth the restrictions.

I toyed with my napkin. "Running a command center is a lot of work. I wouldn't want to be in the way."

"They would not have offered if they thought that," Mom said.

"Hope they have time to take on two trainees." Dimitri interjected. The three of us stared at him, and he shrugged. "You're nuts if you think you're going anywhere without me."

"I don't need you to watch out for me," I argued. Nothing was more important to him than training to be a warrior. If he went to New York, he'd be giving up one of the best training programs in the country. Uncle Chris and Aunt Beth would oversee the training, but they couldn't dedicate their whole day to it like the trainers here did.

Dimitri quirked his eyebrows. "This is not about watching out for you.

How many trainees get the opportunity to learn at a command center, especially a big one like that? I bet not one of our friends would pass up the chance."

The look I shot him said we both knew he was full of it, but he went on as if he hadn't noticed. "In fact, now that I have the idea in my head, I'm going to be totally bummed if we don't go."

"Give it a try, Dani," Mom said. "If you don't like it there, you can come home."

I dipped my chin to think about it. Leaving home would not stop the pain, but getting back to training in a new place might help. It certainly couldn't hurt.

Dimitri's expectant face was the first thing I saw when I raised my head, and his mouth curved into a smile before I even had a chance to speak.

"Okay. I'll go."

My foot connected a few inches from Mason's groin, and he froze out of instinct as if bracing for the pain. It was all the distraction I needed. I moved in and struck the side of his knee with my shin then followed it with a rapid leg sweep. I was on him before he hit the floor, hooking my legs around his and pinning him face-down on the mat.

Hoots filled the training room as I released him and stood. I extended a hand to him, and he accepted it with a sheepish smile.

He straightened his T-shirt. "How the hell do you move so fast?"

Dimitri tossed me a towel, and I blotted the sweat from my face. "Genetics."

"Pay up, Mason," called a warrior named Brock, who looked like he belonged on the cover of a surfing magazine.

Mason shot his friend an accusatory look. "You knew she was that good when you made the bet."

Brock grinned. "You know I only bet on a sure thing."

"Well done, Dani." Uncle Chris's eyes shone with pride when Mason and I walked over to join them. "I swear you get faster every day."

"Not fast enough to beat you," I said, reaching for my water bottle.

"Give it time." He tipped his chin at Mason. "Thanks for helping out."

Mason ran a hand through his mussed black hair. "Happy to. I like to have my ass handed to me occasionally. Keeps me on my toes."

"I'll let Beth know." Uncle Chris smirked at him. "She'll be happy to do that for you."

Mason held up his hands. "Let's not get carried away. I suffered enough at her hands when we were kids."

Laughing, Uncle Chris looked at Dimitri and me. "Good job, you two. Let's call it a morning."

I retrieved my sword from the wall rack, and we left the training room. Across from us, a four-person team stood in front of a row of lockers, gearing up for patrol, while another team stowed their gear away. A few of the warriors called to Chris as we passed them.

Mason and Brock went to chat with the other warriors. Dimitri, Uncle Chris, and I walked to the stairs at the end of the floor. The building had an elevator, but it was only used for moving stuff between the floors.

Uncle Chris stopped at the door on the second-floor landing. "Get cleaned up, and we'll do our call."

Dimitri and I continued to the fourth floor. Entering my room, I hung my sword on the wall and grabbed my toiletries and a change of clothes. My room didn't have an en suite, so I headed to one of the four communal bathrooms on our floor.

Ten minutes later, I stood by my window and brushed my damp hair. I stared absently at the buildings across the street and listened to the traffic below. Three weeks in New York City, and I still wasn't used to not seeing trees outside my window. The city was big and exciting, and I loved the diversity, but I still preferred the forest, the wide-open spaces, and the fresh air.

I wrinkled my nose. The thing I disliked most about New York was the smell. The humans here didn't seem to notice it, but it was overpowering for my heightened sense of smell. It changed slightly depending on what part of the city you were in, but the mingled odors of garbage, exhaust, and human waste were always present to some degree. Aunt Beth said it was a lot worse in the summer, and I didn't know how any warrior could stand it.

I pulled my hair back into a ponytail and took the stairs to the second floor. The building had four stories and a private underground garage. The first floor housed the training rooms, weapons, gear, and holding cells. The third and fourth floors were living quarters. The second floor was the heart of the command center. It held the control room, medical ward, kitchen, and living area. Any warrior who wasn't on a job or sleeping could usually be found there.

Dimitri waved to me from the office off the control room. I entered the room where Aunt Beth and Uncle Chris sat on a couch waiting for me. Dimitri closed the door, and we all sat facing a large wall screen.

I'd barely gotten comfortable when the screen lit up and my father appeared. A moment later, my mother sat beside him. We saw Mom four times a week when she came for my magic training, but twice a week, we did a group video call. Dad kept us up-to-date on the investigation, and we showed him Dimitri and I were doing well.

"We have news about Caladrius," Dad said after our usual greetings. "Valstrom finished reverse engineering their diabetes drug Nexovir."

I held my breath as the room went silent. Weeks ago, the Valstrom scientists discovered an unknown compound in the drug, but it didn't match anything in their database. They had been trying to identify it ever since.

Dad didn't keep us in suspense. "The mystery compound they've been studying is a hormone secreted from the pancreas of a Sati."

"A Sati?" Uncle Chris echoed.

"What's a Sati?" Dimitri asked. He looked at me, and I shrugged. It was impossible to remember every single species from our books.

Dad leaned back in his chair. "It's a primate from the mountains in China. It resembles a gray, hairless chimpanzee."

"With claws and fangs," Uncle Chris added. "Why did it take so long to identify it?"

"Valstrom said the hormone has been genetically modified so it's almost unrecognizable," Mom said.

"Putting aside the fact they know about the existence of a hairless primate from the mountains in China, why would they want one of its pancreatic hormones?" Dimitri asked.

"Insulin." I looked from Mom to Dad. "The pancreas produces insulin."

They nodded.

"This is proof Caladrius is doing illegal experiments," I burst out. "What are we going to do?"

Dad rubbed the back of his neck. "We've been over their lab twice, and we found nothing there. They have a secret lab somewhere, and we have to find it."

"It could be anywhere." My shoulders fell. Caladrius had proven to be smart and evasive. I had no doubt Dad would get them, but it could take months. What if Summer didn't have that long?

"Do you think they know you're onto them?" Dimitri asked.

"Yes." Dad picked up something and held it for us to see. It was a headshot of a thirtysomething dark-haired man in military fatigues. "Of the four men who tried to sneak into Westhorne, he's the only one we've been able to identify. His name is Austin Cain, and he's an ex-Marine. After he left the military two years ago, he completely went off the grid."

"Austin Cain was working for a private security firm under the name

Dean Roberts," Mom said. "One of their clients is Caladrius Pharmaceuticals."

I sat up straighter. "I knew it."

"So, now you'll question Julian Cross?" Dimitri asked.

Dad tossed the photo on the desk. "When we find him. He was supposedly on a ski trip in France, but it turned out to be a body double. The last time the real Julian Cross was seen was at a charity event four days ago."

"He's too well known to disappear for good," Aunt Beth said. "I find it hard to believe he would abandon a billion-dollar company after what he did to make it a success."

Uncle Chris nodded. "I agree. From what I've seen of him, he enjoys the limelight too much to give it up."

"Someone in the company must know where he is," I said in frustration.

"We'll find him," Dad assured me. "If he's hiding it's because he knows we are getting close."

A knock sounded on the door, and Mason stuck his head in. "Sorry to interrupt. We got a call from the wrakk in the Bronx. They have six Gulaks tearing up the place."

"It's always Gulaks," Aunt Beth muttered, standing.

"We'll let you go," Dad said.

"Eldeorin and I will see you tonight, Dani," Mom called as we said goodbye.

Aunt Beth moved to my side as we left the office. "How is your magic training coming along?"

"Great. Mom says my control is better than hers was before liannan. Eldeorin said it's because Mom didn't train with him until after liannan. If she had, she would have had better control when her magic got stronger."

"Does Eldeorin know when your liannan will come?" Aunt Beth asked.

I grimaced. "No, but he thinks it will happen soon. You'd think it would have happened by now with all the glaen I've drunk and the time I've spent with him."

"Hey, Dani." Uncle Chris grinned at me. "Want to ride along?"

"Seriously?" I looked at Dimitri, who was almost bouncing with excitement. He and I hadn't been allowed to go on a call since we got to New York.

Uncle Chris chuckled. "We're leaving in three minutes."

Dimitri and I sped upstairs to change and grab our weapons. We were in the parking garage waiting when Uncle Chris, Mason, and Brock got there.

Uncle Chris drove, and I rode shotgun. As we left the building, I was struck by the eerie sensation of being watched. It wasn't the first time I'd felt it since I came here, but I figured someone was always watching you in a city with millions of people.

I'd never been to a demon market, and I was more excited to see it than the Gulaks. This wrakk was in a nondescript warehouse behind a strip mall. The main entrance had been moved to the back of the building to make it as inconspicuous as possible.

We parked in the back, and Uncle Chris led us into the building. I was behind him, and I came up short when I met an invisible wall. This had to be the demon ward, which kept most non-demons out. Mom told me once it was like walking through a wall of Jell-O because of her Fae side, and that was exactly what it felt like for me.

I pushed through and was met with shouts, cries, and the sound of breaking wood. Ahead of us a row of stalls blocked our view, but it wasn't hard to tell what was on the other side. Uncle Chris motioned for Dimitri and me to bring up the rear as he hurried toward the racket.

We rounded the first row of stalls, and I craned my neck to see everything as we passed by. There were vendors selling meat, produce, bread, clothing, housewares, medicine and so much more. I hoped we had some time to look around after the Gulaks were taken care of.

I had never seen so many demons in one place. There were Vrell demons, gray-skinned Mox demons with long, white hair, pale Femal demons with red eyes, short, furry, orange-eyed Quellar demons, and a few short, thin Ranc demons with small curved horns.

Everyone watched us as we ran by. At one time, it had been rare to see a Mohiri in a wrakk, and demons would have never contacted us for help. My mother changed that when she forged a connection with the demon community years ago. Most of them loved her, and they even had a special name for her. They called her *talael esledur,* which meant "kind warrior."

We found the Gulaks in the next row where they had destroyed four stalls and beaten up the owners. One Gulak had a Quellar demon by the throat, bellowing for the much smaller demon to pay up or else.

"I don't think your protection services are required here anymore," Uncle Chris called.

All six Gulaks looked in our direction, and the one holding the Quellar demon dropped him. I thought for sure they would back off when they saw five armed Mohiri, but no one ever accused Gulaks of being smart. They grabbed the cutlasses they wore on their hips and faced us.

Dimitri and I stayed back when Uncle Chris, Mason, and Brock advanced. The Gulaks became emboldened when they realized they had to fight two less warriors. They growled and charged.

Uncle Chris met the first one in a clash of blades. He was so fast he disarmed the Gulak before the demon knew what was happening. The Gulak, realizing he didn't have a prayer of winning, spun and ran away. At this rate, it was going to be a short fight.

"Excuse me," said a timid voice behind me.

Dimitri and I turned to face a female Mox demon, who looked distraught and scared. Her gaze flitted nervously between the two of us.

"Don't worry. The Gulaks will be gone soon," Dimitri told her.

"It's my daughter, Nali," she said in little more than a whisper. "I can't find her."

I glanced back at the fight and said, "We'll help you find her. She couldn't have gone far in here."

"She's probably hiding," Dimitri said. "Where did you see her last?"

The Mox demon brought us to a clothing stall in the second to last row. Her eyes darted around like she expected someone to jump her. "We were here."

We searched the area around the stall but saw no sign of the girl. We decided to split up with Dimitri going one way and the two of us going in the other direction. As we searched, the Mox demon didn't speak, except to call her daughter's name.

I stopped abruptly as we walked behind the last row of stalls. "I think I hear her." I listened again and picked up what sounded like a child crying. Fearing she had run into the fleeing Gulak, I hurried toward the sound.

The crying stopped as I neared the loading bay. The large door was closed, but a small door stood open, giving me a glimpse of the back of the strip mall. The Gulak must have run out this way.

I went to the door and looked out. A few yards to my left, a little Mox girl sat rocking on the icy asphalt with her knees drawn up to her chest. One of her sleeves was torn and stained with black demon blood.

"I found her." I pushed through the demon barrier into the cold sunshine and ran to the girl.

She raised her head and looked past me with terrified eyes. I drew my sword as I whirled to face the Gulak demon.

I felt a sharp sting in my thigh. Four men stood less than ten feet away with guns pointed at me. A wave of dizziness hit me, and I stared in confusion at the tranquilizer dart embedded in my thigh.

"I am sorry," cried the Mox female. "They said they would kill Nali if I did not help them."

I stumbled for the door, but my legs were too heavy. My legs buckled, and

18

———————

I woke to a pounding in my head so loud I couldn't hear anything else. I was lying on my right side, and there wasn't a part of my body that didn't hurt.

Cracking my eyes, I squinted until a bare white wall came into focus. My gaze slid along the wall to a tiny sink and toilet you would expect to find in a prison cell.

A prison cell? I moved to sit up and almost tipped forward onto the floor. I braced my hands on the bed and steadied myself until the room stopped spinning.

I took a few slow deep breaths and lifted my head to look at my surroundings. As soon as I did, I wished I hadn't. I was in an eight-by-ten-foot cell, which was completely white except for one wall that appeared to be made of Plexiglas. It had a slot at waist level near the door and another slot at the bottom. The door was made of the same transparent material, and I could make out an electronic lock on the outside.

Across from my cell was another one holding a Gulak demon, who was growling and banging his fists against the barrier. It took my groggy mind a few seconds to realize his banging matched the pounding in my head.

"Could you maybe stop that for a minute so I can think?" My voice came out as more of a raspy stage whisper.

The Gulak stilled, glared at me for a few seconds, and went back to making a racket. He had been quiet long enough for me to hear other growls and sounds nearby.

Standing on unsteady legs, I noticed my outfit for the first time. My clothes were gone, and in their place was a pair of pink hospital scrubs and white cloth slippers.

I walked to the barrier and touched it. It felt like acrylic, but it was warm to the touch, and there was something not quite right about it. I pressed my palms to it and felt a faint pins and needles sensation. The wall was infused with warlock magic.

Excited, I moved to the door. If they were relying on a warlock ward to reinforce the cell, I might be able to weaken it.

I summoned my magic and let it pool in my hands until they glowed. Placing them against the door, I pushed my magic into it and immediately came up against a barrier. I fed more magic into the door. My hands prickled uncomfortably, and it grew in intensity until I had to pull them away.

I wiped sweat from my upper lip. I didn't understand it. Fae magic was stronger than warlock magic, so I should be able to break through the ward. Maybe I wasn't strong enough yet. Or could Eldeorin's binding ward be limiting my magic? It was supposed to prevent me from accidentally lashing out at other Mohiri, not weaken me.

"Damn it." I slapped my hands against the door, startling the Gulak, who paused his rant to stare at me.

Feeling other eyes on me, I looked at the cell on his right and saw a Ranc demon staring back at me with catlike eyes. On his left, another Gulak paced restlessly. All three demons wore a black metallic collar.

I shivered, suddenly cold, and rubbed my arms until I realized the cold was inside my chest. It could only mean one thing – there was a vampire nearby. A sliver of fear went through me. Had I been captured by vampires, or was there a vampire in one of these cells? I sent up a silent prayer it was the latter.

Turning away from the barrier, I studied my cell, which didn't look like any cell I had seen in movies or on TV. The only word to describe it was sterile. Aside from the toilet and sink, everything in here was white. The bed was nothing more than a mattress on a platform two feet off the floor with white blanket and a thin pillow.

The walls were bare except for recessed lighting and small vents along the top. Even if I could reach them, the vents were hardly big enough for a cat to squeeze through. I walked over to touch one of the walls. They were made of the same acrylic-like material, and I detected warlock magic in them, too.

I sat on the bed to evaluate my situation while trying to keep my calm. I was in a cell designed to contain someone a lot stronger than a human. The bare sterility of the cell and my outfit indicated I was in some kind of medical facility. But what kind of medical building had cells? My gut twisted as a horrifying realization hit me. These were laboratory cages, which made us laboratory animals.

Sliding across the bed, I sat with my back against the wall and my hands tucked into my armpits. I forced myself to take deep breaths and tried to calm my racing heart. Fear wasn't going to help me get out of here.

A door opened, and a chorus of shouts and growls went up as footsteps approached. I stayed on the bed and watched four male guards wearing black uniforms and helmets stop outside my cell.

One of them stepped forward and held up a pair of handcuffs. "Approach the wall and put your hands through the slot beside the door."

I sized up the four of them, calculating my odds, and decided not to risk it. Even if I managed to take them all down, I had no idea what lay beyond my cell or how many more guards stood between me and freedom. I needed to find out what I was up against before I planned an escape.

I got off the bed and walked over to the door. I stared at the guard who had spoken, but his face was impassive. "Where are you taking me?"

"Put your hands through the slot," he said again in a flat voice.

The thought of having my hands bound unnerved me, but not as much as being locked in here. Reluctantly, I did as he instructed, and he secured the cuffs on my wrists. They looked like ordinary handcuffs, but I detected the same warlock magic in them as soon as they touched my skin.

"Step back," the guard ordered. I obeyed, and he used a silver key fob to unlock the door. He held the door open and motioned for me to leave the cell.

I stepped into a long hallway lined with cells on both sides. The guards led me down the hallway past so many demons it made my head spin. In addition to the Gulaks and Ranc demons, there were Vrell, Mox, Femal, Quellar demons, and more. The last three cells contained an incubus and two vampires. The vampires bared their fangs at us, but stayed at the back of their cells. Every demon in the cells wore the same black collar.

One of the guards used a key fob to unlock the heavy door at the end of the hall, and we entered a small room with three other doors. We took the one on the right, which led to another long row of cells. The first two cells contained werecougars, and my breath caught at the sight of them. Were these the two teenagers from the Oregon pride?

After the werecougars, there were two gray, hairless chimpanzee-like creatures. I remembered my father's revelation about Nexovir containing a hormone from a Sati pancreas. If I had any doubt about where I was, it disappeared.

My steps faltered when we reached the next cell, and I saw a golden-haired werewolf inside. Wasn't the one from Montana brown? If so, who was this one? There were shaved spots on both front legs, and he wore a black metal collar. It looked like the collars the demons wore, only wider. I stared into his dull eyes and saw a wolf who had been completely broken.

Tears blurred my vision as the guards pushed me past the werewolf. I caught a glimpse of the cell across from his. It contained a sleeping black werewolf with gray around his muzzle. He wore the same metal collar, and he had a shaved patch on his hip, which showed a fresh scar. We hadn't heard about an older wolf being taken so he had to be a lone wolf.

When I saw the red werewolf in the cell across from him, a cry tore from my throat. I pulled out of the guards' grasp and pressed my hands to the barrier. "Summer?" I called to the wolf curled up in the corner facing away from us.

The werewolf didn't move. I didn't need to see her face to know it was Summer, and I banged on the barrier, calling her name. I fought the guards when they pulled me away, but they forced me through another door. I needed to get back to her and find a way to get her out of this place.

I was barely aware of us entering an elevator until it started to ascend. I looked at the button panel, surprised to see the floors were in descending order. We left level four and were going up to level two. That could only mean one thing – we were underground.

The elevator stopped, and the doors opened to a huge laboratory separated into smaller labs by glass partitions. The lab was a hive of activity, and everywhere I looked there were people in white coats. None of them paid us any attention as the guards led me through the maze of labs.

I couldn't see what any of the people were working on until we passed a lab where a group of scientists stood around a surgical table. One of the scientists moved, and I was horrified to see a Sati strapped to the table. Tubes ran from its mouth, and it appeared to be unconscious as they performed some kind of surgical procedure on it.

I pictured Summer strapped to a table like that, and I knew what it meant for your blood to boil. Magic burned hot at my core, but I had no way to release it. It didn't react to the human guards, and I wasn't strong enough to manipulate the small amount of moisture in the humidity-controlled lab. I had never felt more impotent and helpless.

We stopped at yet another door. One of the guards spoke into a radio, and after a short pause, he opened the door and ushered me into a large office. The room was a sharp contrast to what I had seen of this cold, sterile place so far. The office was decorated in warm hues with polished oak furniture. Two plush leather chairs faced the desk, and a separate seating area held a tan leather couch and a coffee table. Framed landscapes adorned the walls, and a large oriental rug lay beneath the desk. Instead of a window, a massive screen behind the desk displayed a tropical beach landscape.

The guards directed me to sit in one of the chairs and shackled my legs. Then they left, closing the door behind them.

A door on the side of the room opened, and none other than Julian Cross walked in. He wore dress pants and a gray shirt, and he smiled like he was in front of the cameras at a celebrity gala.

He crossed the room to sit on the edge of the desk five feet away from me. "Danielle, it is such a pleasure to meet you," he drawled in a smooth southern accent.

"Excuse me if I don't shake your hand." I held up my cuffed hands. Inside, I was trembling with rage. If my legs weren't shackled, I would jump out of my chair at him.

He assumed an apologetic expression. "You'll have to forgive me. A man in my position cannot be too careful with security."

"I imagine kidnapping and experimenting on people creates a lot of enemies," I retorted.

Julian's smile slipped a fraction, but he recovered quickly. "We don't experiment on people. The work we do here helps people."

"Tell that to the prisoners in your cells."

"Those are not people. They're inhuman." He looked so incredulous I thought he truly believed it – or maybe he told himself that so he could sleep at night.

I glared at him. "Most of them are intelligent beings capable of the same emotions as any human. That makes them people. When shifters are in their human form, they are essentially human. Even a doctor would have trouble telling them apart."

"Let's assume you are right. Don't you think the millions of people our research will save is worth the sacrifice of a few?"

"How many is a few? Hundreds? Thousands?" I fought to keep my anger in check. "And what gives you the right to decide that?"

Julian sighed and stared at one of his paintings. "I wish I could make you see how important our work is. For centuries, scientists used animals in their research for the good of mankind. This is merely the natural evolution of science."

"And if it happens to make you and your shareholders a lot of money, that's a side perk," I said.

"I'm sure you have heard the adage 'It takes money to make money.'

Research and development are expensive." He raised his hands and gave me a *what can you do* smile. "And shareholders do expect good returns on their investments."

There was so much I could say to him, but it wouldn't change his mind or convince him to stop. He could spout all the BS he wanted to justify his actions, but we both knew this was about making money. People like him could never have enough, and they'd do whatever it took to make more.

"Where do I come into your grand plan?" I asked between clenched teeth. "Am I a person?"

His eyes widened. "Of course."

"Then why am I here?"

An excited gleam entered his eyes, and he walked around the desk to sit in his chair. "I have over a hundred specimens of various species here, and my people bring me a new one every week."

A hundred? Shock reverberated through me, and I almost missed what he said next.

"My people are the best at what they do, but there is one thing they have been unable to find for me, despite the unlimited resources I've poured into it." He smiled wryly. "It's my Holy Grail, so to speak."

I immediately knew what he was talking about, but I feigned ignorance.

"I'm sure you are aware of the medicinal properties of troll bile. Imagine what we could do with it." His expression became a little fanatical. "We could make pharmaceutical advances that would otherwise take decades. It would revolutionize medicine."

"What does any of that have to do with me?"

"Everything." He leaned forward and rested his arms on the desk. "I've spent the last five years trying to locate a troll, but as you know, they are impossible to find. So, it came as a shock to learn someone in the US used to sell troll bile on the black market over twenty years ago. Plenty of people have tried to sell fake bile, but this was authentic."

I clenched my hands in my lap. "Twenty years ago, I wasn't even born yet."

"No, but there was another girl." He paused for dramatic effect. "You have no idea what it took to learn her identity. First, I had to find the middleman she used to sell the bile. He claimed his source stayed anonymous, which was plausible for someone with access to troll bile. Other people, who were in the business at the time, said the girl wasn't real. She was made up to hide the seller's real identity."

Julian's expression was one of admiration now. "She covered her tracks well. Fortunately, technology has come a long way since then. We ran exhaustive searches on the dark web until we found mention of a man, Yusri al-Hawwash, who also went to great lengths to obtain troll bile. His search led him to a small town in Maine called New Hastings, to a girl named Sara Grey."

I couldn't hide my apprehension fast enough, and he gave me a knowing smile as he continued.

"We went to New Hastings and learned Sara Grey ran away from home when she was eighteen. Not a soul in the town knew where she went, but they did know of her uncle, who lives in North Carolina now. It wasn't difficult to dig into his life and find out his niece is married with twins and lives in Idaho."

He smiled, clearly pleased with himself. "Shall I go on?"

"Why stop now?"

He played with a tablet on the desk, and an aerial view of Westhorne appeared on the screen behind him. I could make out the geographical landmarks, but the manor and main grounds were blurred. So were the houses at the lake.

"Imagine my surprise to discover Sara Grey lives at a Mohiri stronghold in Idaho. It put a serious wrinkle in my plans. I thought I was dealing with a forty-year-old woman, not the Mohiri. I'm sure you know surveillance of the stronghold is impossible. All satellite and aerial photos are distorted like this one, and drone photography does not work. The entire area is protected by a sophisticated security system. In the end, we sent in a team to locate and retrieve her. Our team never returned."

Those men had been after my mother? I didn't know whether to be scared or to laugh at the idea of anyone trying to "retrieve" her. Unlike Hugo and Woolf, she would have left the men alive, but they would have woken up in federal custody or in the middle of the Sahara.

Julian removed the aerial photo from the screen. "We continued to monitor the uncle, which is how we learned Sara's twins had gone to stay in New York City. It took a few weeks to trace them to the building they were staying at. All we had to do was watch and wait for the right time to make our move."

Having managed to wrestle my emotions under control, I said, "You went to a lot of trouble to find her, but to what end? And what does kidnapping me accomplish?"

"Your mother sold troll bile at least three times, which means she knew how to obtain it. My plan was to take her and convince her to bring me to her source. That didn't work, so I made a new plan. Your mother will give me troll bile in exchange for you."

I raised my bound hands to rub my throbbing temples. "Trolls are among the deadliest creatures on the planet. Did you ever stop to wonder how a Mohiri teenager was able to get her hands on their bile? Maybe there's a reason she wasn't afraid of them."

"Are you suggesting I should be afraid of her?" he asked with a patronizing smile.

"I'm saying you should let me go before she and my father find you."

For a moment, his pleasant façade slipped, revealing the dangerous calculating man underneath. He stood and came around to sit on the edge of the desk again. "No one is going to find us. Westhorne is not the only place that can hide itself. This is an underground facility in a remote area, and it's concealed by a powerful warlock glamour. You could fly fifty feet above this place and never know it's there."

"For a man working for the good of mankind, you've gone through a lot of trouble to hide." I wondered how long he'd be smiling if I told him my mother could see through warlock magic.

"Caladrius is not the only pharmaceutical company exploring this new field of science. Our competitors have been trying for years to get their hands on our research." A beep came from his tablet, and he picked it up. He frowned and touched the screen. "I'm afraid that's all the time we have today. We will talk again tomorrow."

He stepped away as the door opened, and one of the guards came over to unshackle my legs. As we left, I looked back and saw Julian looking at his tablet as if he had already forgotten I was there.

The four guards escorted me down to the holding cells. The second they opened the door to the shifter section, we were met with loud snarling and banging. The guards hesitated, and two of them pulled out shock batons before they entered.

Something slammed into the wall of a cell, which had been empty earlier. The guards moved to the other side of the hallway as we drew even with the cell and paused to look at the crazed creature inside.

I had never seen a werewolf in such a state as this. His dark fur was matted and filthy, and he was foaming at the mouth as he threw himself at the barrier. He wore a collar like the others, and there were fresh shaved patches on his forelegs. I'd heard of werewolves going feral, but this was beyond that. Whatever tortures they were subjecting him to here had driven him insane.

"Quiet," ordered one of the guards. "Don't make us use it on you again."

"Use what?" I looked at the guard's angry face and saw fear in his eyes.

The wolf slowed for a few seconds, and then he lunged at the barrier, snapping and spraying the glass with flecks of foam. The guard who had spoken took out a device, which looked like a small remote control, and pointed it at the wolf.

He pressed a button, and I cried out as the wolf spasmed like he had been electrocuted and collapsed on the floor. The collar around his neck was lit up with small red lights.

"You monster," I screamed as I yanked my arm away from the guard holding it and threw myself at the one with the device. He wasn't expecting the attack, and he went down with me on top of him.

The other guards jumped in to pull me off him, but not before my knee landed solidly between his legs. He let out a high-pitched sound and rolled onto his side, cupping his groin.

One of my captors struck the side of my head with a baton, and I saw stars. He raised the weapon again, but another guard grabbed his wrist.

"What the hell are you doing?" the man asked. "Julian said she's not to be harmed."

"You saw what she did to Matt," argued the one with the baton.

The first man took my arm. "Doesn't matter. You know how Julian is about having his orders followed."

I tucked that bit of information away as they led me past the cells. When we came to Summer's cell, my heart sank because she wasn't there. Neither was the golden-haired wolf. I remembered the Sati in the lab and felt sick. What were they doing to her and the other wolf?

The guards brought me to my cell and shoved me inside. After they removed my cuffs and left, I couldn't stop thinking about Summer and the other wolves. They had driven the crazed wolf insane with their treatment of him and then punished him for being what they'd made him into.

If he was the Montana wolf, he'd been here over four months. No werewolf could handle captivity that long even without the experimentation. They needed to run often and hunt at least once a month, but Caladrius didn't care about that. They needed their specimens alive, not sane.

"Oh, Summer." I let the tears come as I went to sit on the bed. I had been so focused on finding her I didn't think about what mental state she'd be in when she was rescued. Would she still be the girl I knew when we got out of this place?

I thought about Mom, Dad, and Dimitri. They had to be going out of their minds with worry. Mom would have contacted Aine and Eldeorin by now, and they'd be out looking for me. The United States was a big country, and that was a lot of ground to cover, even for faeries.

We couldn't wait for rescue. I needed to get Summer away from this place.

Once I got her to safety, I would contact my parents, and we'd come back for the others. I hated to leave them behind, but Summer was my priority.

I began mentally cataloguing everything I'd seen between here and Julian's office. What route had we taken? How many other guards did I see? Was there something I could use as a weapon? How would I get my hands on one of the key fobs the guards carried?

I needed to see more of this place. Hopefully, Julian would send for me again and give me an opportunity to plan an escape.

I lay down on my side and closed my eyes. "Hold on a little longer, Summer. I'm going to get you out of here."

<hr>

Julian wasn't alone when the guards took me to his office the next morning. A petite young woman with a spiky blue pixie cut lounged on the couch in his sitting area. She looked to be in her early twenties and wore an oversized T-shirt and black jeans. She didn't take her eyes off the book in her hands when I was escorted in and deposited in the chair I'd used yesterday.

"I hope you slept well," Julian said as he took his seat behind the desk. Today he wore jeans and a blue shirt, and the wall screen showed the New York City skyline.

"I can't remember having a more comfortable bed," I replied dryly.

He smiled. "Perhaps we can find you nicer accommodations."

"Why do I think there's a big *if* attached to that offer?" I asked, noticing an air of anticipation around him. He wanted something from me.

He leaned back in his chair. "It occurred to me after you left yesterday that maybe your mother isn't the only one in your family who knows where to find troll bile. That seems like something she would share with her daughter. If you were to help me obtain some bile, there would be no need to involve your mother. I'd have what I want, and you'd be back with your family before you know it."

"You're going to let me go, knowing I know your identity and what you are doing here?"

"Well, no." He chuckled. "I have someone who will take away your memories of your time here."

I glanced at the blue-haired girl, and Julian waved a hand dismissively. "Not Willow. She has a different set of skills."

Willow looked up from her book briefly and went back to reading. Her eyes were as blue as her hair, making me suspect she must have colored contacts.

Other than faeries, there were two beings I knew of with the ability to alter memories. A warlock could do it, but it would take a very powerful one to mess with a Mohiri mind. A Hale witch would drive a Mohiri insane in the process, and I didn't think Julian wanted that outcome.

"A warlock?" I asked.

Julian nodded. "He's the best money can buy. Any employee who leaves this facility has their memories modified."

"Do they know that?"

He gave me a conspiratorial smile. "No, but they are compensated well for their time here. And the process is quite safe."

A new realization struck me. He thought I was a normal Mohiri, and he had no idea warlock magic wouldn't work on me. I might not be strong enough yet to physically get through the wards here, but I could detect them. If a warlock somehow managed to get inside my mind, he wouldn't be able to mess with it.

Armed with this new information, I lifted my head. "And if I can't tell you where to find the trolls?"

"Then I'll go with my plan to trade you for your mother's help. But I hope that will not be necessary." He stood and went to a sideboard to pour himself a glass of amber liquor. "Would you care for something to drink?"

"No, thanks."

He returned to his chair and took a sip of his drink. "Tell me, Danielle, have you ever seen a troll?"

Remy's face flashed in my mind. "In drawings."

"Not in person?" Julian asked.

"No."

He ran a finger along the rim of his glass. "And have you ever seen troll bile?"

"No." Again, my mind went back to Remy, but this time, I thought about the vials hidden at the back of the cave.

Julian cast a glance in Willow's direction. I followed his gaze and saw her shake her head.

"Danielle," he said, bringing my attention back to him. "Do you know what an Emote is?"

I gave a small intake of breath. "Yes."

His smile didn't waver. "Then you will understand why my friend Willow says you didn't answer either of my questions truthfully."

I didn't reply because it was no use denying it. There was no better lie detector than an Emote. Instead of being angry, Julian looked pleased. Why shouldn't he? He had finally found someone who had seen a troll. Not that it would help him because I'd never betray Remy.

"I understand why you lied about it," Julian said. "You have no reason to trust the person who is holding you against your will."

And the person imprisoning and experimenting on people, I thought.

He put his hands together as if in prayer. "What can I do to change that?"

Holding up my cuffed hands, I gave him a pointed look.

"Anything but that." He thought for a moment and touched his tablet screen. "I'm going to show you some of the work we are doing here. Once you see the importance of our research, you'll better understand why I took such extreme measures."

Nothing he showed me here could sway my opinion of him or change my mind, but I didn't say that. I would take every opportunity available to study my surroundings and figure out the layout of the lab.

The door opened, and two of the guards entered. Julian walked around the desk and started to extend his hand to me in some warped display of gallantry. I stood quickly before he reached me, pretending I didn't see his gesture. If he touched me, I wouldn't be able to hide my disgust or contempt for him.

He stopped and dropped his hand. Smiling, he waved at the door. "Shall we?"

I began to step around the chair, which put me within arm's reach of him, and I stumbled as shock coursed through me.

Julian Cross was a demon.

19

Julian reached out to steady me, but I moved away. It took a supreme effort to smile and act as if nothing was wrong.

He was a demon, but what kind? I'd know if he was a vampire, and he didn't have the eyes of an Incubus or Tana demon. What other demons had a human form? None I could think of.

"Are you okay?" he asked, sounding almost sincere in his concern.

"Yes." I rubbed my forehead as if it hurt. "I'm a little dizzy from the blow to my head yesterday."

His brows pulled down. "You took a fall?"

"One of the guards hit me with his baton on the way back to my cell," I said, grateful now for the distraction.

Julian's face hardened as he spun toward the guards at the door. "Is this true?"

One of them spoke. He was the guard who had stopped the other one from hitting me again.

"She attacked Matt when he shocked the crazy wolf, and Donovan struck her," the guard explained. "It won't happen again."

"See that it doesn't," Julian said in a voice that sent a chill down my spine.

"Yes, sir." The guard opened the door for us, and I walked out ahead of Julian, careful not to touch him. Most demons couldn't sense Mom's Fae magic when it was dormant unless she made physical contact with them. The same had to be true for me.

Julian told three of the guards to stay behind because he didn't want too many of us crowding the labs and interrupting work. He walked beside me, and the single guard fell in behind us.

I was torn between worrying Julian would brush against me and dreading what I would find in the labs. If I saw Summer strapped to a table, I was going to lose it.

Julian steered me toward a lab where a woman in a white coat studied something under a microscope. In a corner of the lab stood a stack of four small cages, each containing a rat-like creature with yellow eyes and large curved incisors.

"Did you know Bazerat stem cells have ten times more regenerative ability than human stem cells?" Julian asked. "We are on the cusp of developing a treatment to regrow cells destroyed by brain damage. Imagine a stroke victim or someone with a traumatic brain injury able to regain full brain and body function."

We moved to the next lab where two people were comparing MRI images from two brain scans. I couldn't see a difference, but whatever the scientists saw excited them.

"These are before and after scans of someone with frequent migraines," Julian explained. "The test subject is on a protocol we developed to prevent migraines."

I stared at him. "A human test subject?"

He laughed. "We have several employees who suffer from migraines. They volunteered to take part in a preliminary trial."

The next three labs we visited were working on projects to help with chronic pain, obesity, and asthma. At each one, Julian made sure to mention how millions of people would be helped by the drug. I wasn't unsympathetic to the people suffering from these conditions, but Julian's methods were cruel and unethical.

As we did our tour, I mapped the layout in my mind. There were two elevators and two doors, which led to stairs, and they all had guards posted near them. Every door required a key fob to open it, which meant I needed to get my hands on one of them. There were security cameras around the lab, but not as many as I'd expect in a place like this. Julian must have decided he didn't need them here. It wasn't likely someone would break into their secret underground facility.

An older woman in a lab coat called to Julian, and we entered her lab. The security guard stayed outside as he had with every lab we'd visited. I didn't know if guards weren't allowed in the labs or if, like me, he didn't want to see what happened there.

Julian and the woman went to a workbench where she had some papers laid out and began a discussion. Squeaks drew me to another workbench next to a tall refrigerator with glass doors. I found a cage with a large towel draped over it. The front of the cage was uncovered, allowing me to see it was full of naked imps.

Having grown up with Eliot, Orwell, and Verne, it was easy to forget most imps were wild, mean little demons. This lot squeaked angrily and bared their sharp little teeth at me. Some of them made rude gestures, which made me smile. Most people considered imps vermin and didn't see them as intelligent creatures despite their humanlike mannerisms.

"Stay away from those," the woman barked. "They are part of an important project I'm working on."

"Just looking," I called back.

She resumed her discussion with Julian, and I turned back to the imps. There had to be more than three dozen of them crammed into the cage, which gave them little room to move around. Attached to the bars were a water bowl and a food feeder. The feeder contained something that looked and smelled like canned dog food, and I wasn't surprised to see it hadn't been touched.

My lips pressed together at their state of undress. Imps normally wore loincloths, additional proof of their rational thinking. These imps had been stripped of what little clothing they had and were being treated worse than lab rats.

I moved a little closer to the cage, setting them off in a flurry of squeaks and chattering. Under my breath I said, "Quiet."

The imps went still and gaped at me, not because I'd spoken to them, but because I'd spoken in their language.

I didn't realize what I was going to do until I began formulating a plan. I whispered the word for *free*. A few imps stirred from their shock and nodded fervently.

"Move back," I whispered.

The imps stared at me in confusion for a few seconds then crowded at the back of their cage.

I shot a glance at Julian and the woman, who were still poring over her papers. Satisfied they were distracted, I summoned the magic in the water bowl. The imps froze, and their eyes rounded with fear when they sensed Fae magic, but I had no time to reassure them.

After all my practice with Mom and Eldeorin, it was easy to draw water from the bowl and feed it into the lock on the cage door. I concentrated on the lock, and in my mind's eye, I saw the internal mechanism. It was a basic cylinder lock, and I would have opened it in seconds with a pick.

Julian's voice broke my concentration. He and the woman were no longer bent over the papers, and they appeared to be finishing their conversation.

I focused on the lock again. Six inches separated me and the cage, so if anyone looked this way, they would see I wasn't touching it. The cage itself was hidden from view by the refrigerator.

The lock clicked as Julian told the woman he'd schedule a meeting for tomorrow. Sensing freedom was near, some of the imps started for the door, but I couldn't have them spilling from the cage while I was there. I pulled the water from the lock, pooled it around the door latch, and froze it.

The imps ran at the door and tried to push it open, but it wouldn't budge. They glared at me, and I whispered, "Soon" as I walked toward Julian.

My heart raced a little as we left the lab, and it felt good to not feel totally helpless. I didn't know if freeing the imps from the cage would help them, but at least they had a chance.

Ten minutes after we continued our tour, shouts rang out across the floor. Julian hurried toward the noise, and the guard pushed me after him. It wasn't long before I saw the first little bald demon running along the top of a glass partition.

I hid my smile at the chaos around me. There were imps everywhere and people running after them. Unfortunately for the lab workers, imps were fast and good at hiding. In a few hours, they'd find a way inside the walls, and it would be all over.

"What is going on here?" Julian shouted as an imp ran between his legs. "Aubrey?"

The older woman hurried toward us, red-faced and holding a paper towel against a bleeding cut on her right hand. When she saw me, her lips curled.

"You did this," she bit out. "You freed them."

"Me?" I injected confusion into my voice.

Julian held up a hand. "Danielle was with me. She couldn't have done it."

Aubrey shook her head. "She must have unlocked the cage while you and I were talking. You heard me tell her to stay away from them."

"How? Telekinesis?" I showed her my cuffed hands.

"I don't know how, but you did it," she snapped.

Julian stepped between her and me. "Aubrey, if she unlocked the cage, the imps would have escaped before we left your lab."

"Then how did they get out?" she pressed. "I locked the cage myself this morning, and she's the only other person to go near it since."

The guard spoke from behind me. "There is a security camera near your lab. Maybe that will show how they got out."

Aubrey shot me a smug look. "Excellent idea."

How could I have forgotten to check for cameras? If Julian discovered what I could do, I might end up on a table in one of these labs.

"We can check the footage in my office," Julian said.

On the way back to his office, I frantically thought about how to explain away whatever was on the camera. I had come up with nothing by the time Julian picked up the tablet on his desk and brought up the security app. I glanced at the couch, but Willow was gone. I hoped Julian didn't call her back to verify I was telling the truth.

"Here it is." He pressed something, and a camera security feed appeared on the large screen. It showed most of Aubrey's lab including the cage, but the angle of the camera didn't capture the front of the cage. I tried to remember if I had touched it at all.

Julian went back to the moment we entered the lab. While he was speaking to Aubrey, I looked around and walked over to the cage. We could hear the imps making a racket and then going quiet. I moved closer, and Aubrey could be heard telling me to stay away from the imps. After that, I appeared to watch the imps until I left with Julian.

I let out a breath as Julian stopped the video and looked at Aubrey. "As you can see, she didn't touch the cage."

Aubrey still didn't look convinced, but there was nothing she could do other than complain about having to redo the experiment she'd been working on for weeks. She cast me a glare as she stomped out of the office.

"That tour was more exciting than I planned," Julian joked. "I hope you came away with a better understanding of all the good we are doing here."

"I did," I said, deciding it was better to placate him a little.

The corners of his mouth turned down playfully. "But you still don't trust me."

"Would you if you were in my shoes?"

His smile was a little more forced than usual. "I will just have to work harder to convince you."

I thought about Summer and the other wolves in the cells below, and it was all I could do not to tell him nothing he said would convince me. He was only letting me out of my cell for these meetings, and I couldn't afford to anger him.

His phone rang, and he answered it. He frowned at whatever the person on the other end said to him. "How did they get in there?" Pause. "No. That is sensitive equipment. Wait for me."

Hanging up, he said, "It looks like I'll have to cut our time short today."

I almost smiled at the note of aggravation in his voice. I didn't have to ask who *they* were. Freeing the imps had been worth the risk of almost getting caught. I hoped they wreaked havoc and gave him nothing but headaches.

The four guards escorted me to the elevator. I had to suppress a grin when a harried-looking young man ran past chasing an imp clutching a USB drive in his tiny fist.

I thought about Summer as we neared the cells. She was in her cell when the guards came to get me earlier, but she had been unresponsive when I called to her. I wished I could let her know I was here and she was no longer alone.

Summer was still asleep when we entered the shifter section. What were they doing to her? She had lost weight in captivity, and her once lustrous fur was dull. It gutted me to see her like this, and it made me so enraged I wanted to turn this place into rubble.

The crazed werewolf was going nuts in his cell again, and a guard took out the controller they'd used yesterday to activate his collar.

"Don't," I pleaded. "Can't you see he's in pain?"

The guard paused with his finger over the button. Before he could decide what to do, the wolf stopped ranting and stood quietly with his head down like he had yesterday.

"I think he likes you," another guard joked.

The guard holding the device lowered it. "So, all it takes is a pretty girl to get your attention." He walked over and tapped on the glass. The wolf slammed into the barrier, and the man jumped backward, causing his friends to snicker.

Back in my cell, I paced the floor, trying to make sense of what I'd learned today. How could Julian be a demon? David and Kelvan had scoured his life and his family history back to his birth. He'd grown up in a prominent Atlanta neighborhood, attended high school, and gone to Yale. He'd had leukemia when he was seven, and his younger sister had diabetes. He claimed she was the reason he had developed Nexovir.

None of it added up, but I wasn't mistaken. He *was* a demon of some kind. Did the people here know what he was? And was he in this for the money, or did he have a more sinister plan?

My question kept me awake most of the night, and I was bleary-eyed when the guards took me to see Julian the next morning. He asked me more questions about the trolls and troll bile, and I was too tired to formulate answers that would fool Willow. By the time I left his office, he knew that I knew where to find troll bile, and he figured it was only a matter of time until he got the location out of me.

"Name your price," Julian said to me the following day after another round of questions didn't reveal the information he wanted.

I considered negotiating for Summer's release and mine, but I didn't trust him. If I showed him I cared about her, he would most likely threaten her to get what he wanted instead of letting us go. I wished I knew what kind of demon he was. It might help me understand what drove him and what he wanted most.

"Have you contacted my parents with your ransom demands?" I asked instead of answering his question.

"I'm still hoping you and I can come to an agreement. There must be something you want." He tapped a finger on his desk, and my scalp prickled with unease when his lips curved into a calculating smile. "I hear you have a fondness for the werewolves."

"They're in pain, and I have a heart."

"I think it's more than that. The guards say you call one werewolf by name." He gave me an assessing look. "How would you know her name?"

My pulse jumped, and I fought to keep my calm expression. "I know she's from the Maine pack, and she went missing in October. We've been searching for the missing wolves."

He looked at Willow, who nodded. My shoulders almost sagged in relief.

"And what of the other werewolf?" he asked. "I hear you are protective of him. You deny knowing him?"

"All I know about him is he's from Montana, and he also went missing in October. Like I said, we've been searching for them."

Julian looked to Willow again, and she confirmed I'd told the truth.

He seemed to ponder something, and I was afraid of what he would ask me next. But he told me we were done for now. When the guards escorted me out, he called one of them back, but I couldn't hear what they talked about. He was up to something, and I was afraid to find out what it was.

When we entered the shifter section, the crazed wolf was pacing his cell. He snarled and lunged at the barrier as soon as we walked into view.

One of the guards used his key fob to open the cell across from the wolf and told me to go inside. "Julian thought you might be happier with the werewolves," he said as he removed my handcuffs.

I hid my excitement, not wanting to give them anything to carry back to him. The moment they left, I pressed my face to the barrier to see into Summer's cell, but only the front was visible from this angle.

"Summer, can you hear me?" I called softly. "Are you there?"

There was no answer. I rested my forehead against the glass. I was so close to her, but I might as well have been miles away.

I opened my eyes and looked at the wolf across from me. He was still pacing, but his growling had stopped.

"Bryce," I said tentatively, unsure if he would even remember his own name in this state.

The wolf stopped pacing, but he didn't look in my direction.

Encouraged, I said, "My name is Dani, and I'm going to do whatever I can to get you all out of here."

He didn't move or acknowledge me in any way.

"Do you understand me?" I asked and got no response.

"This would be a lot easier if you were in human form," I muttered, rubbing my tired eyes.

My head shot up. I hadn't seen any of the shifters in their human form in the three days I'd been here. I stared at the wolf's collar, which was half hidden by his wild matted fur. Could those collars somehow prevent were-wolves and werecougars from shifting? But how? The only way to stop them from shifting was silver, and I'd seen no silver on the collar – unless it was on the inside.

Please, no. I pressed my hands to the barrier, overcome by the unimagin-able cruelty of such an act. If I was right, it was no wonder Bryce was out of his mind. Silver was lethal to shifters, but the right amount would make them tired and weak without killing them. Prolonged exposure could drive them insane.

I already knew why the lab wanted to keep the shifters in their animal form. As I'd said to Julian, in their human form shifters were essentially human.

The door at the end of the hallway opened, and six guards appeared pushing a large flatbed cart. They stopped in front of my cell, but it wasn't me they had come for.

"No," I uttered when one of them held up the controller and activated Bryce's collar. The wolf jerked and collapsed, and the other guards entered his cell with silver chains. They quickly bound him, and together, they lifted him onto the cart, straining under his weight.

"Where are you taking him?" I asked hoarsely.

The guards didn't answer or glance my way as they pushed the cart out of the section. I tried not to think of what they were going to do to him. The golden wolf had been gone for two days, and I was afraid he might not come back.

Two guards came with a food cart and slipped trays through slots in the bottom of the barrier. The shifter trays held raw meat. Mine had a sandwich and a cookie. I ate and lay down on the bed to think. There was nothing else to do here.

I dozed off and woke to the sound of the guards returning with Bryce. They hoisted him from the flatbed and dumped him on the floor of his cell like he was a bag of trash. How did people become so cruel and devoid of empathy? I hadn't seen a single person in this place who seemed to have an ounce of compassion for their test subjects.

I sat on my bed and watched the unconscious werewolf. It wasn't long before he roused and tried to stand, and it took several attempts to get to his feet. He was wet, and he shook out his fur, sending water droplets everywhere.

He seemed unusually subdued, but this could be normal after they returned him to his cell. He stood facing the back of his cell, moving his head back and forth as if trying to shake off whatever they'd done to him.

I got up and walked to the front of my cell. "Bryce, are you okay?"

The wolf turned toward me and lifted his head to look at me for the first time. His beautiful amber eyes met mine, and I staggered as the world tilted beneath me.

"Ronan?"

20

It's not him.

Bracing my hands against the barrier, I closed my eyes and took several tremulous breaths. The last three months had been hell, and now I was a prisoner. It was too much, and my mind was playing tricks on me. After all this time, it was impossible for the two of us to be here in this horrible place.

I opened my eyes and looked at the floor near the wolf's feet. Slowly, my gaze moved up his front legs to his broad chest and shoulders. His fur was dark brown, but I imagined it lightening to a warm brown when it dried. I lifted my eyes to his face, and a sob caught in my throat. I would know his face anywhere.

"Ronan," I said in a raw whisper. "It's really you."

Solmi? My Mori asked plaintively. It couldn't sense Ronan's Mori when he was in wolf form, but my Mori felt my emotions. I rubbed at the ever-present ache in my chest. It had dulled since I left Westhorne, but I didn't think it would ever go away.

Ronan cocked his head, but I saw no recognition in his eyes. I thought of the golden wolf's blank stare, and terror rose in me. Was this still the Ronan I knew?

"It's me, Dani," I said in a louder voice. "Don't you remember me?"

He tilted his head in the other direction, showing he heard me, but I could have been looking at a stranger.

"What have they done to you?" It was hard to talk around the lump in my throat, but I refused to give in to tears. If I started, I might not be able to stop.

He lay on the floor, his eyes never leaving mine. Did some part of him recognize me, or was he reacting to the sound of a kind voice?

I lowered myself to the floor and sat cross-legged, watching him. *He's real,* I told myself when I began to question again if I was cracking under the stress.

But how did he get here? He was supposed to be in Alaska. How had he ended up a prisoner of Caladrius? Ronan was no inexperienced young wolf they could take easily.

"I missed you so much," I whispered. "But I would wish I never saw you again if it meant you were free of this hellish place."

I lay on my side facing him, not wanting to let him out of my sight for a second. He stared back at me, unblinking, and I prayed my Ronan was still in there.

"Please, Ronan," I begged softly. "Please, come back to me."

I jolted awake to the sound of a door opening, and it took a moment to remember why I was sleeping on the floor. I bolted upright and looked at Ronan, afraid to discover I'd dreamed the whole thing. He was still there, but on his feet, his teeth bared as he waited for whoever had opened the door.

Two guards arrived with the food cart. They slid the trays into each cell and left without saying a word. I glanced down and saw another wrapped sandwich and a cookie on my tray. On Ronan's tray was a pile of bloody meat. He ignored it, apparently having as little interest in food as I did.

I still couldn't believe it was him. I had finally accepted I'd never see him again, and here he was standing ten feet away from me.

The door opened again, and I tensed. The only reason guards would be here was to take someone away or return them to their cell. Summer had been gone since yesterday, and I prayed they were bringing her back.

The last person I expected to see was Julian Cross. He strolled up to my cell as if he was a friend popping in to say hi, but the cunning look in his eyes sent a trickle of fear down my spine. What was he up to now?

"Good morning, Danielle," he said in a jovial tone.

Ronan went berserk, slamming into the barrier so hard I thought he might break it. Unperturbed, Julian reached into his breast pocket and held up one of the controllers the guards carried.

"Tell him to stop, or I will use this," he said over the noise.

I shook my head. "I can't make him stop."

Julian's finger hovered over the button. "I think you can."

My eyes went to Ronan. I'd seen what the collar did to him, and I couldn't bear to watch him hurt like that again.

"It's okay," I called loudly. "Calm down."

Julian leaned closer to the barrier. "Maybe it will help if you use his name. What did you call him? Oh, yes. Ronan."

Ice flooded my veins, and for several seconds, I couldn't move. He knew, and he had come down here to cash in on that valuable bit of information.

"Go ahead. Tell your friend Ronan to be quiet," Julian said.

I swallowed dryly. "He doesn't know who I am. I don't think he knows who he is anymore."

"That may be so, but he does respond to you. On some level, he recognizes you or your voice."

I stepped away from Julian so I was facing Ronan fully. "Ronan, stop, please."

He continued to rage for another thirty seconds before he calmed down.

"Fascinating." Julian returned the device to his pocket. "Now that we can hear each other without shouting, let's talk about your friend. First, how were you able to lie about knowing him and fool my Emote?"

"I didn't lie. I thought he was a werewolf from Montana named Bryce. I didn't recognize him until they took him away and cleaned him up."

Julian seemed to accept the explanation. "After talking to the guards, I was very curious about your interactions with the werewolves. I reviewed the security feed for this section for the last twenty-four hours, and it was quite enlightening."

I didn't respond as I waited for him to get to the reason for his visit. He didn't make me wait long.

"Your friend Ronan is not like the other werewolves here. They have become subdued over time, but he gets more feral every day, and it takes twice as much sedative to keep him under for tests." Julian paused and looked at Ronan, who curled his lip to show his fangs. "As you can imagine, my scientists are intrigued."

I crossed my arms. "Everyone is different."

"That's what I said. But you know scientists. They are eternally curious and looking for puzzles to solve. Yesterday, they did MRI scans on him and made an interesting discovery. The scans revealed a mass of some kind in his brain." He took a small handheld tablet from his back pocket and held it up for me to see an MRI image with a shadow at the back of the brain. We thought it was a tumor, but I suspect it's something more."

I felt sick.

Julian was enjoying himself. "I could be wrong, of course. Who ever heard of a werewolf with a Mori demon? It should be impossible. But it explains so much, such as why he responds to you. Look at him." He pointed at Ronan. "That wolf wanted to rip my throat out a few minutes ago, and now he's as calm as a lap dog."

My nails dug into my palms so hard they drew blood. I was anything but calm, and I fought hard to hide it.

"I'm faced with a dilemma, Danielle," he said. "My scientists want to take a closer look at the mass in Ronan's head. However, to do this they'll need to dissect his brain."

I began to tremble with the effort to hold back the magic trying to erupt from my core. I didn't know if I could hurt Julian from behind his warlock ward. All I would do was reveal my only weapon.

Julian continued. "I, myself, relish the opportunity to study a Mori demon. But I think your friend might be more valuable alive. Don't you agree?"

I couldn't answer him. To do so would loosen my fragile hold on my rage.

"I can see this conversation is upsetting you." He tucked the tablet back into his pocket. "I'll come back tonight. That should give you enough time to think of ways Ronan can be of value to me. I'm sure you'll come up with something mutually beneficial to us both."

Julian didn't try to mask the malicious triumph in his eyes as he turned and walked back the way he'd come. He was done with all the pretense, and he was letting me know his patience had run out. Either I gave him what he wanted, or he killed Ronan.

My legs gave out the second the door closed, and I sank to the floor. I looked at Ronan, who watched me silently. If he understood Julian's threat, he didn't show it.

Cradling my head in my shaking hands, I pushed back the panic threatening to overcome me. I couldn't let them hurt Ronan. I had to give Julian what he wanted and hope it distracted him long enough for me to get us out of here.

It felt like I was about to betray Mom and Remy. But they would want me to use the bile if it meant saving us. It wasn't like I would lead Julian to the trolls. I'd tell him where to find the cave and the bile.

I lifted my head and stared at Ronan as something my mother said came back to me. Only someone with Fae magic could get through Remy's ward. Julian couldn't retrieve the bile on his own, and if I told him why, he'd know what I was. If I went with him, I might be able to escape, but I'd be leaving

Ronan and Summer here with no idea if I could find this place again. Julian was too smart to let me leave here without a blindfold. He might even knock me out for the trip.

"I don't know what to do," I told Ronan, and he cocked his head. I would have given anything to hear his voice, to have him reassure me everything would be okay.

Unable to sit and do nothing, I paced my cell, hoping an answer would come to me. The minutes turned into hours, and my desperation mounted. Julian said I had until tonight, but I didn't know when that was or how much time I had left.

The section door opened, and footsteps approached. When I saw the guards pushing the flatbed cart, I ran to the barrier. In his cell, Ronan was going wild again.

"Where's Julian?" I called to the guards. "He said he would come back."

The guards acted like I wasn't there. I pounded on the barrier and shouted at them, but they didn't say a word.

"Ronan," I screamed when they activated his collar to knock him out. I kept screaming and beating the glass as they loaded him onto the cart and took him away.

Pain tore through me, and I couldn't breathe. I was back in his cabin at Westhorne losing him all over again, and this time, it would destroy me.

A crash of metal came from behind me. I spun to face my cell, but it was empty. My gaze fell on a white object on the floor beneath the sink, and I started toward it.

Something bounded off my head and landed on the floor. I stared down at the small silver device in confusion. Was that...a key fob?

I tilted my head to look up, and that was when I knew I had lost my mind. It was the only explanation for the four tiny faces staring back at me from the air vent.

"Are you really here?" I asked stupidly.

The imps bobbed their heads. One of them chattered and pointed at the key fob. I could make out only one word. *Free.*

I snatched up the fob and hugged it to my chest. "Thank you."

The imps grinned, looking pleased with themselves. I ran to the door and tried to see the reader on the other side. I reached through the slot beside the door and stretched my arm as far as I could, but the reader was six inches out of my reach.

I frantically looked around the cell, but all I had was bedclothes and a vent cover.

There has to be something. I was too close to give up now.

One of the imps chattered and pointed at the door.

"I can't reach the lock."

He pointed lower, and I spotted the tray with my untouched meal. I picked up the tray and set it on the bed.

"Is this what you want?" I held up the wrapped sandwich. "Are you hungry?"

They nodded, and I realized I had no way to get the food to them. I sized up the vent and the distance. I could do that.

I picked up the sandwich and went to stand beneath the vent. "Move back."

They knew what that meant, and they disappeared from sight. I took aim, jumped, and threw the sandwich at the vent. It sailed through the opening, and I heard grunts as it hit the imps.

"Sorry," I called. I took the cookie and threw it, too. It skimmed past one of the imps as he stuck his head out.

He disappeared again, and I heard paper ripping as they dug into their meal. I knew I should have eaten the food myself to keep up my strength, but the thought of food made me nauseous.

I picked up the tray to carry it to the slot and stopped mid stride. My stomach quivered with excitement as I grabbed the key fob from the bed. This could work.

I went back to the slot near the door. Placing the key fob on the tray, I eased the tray through the slot and toward the reader. My heart leapt when it reached the reader.

"Careful," I said between gritted teeth as I tipped the tray toward the door. I lined the key fob up with the reader and sent up a silent prayer. I held my breath and tipped the tray more until the key fob fell forward on the scanner.

The reader chirped and clicked as the lock released. I almost dropped the tray in my excitement. I pushed the door, and I wanted to cry when it opened.

The imps chattered. I looked back at them and smiled. "Yes, free."

I hurried to the werecougar cells at the end of the hallway. They were asleep, but they came awake quickly when I rapped on the barrier. They stared at me like I was an apparition.

I held up the key fob. "We're getting out of here."

The cougars ran to each other when I freed them. The male licked the female's face, and she pressed herself against him.

"Are you Felix?" I asked the male.

He stared at me in surprise and nodded.

"I'm from the Mohiri stronghold in Idaho, and I met your sisters Fanny and Felicity in the mountains." I looked at the female cougar. "You must be Lena."

She nodded.

I tucked the key fob into the breast pocket of my top. "Do you mind if I look at your collars to see if I can remove them?"

Felix stepped up to me, and I studied the collar. I ran my hands along the metal, but I couldn't feel a release or even the seam where it joined.

"We need to find something to break them," I said. "Do they have silver in them? Is that why you don't shift?"

They nodded sadly.

"Can you still run?" I asked, and they nodded again.

"Good." I went to unlock the cell holding the old black wolf. His eyes fluttered open and closed again when I called to him. If he couldn't make it on his own steam, we'd have to come back for him.

A fresh wave of panic hit me when I walked past Ronan's empty cell. I had to find him before Julian carried out his threat. I couldn't leave here without him or Summer.

I looked down at my scrubs. If I went searching for them dressed like this, I wouldn't get far. I needed to find clothes, maybe a lab coat so I could blend in. The werecougars would have to stay out of sight because it was impossible to disguise them.

"I'm going to look for some clothes," I told them. "Wait here for me."

I started for the door at the end of the hallway and came to a halt when I saw the security camera above it. I forgot about the cameras. I didn't know if Julian had someone constantly monitoring them, but the guards would have come by now if that was the case. Either way, there was nothing I could do about it.

I went to the door and pressed my ear to it. Hearing nothing, I used the key fob to open it. I followed the route the guards always took when we left the cells and emerged in front of the elevators. On either side of them was a hallway, and I took the one on the right.

All the doors had readers, but I had no idea what waited on the other side. At the end of the hallway, I said a silent *YES* when I located a large locker room. On a rack hung a row of freshly laundered guard uniforms. I found one in my size, changed into it, and went in search of boots. I found not only boots, but a helmet, a radio, and a shock baton.

I was lacing up the boots when two people entered the room. Hidden behind the second row of lockers, I went still and listened.

"What a day," a woman groaned. "I spent the whole afternoon hunting those little demon bastards on three. The white coats are all in a tizzy because the imps chewed up a bunch of wires in one of the surgical suites. They acted like it's our fault the imps got out."

"I heard about that. At least, you weren't stuck down here in the zoo," a male voice said. "These things give me the creeps, and that big werewolf scares the shit out of me. We had to knock him out twice when we transported him today. They don't pay us enough for this."

I sucked in a breath. *Ronan.*

A helmet thumped down on a bench, and the woman said, "You won't have to deal with him much longer. One of the white coats told me he's scheduled for termination."

My boot lace snapped. The female said something else, but I barely heard it over the blood pounding in my ears.

"Yeah, that's what I was told, too. We had to stick him in the storage bay until they're ready for him," the man said.

I whipped my head in their direction. Storage bay?

"Why not leave him in his cell until then?" the female asked. "It's a lot more secure."

The man made a sound of annoyance. "Matt said Julian is playing head games with the girl to make her talk. It doesn't matter what she tells him. That werewolf will be on a slab this time tomorrow."

I shook with suppressed rage. I knew I couldn't trust Julian, but hearing these guards speak of his plan to kill Ronan made me wish I had five minutes alone with him without my restraints.

Footsteps came toward me, and the female guard said, "I'll change and meet you in the cafeteria."

"Okay," called the male as he left the room.

I had nowhere to hide, so I turned and pretended to look for something in a locker. The female gave a little gasp and stopped walking abruptly.

"You startled me," she said, laughing. "I didn't know anyone was back here."

I didn't answer, and she came closer. "Did you hear me?"

Her hand touched my shoulder, and I whirled to face her. Before she could utter a word, I had her pressed against the lockers with a hand over her mouth and the baton across her throat. She struggled, but she had no real fighting skills.

"Where is the storage bay they are holding the werewolf in? How many guards are there?" I asked in a low voice. "And if you yell for your friend, I will stick you both in the cells with the vampires."

The whites of her eyes showed, and she looked ready to hyperventilate. I lifted my hand from her mouth. "Talk."

"You go past the elevator and turn right at the end of the hall," she rasped. "It has double doors."

"What kind of security is there?"

Her throat worked. "N-none. They might have left some guards with the werewolf."

"For your sake, I hope you're telling the truth." I spun her and put her in a sleeper hold. When she was out, I divested her of her key fob, flashlight, and name tag, and put her in a small bathroom at the back of the locker room.

I did a quick search and found nothing to remove the shifter collars. Hopefully, we'd find something in the storage area.

Grabbing the helmet, I ran back to the holding cells. The werecougars were pacing the hallway when I let myself in.

"Took longer than I expected." I hurried past them to the door on the other end and unlocked it. I entered the demon section and went straight to the cells holding the Vrell demons.

I freed the first one and thrusted a key fob at him. "Free everyone – except the vampires. I'm taking my friends and getting the hell out of here."

The stunned Vrell demon took the key fob. I didn't wait for him to speak. I turned and ran back the way I'd come, ignoring the demons staring at me from their cells. Back in the shifter section, I told the werecougars where I was going.

"You better come with me," I said as I headed for the door. "You can't go anywhere here without a key fob."

They followed me out of the cells. I put on the helmet when we reached the main elevator and ran to the storage area. There was no telling when someone would discover we were missing and raise the alarm.

When I reached the double doors, I slowed and turned to Felix and Lena, who were right behind me. "There might be guards inside. I'll go first to check."

I unlocked the door and opened it. Seeing no one, I motioned for the cougars to follow me and quietly closed the door behind us.

The storage area looked like the interior of a small warehouse. The walls were lined with industrial shelving full of boxes and crates, and a forklift stood beside several pallets of boxes.

Voices and laughter came from my left, along with the clang of something striking metal. I followed the noise and peered around a corner at a sight that ignited my rage.

A cage sat in the middle of the floor. Inside the cage stood Ronan, snarling at two guards banging their batons against the bars. Their helmets were on the floor a few feet away, so I saw their amusement when one of the batons shocked Ronan, making him yelp.

"Stay here until I call you," I told the cougars, and I walked around the corner. I was almost to the cage by the time the guards noticed me.

"Tracy, I thought your shift was over," one of them said before he realized the face beneath the helmet wasn't hers. "Hey, you're supposed to be in –"

He didn't get to finish that sentence. I pulled my baton and slammed it against the side of his head. His friend went for his baton, but I was on him before he could get it out of the holster.

"How do you like this?" I ground out as I used the business end of the baton to give the guard a taste of his own medicine. His clothes protected him from the full force of the shock, but it was enough to make him spasm and collapse.

I dropped the baton and ran to the cage. The door was locked, and I had to search the guards for the key. Ronan stood quietly watching me as I unlocked the door and opened it. I moved back to let him out, but as soon as he stepped out of the cage, I threw my arms around his neck and buried my face in his thick fur. He smelled like antiseptic and chemicals, but underneath was his familiar woodsy scent.

He didn't react to my hug, and I tried not to let it bother me. For now, having him with me was enough. There were so many things I wanted to say to him, but this was not the time. We needed to find Summer and get out of this place.

I let him go and stepped back. At a sound behind me, I looked to see Felix and Lena walking toward us.

"Help me look for something to get those collars off," I said.

We did a quick search, which turned up nothing, but I did find a wall map of the facility. This place was bigger than I'd thought. The first level was living quarters, and the second and third levels were labs and a surgical area. The bottom level housed the guard quarters, storage, mechanical rooms, and the cells. There were two whole cell areas I hadn't seen, but we had no time to check them out.

I wanted to jump up and down when I saw the words NORTH EXIT on the top level near the stairwell. This was it, our way out. It would most likely be guarded, but we'd deal with that when we got there. One hurdle at a time.

"I need to find my friend Summer," I told the cougars. "She's a werewolf, and she's been gone from her cell for two days. Do you know where they might have taken her?"

Felix stood on his hind legs and placed his paw over an area on the level above us, which said OBSERVATION.

"Is that area guarded?" I asked him, and he nodded.

I puffed out a breath. "Okay. When we get to that level, you three will stay on the stairs while I go in to look for her. First, I need to hide these guards in case someone comes in."

I dragged the two guards out of sight behind the forklift. A thought occurred to me. I searched their pockets and found a collar transmitter, which I stomped to pieces with some satisfaction.

The guards were going to wake up with bad headaches, but they deserved much worse. If I had my way, everyone here would spend years in cells like the ones they'd kept us in.

We left the storage bay and made our way to the stairwell. Like the elevators, it required a key fob to gain access. I went first, hoping we didn't encounter anyone on the stairs. I was confident I could take them, but I couldn't risk a guard activating the shifters' collars. I didn't know if all the guards carried a universal controller for the collars or if there was a specific controller for each collar.

We reached the first landing without incident. I unlocked the door and went into what resembled a surgical wing of a hospital. On my right was a corridor with a sign above it, which read SURGERY. Ahead of me was another corridor lined with doors. The first one was a cleaning supply room, and beside it was a room for soiled equipment and materials to be cleaned and sterilized.

This level had low lighting, and it was quiet except for the hum and beep of machines and the murmur of voices. I walked down the corridor, and the voices got louder until I reached the partially open door of a staff lounge. Inside, two women in green hospital scrubs sat at a table drinking coffee, and they didn't spare me a look as I walked by.

I slowed at a nurses' station where a man in scrubs typed on a keyboard. He gave me a harried, inquisitive look as I approached.

"I'm checking to make sure the imps didn't come back," I said.

The man sneered. "You guys should have caught them by now. We're down to one surgical room until we get the other two repaired."

"We're working on it." I walked past him, and my pulse jumped at a sign marked OBSERVATION above three glass-walled rooms.

The first two were empty, but there was a shape draped with a sheet in the third one. I entered the room and walked around the machines hooked up to the person on the bed. My heart plummeted when I saw golden fur, not red.

"You're not supposed to be in here," barked a man from the doorway. He was the one from the nurses' station.

I left the room. "I thought there were two werewolves here."

"Dr. Clark had his moved to his private lab upstairs for closer observation." The man eyed me suspiciously. "Why do you care where it is?"

"Because *she* is my best friend," I wanted to say before I punched him out. I couldn't do either, so I shrugged. "Just curious."

I headed back to the stairs with a crushing weight on my chest. Even if I could find Summer in the maze of labs on the second level, I'd never be able to move her. There were too many people there and guards at every exit.

If it were only me, I'd attempt it, but I couldn't risk Ronan getting caught and locked up again. We'd never get another chance like this. As much as it killed me to leave Summer behind, the best thing I could do for her was escape and get help.

Ronan, Felix, and Lena watched me quietly when I rejoined them, and I shook my head. "She's not there. We need to leave without her."

I continued up the stairs, and they followed. On the second-floor landing, I stopped and looked at the closed door. Summer was in there. After all these months, she was so close, and I was abandoning her.

"I'm sorry, Summer," I whispered. "I promise I'll come back for you."

Felix nudged me with his nose, and I climbed the last flight. I was almost at the top when the lights started flashing red and an alarm rang out. I looked back at the others as a door opened somewhere below us and boots pounded the stairs.

It was time to run.

<h1 style="text-align:center">21</h1>

I opened the door and peeked out at a room with bare concrete walls and floor. Seeing no one, I stepped into the room and saw a door on my right. On my left was a set of huge steel doors with no handles. Next to them was a card reader.

The door on my left opened, and a guard ran out. "We need to lock down the stairs." He skidded to a stop. His eyes widened, and he backed up, tripping over himself. I started to give chase, but Felix ran past me and pounced on him. The guard let out a strangled scream as the werecougar pinned him to the floor.

Three more guards brandishing batons spilled into the room. They advanced on us, and one of them spoke into his radio, calling for reinforcements.

I went for the one with the radio. He brought up his baton, but I knocked it out of his hand with my stolen baton. He dropped into a fighting stance, and we traded a few blows. He was better than I expected based on what I'd seen so far from the other guards, but he was slow. I sent a kick to his midsection, and he slammed into a wall. He crumpled to the floor, and I spun to take on the next one, but Ronan and Lena had already pinned them.

I knocked out the guards with my baton as shouts echoed up the stairs. I ran to the large doors and held my key fob over the reader. Nothing happened.

I tried a few more times to no avail. *Come on.* Freedom was on the other side of this door. There had to be a way out.

A sign near the door caught my eye. THESE DOORS ARE AUTOMATI-CALLY SECURED DURING A LOCKDOWN. THESE DOORS ARE AUTO-MATICALLY UNLOCKED DURING A FIRE EMERGENCY.

"Great. Where's a match when I need one?" I spun and ran to the door the guards had used, calling to the others, "Keep them out as long as you can."

The door opened to what had to be the living quarters. A dozen or more heads poked out of open doors to see what was going on.

"Get back inside," I ordered in my most authoritative voice. "We have a situation."

I was surprised when they obeyed without question. I looked for a fire alarm to pull, but of course, they wouldn't make it that easy.

I pushed open the door to a small lounge and saw sprinklers in the ceiling. I wet my hands under the faucet and hopped up on a chair to wrap my hands around the sprinkler head. And then I summoned my magic.

Most sprinkler systems worked by detecting heat or smoke. I couldn't create smoke, so I used the water magic to heat the metal until...

Water sprayed from the sprinkler a second before the fire alarm went off. I jumped off the chair and ran back to where I'd left the others.

I'd been gone less than a minute, but it was enough time for the guards in the stairwell to reach the door. They pounded on the door and pushed at it, but they were no match for Ronan.

I reached the exit doors as they emitted a series of loud clicks and began to part. Beyond them was a concrete tunnel wide enough for a jeep or truck. I couldn't see light at the other end, but there was something better. I smelled trees.

I ran to Ronan. "Go. I'll hold them off until you get outside." He didn't budge, and I had no idea if he could even understand me. I put my hands on either side of his head. "Listen to me. They could have a controller to activate your collar. I need you to get out of their range. If you fall, I won't leave you, and they'll get us both."

What I didn't tell him was if anyone got captured, it should be me. Julian would kill him and maybe the werecougars, but I was too valuable. He needed me alive if he ever wanted to get his hands on troll bile.

The door threatened to give away under the assault, and a dozen guards could come through the other door at any second.

"Go, please," I pleaded. "You trained me. You know I can do this."

It felt like an eternity passed until he nodded. I braced my hands against the door, knowing I couldn't hold it for long, and said, "Now."

He stepped away from the door, and my arms almost buckled under the force. I gritted my teeth and held firmly as he, Felix, and Lena, ran into the tunnel. I prayed they found a way out on the other end.

"They'll be here in two minutes," said a man on the other side of the door.

I could take my chances with this bunch or wait and face twice as many. I jumped back from the door, and it burst open. Two guards fell through, and three more stood behind them. Surprise registered on their faces when they saw I was alone.

I could outrun them, but I couldn't lead them to Ronan and the others until I knew they were out. Backing away, I gripped my baton as they advanced. The guards formed a loose circle around me, but none of them attacked. They were stalling until backup arrived.

Pulling off my helmet, I tossed it aside and grinned at the guard in front of me. "Let's do this."

I lunged forward and delivered a strike to his throat. As he staggered backward, gasping for air, I faced the others and activated my baton. The crackle of electricity filled the room.

The four guards raised their batons and charged me at once. Using my baton, I blocked their attempts to shock me and launched my own attack with a series of rapid knee strikes to groins, palm-heel strikes to noses, and elbows to throats.

The door to the living quarters opened, and four more guards spilled out. The one in the lead carried a tranquillizer gun like the one used on me in New York.

"There's no way out of this," he said, walking cautiously toward me.

I grabbed the closest guard and pulled him in front of me as a shield. "There's always a way."

Hot pain shot up my calf, and my leg muscles stiffened like I was no longer in control of them. I fell to my knees as a dizzying current of electricity swept through me. Looking down, I saw one of the fallen guards holding a baton. The others began to close in.

A savage growl echoed off the walls along with the scrape of claws on concrete. The guards spun toward the tunnel entrance, but I couldn't make my body obey me. I didn't need to look to know what – or who – was there.

"Shoot it," someone shouted.

The guard with the gun swung his arm up and fired twice. His eyes bulged, and he fired two more times. Behind him, the others were scrambling unsuccessfully to unlock the door, which had closed behind them.

The shooter screamed as the massive werewolf leaped over my head. Ronan's jaws snapped the guard's neck, and he shook the man several times before tossing the limp body aside.

The guards at the door spun and came at Ronan with their batons. He swatted away one with his paw and pounced on another.

The third guard managed to press the baton to his side, but it only served to enrage Ronan further. He bit down on the guard's shoulder and threw him against the wall. The guard slammed into the concrete so hard his ribs cracked.

Ronan started toward me, his eyes wild and his snout glistening with blood. He looked like a crazed beast, but I wasn't frightened. I could never be afraid of him.

The grind of metal drew my attention to the tunnel doors. They were closing. During the fight, the fire alarm had stopped, and it must have triggered the doors to lock down again.

I tried to stand, but my legs refused to cooperate. I looked up at Ronan. "I can't walk. You need to get out before you're locked in here."

Lowering his head, he snagged the shoulder of my stolen guard uniform with his teeth and lifted me to my feet. He crouched beside me and made a chuffing sound. I could almost hear his voice saying, "What are you waiting for?"

I grunted as I grabbed my leg and lifted it over his back until I straddled him. I wrapped my arms around his neck and held on for dear life.

Ronan stood and ran for the opening between the two doors, which was getting smaller by the second. I squeezed my eyes shut. We weren't going to make it.

Cold air washed over my face, and the scent of spruce and pine filled my nose. I inhaled deeply. Nothing had ever smelled so good.

I opened my eyes as Ronan slowed to a stop beside Felix and Lena. We were inside an old building missing its windows and doors. I glanced behind me at a concrete structure, which looked like the entrance to a doomsday shelter.

Ronan went to the doorway and stepped outside into what resembled an old gold mining set from a movie, complete with a boarded-up mine entrance. There were a few dilapidated buildings and a newer one with two large doors. Around us were trees and snow, and we could see a mountain in the distance.

"There." I pointed at the building. We couldn't stay here long, but it could have a vehicle or a map to tell us where the nearest town was.

The big door was closed, but a small door beside it was unlocked. I reached out to turn the knob, and Ronan shoved the door open.

The building turned out to be a hangar. Inside, we found a helicopter and all the tools and equipment for maintaining an aircraft. There were also two snowmobiles and an ATV, but no sign of any keys. Not that it mattered because the others couldn't ride them in their animal form.

"How are they transporting all the people and equipment to and from this place?" I wondered out loud.

I was able to move my legs again, so I got off Ronan's back to look for a phone or radio. Spotting a bulletin board and a map on the wall, I hurried over to check them out. My jaw dropped when I saw the map. "You have got to be kidding me."

We were in the middle of the Yukon.

There wasn't a town within two hundred miles, at least, not one shown on this map. We might as well have been in Siberia.

A sound caught my ears, and I turned to the others, who stood behind me. Their ears were erect, and Ronan's head was swiveled toward the door.

I ran to the door and listened. In the silence, it was easy to hear the distant whine of snowmobiles.

"They're coming. Let's get out of here."

I ran outside with Ronan, Felix, and Lena at my heels, and we took off in the opposite direction. At the edge of the trees, I looked back at the buildings and stumbled when they flickered in and out of sight. It was the warlock glamour Julian had boasted about.

I memorized the angle of the lab from the mountain so I could find my way back here. "I'm coming back for you, Summer," I said and plunged into the trees.

Under the cover of the thick evergreens, there was less snow, which made running easier. I worried about the trail we were leaving, but we could do nothing about it. We had to put as much distance between us and Caladrius as possible.

Ronan took the lead, setting a pace I could match. Out of the four of us, he had the most experience in the wilderness, and he led us on a twisting route to stay under the trees, which would make pursuit more difficult. Every now and then, we heard an engine, but they didn't seem to be gaining on us.

Freedom had given the werecougars new energy, and they kept pace with us despite the collars. After a few miles, though, their breathing became labored, and I knew they'd need to rest soon. Ronan's collar seemed to have no effect on him other than preventing him from shifting.

We came to a small river and crisscrossed it several times to hide our trail. Hoping we'd lost our pursuers, I suggested we stop to drink and have a short rest. I examined their collars again, and this time I detected something I'd missed back in the lab.

"These collars are infused with the same warlock spell used in the cells," I said unable to contain my excitement. "Now that we're away from the wards, I might be able to break it."

Even in their cougar forms, Felix and Lena's surprise was evident, and I remembered they had no clue I was anything but a Mohiri. I was thinking of the best way to explain it when the sound of engines reached us.

"How did they find us so fast?" I asked as we jumped to our feet and took off running again.

The answer hit me, and I couldn't believe I hadn't thought of it sooner. It was the collars. They were tracking the collars.

The ground started to rise as we got closer to the mountains. We reached a stretch of rocky terrain, and I jumped up on a boulder to look back the way we'd come. Half a mile away, four snowmobiles sped toward us. Even if they knew where we were, they wouldn't be able to follow us on snowmobiles on these rocks.

A new sound split the air, and my breath caught in my throat. It was the unmistakable *whop-whop-whop* of a helicopter.

"Run," I yelled as the helicopter came into view.

We sprinted over the uneven ground, made treacherous by icy patches. One misstep could mean a broken leg and certain capture. None of us dared look back, but we could hear the relentless metal beast closing in on us until the thump of its rotors drowned out our labored breaths.

"Faster," I shouted. Even if I had destroyed the controller for Ronan's collar, Felix and Lena's could still be activated. We had to keep as much distance as possible between us and the helicopter.

Something bounced off a rock a foot away from me. Another object hissed past my head to embed itself in a small patch of ice directly in front of me. Horror filled me at the sight of the quivering red feathers. They were shooting tranquillizer darts at us.

I started weaving back and forth evasively and noticed the others doing the same. We put on a burst of speed to reach the trees five hundred yards away.

I yelped when a dart flew by me so close its tail brushed my cheek. Ronan, who was ahead of me, was the biggest target, but no darts went near him. Was it because they knew their darts wouldn't work on him?

They're shooting at me. I dodged a rock instead of leaping over it, and my suspicions were confirmed when a dart struck the rock. Julian didn't care about the shifters because he could always get more if they evaded him. It was me they were after.

We were twenty yards from the trees when I felt a sting on my shoulder. I yanked the dart out, but not before it injected the sedative. I ran a few yards until dizziness hit me. My limbs started to feel heavy, and I staggered.

"Ronan," I said on a gasp as my knees began to buckle.

He was beside me in an instant. His jaws closed around the back of my coat, and he lifted me until only my feet dragged on the ground. I teetered on the edge of consciousness as he carried me into the woods.

It was night when I awoke. I stared in confusion at the ground moving past beneath me. Why was I upside down? And who had taken a hammer to my head?

I moaned, and the ground stopped moving. It was a minute before the disorientation wore off enough for me to realize I was draped across Ronan's back. How the hell did I get up here?

I lifted my upper body and slid off him. I intended to stand, but my body had other ideas, and I landed on my ass. Ronan turned to look at me as Felix and Lena walked into my line of vision.

I gave them a weak smile. "I'm okay. Just give me a minute."

It took more like ten minutes for the aftereffects of the drug to wear off. By then, my backside was wet and I was freezing. It was easy to forget the cold when you were running for your life. Bracing my hand against a tree trunk, I stood on legs that were still a bit wobbly, but they held my weight.

"We lost them?" I asked hopefully.

Lena shook her head. At that second, we heard the distant thump of helicopter blades. They knew we were in the vicinity, but they couldn't find us in the trees. I stared at the ground covered in less than an inch of snow. That explained why the snowmobiles hadn't come after us.

"We need to keep moving." I took a few cautious steps to make sure I wouldn't fall on my face. "I need to walk this off and clear my head. Then I'm going to try to get those collars off you. We'll never lose that helicopter while you're wearing them."

We walked for an hour before I was strong enough to run. It took another two hours for me to get back to my normal speed. The whole time, the helicopter hovered nearby. Shouldn't they need to refuel by now? Maybe they'd done that while I was out. For all I knew, Julian had a whole fleet of helicopters.

It was starting to get light when we heard the muted roar of water. We headed that way and reached a fast, churning river a few minutes later.

"Let's stop here," I said after we'd all drunk from the icy river. I rubbed my cold hands together. "Who wants me to try their collar first?"

Felix walked over to me. I curled both hands around the collar and felt the warlock magic in it. Doubts assailed me. I'd never tried to break a warlock spell, and this was a strong one.

"I've never done this, so no promises," I told Felix as I summoned my magic.

The moment the two magics connected, I saw the intricate warlock spell woven around the collar like fine mesh. I studied it closely and discovered it was two spells, one on top of the other. I found no beginning or end and no obvious weak area to attack.

I tested a spot, and an unpleasant tingle shot up my arm. I pushed harder. The tingle became a painful burning sensation. Gritting my teeth, I tried again and gasped as invisible fingers closed around my throat, choking me.

Coughing, I released the collar. Ronan and Lena had come closer and were watching me with worried eyes.

I put up a hand. "I'm fine. The spell is stronger than I expected."

That was putting it mildly. The warlock who made the spells had to be a powerful one. My knowledge of warlocks was limited to what I'd learned from Mom and Eldeorin, but I knew it required a lot of skill and magic to layer a protective spell on top of a binding spell. I also knew I wasn't strong enough to break this spell on my own.

Fortunately, I wasn't alone. I bent to scoop up handfuls of snow, which I packed around the collar until it was completely covered. Placing my hands on it, I called to the water magic, bolstered by its reassuring warmth. I sent the magic into the collar and felt the warlock's spell attack it. It gave me the opening I needed to focus my magic on the binding spell. Without its outer layer, the spell was weaker and no match for my magic.

The snow around the collar glowed a brilliant white. The warlock spell collapsed, and a second later, the collar split in two and fell to the ground.

Jubilant, I leaned down to reach for it and paused as dizziness hit me. Shaking it off, I picked up the two pieces and got my first look at the thin veins of silver running through the inside of the collar. As I suspected, it was enough to affect the shifters without killing them.

Ronan, Felix, and Lena stared at the collar in my hands. Ronan seemed as surprised as the others, making me worry again he had forgotten me and his wolf responded to me only because of my Fae affinity with animals.

"I guess I should tell you I'm half Fae," I said lightly to Felix and Lena, enjoying their astonishment. "I'll tell you all about it when we aren't running for our lives."

I looked at Felix. "Do you feel better without the collar?"

He nodded.

"Can you shift?" I asked.

He closed his eyes and shook his head.

"You've been exposed to silver for a long time. It might take a little while for the effects to wear off." I tossed the collar on the ground. "The main thing is they won't be able to track you anymore."

He nudged Lena in my direction, and I smiled. "Okay, Lena, you're next."

She quivered with excitement as I packed snow around her collar like I'd done with Felix's. I placed my hands on the collar, but the moment I summoned the water magic, a fresh wave of dizziness washed over me. I placed my hand on Lena's back and closed my eyes as I waited for it to pass.

I looked up into Felix's anxious eyes. "I must have used more magic than I thought the first time. I think I should wait an hour or so before I do it again."

The helicopter chose that moment to swing low and circle directly above us. We had stayed in one spot for too long.

"We can't stay here. Which way should we go?" I asked Ronan.

If we followed the river downstream, we were likely to come across larger bodies of water, which meant civilization. Going upstream would bring us deeper into the mountains. It would make pursuit harder but take us farther away from help. Crossing the river meant going into the open and making ourselves easy targets for the shooter in the helicopter.

Ronan looked in both directions and seemed to weigh our options. Whatever he decided, I would go with him. I didn't want to let him out of my sight ever again.

He looked at me and started to walk downstream. I moved to follow him and stopped to snatch up the collar from the ground. "Wait." I went to the edge of the riverbank, which was hidden from above, and pitched the two pieces into the river. I watched in satisfaction as they disappeared beneath the surface.

"If they track your collar here, maybe they'll think you fell in," I said to Felix. "Can't hurt."

We ran for what felt like hours, careful to stay under cover. A few times, we had to veer away from the river when we came to a break in the trees. The whole time, the helicopter stayed with us like a predator stalking its prey, waiting for a chance to swoop in for the kill.

An hour into the run, my stomach growled, reminding me it had been almost a day since I last ate. The others had to be starving. Werewolves required twice as much food in their animal form, and I assumed werecougars were the same.

The sun was high in the sky when we reached a place where the river was wide and slow for a few hundred feet before becoming a raging torrent again. I spotted a moose drinking from the river on the other side and called for a short rest stop. There should be plenty of wildlife to hunt, and Ronan, Felix, and Lena needed to eat soon, or they'd collapse from hunger and exhaustion.

Out of sight of the helicopter, I called them all together. "Felix, you can move around without your collar. Do you think you could hunt while I remove Ronan's and Lena's collars?"

He looked at Lena, clearly reluctant to leave her. Then he nodded and ran off.

I looked at Lena. "You ready?"

She came to stand next to me, and I did everything the way I had with Felix. As it had the last time, the warlock's protective spell attacked the water magic, allowing my magic to target the binding spell.

A burst of light enveloped us and sent me flying backward. I landed on my back, stunned, and stared up at the tiny patches of blue sky visible through the tree canopy.

Ronan's big head appeared above me. I reached up and touched the face as dear to me as his human one. While his face was exactly as I'd remembered it, his amber eyes were missing their familiar warmth. I searched them for any indication he remembered me, but I didn't find one.

"Is Lena okay?" I asked hoarsely.

The werecougar came into view. I checked her face before my eyes dropped to her bare neck.

"It worked." I pushed myself to a sitting position and then to my feet. I almost fell on my ass again when I looked around me. For at least fifteen feet in every direction, there wasn't a trace of snow on the ground.

"Did I do that?" I asked and did a mental facepalm. Who else could have done it? I turned to Lena. "Did I hurt you?"

She shook her head, and some of the tension drained out of me. I walked over to where we'd been standing and picked up the two collar pieces. It looked like Felix's collar, but obviously something was different. Could the warlock spell have been stronger on this one?

I looked at Ronan's collar. I wanted to get that thing off him, but I was afraid to touch it after what had just happened. What if the warlock spell was stronger on his, too? What if I hurt him?

"Maybe we should wait a bit before I do yours," I said.

Felix ran up to us, ten minutes later, with a large snowshoe hare dangling from his mouth. He dropped the hare and went to Lena, who rubbed her head affectionately against his.

The hare wasn't going to be enough to satisfy all three of them, but it would provide some fuel until we stopped again.

A twig snapped. The four of us froze, and I trained my ears on our surroundings. It could be an animal, but I doubted it with three dangerous predators nearby. I tuned out everything but the sounds of the woods. A branch creaked in the breeze, a woodpecker drummed against a tree trunk, water trickled over rocks in the river.

Then I heard it, the quiet crunch of snow under a boot less than twenty yards away. Ronan's ears twitched. He heard it, too. How the hell had they gotten so close to us?

"Run," I whispered.

The four of us took off downriver at the same time. I didn't look back to see if our pursuers were behind us because they couldn't catch us on foot. After a few minutes of running, I realized I had Lena's collar in my hands, and I tossed the two pieces into the fast-moving river.

We evaded the people on foot, but the helicopter stayed with us. At one point, there were two helicopters, which answered my question about them needing to refuel. They took turns tracking us.

There was no shortage of woods to hide in here, but with Julian's people hunting us on the ground and from the air, eventually our luck would run out. None of us could keep up this pace without rest or food.

I had to get that collar off Ronan. It was the only way we were going to make it.

The banks grew steeper, muting the roar of the river and making the helicopter more audible, as if we needed a reminder it was there. Thick gray clouds moved in to block out the sun, and I smelled the change in the air. A storm was coming. I didn't want to get caught in it, but the helicopter would have to be grounded until the storm passed.

It wasn't long until the snow came. It started out as a light flurry and changed to thick heavy flakes, which coated the shifters' fur. We needed to lose the helicopter and find shelter before this got bad. Ronan, Felix, and Lena's coats would protect them, but I wasn't dressed for a snowstorm.

Ahead of me, Ronan's ears went erect. His hearing was better than mine, which meant he'd picked up something I couldn't hear yet.

He sped up, looking back to make sure I kept up with him. Neither of us had to worry about Felix and Lena. Werecougars were second only to cheetahs in speed. Without the collars, our new friends had enough energy to outrun Ronan.

A few minutes passed before we heard the whine of snowmobiles. Fear sent a fresh burst of adrenaline through me.

The snowmobiles grew louder. I looked down at the river. Alone, I could do it, but werecougars were not the best swimmers in their animal form.

One of the werecougars growled. I risked a glance to my right and caught a flash of blue and yellow through the trees. The snowmobile wasn't coming at us, it was going past us. They were trying to cut us off.

Ahead of me, Ronan barked. My stomach pitched, and I peered past him expecting to see Julian's people waiting for us. Instead, I saw – was that a bridge?

Hope burst to life in me as I stared at the rope bridge strung across a high narrow gorge. This was no fraying old bridge like those I'd seen in movies. It couldn't be more than ten years old with solid wood planks and thick rope secured to sturdy posts on both sides. Ropes crisscrossed along the sides to prevent people from falling. There were Indigenous groups in the Yukon, as well as trappers, miners, and people who chose to live in a remote location. The bridge could have been built by any of them. We might be close to a cabin or even a small settlement.

We skidded to a stop at the bridge. It was no more than one hundred feet long, but it might as well have been a mile. It was out in the open, making us easy targets for a shooter in the helicopter.

"We have to do it," I said. "It's our only chance."

The snowmobiles changed course and headed straight for us. The helicopter must have warned them about the bridge. Their headlights shone brightly in the gloomy woods as they closed in on us.

"Felix, Lena, you go first. Ronan and I will be right behind you." I frantically waved them ahead of us. "If anything happens and we get separated, run. Don't worry about us."

The werecougars ran onto the bridge. When they were ten feet away, they stopped and looked back at us.

"The bridge looks strong, but we should spread out our weight," I told them. I turned to Ronan. "You next."

He shook his head and nudged me toward the bridge. I started to argue and saw the snowmobiles bearing down on us. We were out of time.

I followed Felix and Lena onto the bridge. They were already a quarter of the way across it, and their movement made it sway.

"Stay close," I called to Ronan as I began to run. The snow was coming down harder, and the wind was picking up.

The bridge creaked when Ronan stepped onto it. I slowed to look back over my shoulder at him, and felt faint at the sight of the man running toward the bridge with a gun in his hands.

"Ronan," I shouted.

He sped up, and I began to run again. Felix and Lena were over halfway. They were going to make it.

I was almost at the midway point when the helicopter swooped down to hover close enough for me to see the faces of the pilot and co-pilot. The aircraft turned so the open side door was facing me. A man crouched inside, pointing a gun at me. Beside the man was Julian Cross.

"It's over, Danielle," Julian shouted above the thumping of the blades. "Stop now, and I'll let your werewolf go."

"No," I yelled back. He needed Ronan to use as leverage against me, and he'd already proven his word meant nothing.

Julian said something to the other man. The gun swung toward Ronan, who had caught up to me. Reaching into a pocket, Julian took out an object and held it up. Fear clawed at my chest when I saw a gleaming silver bullet.

"He dies if you don't give up," Julian said.

I shook my head. "He dies if I do."

Ronan snarled and pushed me toward the other side of the bridge where Felix and Lena waited for us. I looked back to see a man on the bridge pointing a dart gun at me. This had all been a diversion so Julian's man could get close to us.

The man on the bridge pulled the trigger, but Ronan blocked me with his much larger body. If the dart hit him, he didn't show it. How many of those could he take?

He pressed his nose to my back again, propelling me forward. We made it ten feet when two shots rang out.

Ronan jerked and fell against the rope handrail. The bridge tipped precariously under his weight, and I found myself staring at the river a hundred feet below.

I reached for him. Blood oozed from a bullet hole in his shoulder and another in his hip. He looked at me with pain-glazed eyes, and, for a second, I saw recognition in them.

"Stay with me, Ronan," I begged him. "I can't lose you again."

His eyes closed, and his body slumped against the rail. I grabbed one of his front legs and clung to it, but I was no match for the dead weight of a werewolf.

"Ronan," I screamed as he slipped from my grasp.

22

For a moment, time stood still. The snowflakes were suspended in the air, Julian's mouth was open in a shout, his hand outstretched, and the man running toward me froze mid-stride.

The world sped up again, and I jumped.

Ronan hit the water and went under a few seconds before I plunged into the river. The shock of the icy water almost took my breath away, and a thousand needles pricked my skin. It took me several precious seconds to recover and orient myself.

The river was fast and deep, and I let it carry me as I searched for Ronan. I caught a glimpse of something dark, but it vanished. I saw it again and reached for it, only to have the current snatch it away from me.

Taking a deep breath, I dived under. My eyes adjusted to the murky water, and I spotted a dark shape a dozen feet away. I started toward it, only to discover it was a tree.

Where are you? I looked around me desperately as I fought my rising panic. I barely registered the numbness creeping into my body. What if he was snagged on something, and I'd gone past him? What if I'd lost him forever this time?

"You can't have him," I screamed into the water. "Give him back to me."

Heat enveloped my body, and the water around me glowed with millions of sparkling lights. They spread out in all directions, attracting more as they went until it was as bright as day beneath the surface.

A large blob of magic moved against the current toward me. I swam for it and almost sobbed in relief when I saw the shape inside. Wrapping my arms around his neck, I broke the surface and sucked in air.

There was no sign of the bridge or the helicopter, but they were the least of my worries. Ronan was alive, but I could feel his life force weakening. I scanned the sides of the gorge for a place to land, and all I saw was sheer rock walls.

The river carried us around a bend, and I caught sight of a break in the wall. A large chunk of rock had broken away, making it look like someone had scooped out part of the wall. When I swam to it, I saw a ledge just below the surface of the water. It would have to do.

I used the water magic to hoist Ronan onto the ledge and climbed up beside him. The wind had picked up, and the water lapped at us, but the magic insulated us from the cold. Pulling his head onto my lap, I stroked his fur. It terrified me to see him like this, and I wished my mother was here.

I laid my hand on his side, feeling his faint heartbeat and the shallow rise and fall of his ribs. I'd never done this, but to do nothing would mean certain death for him.

Taking a steadying breath, I pushed my magic through his ribs and into his lungs, which were half full of water. If he were human, he would already be dead. I carefully drew the water from his lungs, up his windpipe, and out of his mouth. When I checked his lungs again, they sounded clear.

I laid my hands over the bullet wound in his shoulder. Removing a silver bullet wouldn't be nearly as easy, and I was thankful he couldn't feel pain while unconscious.

Above the roar of the river came the sound of the helicopter. I pressed myself to the wall beneath a small overhang, praying it was enough to hide us from above. The helicopter did a slow pass and came back. They knew we were here somewhere because of that damn collar, but they couldn't find us.

Furious, I wrapped my hands around the collar. The warlock's protection spell shattered under the onslaught of water magic, and the binding spell followed. I raised my arm and flung the collar halves as far away from me as I could. Julian knew by now I'd never leave Ronan, so he'd go wherever the collar went.

I covered the bullet wound with my hands again and sent my magic into him. I found the bullet lodged in one of his powerful shoulder muscles, and I directed a stream of magic at it. I was going to work the bullet loose and extract it from him.

My hands began to glow and get hotter until steam rose off them. Magic poured into Ronan, and he shuddered when it encased the bullet. It didn't stop there. It branched off and spread through him until it found the second bullet embedded in his hip. It surrounded the bullet and stalled like it was waiting for me to do something.

I imagined how to ease the bullets from his muscle and bone, moving carefully as not to hurt him. The moment I had the thought, magic surged in me, and my whole body glowed. My magic hit the bullets with the speed of a lightning strike, and when it receded, not a trace of silver could be found in his body.

What the hell was that? I lifted my hands to inspect Ronan's shoulder wound, but it was gone as if it had never existed. I probed him with my magic and found only healthy tissue and bone.

Ronan's head moved. I leaned over him as his eyelids flickered open, and his dazed amber eyes met mine. Smiling tearfully, I stroked his face. He released a shuddering breath, and his eyes closed, but this time it was in sleep.

The helicopter continued to circle until the weather got worse, forcing it to leave. We couldn't stay here either. I was tiring from expending so much magic, and we needed to get out of the river before I was too drained.

When the light began to fade, I woke Ronan. His eyes were clearer, and he sat up with little effort.

"The helicopter is gone, but Julian most likely left men on the ground to watch for us," I said. "We'll ride the river until we find a place to go ashore."

He nodded. I put an arm around his neck, and we slipped off the ledge, letting the current take us. We left the gorge behind us, and the riverbanks got lower. It was almost dark when I saw a spot on the far bank where we could land. We swam toward it and collapsed onto the ground.

I shivered so violently my teeth clacked together and my limbs seized from the extreme cold. I tried to use the water in my clothes to warm me, but I didn't have the strength.

Ronan stood and shook himself, then he crouched beside me, his eyes watching me expectantly. I forced myself to my knees, falling twice before I was able to get on his back. I wrapped my arms around his neck as he stood and started up the low bank.

The thick woods sheltered us from the snow and some of the wind, but I was too numb to feel the cold anymore. It was sheer will that kept me holding on to Ronan as he took us away from the river. If we didn't find shelter soon, I would not survive the night.

When he stopped walking, I couldn't open my eyes to see where we were. I felt him digging, and then I was sliding off him. He pushed me with his nose, and I rolled into a shallow hole. He lay next to me on his side and chuffed until I rolled over and curled into him. His fur was still wet, but heat radiated from him. Eventually, I stopped shivering and fell asleep.

I awoke disoriented with no idea where I was or how I'd gotten here. The events of the last few days came back in a rush, and I shivered at the memory of how close Ronan had come to dying. I wondered where Felix and Lena were and if they'd escaped. I realized guiltily it was the first time I'd thought of them since I last saw them on the bridge.

Werecougars were more than capable of taking care of themselves in the wilderness, and without those horrible collars, they could easily evade Caladrius. Of the four of us, I was the least equipped to survive out here in winter.

As if to prove that point, my stomach growled loudly enough to wake Ronan. He stretched and stood, and I immediately missed his warmth when he walked a few feet away to shake off six inches of snow that had accumulated during the night.

Reluctantly, I followed him. It was morning, and the snow was still falling. I looked down at where we'd slept and saw a hollow beneath two fallen trees. Snow had piled up around them, creating a nice temporary shelter – if you had a werewolf to keep you warm.

I scanned the area and saw no signs of life other than us. Even so, I kept my voice low.

"We need food and a better shelter," I said. "This storm is going to last at least another day."

We set out with him in the lead. I had lost all sense of direction, but I had complete faith in him. My damp clothes and wet boots made for a cold, miserable hike, and my stomach hurt from hunger. On top of that, my magic was acting weird. One minute, it flooded me, making me so hot I began to sweat. In the next, it receded, leaving me cold and tired.

In the last twenty-four hours, my magic had done things I couldn't explain. I thought about the magic bringing Ronan to me in the river, and how it had obliterated those bullets. My fear for Ronan had driven me to use more of my magic than ever, and being submerged in the river must have amplified my magic. It was the only way I could have done those things and kept us warm as long as I had.

The snow was deep in places with less tree cover, and it made walking harder. At least a foot and a half of snow had fallen since yesterday, and I suspected we'd see another foot before the storm was over. Around us, the frozen wilderness was both breathtaking and desolate, and we appeared to be the only living things moving out here.

We stopped at the base of a tall hill too small to be called a mountain.

Ronan ushered me under the thick branches of a large tree where the ground was bare, and I sat wearily with my back against the trunk. I couldn't remember the last time I was this tired.

"Where are you going?" I asked when he turned to leave. I started to follow him, and he pressed a paw to my chest. Reluctantly, I sat again. I didn't want to be separated from him, but it was more practical for him to search for shelter alone and come back for me. He could cover more area without me to slow him down.

After he left, the world became eerily quiet, and the only sound was the nearly inaudible whisper of falling snow. I got up to relieve myself and then sat to wait for Ronan to return. Walking had staved off the worst of the cold, but it settled into me now. I pulled my legs tightly to my chest and tucked my hands between them as I called my magic to warm me. It responded but only enough to keep me from freezing.

As miserable as I was, I also counted my blessings. We were no longer prisoners, Ronan was alive, and we were together. I couldn't think past today or what would happen when this ordeal was over.

Several hours passed before he returned. He stuck his head under the branches, gave a little bark, and disappeared again. I crawled out to find him prancing eagerly. The snow had stopped, but it was only a temporary lull in the storm.

We followed his tracks for almost an hour until they changed direction and started going uphill. The climb was difficult, and Ronan kept looking back to check on me. I smiled to reassure him even though my legs threatened to give out if we didn't stop soon.

Thirty minutes into the climb, I saw a dark patch ahead of us, which turned out to be the entrance to a small cave. I climbed inside and discovered an opening at the back, leading to a larger cave. I had to duck to get through the opening, but the cave was tall enough for me to stand upright. It took my eyes a minute to adjust enough to make out my surroundings.

My gasp echoed off the rock walls. In the center of the floor was a circle of blackened stones with the remnants of an old campfire inside. At the back of the cave lay a roll of furs tied with rope, a stack of firewood, kindling, a small axe, and a weathered wooden box. I lifted the box cover and found waterproof matches, a dented cooking pot, a bowl, utensils, a pocket knife, an empty canteen, and an old canvas rucksack. I opened the sack and almost cried when I saw four cans of food inside, along with a leather pouch of dried meat and a small satchel of dried herbs for tea.

"How did you find this?" Giddy with excitement and relief, I stood and spun to face Ronan, who stood in the opening. Against a side wall stood a pair of broken snowshoes, some metal hunting traps, and a weird contraption constructed from a large fur stretched between four sticks tied together with rope. I stared at it for a moment before I realized it fit in front of the opening as a windbreak.

There was no scat or signs an animal had been here recently. The oiled traps looked like they'd only been here a month or so. Based on its contents, I guessed the cave to be a trapper's overnight shelter. I hoped they didn't mind two desperate people using some of their supplies.

I ran over and threw my arms around Ronan's neck. "This is perfect." After the last few days, the cave looked as good as a five-star hotel.

He chuffed softly and rested his chin on my shoulder. I could have stayed there like that for hours, but my stomach reminded me how hungry I was.

I let him go and stepped back. "I'm going to start a fire and melt some snow for drinking, and we'll eat. We won't be full, but we won't starve either."

I grabbed the cooking pot and went outside to fill it with snow. As I carried it inside, I met Ronan going out. I busied myself with building the fire and setting the pot on one of the rocks to melt the snow. Standing, I held my cold hands over the fire and watched smoke drift up to a small crevice in the ceiling. It was a perfect chimney.

A cold breeze came from the outer cave, and I went to place the framed fur in front of the opening. Ronan hadn't come back inside, so I walked to the entrance to look for him. He wasn't there. I called for him, but he didn't answer. He couldn't have gone far.

Retreating to the inner cave, I put the frame up to block the wind and laid some of the furs on the floor beside the fire. They were soft and well cared for, and they'd make a warm bed tonight. We were so lucky he'd found this cave.

The frame rattled when a gust of wind blew through the entrance. The storm was picking up again, and it promised to be worse than yesterday's. I glanced at the stack of firewood. We should have enough wood to get us through two days.

The snow in the pot had melted, so I poured the water into the canteen. Having nothing else to occupy me, I sat, but I couldn't stay still for long.

Where was Ronan? I got up and went to peer out over the frame. Outside the entrance, snow swirled. My gaze went to the metal traps, and terrifying images of him caught in a hunter's trap filled my mind.

I began to pace the cave. I was minutes away from going to look for him when a noise came from outside. I ran to the opening and looked out as Ronan dropped two snowshoe hares on the floor. Relief hit me so hard I forgot to scold him for leaving without telling me. He shook out his fur, showering the small cave with snow, and I moved the frame aside for him to enter the larger cave, which had warmed up nicely.

"Did you eat?" I asked.

He nodded and sat near the fire.

I went to the box, took out a can of beef stew, and dumped it into the pot to heat. It was lukewarm when I dug into it with the spoon, nearly moaning at my first food in two – or was it three – days. It felt like we had been running from Caladrius for a week.

I was so hungry I planned to go back for the second can of stew, but by the time I finished the first one I was a little nauseous. It probably wasn't a good idea to eat too much all at once. I took the pot to the entrance, cleaned it with snow, and filled it with snow to melt. The canteen couldn't hold enough water for the two of us.

Back inside the cave, I put up the frame and removed my damp coat. I sat on the fur across from Ronan and tugged off my wet boots, placing them near the fire to dry. I would have given anything for clean, dry clothes. When we got back to civilization, I was taking an hour-long shower and not feeling a bit guilty about it.

I looked at Ronan across the fire. This was the first time since we left our cells that we'd been alone together and weren't running for our lives. There had been no time for me to recover from the shock of seeing him in that cell or to process all the emotions currently crowding my chest.

I wished I could talk to him. I missed his voice and his face so much. At the same time, I was afraid of what he would say. Caring for me out here didn't mean anything had changed between us.

Warm and fed, I yawned as the exhaustion and fear of the last few days caught up to me. I spread out the rest of the furs, put another log on the fire, and got into my makeshift bed.

"I'm going to rest a bit," I said as I balled up a fur to use as a pillow.

He chuffed and lay facing the entrance with his head on his front paws. It was the first time he looked peaceful and content since we found each other again.

I burrowed under the furs and closed my eyes. I fell asleep listening to his breathing and the wind howling outside our little refuge.

I woke up shivering and feeling like I had barely slept. Pushing the furs off my head, I braced myself for the cold cave, and I was surprised to see the fire crackling merrily. Ronan must have added wood throughout the night. I looked around and found him sitting by the opening, peering out over the frame.

I moved to sit up and groaned. Every muscle in my body ached, and my head started to pound the moment I was upright. What I wouldn't give for some nasty gunna paste.

Ronan turned his head toward me, his eyes worried.

"Good morning." I smiled and wrapped a large fur around my shoulders. "I never thought I'd say this, but I think the Yukon wilderness is kicking my ass."

The floor was like ice under my feet when I got up, so I pulled on my dry boots before I walked over to him. I peered out, shocked to discover it was still dark. It was no wonder I felt like I hadn't slept long. The storm had stopped, which also surprised me. I'd been sure it would last into tomorrow.

I glanced at the floor of the outer cave and saw the hares were gone. In their place was a fox. Ronan must have been hungrier than he let on to have eaten both hares and gone hunting again.

I shivered again and thought about the dried herbs in the box. Some hot tea would help ward off this chill. Turning to the box, I came up short when I saw the stack of firewood was down to a few logs. There was no way we burned through all of it so fast.

A horrible thought came to me, and I looked at Ronan. "Was I asleep for more than a day?"

He nodded.

Alarmed, I asked, "Two days?" He shook his head, and I asked, "A day and a half?"

He nodded again.

I swayed at the revelation. I'd been exhausted yesterday when we got to the cave, but tired enough to sleep for a day and a half? And why did I feel like I'd gotten no more than an hour of sleep?

Ronan moved closer to steady me, and I leaned against him, filled with intense longing. I wished more than ever he would shift and wrap his arms around me. Emotions welled in me, and tears leaked from the corners of my eyes.

I kept my face averted and went to pull on my dry coat. Discreetly, I wiped the wetness from my face as I set the pot of water on the fire to boil for tea. When I looked up, he was still watching me like he wanted to help but didn't know how.

The tea was good, but it did nothing to stop the shivering. If anything, I got colder, and my headache grew worse. I bundled up in the furs again and curled into a tight ball, but nothing helped. It felt like the marrow in my bones was turning to ice.

Ronan lay beside me, and I lifted the furs to press my body against his. With him next to me and the fire at my back, I should be toasty warm, but I was colder than ever.

I fell asleep from sheer exhaustion, and it was light outside when I woke again. The fire was still going, and a pile of broken branches lay where the wood stack had been. Ronan lay on the other side of the fire, his fur wet from a recent trip outdoors.

My throat was dry and scratchy, so I reluctantly threw off the covers to get some water. He lifted his head, and I motioned for him to stay. I picked up the canteen and swished the water inside. It was almost full.

Uncapping it, I put it to my lips and tipped it, but nothing came out. I shook it again, and this time, no water sloshed. I held it close to the fire and peered inside. The water had frozen solid.

I gripped the canteen tightly with numb fingers. I'd unconsciously frozen the water, but how? I hadn't even summoned my magic.

A sliver of dread went through me. I walked over to the cooking pot and touched the water with one finger. Nothing happened. Maybe I was overreacting. I'd used a lot of magic removing the collars and saving Ronan in the river, so I shouldn't be surprised if it was a little out of whack.

Placing my hands on either side of the canteen, I summoned my magic to melt the water. It felt normal, and I relaxed as I pushed it gently into the canteen.

The canteen exploded. My magic reacted automatically and formed a bubble around me to protect Ronan from flying shards of ice and metal.

He stood, and I put up a hand. "Stay away. There's something wrong with my magic. It's like it's amped up, and I have no control over it."

The second the words left my mouth, I knew what it was. I backed away from him until I was pressed against the wall. *No, no, no. Not now.*

"It's liannan," I said in a voice choked with fear. "You have to leave and get far away from me."

He shook his head and took a step toward me.

I threw up my hands. "No. I'll hurt you, and I would rather die."

Ronan ignored me and kept coming. I side-stepped until I was in front of the opening. "Don't you get it? My magic will kill you. My mother couldn't be in the same room with my father or any other Mohiri until after liannan."

Picking up the frame, I backed out of the cave and replaced it. This close to the entrance, I should have been freezing, but I was burning up inside. Sweat broke out on my face, and to my horror, my skin began to glow.

I ran outside. Snow melted under my feet, and I felt like I was going to combust. My body was lit up like a beacon.

I spun when I heard Ronan coming after me. I called to the magic in the snow and sent it to the cave entrance, where I transformed it into ice. In seconds, the entrance was sealed off with two feet of ice. It would hold him long enough for me to put distance between us.

Ronan's howl, followed by the scratch of his claws against the ice, sent me running down the hill. I didn't know where I was going, only that I had to get as far away from him as possible.

I ran for miles until I came upon the burnt-out shell of a log cabin. I crawled under what was left of the roof and sprawled on the floor. "I'm scared, Mom. I wish you were here."

Heat built up in my chest, and the glow emanating from me lit up the scorched interior of the cabin. I grabbed my head when the headache I'd forgotten about came back with a vengeance. There were explosions of light behind my eyes as the pain increased until I couldn't take it anymore and passed out.

The sun was warm on my face. Smiling, I opened my eyes to discover I was floating on a gentle river as warm as bath water. I looked at the grassy bank and saw my parents, standing with their arms around each other as they sadly watched me go by. Next, I saw Dimitri. He sat with his head on his arms. I called to him, and he raised tear-filled eyes to mine. Why was my family upset?

I rounded a bend in the river where my grandparents and Uncle Nate waited. They all looked like they had been crying. I couldn't understand how anyone could be sad on a day like this.

The river picked up speed, and I barely had time to wave at all my uncles and aunts as I passed by. When I saw Summer with Uncle Peter and Aunt Shannon, I waved wildly at her, but she didn't seem to notice me. She stared at the river, her eyes empty of emotion, and I wanted to go to her, but the river carried me away.

There was a faint roar up ahead, and plumes of mist came off the river. But I was distracted by a figure running along the opposite bank, keeping pace with me. His shape kept changing between a man and a wolf, and he was calling to me. It was Ronan. He'd come back.

"Don't leave me," he called.

Something tugged at my chest, and I drifted closer to him. "I don't want to go."

He ran down the bank to the water and reached out to grab my hand. The current pulled at me, but he would not let me go. "I gave you up once. I can't do it again."

The river became turbulent as it tried to rip me away from him. Ronan's eyes were pleading as he held out his other hand. "Please, stay with me."

I reached for him. The moment our hands touched, the river released its grip on me. Ronan lifted me from the water, and we fell back on the warm grass. He sat cradling me in his arms, a hand stroking my hair. "I love you, Dani."

I opened my eyes and smiled up at him. "I love you, too."

He made a choked sound, and his reddened eyes filled with joy. "Thank you, God," he said hoarsely.

"I'm so tired," I rasped, struggling to stay awake. "Will you stay with me?"

He kissed my forehead. "Forever."

I sighed happily. As sleep claimed me, I heard a contented whisper in the back of my mind. *Solmi.*

23

———————

I came awake to the cheerful crackle of a fire. Staring at the flames dancing in the firepit, I listened to the wind whistling through the outer cave. It sounded like last night's storm had turned into a raging blizzard. We were so lucky Ronan found this cave and we didn't have to spend the night outside.

I snuggled under the furs, not quite ready to leave my cozy nest, and went still when I felt the weight of an arm around me. The arm flexed, pulling me against a hard body, and warm breath caressed the back of my neck. My Mori fluttered, radiating pure joy.

Ronan. I held my breath, afraid to move. If this was a dream, I didn't want to wake up.

"You're awake," said a sleepy voice.

I rolled onto my back. Turning my head, I looked into the warm hazel eyes I'd thought I would never see again. My eyes burned as a wave of emotions crashed down on me.

His face was etched in sorrow and regret as he reached up to brush away the tears coursing down my cheeks. "There is nothing I can say to undo the pain I've caused you. I'll spend the rest of my life trying to earn your forgiveness if you will let me."

My throat was so constricted it was hard to speak. "Your wolf –"

"– loves you," he finished for me. "He always did. It took me leaving you to see it."

"You didn't come back," I whispered, not daring to believe it was true. I thought about those hellish weeks when I clung to a sliver of hope he would change his mind and return.

His eyes darkened. "A week after I left you, I realized my pain wasn't only from breaking our bond. My wolf was grieving the loss of his mate. Imprinting is supposed to be a powerful experience, but it must be different for someone like me. I was on my way back when I was captured. I was so focused on getting to you, I didn't see the trap until I was in it."

My joy at hearing his wolf had imprinted on me was nearly extinguished when I learned how long he had been Julian's prisoner. The whole time I was imagining him running through the forest in Alaska, he was imprisoned in an eight-by-ten-foot cell, forced to endure unspeakable cruelty.

I turned on my side toward him and touched his face. There were shadows under his eyes, and his face was a little thinner after his ordeal, but he was still my Ronan.

"Thinking about you was the only thing that got me through the days," he said roughly. "And the knowledge that one day you would come."

I searched his eyes. "How did you know that?"

"I knew you wouldn't stop until you found your friend Summer." He released a shaky breath. "I never imagined you would be a prisoner there, too."

My voice hardened. "Julian Cross is probably regretting that now. If not, he will soon."

"How did they take you?" Ronan asked. "Why?"

I told him about the ambush in New York and Julian's plan to use me to force my mother to give him troll bile.

"When he realized you cared about me, he threatened to kill me if you didn't help him," Ronan said.

"You heard that? You were so crazed I wasn't sure if you could understand me. Or if you knew me at all."

His thumb stroked my jaw. "I did start to lose my mind eventually. I didn't know you at first, but I sensed you were important to me. It wasn't until we left the river that I started to remember."

"Why didn't you shift then?" I asked. "You have no idea how much I wanted to hear your voice."

"I wanted to, but when you began having magic outbursts in the woods, I realized it wasn't safe for my Mori. The only way to be near you was as my wolf. When you started liannan, a week ago –"

"What?" I propped myself on my elbow and stared down at him. "I went through liannan?"

He frowned. "You don't remember?"

"No, I..." I concentrated on the memory floating back to me. I was in an old cabin, which had burned down, and the pain in my head was excruciating. Another memory surfaced of me lying on the floor of the cave, inside a bubble of light. On the other side of the bubble, Ronan's wolf paced the floor. Then I saw Ronan sitting on the floor with me in his arms.

"You brought me back here," I said as more memories flooded my mind. Most of them were hazy, as if I saw them through fog, but I remembered pain and bursts of light coming from me. And I remembered Ronan.

Why didn't I feel any different? Mom and Eldeorin had made it sound like I would be bursting with magic after liannan. I carefully opened myself to it and gasped at the power roiling inside me like a storm. I quickly locked it down. I should wait until I was alone to test my control.

"How did you survive being that close to me?" I asked him. How had *I* survived without Eldeorin to help me through it?

"After I brought you back here, you got hysterical. I think you were hallucinating about hurting me. You created a ward of some kind around you to contain your magic. I didn't shift until the outbursts stopped." His eyes filled with anguish. "You were feverish, and I had to use snow to cool your body. When it passed, you were so weak you stopped breathing. I thought I was going to lose you."

"You asked me not to leave you." My breath hitched. "You said you love me."

"I do." He smiled tenderly, making my heart swell. "*Inima mea îți va aparține mereu.*"

I recognized those words. He had whispered them to me when he held me the day he left. Everything about that day was seared into my mind. "What does it mean?"

"My heart will always belong to you." He reached up to tuck my hair behind my ear. "I think it was yours from the day we met, but I was too blind to see it."

I lowered my head, and he turned his face to mine. Our gazes locked, and his eyes mirrored my pent-up longing and need. I brushed my lips against his, wanting to savor every second, but at the first taste of him, hunger ignited inside me.

I pushed him onto his back and claimed his mouth with a fierceness that made me dizzy. When he swept his tongue between my lips, heat pooled low in my belly, and blood pounded in my veins to match the tempo of the storm outside.

His heady scent mingling with the smell of his desire triggered some primal part of me I hadn't known existed. *Mine*, I thought possessively as I lifted the furs and slid over to straddle him without breaking the kiss.

Ronan moaned against my mouth and lifted his hips to press his hot body to mine. Pleasure and shock rolled through me when I felt his arousal between my thighs. I became acutely aware of two things. Ronan was naked, and I was in nothing but my underwear.

Panting, I broke the kiss and rested my head in the crook of his neck. Of course, he was naked. It wasn't like he could run out and buy some clothes in the middle of the wilderness. He must have undressed me when I had a fever.

He rubbed my back gently. "It's too soon after your illness. We'll wait until you're ready."

"No." I raised my head to look at him. "I want this. It's just... I've never felt like this."

The gleam in his heavy-lidded eyes wasn't helping. Neither was the feel of his hard body beneath mine. As if he'd read my mind, he made the smallest move, and a bolt of heat shot through me.

"We'll go as slow as you want." His mouth curved into a slow sensual smile. "For as long as you want."

My stomach fluttered with nervous anticipation. I moved over to prop myself on my arm beside him and leaned in to kiss the corner of his mouth. I grazed his upper lip and playfully tugged his lower lip between my teeth before I began a slow exploration of his mouth. Ronan responded in kind, willing to let me set the pace.

I trailed kisses along his jaw and down to the hollow of his throat. Stopping there, I raised my head and tugged the furs down to his hips. His hard, defined body was even more beautiful than it had been the first time I'd seen it, and now I could do something I'd wanted to do that night.

I ran my hand reverently over the planes of his chest and ribcage and down to his taut stomach. He trembled when my fingers traced his navel and dipped to the edge of the fur covering his lower abs. It was a heady feeling knowing I could affect him like this, and it made me bolder.

His body tensed when I slowly pushed the fur down to expose the rest of him. I'd seen naked males. You couldn't hang out with werewolves and not see a lot of body parts. But Ronan was so perfect he could have been sculpted from marble. And he was mine.

I reached out to touch him. My fingertips grazed him, and he let out a low growl. The next thing I knew, I was on my back, looking up into his smoldering eyes. He didn't give me time to recover from my surprise before his mouth crashed down on mine in a searing kiss.

I was weak and trembling with need when his mouth blazed a trail of kisses down my throat to the curve of my breast. Deft fingers unclasped my bra, and he dipped his head again to worship my breasts. Then he was moving lower, and I arched my back as his mouth continued its sensual assault on my sanity.

He rose over me and kissed me again as he settled his body between my legs. Resting his weight on his arms, he gazed down at me with so much love and adoration I was afraid my heart would burst. We needed no spoken words or vows as we made love. We found our release together and shared in our Mori's joy when the bond that had almost been broken was sealed forever.

Later, we snuggled under the furs, and I decided I loved it when Ronan spooned me. It was one of the endless number of things I loved about him. I smiled at the shadows of the fire dancing on the wall of our little haven. "I didn't know it was possible to be this happy."

Ronan kissed the back of my shoulder. "For a long time, I thought I was doomed to live a half-life with no mate or pack. You are everything I believed I could never have. For the first time in my life, I am whole."

I rolled to face him. *Have I told you lately how much I love you?*

His lips twitched. *It's been a few minutes.*

I grinned. *This is going to come in handy at Westhorne, especially around my family.*

"Do you want to live at Westhorne?" he asked. "We've never talked about that."

I pressed a kiss to his jaw. "I want to live wherever you are, whether it is at Westhorne or in the Montana mountains."

He smiled and pulled me closer, tucking my head under his chin. I closed my eyes, blissfully content. Neither of us had mentioned Caladrius, but we both knew what we had to do before we could go home. I wasn't leaving here without Summer. And I was going to keep a promise I made to myself when she disappeared. I was going to make the person responsible for hurting her wish he had never heard her name.

"Are you ready to be amazed?" I grinned at Ronan, whose wolf stood beside me in the middle of a clearing half a mile from the cave.

He snorted and gave a nod.

I took a breath and held out my hand. I had worked on this all day, and I wanted it to be perfect. Summoning the snow's magic, I watched with delight as the entire clearing sparkled. I'd been practicing controlling my new magic for two days, and I was still in awe of it.

In my mind, I created an image, and immediately, a wall of ice sprung up in a wide circle around us. The ice was so clear we could see every detail of the trees outside. When the wall was as tall as the trees, it curved inward to form a globe.

Ronan chuffed, and I looked back at him. "Now for the best part."

I scooped up a handful of powdery snow and held it up to my mouth. I blew the snow off my palm, and it hung in the air for a few seconds before it floated up to the ceiling. It began to grow until it obscured the sky. I snapped my fingers – which was only for show – and the snow drifted down, swirling around us.

Raising my arms, I spun in a circle. "It's a snow globe. Isn't it beautiful?"

I stumbled when I came face-to-face with my naked, smiling mate. He caught me and pulled me against him. "Yes, but not as beautiful as you."

"What are you doing?" I asked, laughing.

He dipped his head and captured my mouth for a long, slow kiss, which turned my legs to rubber. We broke the kiss when delicate ice crystals rained down on us.

"My globe." I pouted. "You made me lose concentration."

"Then we will have to work on that," he said with a suggestive smile.

I wrapped my arms around his neck. "I'm afraid I'm going to need lots of practice."

His husky laugh made me breathless. "I am at your service."

I stood in the opening, looking into the cave we had called home for a week and a half. The furs were rolled and tied, the firepit emptied, and a fresh stack of firewood stood at the back wall. We couldn't replenish the food I had taken, but Ronan had left a few beaver pelts as payment. He said the pelts were waterproof and they made warm winter clothing. In the freezing weather, they should last long enough for the trapper to return.

Turning, I walked to the outer cave entrance and stepped into the sun. Around me was a sparkling winter wonderland. The world seemed so different from the day we found the cave, but I knew it was I who had changed. I felt like a butterfly emerging from its cocoon, transformed into what it was meant to be.

Ronan waited for me in his wolf form. I placed my hand on his back, and he rubbed his head against me playfully. He had changed, too. He smiled and laughed more, free from the loneliness and burdens he had carried his whole life. I warmed when I thought about how we had spent the last two days. He was also a lot more amorous.

"I'm ready," I said, and we started down the hill.

At the bottom, Ronan took the lead again. Yesterday, he had climbed to the top of the hill to orient himself and get the lay of the land. It was all he needed to find his way back to the lab. He had argued against going there without reinforcements, but I'd pointed out it could take us weeks to find civilization. I wouldn't leave Summer in that place a day longer than I had to.

I'd worried we would get there and find an empty facility, but I dismissed it for two reasons. First, it would be a massive undertaking to move everyone and everything there to a new location. Second, Julian believed the warlock glamour hiding his lab was impenetrable. If one of us escapees came back with help, we'd never find it.

We reached the bridge at noon. We crossed it, watching and listening for any sign we weren't alone. Unless he'd sent divers into the river to retrieve Ronan's collar, Julian probably believed we'd drowned or had perished in the blizzard.

It was late afternoon when a twin-engine plane flew low overhead. It was the first sign of civilization we'd seen in weeks.

"I don't think Julian would use a plane instead of a helicopter," I said as the aircraft flew out of sight.

Ronan nodded, and we resumed walking. An hour later, he stopped, and his ears perked up.

"Did you hear something?" I asked.

He shifted. "I think it was another plane. Too far away to tell."

I smiled. "You think maybe we are a little paranoid."

"We have good reason to be." He glanced up at the darkening sky. "Let's rest here, and I'll find something for dinner."

It didn't take him long to return with two snowshoe hares. I used my magic to steam half of one for my dinner, and he ate the rest. Mine was bland and a bit rubbery, but hot and filling. With practice and some seasonings, I might be able to cook one that was palatable.

After our meal, we walked through the night, wanting to reach the lab the next day. Even with all the new snow, Ronan was able to pick up our trail from almost two weeks ago.

It was dawn when he stopped and shifted. "We're no more than five miles from the lab." He pointed at a mountain peak to our left. "It's south of that."

"Great." I started forward, and he caught my arm.

"First, we eat and rest."

I wanted to argue, but he was right. We would both need our strength when we got there. I found a large tree with low branches and barely any snow close to the trunk. Around the tree, snow had piled high to form a little shelter and mute the sounds outside.

"A little redecorating and it'll be just like home," I called to him.

He chuckled. "I'm going to find us some breakfast while you redecorate."

"Sounds good." I grinned as I used my magic to clear away the snow to make a temporary bed. I thought about what we'd do when we reached the lab. We hadn't figured out how we were going to get into the lab, and the plan was to look for other ways in. The south entrance had to be where the snowmobiles came from the day we escaped, so we'd start there.

The thump of helicopter blades jarred me from my thoughts. I scrambled from the shelter to listen. This close to the lab, we were bound to hear a chopper, but the sound rattled me after our previous experience.

The noise faded, but I stayed on alert as I waited for Ronan. He had to have heard it, too, and he'd be on his way back to make sure I was safe.

When half an hour went by with no sign of him, I felt a trickle of fear. Another ten minutes passed, and I couldn't take it anymore. I followed his trail, almost losing it when I came to a rocky area half a mile away. I picked it up again, and I'd gone less than a quarter of a mile, when I heard a phone ringing. I spotted something red on a tree a hundred yards away, and my fear spiked. I drew closer and saw a red scarf tied around the tree. Hanging from the scarf was a satellite phone.

Bile rose in my throat as I approached the scarf and saw multiple sets of footprints around the tree. The tree was at the edge of a clearing where I found more footprints and the tracks of a snowmobile. But it was the sight of three tranquillizer darts embedded in the trunks of two trees that made me want to throw up.

This can't be happening. I untied the scarf with shaking hands and stared at the phone in my hand. It rang again, and I almost dropped it in the snow. I pressed the answer button and held the phone to my ear without speaking.

"Danielle," Julian Cross drawled jovially. "You have no idea how happy I am to learn you are alive and well. I must admit I was quite surprised your werewolf friend survived two silver bullets at close range. He said you were dead, but I had a feeling he was lying."

"Where is he?" I ground out as my anger mounted.

Julian chuckled. "I think you know where to find him. If you don't present yourself here within two hours, the next time you see him, he'll be in specimen jars.

Red tinged the world around me, and the phone casing cracked. "Let him go or so help me..."

"I don't think you fully comprehend the situation," he said, his voice dripping with arrogance. "I am the one with the power here, and your friend will die if you don't surrender."

"No, Dani," Ronan shouted in the background. "Don't –" His words ended in a cry of pain.

"Tick tock, Danielle," Julian said, and the line went dead.

I dropped the phone and ran. Nearly mindless with rage and fear, I barely saw my surroundings as I followed the snowmobile tracks. I was going to destroy Julian Cross. I was going to find my mate, and then I was going to wipe that demon from existence.

The tracks led me to a group of buildings around a large paved area. Directly across from me was a concrete structure exactly like the one we had escaped through. This must be the southern entrance.

I forced myself to slow my breathing. Calming my Mori was one of the hardest things I'd ever done because a Mori acted on primal instinct. I needed to act rationally, not emotionally, if I was going to help Ronan.

I stepped from the woods and walked across the asphalt toward the concrete structure. There was no one in sight, but Julian was expecting me. I wouldn't be alone long.

On my left was a hangar with the door open to reveal a small cargo plane, and in front of the hangar stood two helicopters. To my right was a short runway, which answered my question about how they moved people and equipment to and from the facility.

The entrance doors started to open, and ten guards spilled out. They stood in a line, watching me with their guns drawn, and I wondered if I should be flattered they thought I needed an armed escort.

When I was a few yards away, two of the guards stepped forward. One carried handcuffs, and I held up my hands to let him put them on me. As soon as they touched my skin, the warlock magic in them vanished.

The guards walked me down a short tunnel wide enough to accommodate a large box truck. On the other end was a second pair of doors, which were opened to a concrete room like the one at the other entrance. The only difference was the addition of a freight elevator.

Six of the guards got into the elevator with me, and we descended one level. The doors opened to the lab where most of the people in white coats stared curiously at us as we walked to Julian's office.

Ronan. I called. *Can you hear me?*

He didn't respond, which meant he wasn't on this level. I should have known Julian would keep us apart.

The office door opened as we neared it, and the guards escorted me inside. Willow sat on the couch again with her legs pulled up and a book in her hands. I wanted to punch her when she glanced up with a look of boredom on her face.

Julian sat behind his desk, wearing a triumphant expression. "Danielle, how wonderful to see you again."

"Where is he?" I demanded.

Julian touched his tablet, and Ronan appeared on the screen behind him. Ronan sat on a chair in the middle of a room with six guards in a semicircle around him. He wore handcuffs, and someone had given him a pair of pants.

The rage I was fighting to suppress threatened to erupt when I saw the collar around his neck. I didn't know if it could hurt him in human form, but the sight of it made me want to leap over the desk at Julian. One of the guards held a controller and another guard pointed a gun at Ronan, who looked ready to rip their limbs off.

"Ronan?" I called.

"He can't hear or see you." Julian waved at the visitor chairs. "Please, have a seat."

"I would rather stand." I needed to get close to him. The only way I could think of to save Ronan was to take Julian hostage and force him to release us. Julian valued his own life too much to risk it.

"I insist." He motioned to the guards, and they pushed me down into a chair.

Julian went to pour himself a drink and walked over to sit at the desk again. "I must admit I severely underestimated you, Danielle. My people are still baffled about how you got out of your cell, and it was quite the feat to escape from this place. I don't suppose you want to tell me how you did it."

I scoffed. "Your security is a joke. I've seen better guards in a mall."

His eyebrows rose, and Willow snickered. The guards shifted angrily. Instead of being insulted, Julian threw back his head and laughed. "That doesn't tell me how you escaped from your cell. Or how you removed the shifter collars."

"No, it doesn't." My gaze kept going to Ronan. Other than the restraints, he looked okay.

Julian sat back in his chair. "I wrote you and your werewolf off for dead when you went into the river. Imagine my shock to find you alive and well after two weeks in the Yukon wilderness in the middle of the winter. You must have a guardian angel – or a fairy godmother."

"Mine is a faerie godfather." In my peripheral vision I saw Willow staring at me. *Take that.*

Julian took a sip of his drink and studied me over the rim of his glass. "You are surprisingly facetious for one in your situation."

I shrugged. "I could say the same about you."

His eyes sparkled with amusement. "I've heard the Mohiri are cool and composed when facing an adversary. Like the calm before the storm."

"You have no idea." Magic rolled deep inside me, testing my control. *Soon.*

He chuckled and opened his mouth to speak, but I cut him off. "May I ask you something?"

"Shoot."

I watched his face closely. "What kind of demon are you?" I needed to know what I was dealing with before I made a move.

His eyes widened, and he stopped laughing abruptly. The lack of reaction from the guards told me they already knew he wasn't human.

He regained his composure quickly. "What makes you think I am a demon?"

Come over here, and I'll show you, I thought. "I'm a Mohiri, and I can tell."

Julian glanced at Willow, who nodded. Technically, I hadn't lied.

He observed me for a long moment, appearing to contemplate how to answer me. I was surprised when he finally spoke.

"There is no human translation for what I am," he said. "I call myself a Vanth demon."

"I have never heard of a Vanth demon." The Mohiri database of demonology was vast, so it was impossible to know every demon. But our studies prioritized demons capable of inhabiting a human body.

"I'm not surprised. I may be the only one of my kind in this realm." At my confused expression, he said, "Twenty years ago, an archdemon weakened the barrier between here and my dimension, enabling a number of demons to slip through it into this realm. I was one of them."

I had heard all about the archdemon Alaron. There wasn't a Mohiri who hadn't heard of him or how Aunt Jordan had killed him. She was famous for it.

"How do you have human form?" I asked. "Do you take over a human body like a Vamhir demon?"

His lips curled in disgust. "Do not compare me to those parasites. I don't infect a human body. I replicate it along with their memories."

"And dispose of the original," I said. "How long have you been living Julian Cross's life?"

"Since college. I was living as a waitress when I met him, and he was perfect – handsome, wealthy, and connected."

I glanced at Ronan again. He was deceptively calm, but rage seethed in his eyes. *Give me a little more time,* I begged silently.

I returned my gaze to Julian. "My people know Caladrius is experimenting on demons and shifters. They will come for you."

"They may go after Caladrius, but they won't find me. If they knew where I was, they would have come already." He gave me a smug smile. "You don't think I have prepared a contingency plan? I could leave here today and slip into a new life. I have my research and more than enough money to start over. There is a lucrative black market for medical treatments and drugs. I'll have a new face and a new lab in a new country. All I need is one final piece."

"Troll bile."

"And you will give me that." He picked up his tablet and touched the screen. "Donovan."

The guard holding the gun on Ronan touched his earpiece and nodded. He took a step closer and pointed the gun at Ronan's head. My stomach dropped, but Ronan's expression didn't change.

"Your friend survived the last silver bullet, but no werewolf can survive a bullet to the brain," Julian said. "Tell me what I want to know."

I put my head down and pretended to think about it. Sighing, I lifted my gaze to his. "The bile is in a cave."

He looked at Willow, and his eyes were lit with excitement when they returned to me. "You have seen it yourself?"

"I've touched it."

At Willow's confirmation, Julian clasped his hands to his chest, trying to contain his glee. "How much is there?"

"Three ounces," I replied.

Julian almost levitated off the floor. "Where is the cave?"

I darted my eyes around the room and lowered my voice. "I'll tell only you, and then you have to let Ronan go."

"Yes," he blurted as he stood and started toward me.

My muscles tensed to spring. This was it.

A startled shout came from the screen as Ronan's cuffed hands shot up to grab the gun from the guard. He swung in the other direction and knocked the controller from the second guard's hand.

The other guards jumped on him with batons and someone said, "Get the controller."

I caught the flash of a gun in a guard's hand as a panicked voice shouted, "Shoot him."

"NO." I leaped to my feet and froze as a shot rang out. Ronan's body jerked, and he fell forward. He hit the camera, and the screen went dark.

24

My scream scorched my throat. The handcuff chain snapped, and Julian stared at it in disbelief. Roaring filled my ears, and my blood turned to lava as my vision tunneled until all I saw was him.

"You," I growled, throwing off the guards trying to restrain me. Magic filled me, and electricity rolled across my skin. It didn't hurt the human guards, but they were of no consequence to me. Light burst around my eyes as my entire body began to glow.

"Holy shit!" Willow leaped off the couch. "You're a goddamn faerie!"

Julian's eyes went round with horror, and he backed up, tripping over his chair.

A baton struck my back, but my magic absorbed the electricity. More hit me as I stalked toward Julian, and I swatted them away.

Someone tackled me, and I went down under a dozen guards. I fought like a mindless beast, punching and kicking until the last body rolled off me. I bolted upright and spun toward Julian.

He was gone.

"He's running."

I looked at Willow, who stared at me in awe. She pointed at the other door in the office. "He'll go for the choppers."

Jumping over the prone guards, I raced to the door. It led to a suite of rooms, which had to be Julian's apartment. I ran through the suite and out the other door into a small hallway. A guard with a baton ran around the corner and tried to block me. I grabbed his arm and flung him into the wall.

My rage mounted as I sped through the facility. By the time I burst from the south entrance, I could taste the bloodlust in my mouth.

A plane passed overhead, but the sound was almost drowned out by the thump of helicopter blades. I ran toward the choppers as one of them lifted off the ground with Julian in the pilot seat.

A roar tore from my throat as I released the storm inside me. A spinning column of snow rose a hundred feet into the air around me, and I threw it at the fleeing helicopter. My last sight of Julian was his panicked face as the whirlwind surrounded the aircraft, trapping it in the air.

Ice, I thought, and the snow froze into jagged ice crystals, which nearly obscured the helicopter.

The memory of Ronan jerking when the bullet struck him played on a vicious loop in my head. I curled my hand into a fist. *Crush.*

The whirlwind closed in.

"Dani, no."

I thought I had imagined my mother's voice until a gentle hand covered mine. The whirlwind froze with the helicopter suspended inside it encased in ice.

I fought her magic. "He has to pay for what he did."

"He will, but not like this." She pushed my hand down, and the helicopter lowered to the ground.

"You don't understand," I choked out. "He –"

My Mori stirred. I whirled to see Ronan race through the doors into the sunlight. He came up short when he saw us, his expression a mix of relief and shock.

I ran to him, and he caught me in his arms. "They told me you gave yourself up," he said harshly. "I didn't know what they were doing to you."

"I saw them shoot you." I clung to him, vowing to never let him go again.

Ronan's arms tightened around me. "It went wide. They shocked me with a baton."

"I thought..." My voice broke.

"Don't think about that," he murmured. "It's over."

I pulled back and reached for the collar around his neck. As soon as I touched it, it broke and fell to the ground.

"There they are," Mom said as I registered a new sound. Ronan and I turned our heads to watch a twin-engine plane approach the runway. It looked like the one that had flown over us the previous day.

Mom walked toward us. I let go of Ronan to run to her. We hugged each other laughing and crying. I couldn't believe she was here.

"I should tell you your father is a little wound up," she said when we separated.

"Dad's here?"

"Along with Dimitri and a few others who can't wait to see you." She paused and flicked her hand toward the entrance. I turned and stared at the wall of ice blocking the doors. Behind it, blurry figures moved.

She smiled. "We'll deal with them in just a minute."

"How did you find us?" Ronan asked as the plane landed and taxied down the runway.

"Your friends Felix and Lena called their parents, who called me," she said.

"They made it?" I asked almost dizzy with relief.

"They found a werecougar pride who took them to Dawson City. They couldn't tell us the exact location of the lab, but they narrowed it down to this area. We've been flying around for the last two days, looking for the place."

"I think we saw your plane west of here yesterday afternoon." I looked to Ronan for confirmation on the direction, and he nodded.

"That was us. We searched in a grid pattern," she said. "Today just happened to be the next grid. When we flew over this place, I saw it and came down to remove the warlock glamour."

The plane slowed at the end of the runway. It didn't come to a complete stop before the door opened, and my father jumped out. I felt like a little girl again when he sprinted to us and pulled me into his arms. He didn't speak as he hugged me fiercely, but the tremble in his arms told me what words could not.

When he finally let me go, I saw Dimitri, Grandfather, Uncle Chris, Aunt Jordan, and Uncle Hamid standing behind him.

Dimitri wrapped me in a hug as tight as Dad's had been. "I should have stayed with you at the wrakk," he said hoarsely. "If we hadn't split up…"

I hugged him back. "They would have taken you, too, and Julian would have used us against each other."

"Where is he?" Dad asked with barely-controlled fury as Grandfather stepped up to me for his hug.

"There." Mom pointed to the helicopter, which looked more like an ice sculpture with streaks of blue electricity running through it. "He's inside that, and he's not going anywhere."

Aunt Jordan whistled. "Nice, Sara."

She beamed with pride. "That is Dani's handiwork."

Dad held out a hand to Ronan. "It's great to see you again, though I wish it was under better circumstances."

"You two must have quite the story to tell," Uncle Chris said as he took his turn hugging me.

"You have no idea." I took a deep breath as the adrenaline and fear of the last two hours wore off. And then I remembered why Ronan and I were on our way here today.

"We have to find Summer," I burst out. "The last time I saw her was two weeks ago, and she didn't look good."

"What kind of security do they have?" Dad asked as we hurried toward the ice-covered entrance.

"Armed human guards and electronic locks," Ronan replied. "They use warlock spells for the cells and restraints."

"Cells?" Mom and Dad asked at the same time. I didn't know who sounded scarier.

I grabbed Dad's arm. "There's another entrance. People will try to leave that way."

"We'll take care of it," he said.

We reached the entrance, and I could still see people on the other side. "Leave them to me," Mom said.

The wall of ice melted and drenched the guards, who had no time to react before they were relieved of their weapons. My mother made it all look so effortless.

Once inside, Ronan and I gave them the layout of the place. When we told them about the cells and the prisoners we'd seen there, Grandfather and Uncle Chris said they would handle the bottom level. Dad and Dimitri took the top level, and Aunt Jordan and Uncle Hamid took the second level where the labs were. Mom, Ronan, and I headed for the third level because my gut told me Summer was there.

Julian's guards didn't put up a fight when they saw us. Word must have spread quickly among them that he was no longer in charge. The lab was in chaos, and the people working there were confused and scared. Good. Let them be afraid for a change. If I had my way, every single one of them would end up in a prison cell.

We entered the surgical floor, and Ronan went to check for guards while Mom and I headed for the observation area. The first person I encountered was Aubrey, the scientist I'd had the altercation with my second day here.

"What are you doing in here?" She grabbed my wrist and shouted, "Guards."

I spun her and wrenched her arm behind her back until she grunted in pain. Spotting a cage nearby, I shoved her inside and slammed the door, which locked automatically.

"Get used to this view." I leaned down to look her in the eyes. "By the way, you were right about the imps."

"Imps?" Mom asked when I straightened.

"I'll tell you about it later." I hurried to the observation rooms. The first one held the golden-haired werewolf, who had to be Bryce, the Montana wolf. He was strapped to a bed with a heart monitor hooked up to him. The second room was empty. In the third one was Summer.

"Summer." I ran to the bed. Her fur was dull, and she'd lost a lot of weight. There were so many wires and tubes I was afraid to touch her. "She looks bad, Mom."

"Let me see her." My mother moved around me and laid a hand on Summer's side. Her brow furrowed as worry crept into her expression.

"Who are you?" demanded a thin thirtysomething man with a receding hairline and a pinched face. "What are you doing with my specimen?"

I had him by the throat against the wall before he could blink. "She is *not* a specimen, you worthless piece of garbage."

The man's face turned red as he grabbed my wrist in both hands. He kicked my shin, and I lifted him until his feet dangled.

"What did you do to her?" I shouted in his face.

A machine began to beep rapidly. I looked over at Summer as an alarm sounded from another machine. I let the man drop and rushed to the bed as the heart monitor let out a continuous high-pitched tone.

My mother placed her glowing hands on Summer's chest and pushed magic into her. I touched Summer's head and felt her lifeforce fading.

Fear gripped me. "She can't die."

Mom's face was a mask of determination. "Not on my watch."

I pressed my hands to Summer's side and sent my magic into the frail body. Mom's powerful magic was working on Summer's heart and lungs, and I used mine to heal her other organs damaged by months of silver exposure and whatever else these bastards had done to her.

An eternity passed until Summer's heart and lungs started working on their own again. Mom and I continued healing her weakened body, repairing scarred surgical tissue that hadn't healed properly because of the silver exposure.

Mom withdrew her magic and smiled. "Summer's going to be okay."

I let out a shuddering breath and stroked Summer's head. "I should have tried harder to reach her when we escaped. I left her here with these people."

"You are not to blame for this," Ronan said sternly, walking over to put an arm around me. "Even if you had gotten to her, she was too weak to run. We nearly died trying to outrun the men hunting us."

My mother stopped unhooking machines to look at us. "You nearly died?"

"They shot Ronan with silver bullets when he shielded me from their tranquilizer darts," I said.

"She saved my life," Ronan told her.

I smiled at him. "And you saved mine."

"I'm so sorry for what you went through," Mom said to Ronan. "I'm also very grateful you were with Dani."

He pulled me closer. "So am I."

We broke apart when a loud commotion came from down the hall, and a male voice shouted, "Where is she? Where's my daughter?"

Uncle Peter and Aunt Shannon ran into the room and came up short when they saw Summer. They looked haggard and older than their forty years, and their eyes welled as they went to her.

"Oh, my baby." Aunt Shannon stroked Summer's face with a trembling hand. "Mama's here."

Uncle Peter turned to my mother. "Is she...?"

"She's going to be fine." Mom assured him. "Her body was sick from silver exposure. Dani and I healed the damage, but she's still very weak."

Summer let out a low whine. I hurried around the bed to stand beside her parents as her eyes fluttered open.

"Summer, it's Mom," Aunt Shannon said tenderly, but Summer didn't react to her voice. She stared through us like we weren't there.

Uncle Peter lowered his voice. "What's wrong with her?"

Mom laid a hand on his arm and spoke quietly. "She's been through an extremely traumatic experience, both physically and mentally. She needs time to recover."

Angry tears burned the backs of my eyes as I looked at my catatonic best friend. *They are going to pay for doing this to you.*

"When can we take her home?" Aunt Shannon asked, wiping her eyes.

"Today," Mom told her. "When we get back to Dawson City, I'll fly with you to Maine."

Aunt Shannon hugged her. "Thank you."

Uncle Peter turned to embrace me. "And thank you, Dani. If not for you, we might never have found her."

He released me and raked a hand through his red hair. The gray at his temples hadn't been there last summer, and he looked angrier than I'd ever seen him. "Where is Julian Cross? Tell me he didn't get away."

I was suddenly glad Mom had stopped me from killing Julian. It would have deprived his victims of the chance to confront him for what he had done to them. He needed to answer for his crimes, and death would have been the easy way out.

"We have him, thanks to Dani," Ronan said, smiling at me.

I went to him and took his hand. "Uncle Peter, Aunt Shannon, this is Ronan."

I watched in trepidation as they shook hands. It was normal for a werewolf pack to be wary and unfriendly with lone wolves, and I wanted so much for them to like Ronan. I didn't know what I would do if they spurned him.

Uncle Peter's smile was genial and sincere. "It's great to meet you, Ronan."

"Dani talks about you and your pack a lot," Ronan said at ease with him.

My anxiety drained away as I listened to the three of them talk for the next few minutes. I should have known Uncle Peter and Aunt Shannon would be friendly. I hoped the rest of the pack would be the same.

"I'm going to check on Bryce and see if anyone else needs immediate healing, and then we can get Summer on the plane," Mom said.

"There was an older werewolf in the cells," I told her.

Grandfather joined us. "He's still there. We unlocked his cell, but he didn't wake up. We didn't want to move him until you looked at him."

Mom's lips pressed together. "I'll see to him next."

Uncle Peter extended his hand to Grandfather. "Tristan, thank you again for sending the jet for us yesterday. You have no idea how much it means to us."

"No thanks are necessary," Grandfather said, shaking his hand. "If there's anything you need, just ask."

"What will you do with this place and all the people here?" Aunt Shannon asked.

"I contacted the rest of the Council, and they are going to send a team to oversee closing down the facility," Grandfather said. "There are a lot of prisoners to free, and many will need a ride home. All the humans need to be questioned before we turn them over to the government."

"I'm going to personally interrogate Julian Cross," Dad said as he appeared in the doorway. "That man has a lot to answer for."

I held up a hand. "About that. Julian Cross is not a man. He's a Vanth demon."

Grandfather frowned. "There is no such demon."

"There is now." I repeated what Julian had told me about his origins and how he became Julian Cross.

Grandfather's eyes lit with interest. "We suspected new demons had crossed through the barrier, but this is the first one we've found. Our scholars will be eager to study him."

I smiled at Ronan. "That is what I call Karma."

Mom returned and got Summer ready to transport to the plane. She put Summer to sleep for the trip before Uncle Peter carefully moved her to a gurney and strapped her down. My chest hurt seeing her like that.

"Why is there a woman in a cage?" Grandfather asked as we wheeled Summer past Aubrey, who was surprisingly quiet.

"She's practicing for prison," I said without further explanation.

We ran into Aunt Jordan near the entrance. "It's just as well Hamid and I are here," she said, walking with us to one of the planes. "The Council has asked us to stay here until they can send a team to oversee cleanup. Do you know the place is infested with imps?"

"Don't hurt them," I told her. "I owe them. They helped me escape from my cell."

Her eyebrows shot up. "What is it with you and your mother and imps? Next, you'll be bringing them home with you."

I laughed for the first time since Ronan and I were alone in the woods that morning. Had that only been a few hours ago?

Exhaustion stole over me, and I remembered I hadn't slept in over twenty-four hours. I couldn't wait to shower and sleep in a real bed.

Ronan stood at my back with his arms around me as Summer was loaded onto the plane her parents had arrived in. *We'll be out of here soon.*

It won't be soon enough for me. I looked over at the helicopter-shaped lump of ice. Part of me wanted to see Julian's face when he learned what his fate would be. A bigger part of me was happy to never lay eyes on him again.

Finally, Ronan and I boarded the plane with Mom, Uncle Peter, and Aunt Shannon. The others would take the second plane.

Ronan and I sat in the last row, and I let out a huge sigh when the plane took off. I gazed down at the vast Yukon wilderness. It was breathtakingly beautiful, even if it had tried its damnedest to kill us. It had also brought me back to Ronan, and for that, it would always have a special place in my heart.

Do you think we'll ever come back? I asked him.

He reached for my hand and entwined our fingers. *If you want to.*

I think I will, someday. I laid my head against his shoulder. *There are a lot of other places I want to see, too.*

Where do you want to go first? he asked.

I smiled to myself. *I heard about this cozy little one-room cabin in the Montana mountains with a stone fireplace and a big bed.*

He chuckled and kissed the top of my head. *Just say when.*

"Isn't this homey," Eldeorin said from the open door of the guest cabin. "I'm surprised you can fit a bed in here."

I looked up from the bag I was unpacking. "Hello to you, too."

He entered the small cabin and looked around. "It's been two months since your liannan. It is time to begin your new training."

"Not today. I have plans."

"Nothing is more important than this," he said, taking a step toward me.

I put up a hand. "Dad told me Mom has been planning this dinner for two weeks. You do not want to mess with her today."

That gave him pause. Eldeorin might be ancient and powerful, but he did not like to get on Mom's bad side. He'd never admit it, but he had a soft spot for her.

"Tomorrow then," he conceded.

"What happens tomorrow?" Ronan asked as he came through the door. He walked over and slid an arm around my waist.

I leaned into him. "Now that I've survived liannan, Eldeorin wants to see what my new magic can do."

"I know what it can do. I want to see what you can do with it. I will return tomorrow," Eldeorin said and vanished.

Ronan stared after him. "Is he always like that?"

"Pretty much." I turned in his arms. "I should warn you. Eldeorin likes to pop in unexpectedly. He drives my father nuts."

"Duly noted." Ronan lowered his head and kissed me breathless. He did that a lot. Aunt Jordan told me mated males could barely keep their hands off their mates for the first year or two. No one would hear me complain.

I smiled up at him. "Are you ready for your first family gathering? I have to warn you it will be noisy and crowded."

His eyes lit with amusement. "For you, I will endure it."

"Don't say I didn't warn you." I pressed a light kiss to his jaw and backed out of his arms. "We'd better go. I told Mom we'd be there at five."

We left our cabin and strolled across the sunny grounds hand in hand. We were always touching or holding hands when we left home. The months of pain and separation had left us with emotional scars, and we didn't like to be apart. At night, wrapped safely in each other's arms, we talked about it. Every day, the scars healed a little more.

I thought about Summer, who was also healing from her ordeal. She had come out of her catatonic state a week after we brought her home, and I'd stayed there for another week. She was quiet and withdrawn, but every now and then, I caught glimpses of the old Summer. She was coming back to us – all she needed was time.

My phone vibrated, and I smiled at the name on the screen. I clicked on the text message and showed it to Ronan. It was a photo of a smiling sandy-haired Felix and blonde Lena showing off her engagement ring. Above it were the words **SHE SAID YES!**

Ronan and I visited the werecougars last month, and the four of us had become instant friends. Werecougars and werewolves typically despised each other, but we'd formed a bond during our harrowing escape. Their pride threw a party to show us their gratitude, and even Felicity had smiled at us.

The wedding's in the fall, Felix texted. **We hope you guys can come.**

Wouldn't miss it, I texted back. Something else I learned from our new friendship was werecougar males didn't imprint like werewolf males did. Couples chose their mates.

Dimitri caught up to us on the road to the lake. "About time you two got back. How was Montana?"

"Wonderful." I thought about the past month at Ronan's – our – cabin in the mountains. Four glorious weeks of exploring the mountains during the day and exploring each other at night. My body grew warm thinking about it.

Excited barks came from the woods, and I braced myself as Hugo and Woolf bounded toward us. Woolf pushed between Ronan and me, and Hugo pressed against my other side before they proceeded to slobber all over me.

I shooed them away. "I missed you, too."

Wiping my face with my sleeve, I realized this was the longest I'd ever been away from them. It was also the longest Dimitri and I had been apart since we were born. It sank in that we were adults now, and our lives were taking us in different directions. We'd have holidays and family get-togethers, but it would never be the same.

Why are you sad? Ronan asked over our bond.

I took his hand again. *I'm not. I'm thinking how different it will be not to have Dimitri around all the time.*

"I hope you guys are hungry," Dimitri said. "Mom went a bit overboard with the food. She had the kitchen cook enough turkey and ham to feed a small army and about a dozen sides and desserts. Dad had to borrow some tables from the manor to hold it all."

"I'm starving," I said, laughing.

What had started out as a dinner to celebrate Dimitri and me becoming warriors had grown into a huge family Thanksgiving feast to make up for the one we missed in November. It had saddened me when Ronan confided he had never been to a Thanksgiving dinner, and I wanted to fill his life with all the things he had missed out on.

"Do you know where you're going?" I asked Dimitri.

"New York. Uncle Chris and Aunt Beth will be there until the end of the year," he said. "I wish you were coming with me, but I guess you're planning to stay here."

"We haven't talked about it much." The question reminded me Ronan and I needed to have that conversation. I wanted to see more of the country, but I didn't think I'd be happy living at a command center in a city. I knew he wouldn't. He needed to hunt at least once a month, and he loved to run. I would be happy living here and traveling for jobs, but I didn't want to make him feel obligated to stay here for me.

"I thought..." Dimitri paused. "Never mind."

Voices and laugher reached us before the lake came into view. The first person we saw was Jace, my twelve-year-old cousin, who tackled me like a little linebacker.

"You're here," he yelled in a high voice on the verge of changing.

I ruffled his chestnut hair, which was the same shade as my mother's. "If you get any bigger, you'll bowl me over."

"Hi, Dani," called his fourteen-year-old brother, Daniel, who looked so much like my mother he could have been her little brother.

"Am I invisible?" Dimitri asked in mock indignance. He looked at me. "You can see me, right?"

Jace snickered. "We saw you this morning."

"Let the girl breathe, Jace." Uncle Nate walked toward us, smiling. He was Mom's uncle, which made him our great uncle. He, Aunt Andrea, and the boys lived in Ashville, North Carolina. At fifty-nine, his hair was more gray than brown, but he had the fit and youthful appearance of a man with an active lifestyle.

I hugged him tightly. "I'm so happy you were able to come. I know how crazy your schedule is with the new movie."

"Nothing could keep us away," he said.

Uncle Nate was a famous author of military suspense novels, and one of his series had been made into a wildly successful film franchise. They were currently working on the fifth movie, and he was one of the producers.

"Uncle Nate, this is Ronan," I said when we ended our hug. "Ronan, this is my Uncle Nate."

They shook hands, and Ronan said, "Dani gave me some of your books. I'm enjoying them."

Uncle Nate grinned at me. "I like him already."

We walked less than ten feet before a dark-haired couple swooped in to smother me in hugs. I introduced Ronan to Grandmother Irina and Grandfather Mikhail, and we walked together to the lake.

We entered the house where Ronan and I were besieged by my parents, Uncle Chris, Aunt Beth, Aunt Jordan, Uncle Hamid, Grace, and Grandfather Tristan. I worried Ronan might be uncomfortable surrounded by so many people, but he looked at ease with my family.

Mom ushered us out to the deck for our meal because the dining room couldn't seat so many. Dimitri had not been kidding about the feast. A long table had been set for twenty people, and side tables held food warmers and large serving bowls.

Dinner was noisy and fun. Everyone gave thanks, which took a while because we had a lot to be thankful for this year. There were toasts to Dimitri and me for becoming warriors and more toasts to Ronan and me.

When everyone had eaten all they could, Mom and Aunt Jordan went inside and came out carrying a huge birthday cake with nineteen candles on it. They laid it in front of Dimitri and me as everyone sang "Happy Birthday."

I gave Mom a puzzled look, and she said, "We didn't celebrate your nineteenth birthday in November. What better time than when we are all together?"

After Dimitri and I blew out the candles, Dad stood and went into the house. He came back carrying a long wooden box, which could only contain one thing. Dimitri shifted on his chair in barely concealed excitement.

"Dimitri, ever since you could hold a sword you've been begging me for a pair of swords exactly like mine," Dad said.

"I wouldn't say I begged," Dimitri cut in, and everyone laughed.

Dad walked over to him. "I have been waiting for the day I could give you this. You are going to be a fine warrior, and your mom and I are so proud of you."

He handed the box to Dimitri, who stared at it until I elbowed him. He lifted the lid, and his jaw dropped when he saw the pair of gleaming swords nestled on a bed of black silk. His eyes were wide with disbelief when he raised them to Dad.

"These...these are your swords," he uttered.

"Now they are yours," Dad said. "May they serve you as well as they served me."

Dimitri shook his head. "I don't know what to say."

"That's a first," Grace muttered dryly, setting off another round of laughter.

Mom stood. "Dani, your gift is a little different. It's from Dad and me, but everyone here helped. We consulted with Ronan on it, and he assured us you'll love it."

I whipped my head toward Ronan, who wore a secretive smile. He and I had been gone for over a month. When had she consulted with him? And on what?

Mom held out her hand to me. "Come."

She and I walked down to the bottom deck, and my curiosity grew with every step we took. We stopped, and I looked back at my family, who crowded the steps behind us looking as excited as I was.

"Eldeorin has been teaching me this one, so I hope I get it right." She raised her arm and made a sweeping motion with her hand.

For a few seconds, nothing happened. The air started to shimmer like heat radiating off pavement, and the trees at the other end of the small lake rippled and changed. I squinted as something began to take shape, and I put a hand over my mouth when I saw what it was.

"A house?" I stared at the A-frame log cabin on the other end of the lake. The front of the cabin was mostly windows with a balcony on the second floor and a deck extending out over the water.

I felt Ronan behind me, and I spun to face him. "You want to live here?"

"I want to live wherever you are." He tucked a lock of hair behind my ear. "We can travel and do jobs, and when we come home, it will be to our own house here at the lake."

"But your cabin in Montana?"

"It will make a nice vacation spot, but it was never a real home," he said in a quiet voice. "Here, we'll be near your family, and I can hunt and run whenever I want."

"We're your family, too," Mom told him.

Dimitri called, "You're stuck with us now."

"Are you sure?" I searched Ronan's eyes. I needed to know he wanted this and wasn't doing it only to make me happy.

"Yes." He turned me to face the lake and wrapped his arms around me. "Do you like it?"

"I love it." I was already imagining us waking up in our loft bedroom with a view the lake bathed in morning sunlight.

Ronan moved to my side. "Then let's go see our new home."

I turned with him and saw my parents standing together. I ran and hugged them at the same time. "Thank you."

Mom, Dad, Ronan, and I walked over to the cabin, using a new gravel road that branched off the main road and ran beside the lake. Mom had hidden it with a glamour to prevent me from seeing it before the big reveal. I couldn't believe how sneaky they all were.

Up close, the cabin was bigger than I thought. It had an open floorplan except for a huge stone fireplace and chimney in the center, and at the back of the house was a guest room and bathroom. In the loft, I was delighted to find a smaller fireplace in the master en suite and a view of the entire lake. The house was fully furnished, which meant tonight Ronan and I would sleep in our new home.

"We were gone for five weeks. How did you do all this?" I asked my parents when we returned to the first floor.

My father smiled. "We had two crews working around the clock."

"And while they were building it, I ordered all the furnishings," my mother said. "I had help from Beth and Jordan."

I looked around in awe. "This is perfect."

A flicker of movement on the couch caught my eye, and I turned my head to stare at the two tiny faces peering over the top of a throw pillow. A third one appeared at the side of the pillow, followed by a fourth. I walked over and lifted the pillow to reveal the four imps hiding there.

Mom laughed. "Those are from Jordan. They stowed away in her duffle bag at the lab, so she brought them here as a housewarming gift."

"You're the ones who brought me the key fob," I said, and they chattered eagerly.

I turned to Ronan, who sighed. "You want to keep them, don't you?"

"If it wasn't for them, we wouldn't have escaped." I looked back at the four hopeful faces. "And they have nowhere else to go."

Ronan pointed at the imps. "No stealing, and upstairs is off-limits."

They nodded with less enthusiasm. I decided not to tell him the quickest way to get an imp to do something was to order them not to do it.

Mom gave me a conspiratorial smile and looped her arm through Dad's. "We'll let you two settle in a bit. Come over later because we still need to cut the cake."

As soon as they left, I flung my arms around Ronan's neck. "I can't believe we have our own house. I want to see it all again."

He laughed, and we walked through the whole house a second time. It even had a fully stocked kitchen. All we had to do was get our stuff from the cabin and from my old bedroom.

Ronan showed me a large mudroom at the back of the house. "Your mother had them make it big enough for me to undress and shift."

I stepped outside and inhaled the fresh, earthy smell of the woods, the fragrant wildflowers, and the new foliage. It was good to be home.

"You know what I want to do first?" I asked.

"I can think of a few things," he said from behind me in a voice that had dropped an octave.

"So can I." I looked at him over my shoulder. "Race you to the pool."

His eyes turned to gold. "What do I get if I win?"

"Me."

Ronan flashed me a predatory smile that made my pulse quicken. I bolted for the woods, my laughter trailing behind me.

It wasn't long before I heard him coming, and I picked up speed but not so much he couldn't gain on me. He didn't know I had been getting faster since my liannan, and I could easily keep pace with him now. I planned to tell him, but not yet because he loved the chase.

And I loved it when he caught me.

~ The End ~

ABOUT THE AUTHOR

When she is not writing, Karen Lynch can be found reading or baking. A native of Newfoundland, Canada, she currently lives in Maine with her dogs Kenya, Dax, and Des.